MONKEY KING

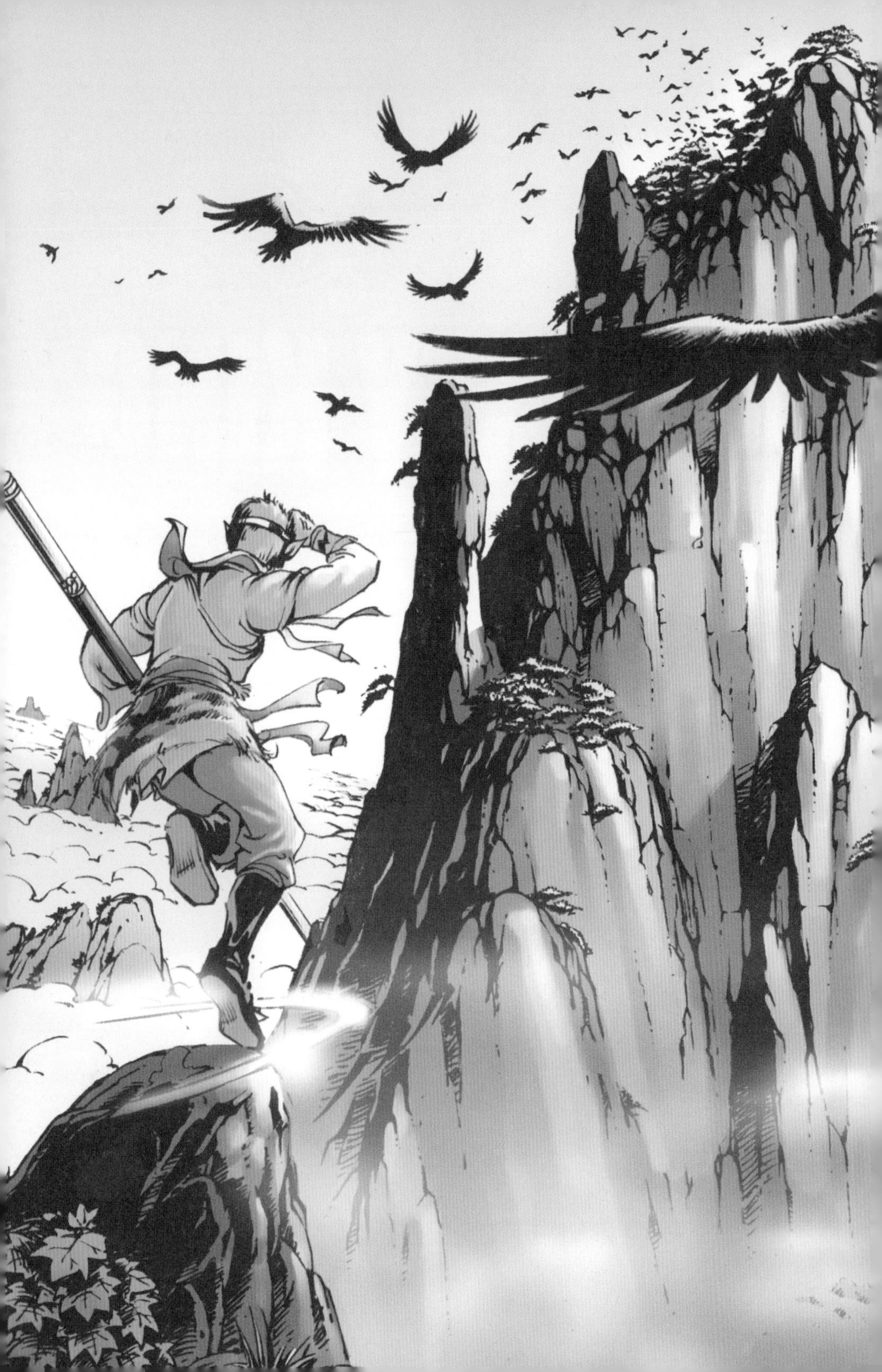

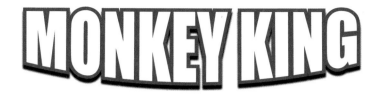

MONKEY KING

Enemies and a New Friend

Created by WEI DONG CHEN

Wei Dong Chen, a highly acclaimed and beloved artist, and an influential leader in the "New Chinese Cartoon" trend, is the founder of Creator World in Tianjin, the largest comics studio in China. Recently the Chinese government entrusted him with the role of general manager of the Beijing Book Fair, and his reputation as a pillar of Chinese comics has brought him many students. He has published more than three hundred cartoons, which have been recognized for their strong literary value not only in Korea, but in Europe and Japan, as well. Free spirited and energetic, Wei Dong Chen's positivist philosophy is reflected in the wisdom of his work. He is published serially in numerous publications while continuing to conceive projects that explore new dimensions of the form.

Illustrated by CHAO PENG

Chao Peng is considered one of Chen Wei Dong's greatest students, and is the director of cartoon at Creator World in Tianjin. One of the most highly regarded cartoonists in China today, Chao Peng's fantastic technique and expression of Chinese culture have won him the acclaim of cartoon lovers throughout China. His other works include "My Pet" and "Searching for the World of Self".

Original story

"The Journey to The West" *by Wu, Cheng En*

Editing & Designing

Sun Media, Design Hongs, David Teez, Jonathan Evans, YK Kim, HJ Lee, SH Lee, Qing Shao, Xiao Nan Li, Ke Hu

Original Chinese edition published by Anhui Fine Arts Publishing House.

Characters

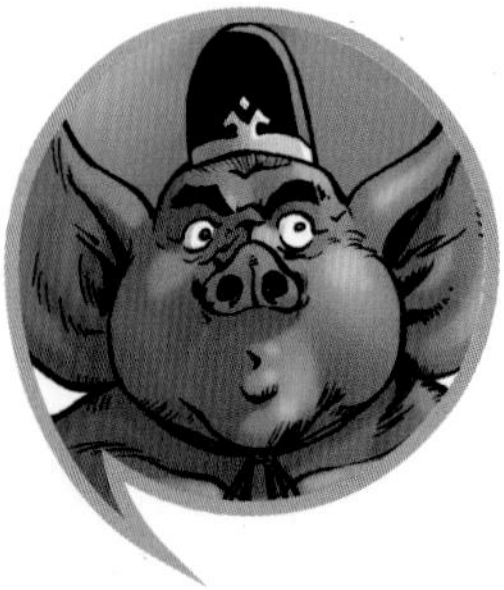

ZHU BAJIE (ZHU WU NENG)

One of four principal characters in The Journey to the West, Zhu Wu Neng is given his name by the Goddess of Mercy, and is then renamed Zhu Bajie by San Zang. (Sun Wu Kong tauntingly refers to him as "Pigsy.") Bajie once served under the Jade Emperor as commander of the armed defense of the Milky Way, but was later banished by the emperor for drunkenly harassing a court lady. Once banished, Bajie entered the womb of a pig and was reborn. Years of moral cultivation allowed Bajie to pass as a person, but his gluttonous nature was revealed once he became betrothed to Gao Cui Lan. The Goddess of Mercy then orders Bajie to follow the same path as Sun Wu Kong: to reject his old ways, embrace Buddhism, and assist San Zang with his journey.

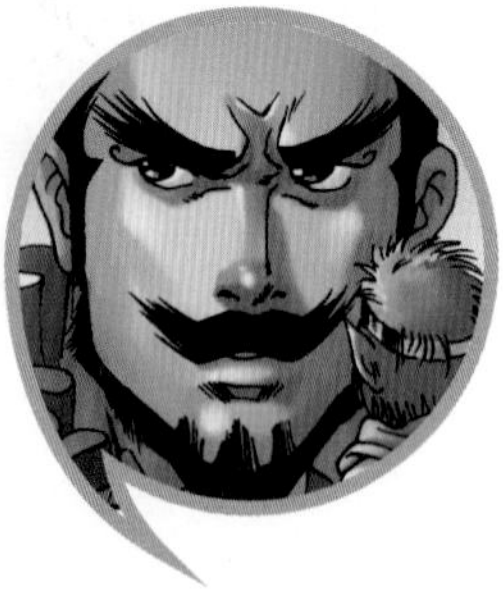

KING OF HEAVEN'S EYES

The King of Heaven's Eyes rules over the western territories of Heaven, and keeps watch over the Earth. In Journey to the West, he allows Sun Wu Kong to borrow BiHuoZhao, which the monkey uses to deflect a fire and save San Zang's life.

THE BLACK BEAR DEMON

The Black Bear Demon is the ruler of Mount Black Wind, who frequently visits with the chief priest of the Buddhist temple where San Zang and Sun Wu Kong spend the night. When the temple is set ablaze, he sees the flames and sets out to help the monks put out the fire. But once he arrives, he is distracted by the luminescent beauty of San Zang's precious robe, and steals it. After the theft, the bear demon engages in an epic fight with Sun Wu Kong, who must enlist the help of the Goddess of Mercy in order to retrieve the robe.

LING XUZI

Ling XuZi is a wolf monster who is friends with the Black Bear Demon. One day, while paying a visit to the demon, XuZi is killed by Sun Wu Kong, who then transfigures into a special elixir XuZi had brought with him as a gift for the bear demon.

Characters

SIR GAO

Sir Gao rules the manor where Sun Wu Kong and San Zang spend some time after the defeat of the Black Bear Demon. He tells the visitors that his youngest daughter, Cui Lan, has been taken prisoner by a pig monster, and asks Sun Wu Kong to free her.

GAO CUI LAN

Cui Lan is the daughter of Sir Gao, who was wedded to Zhu Wu Neng while he was masquerading as a person. Not long after they were married, her husband revealed his true nature, transforming into a pig and taking Cui Lan hostage.

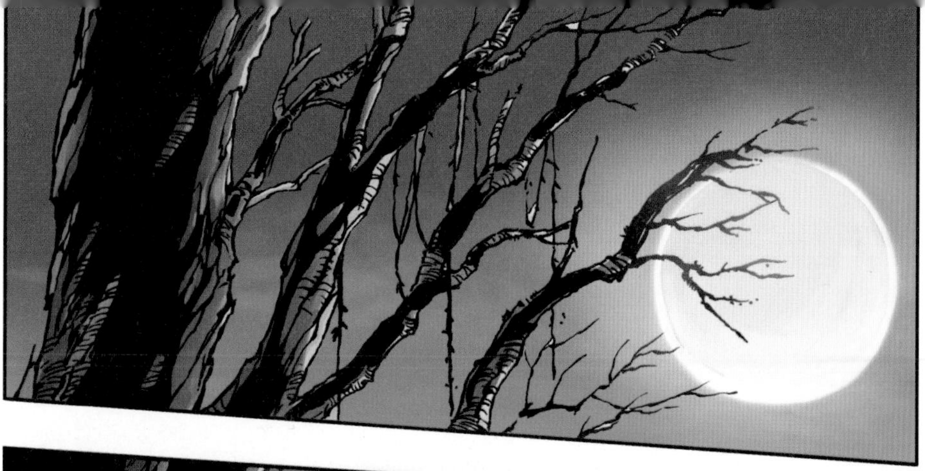

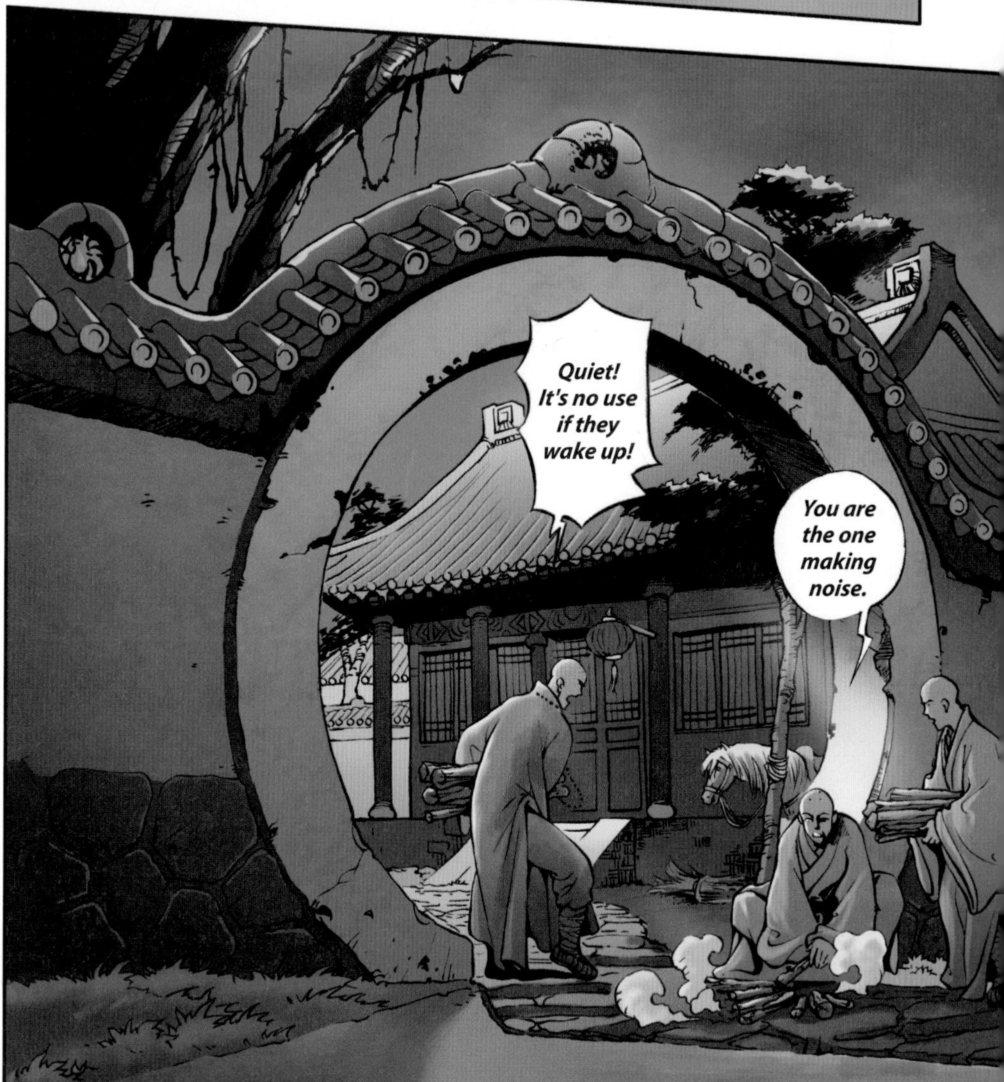
Quiet! It's no use if they wake up!
You are the one making noise.

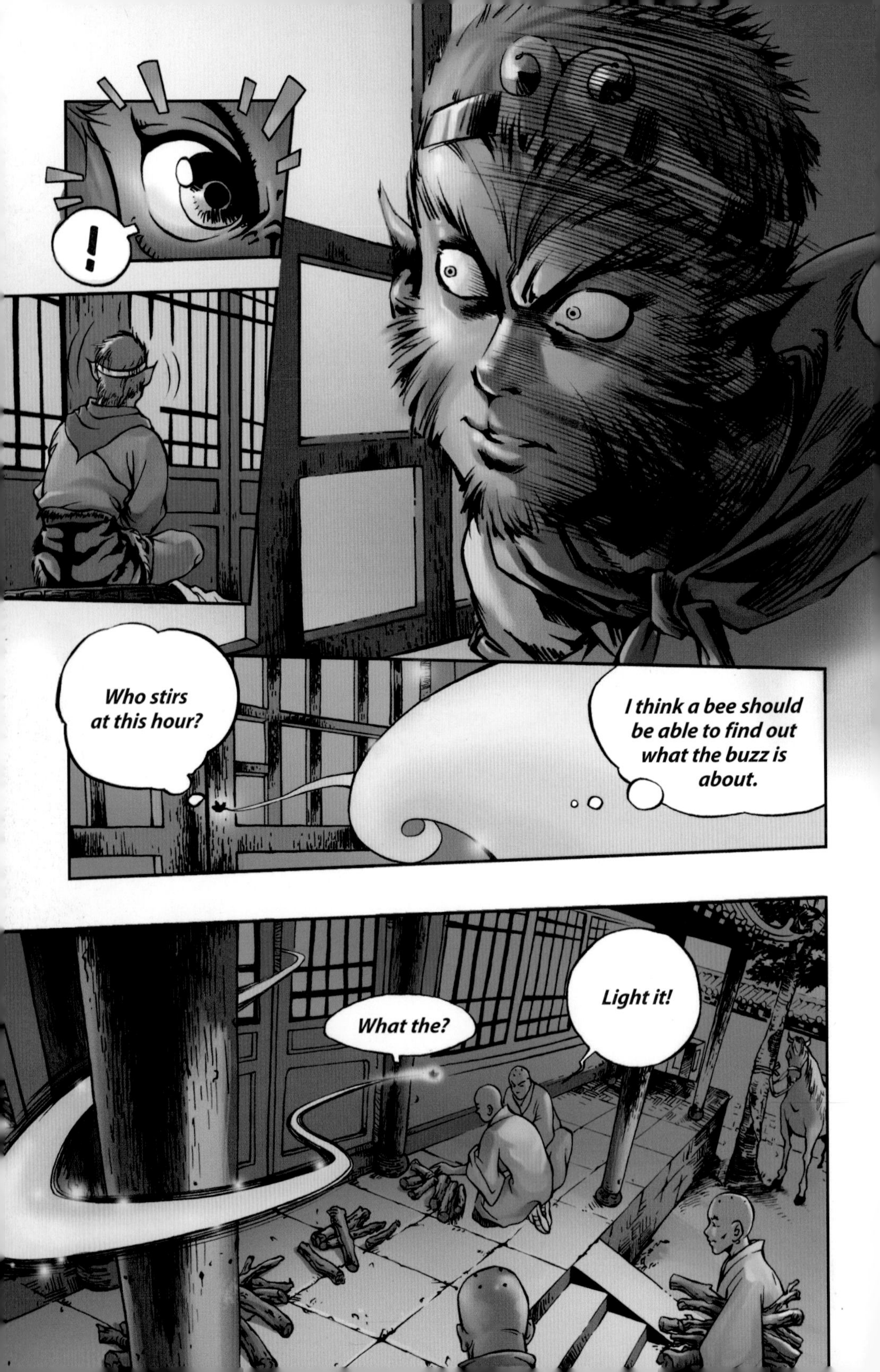
!
Who stirs at this hour?
I think a bee should be able to find out what the buzz is about.
What the?
Light it!

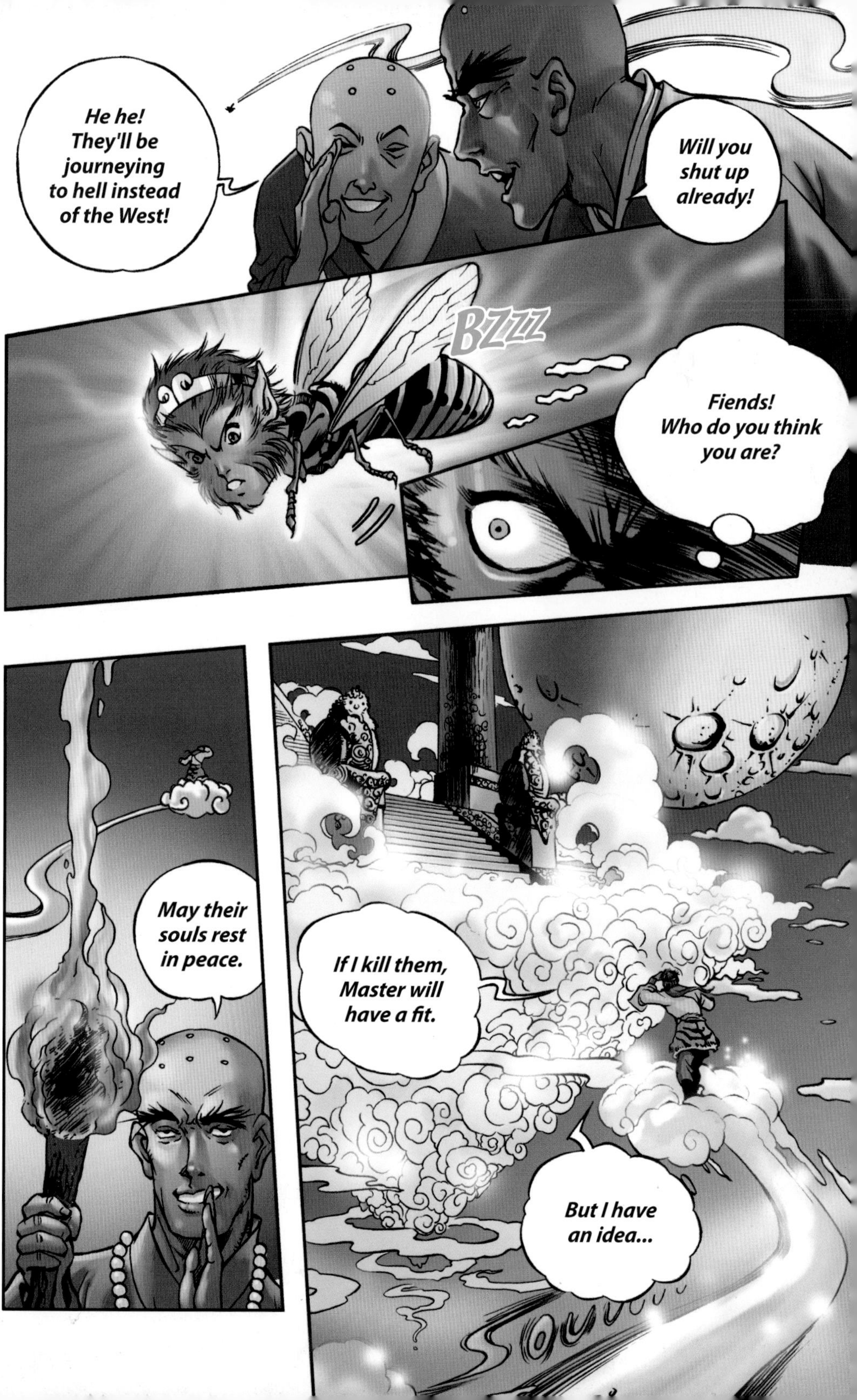
He he! They'll be journeying to hell instead of the West!
Will you shut up already!
BZZZ
Fiends! Who do you think you are?
May their souls rest in peace.
If I kill them, Master will have a fit.
But I have an idea...
SOUUUU

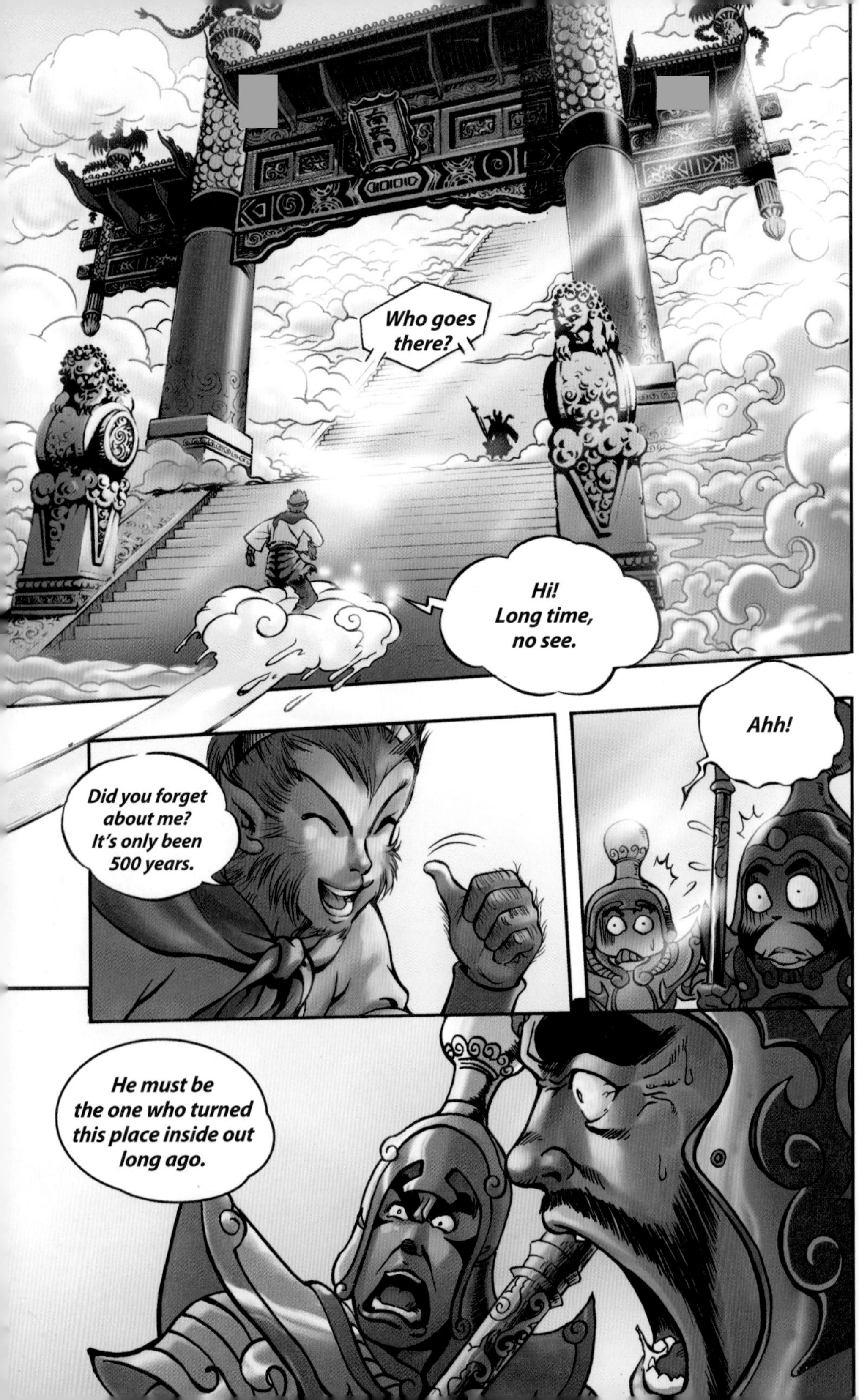
Who goes there?
Hi! Long time, no see.
Did you forget about me? It's only been 500 years.
Ahh!
He must be the one who turned this place inside out long ago.

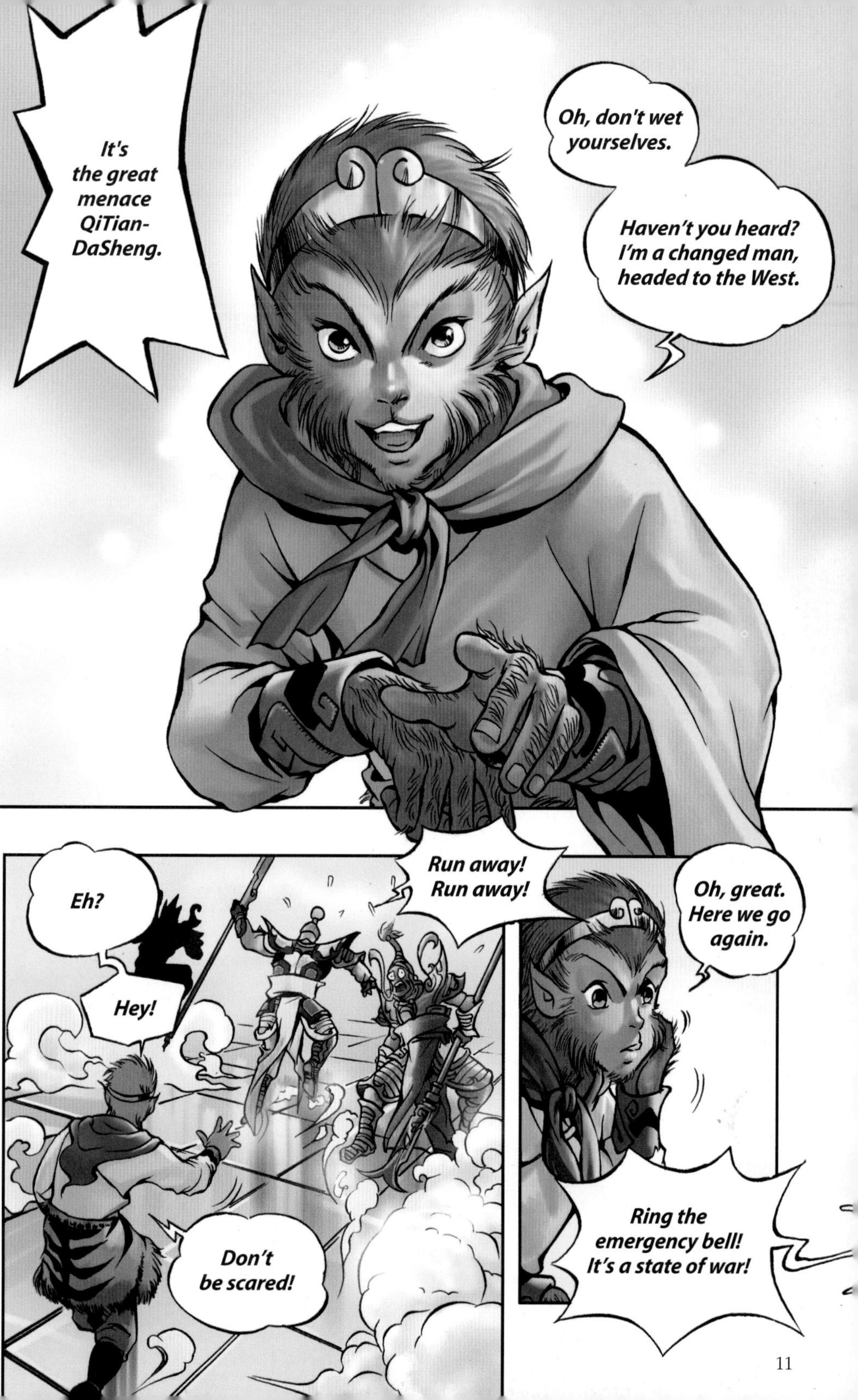
It's the great menace QiTian-DaSheng.
Oh, don't wet yourselves.
Haven't you heard? I'm a changed man, headed to the West.
Eh?
Run away! Run away!
Oh, great. Here we go again.
Hey!
Don't be scared!
Ring the emergency bell! It's a state of war!

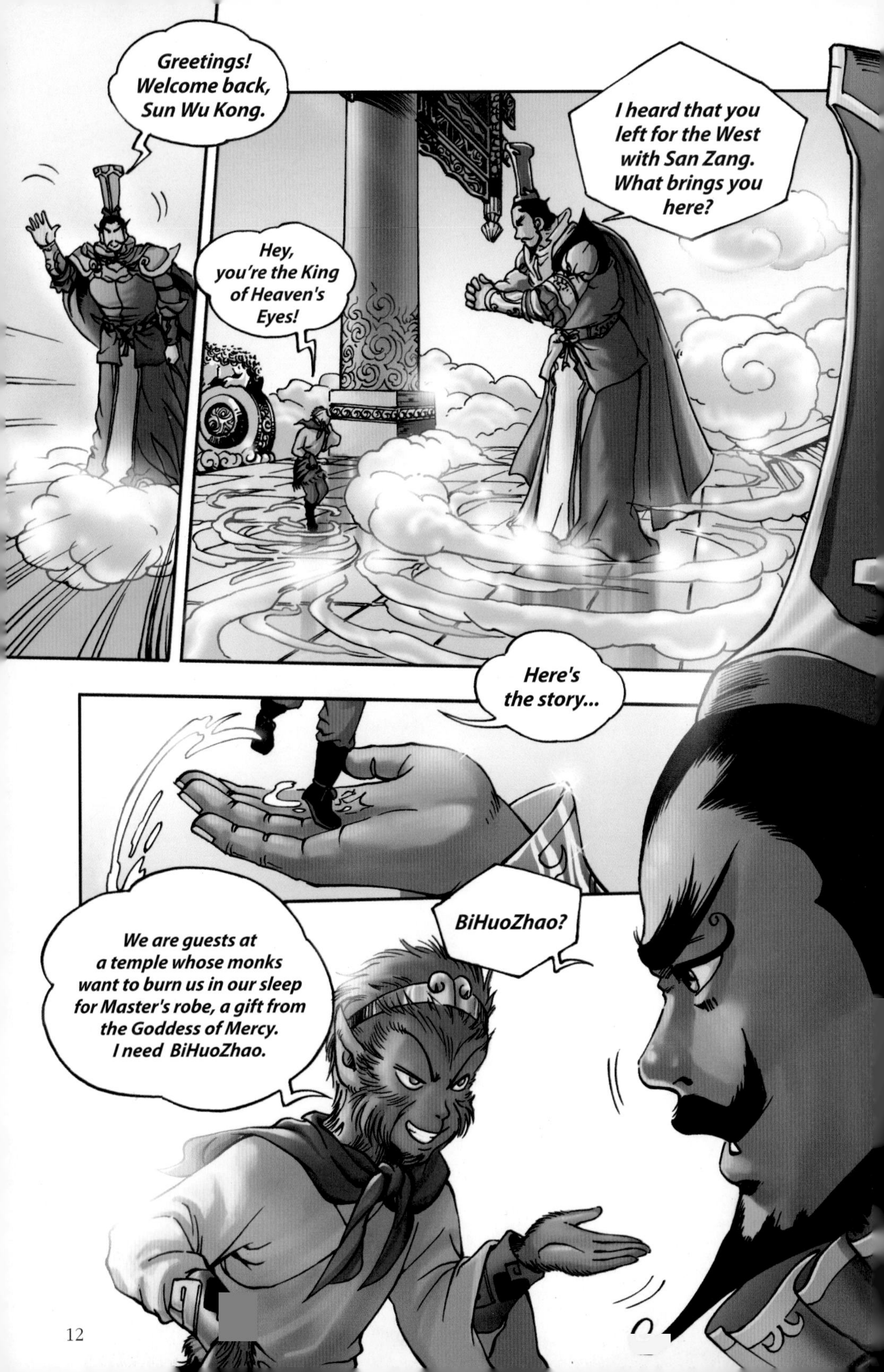
Greetings! Welcome back, Sun Wu Kong.
I heard that you left for the West with San Zang. What brings you here?
Hey, you're the King of Heaven's Eyes!
Here's the story...
We are guests at a temple whose monks want to burn us in our sleep for Master's robe, a gift from the Goddess of Mercy. I need BiHuoZhao.
BiHuoZhao?

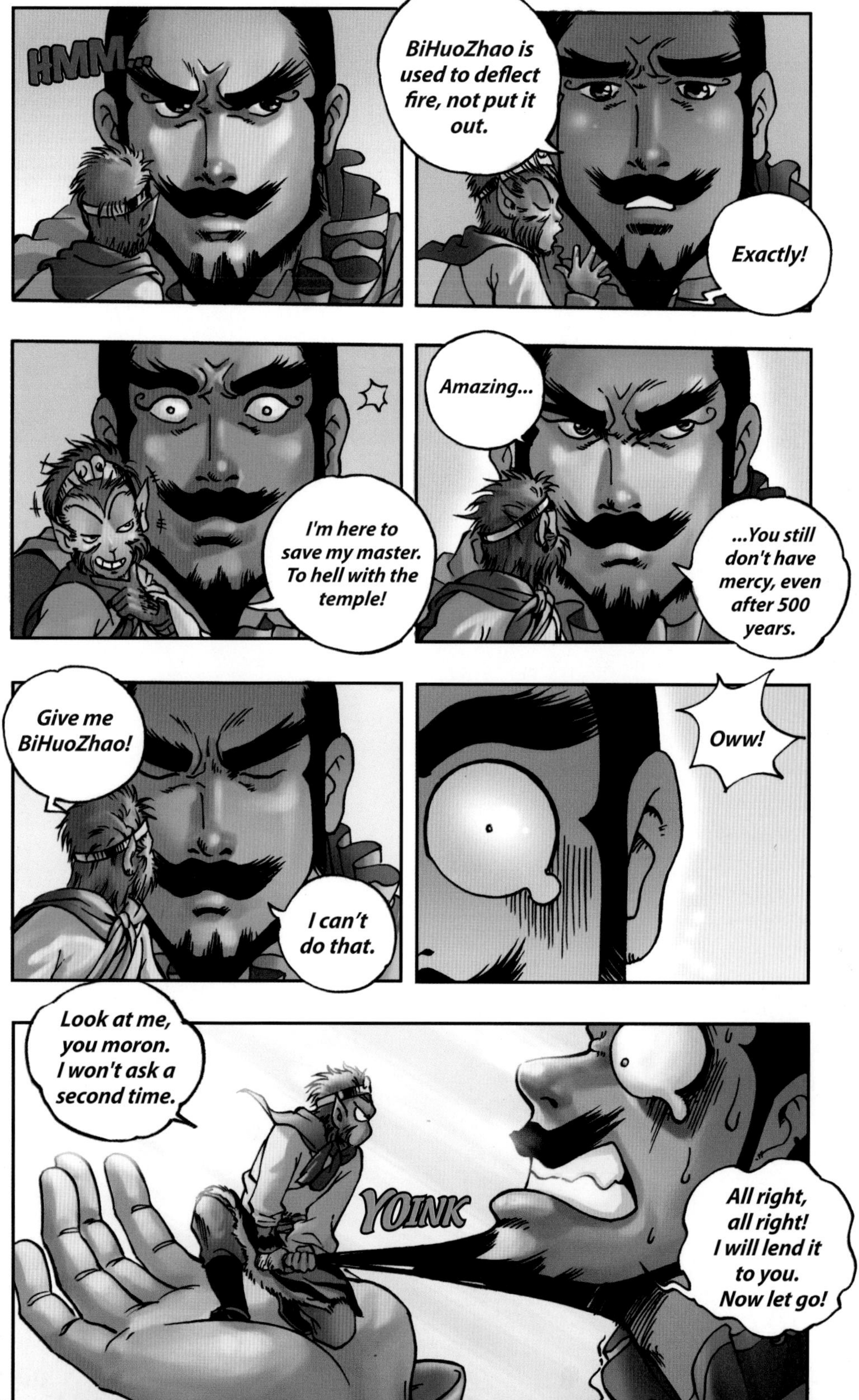
HMM...
BiHuoZhao is used to deflect fire, not put it out.
Exactly!
I'm here to save my master. To hell with the temple!
Amazing...
...You still don't have mercy, even after 500 years.
Give me BiHuoZhao!
I can't do that.
Oww!
Look at me, you moron. I won't ask a second time.
YOINK
All right, all right! I will lend it to you. Now let go!

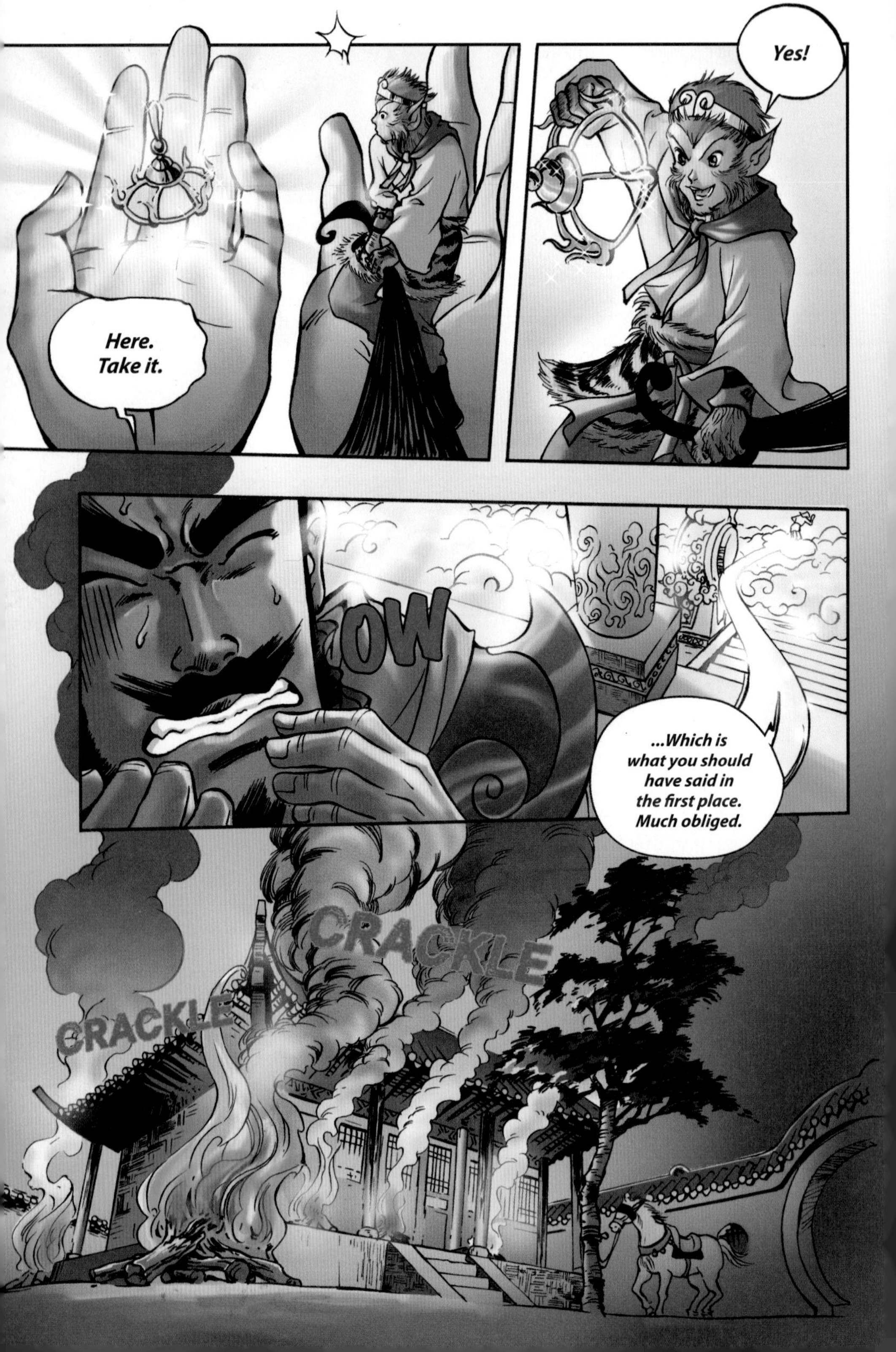
Yes!
Here. Take it.
OW
...Which is what you should have said in the first place. Much obliged.
CRACKLE
CRACKLE

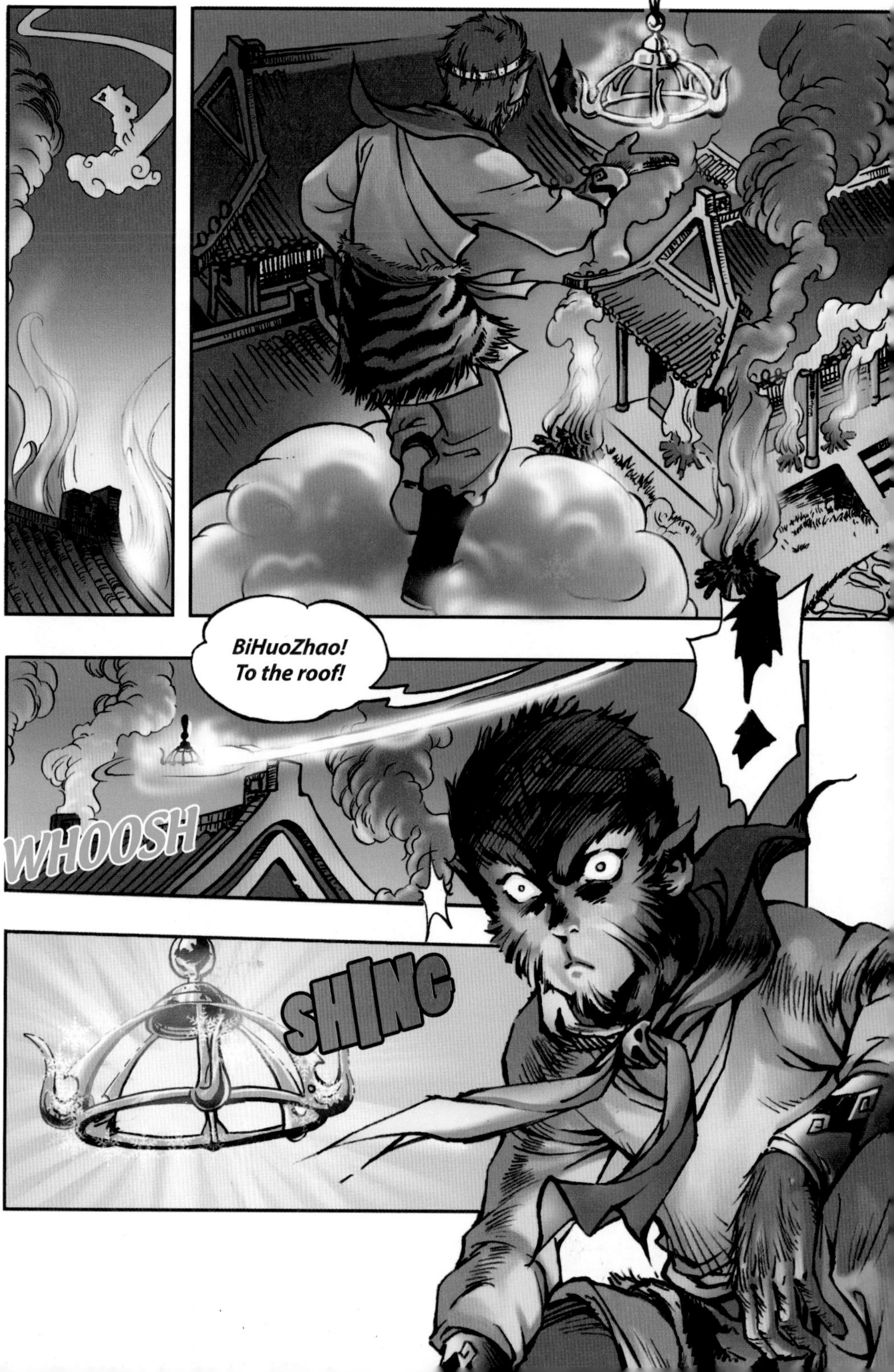
BiHuoZhao!
To the roof!
WHOOSH
SHING

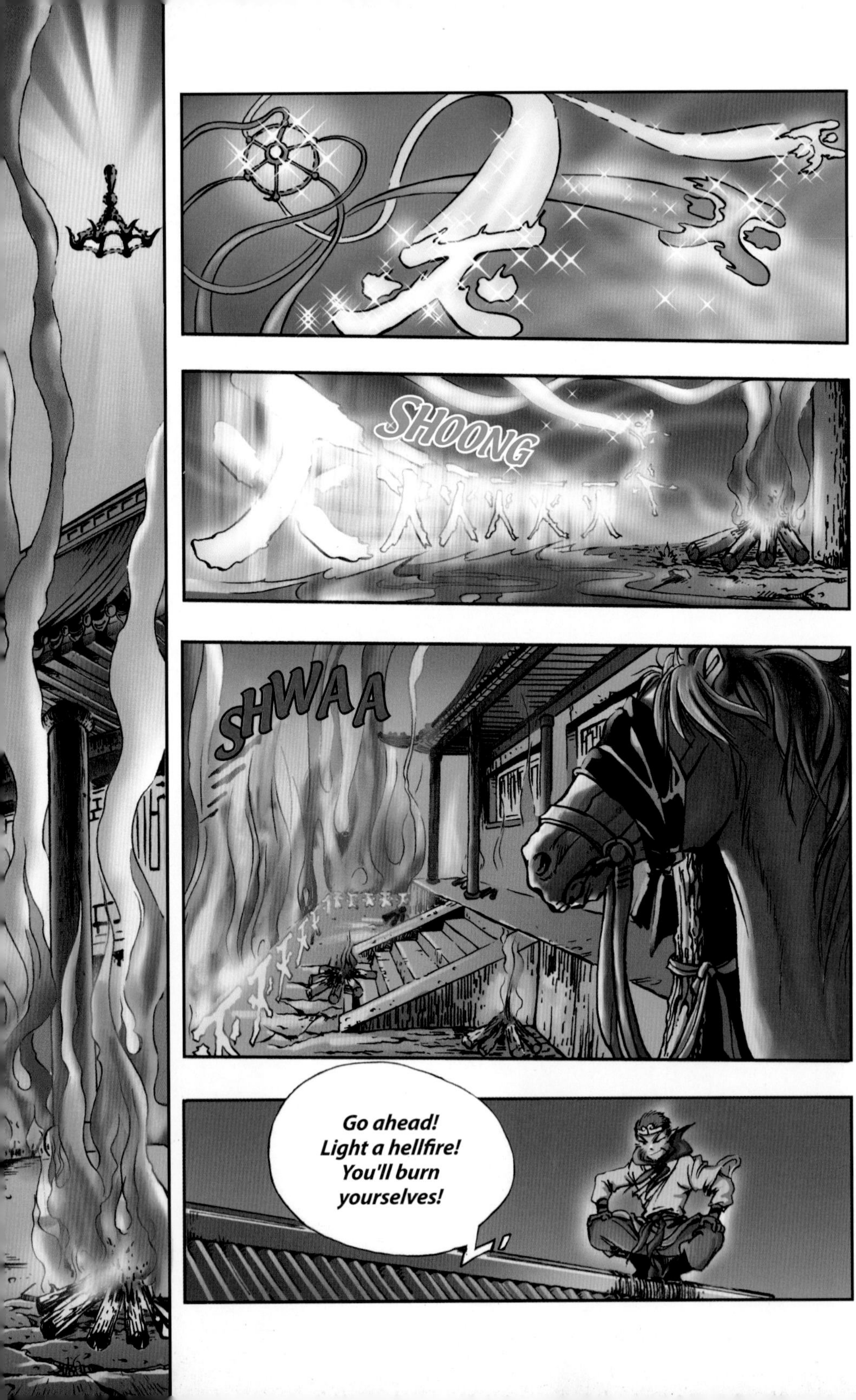
SHOONG
SHWAA
Go ahead! Light a hellfire! You'll burn yourselves!

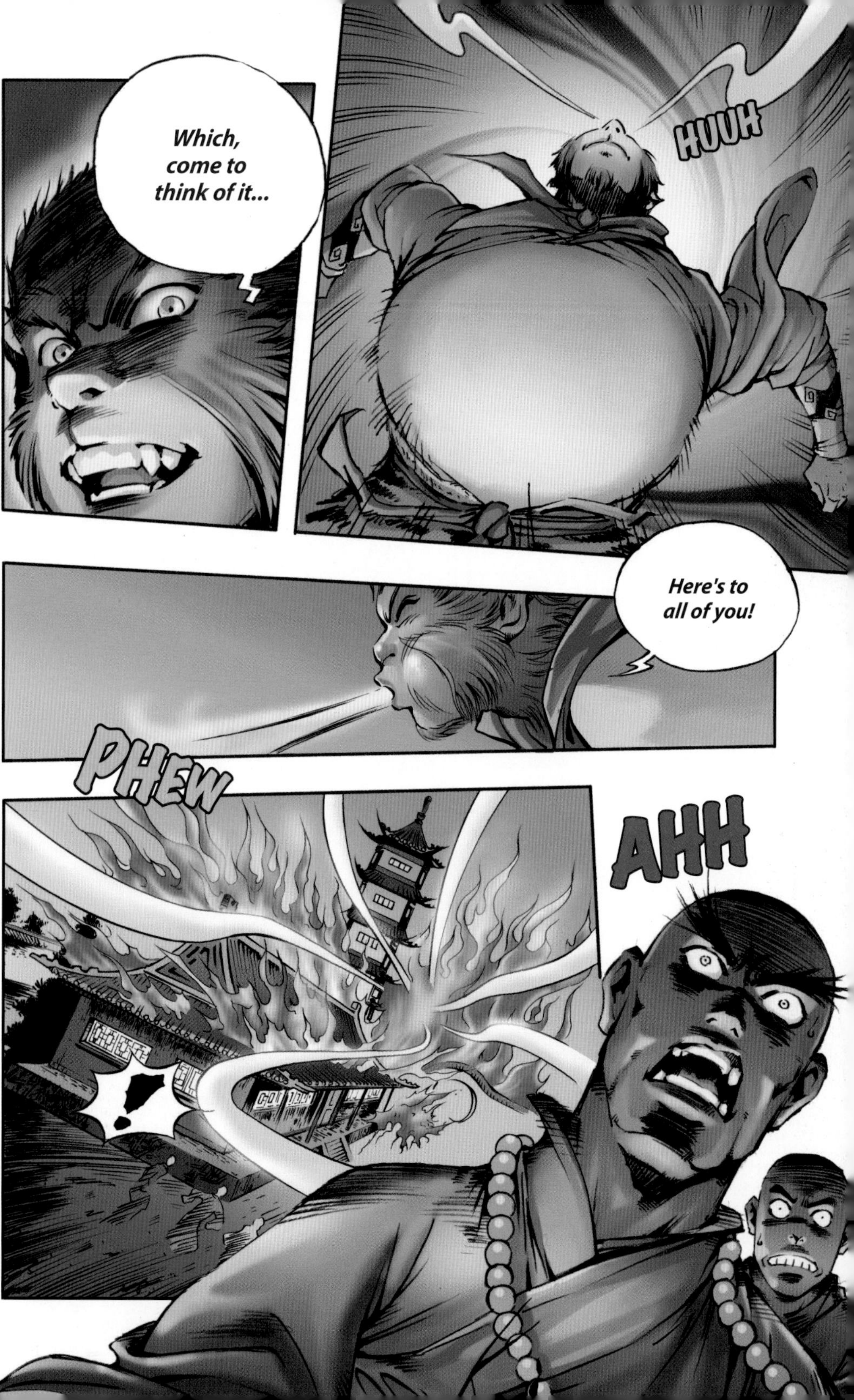
Which, come to think of it...
HUUH
Here's to all of you!
PHEW
AHH

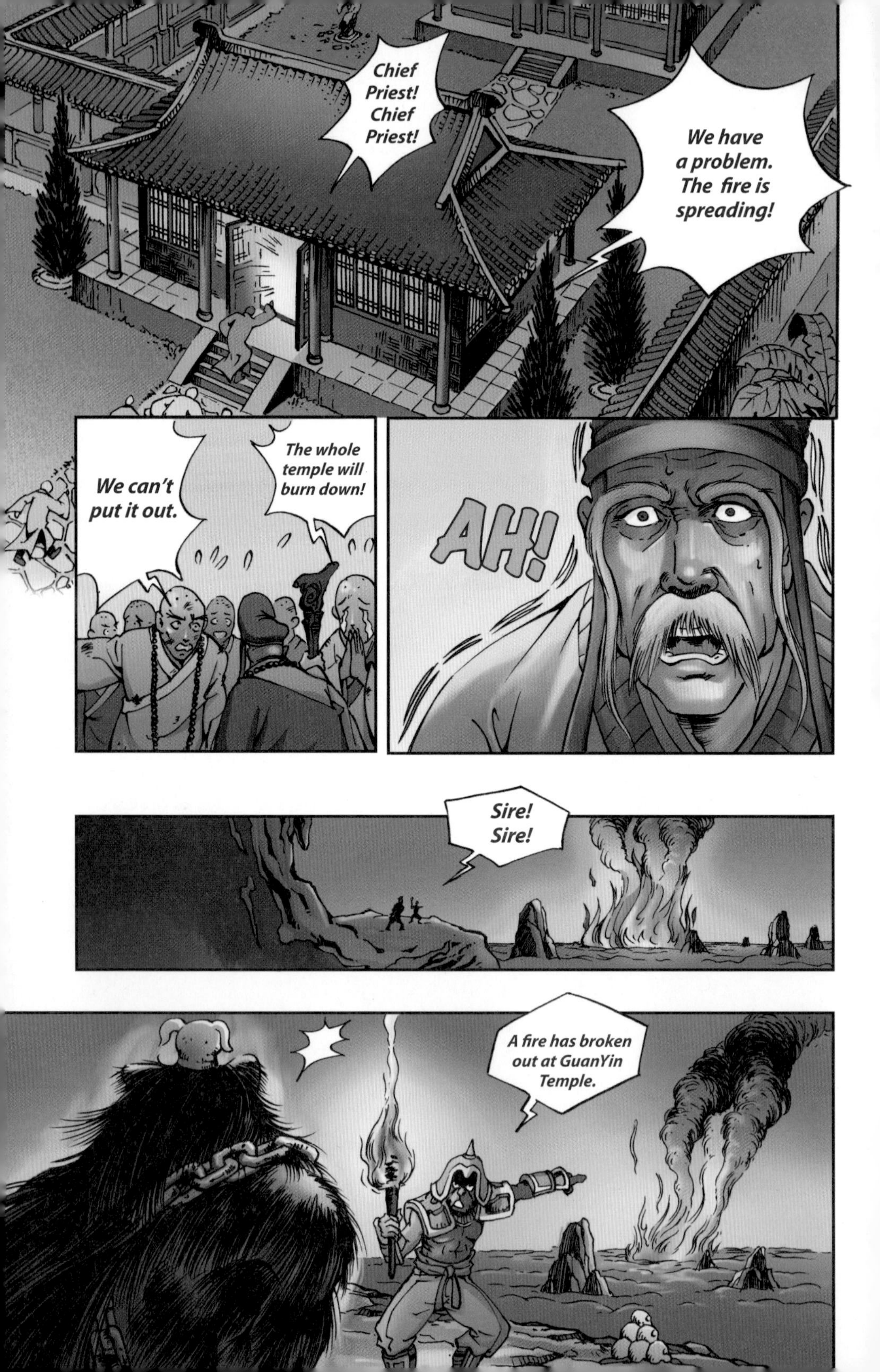
Chief Priest! Chief Priest!
We have a problem. The fire is spreading!
We can't put it out.
The whole temple will burn down!
AH!
Sire! Sire!
A fire has broken out at GuanYin Temple.

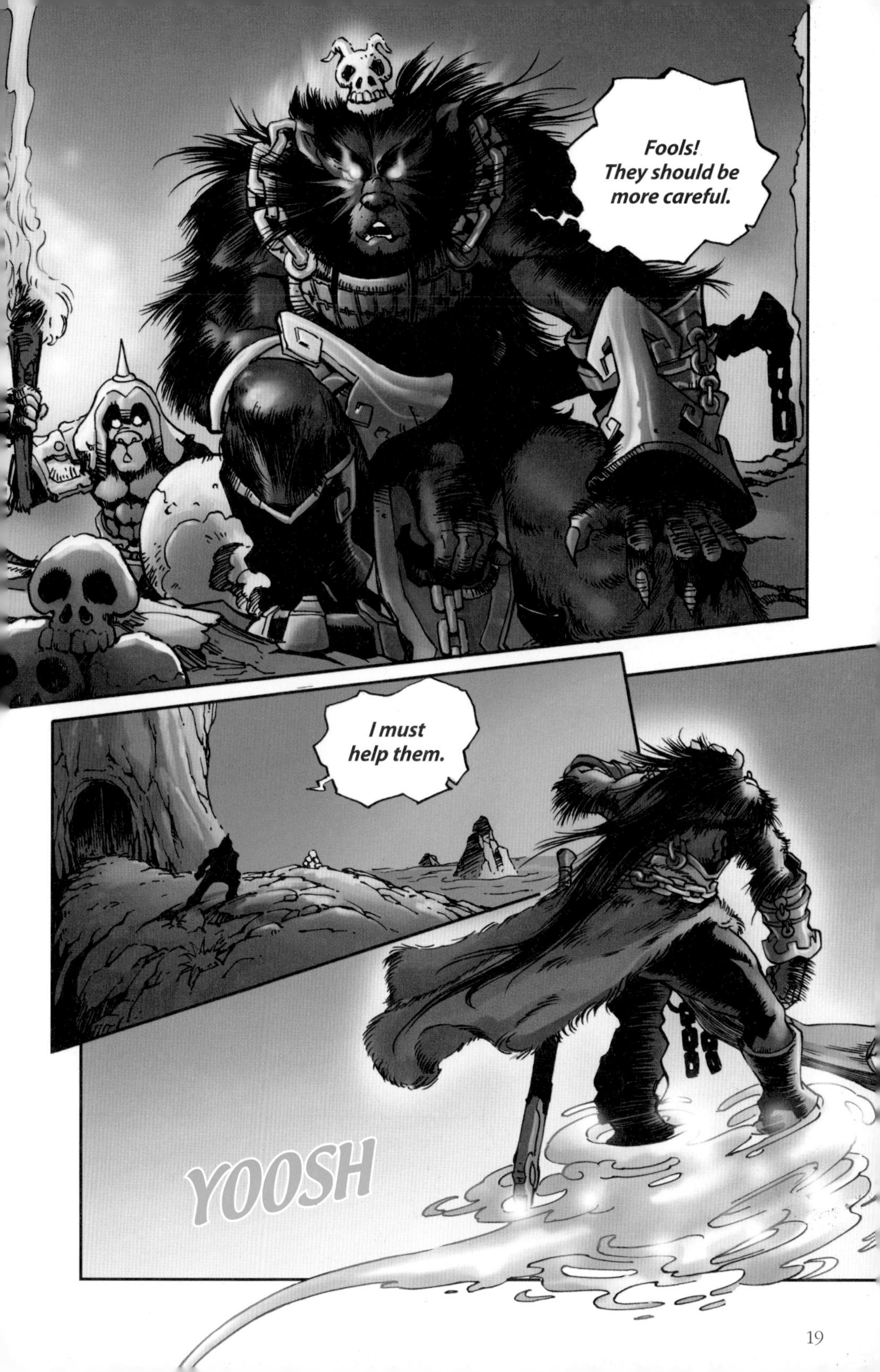
Fools!
They should be
more careful.
I must
help them.
YOOSH

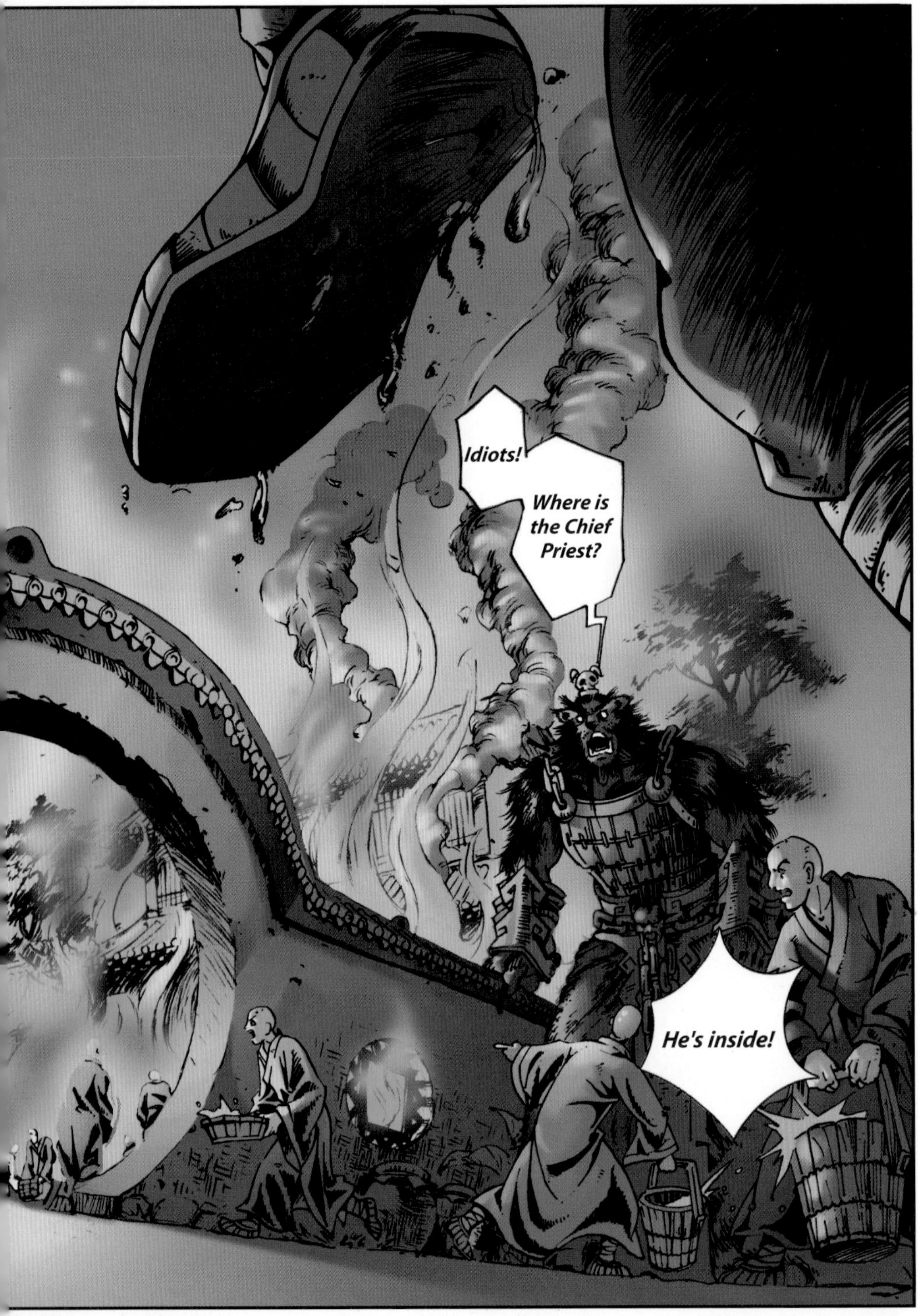
Idiots!
Where is the Chief Priest?
He's inside!

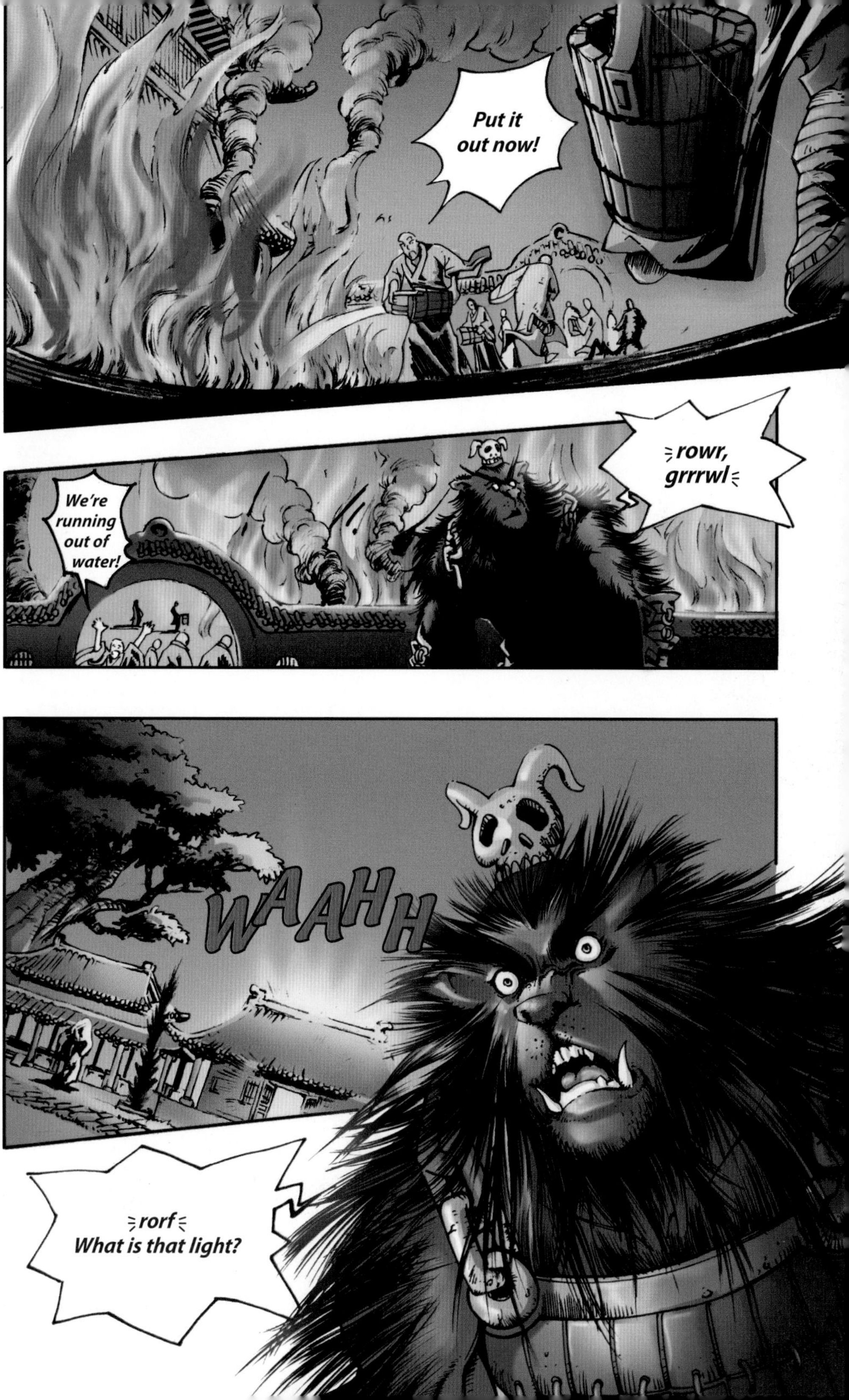
Put it out now!
rowr, grrrwl
We're running out of water!
WAAHH
rorf
What is that light?

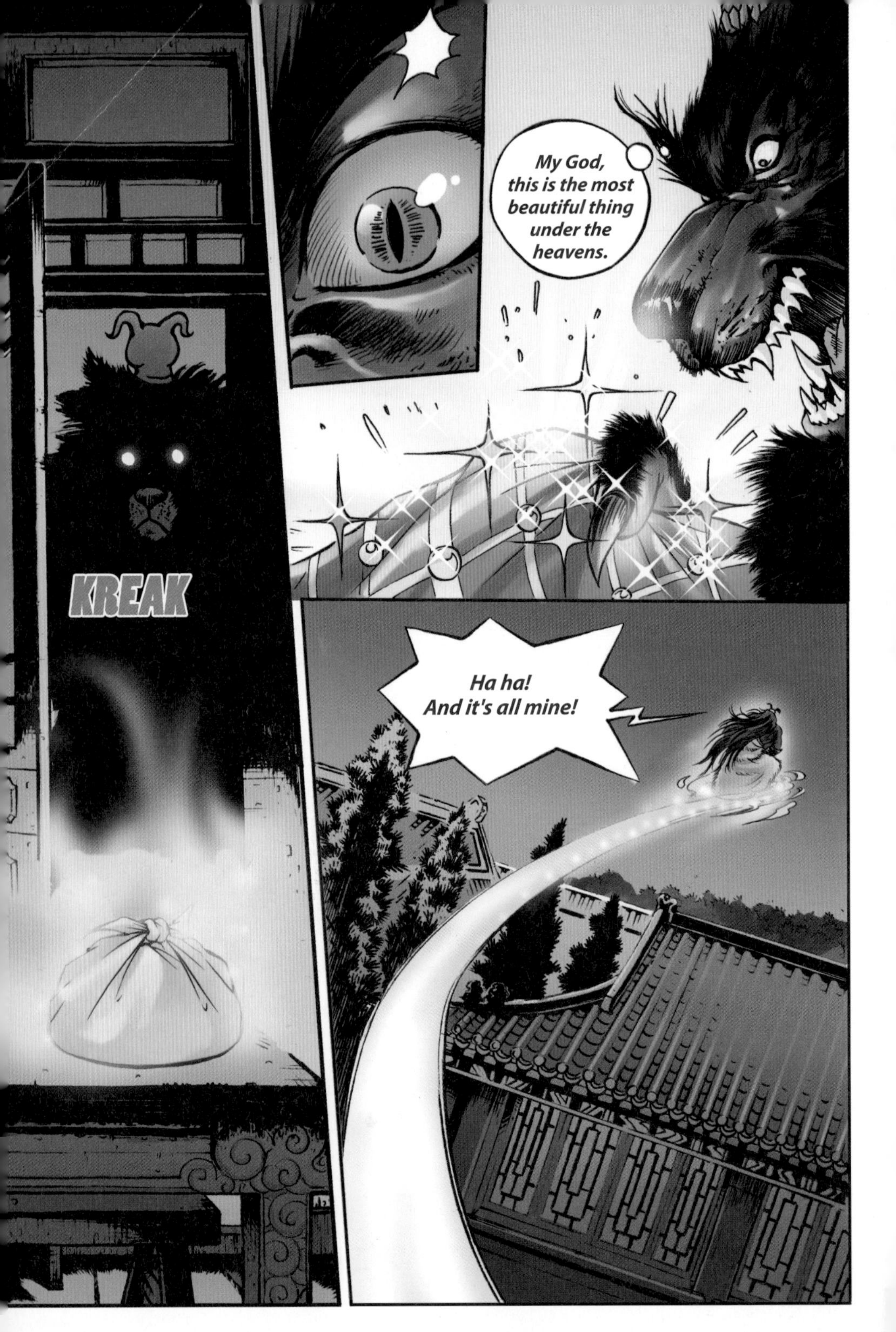
KREAK
My God, this is the most beautiful thing under the heavens.
Ha ha! And it's all mine!

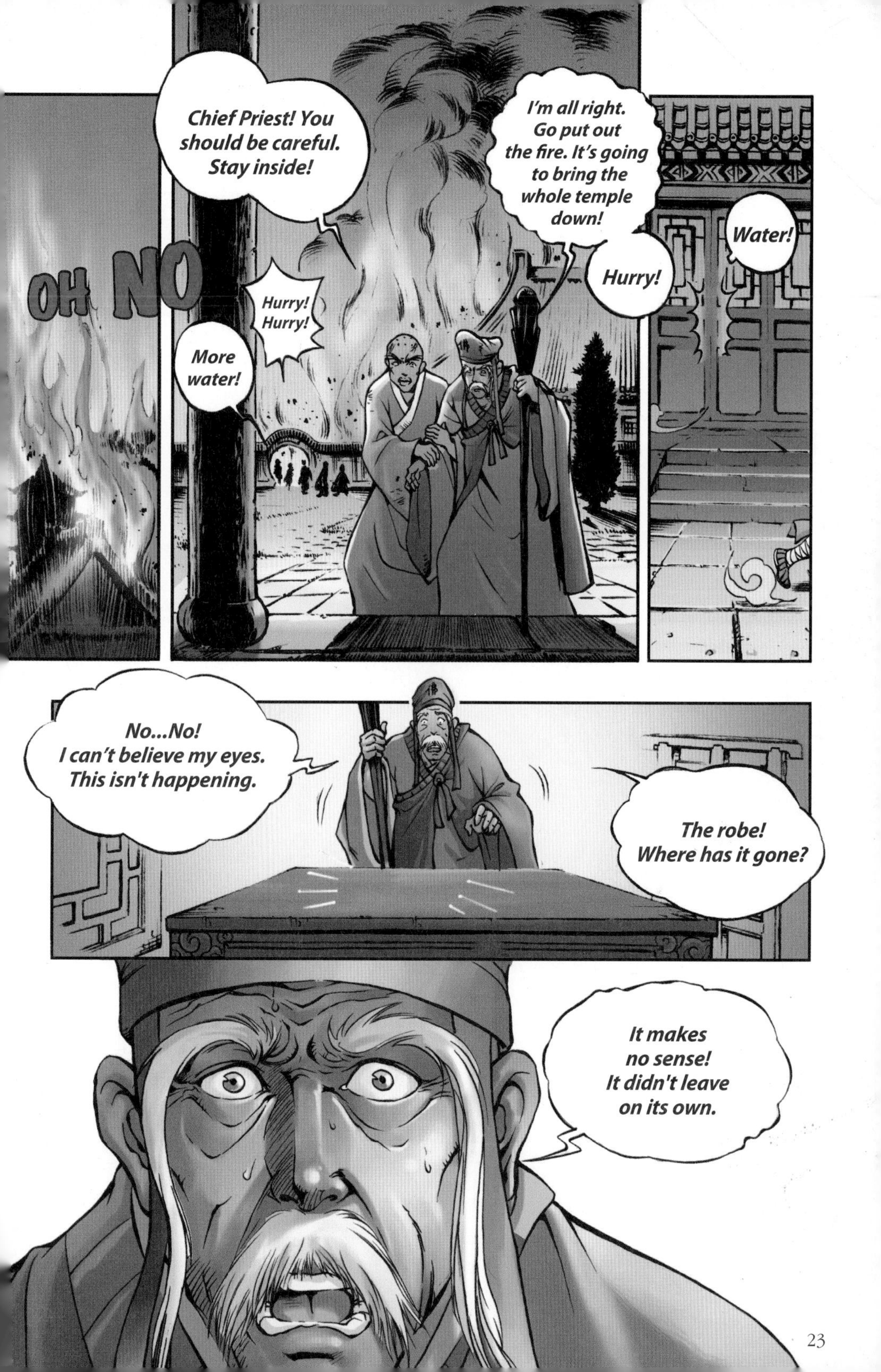
OH NO
Chief Priest! You should be careful. Stay inside!
I'm all right. Go put out the fire. It's going to bring the whole temple down!
Hurry!
Water!
Hurry! Hurry!
More water!
No...No! I can't believe my eyes. This isn't happening.
The robe! Where has it gone?
It makes no sense! It didn't leave on its own.

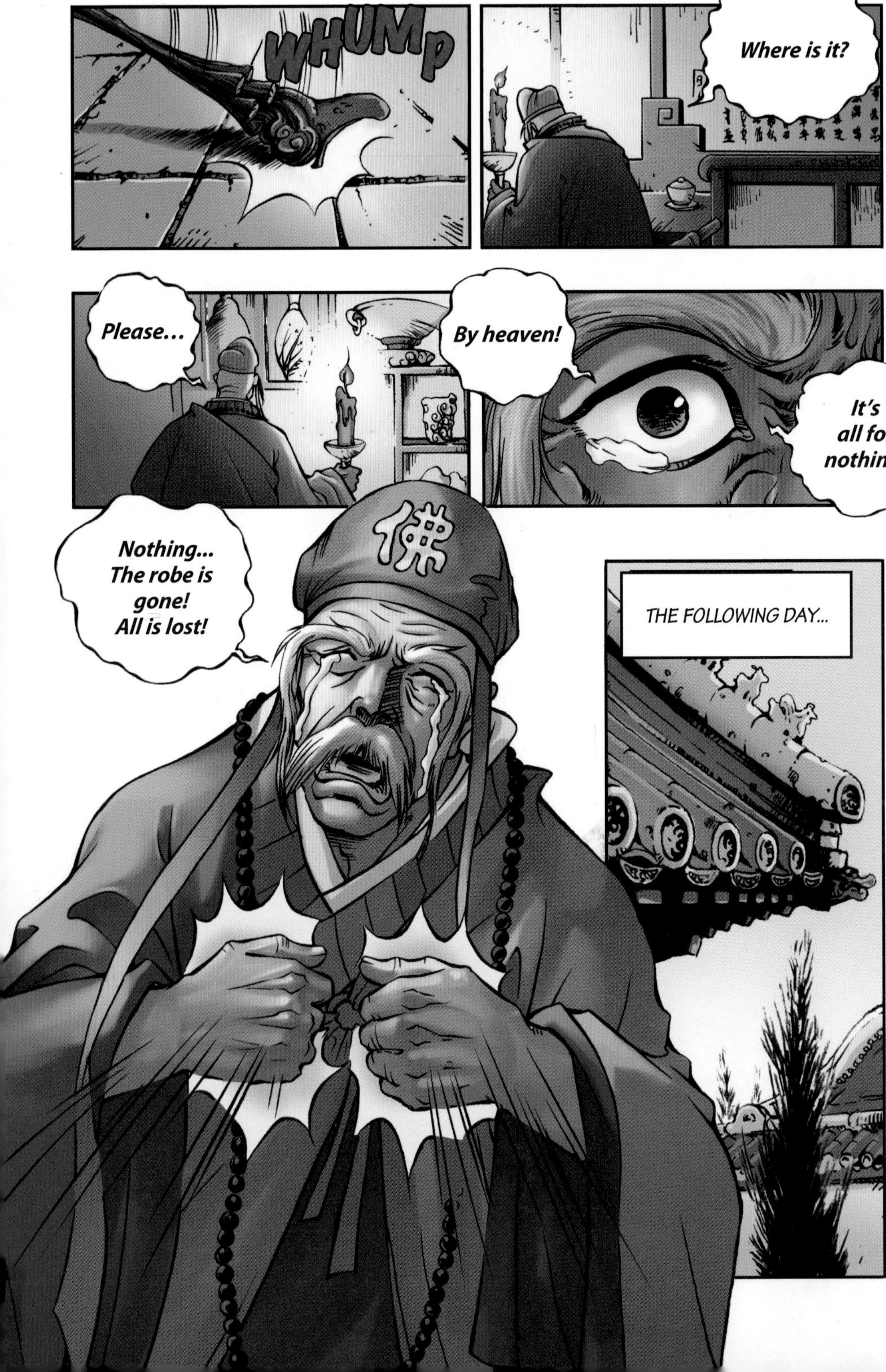
WHUMp
Where is it?
Please…
By heaven!
It's all for nothing!
Nothing... The robe is gone! All is lost!
THE FOLLOWING DAY...

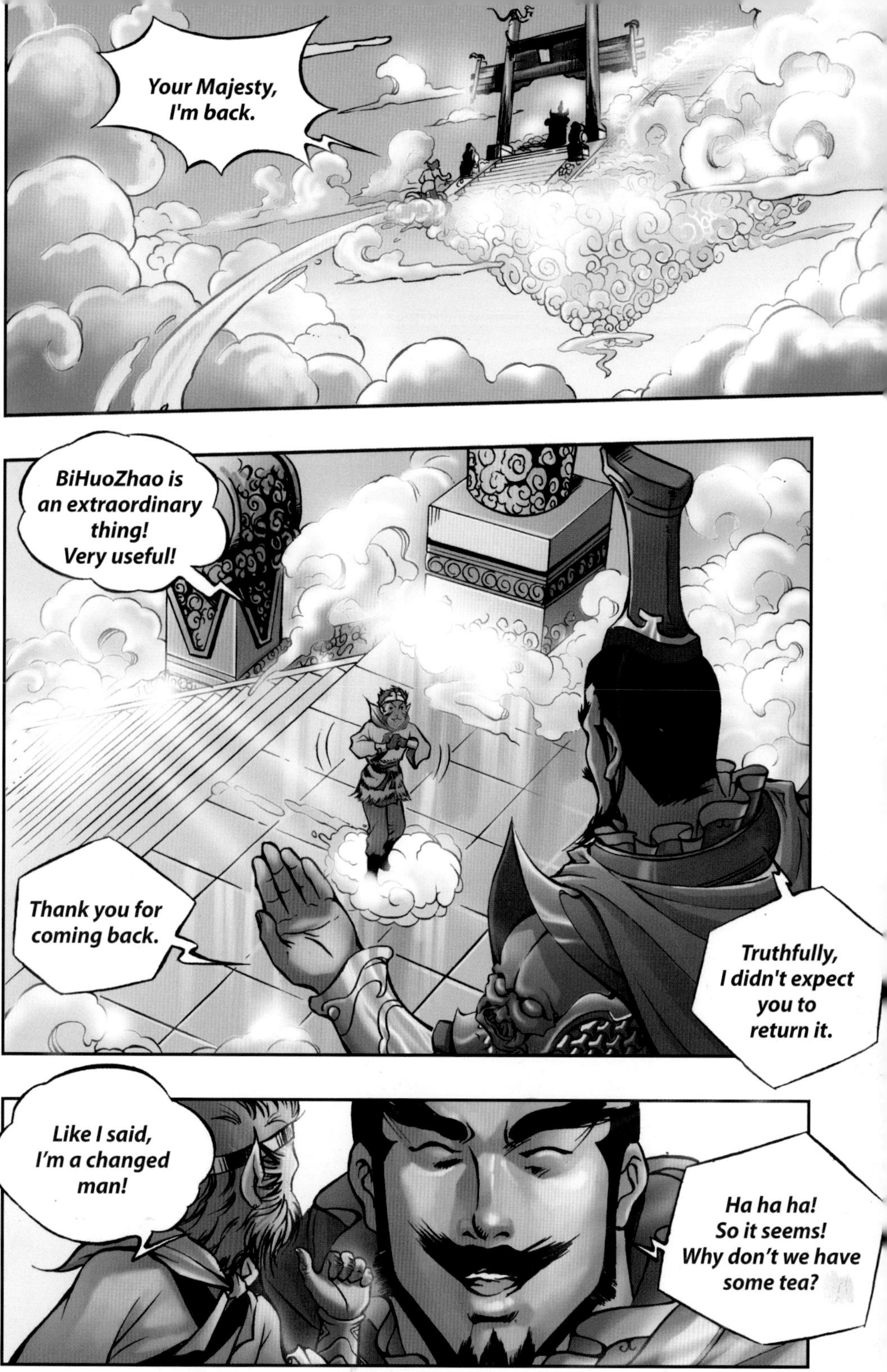
Your Majesty, I'm back.
BiHuoZhao is an extraordinary thing! Very useful!
Thank you for coming back.
Truthfully, I didn't expect you to return it.
Like I said, I'm a changed man!
Ha ha ha! So it seems! Why don't we have some tea?

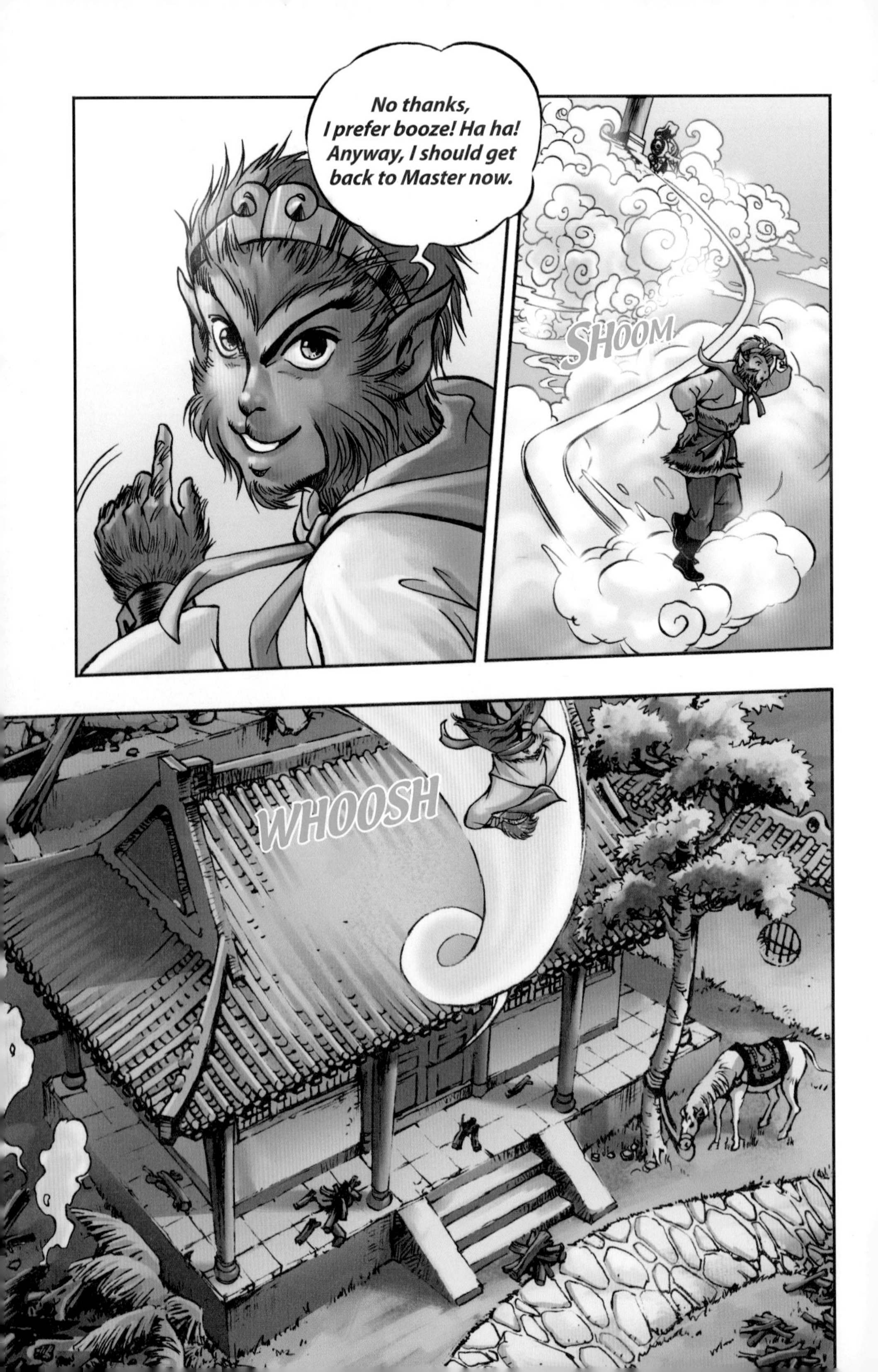
No thanks, I prefer booze! Ha ha! Anyway, I should get back to Master now.
SHOOM
WHOOSH

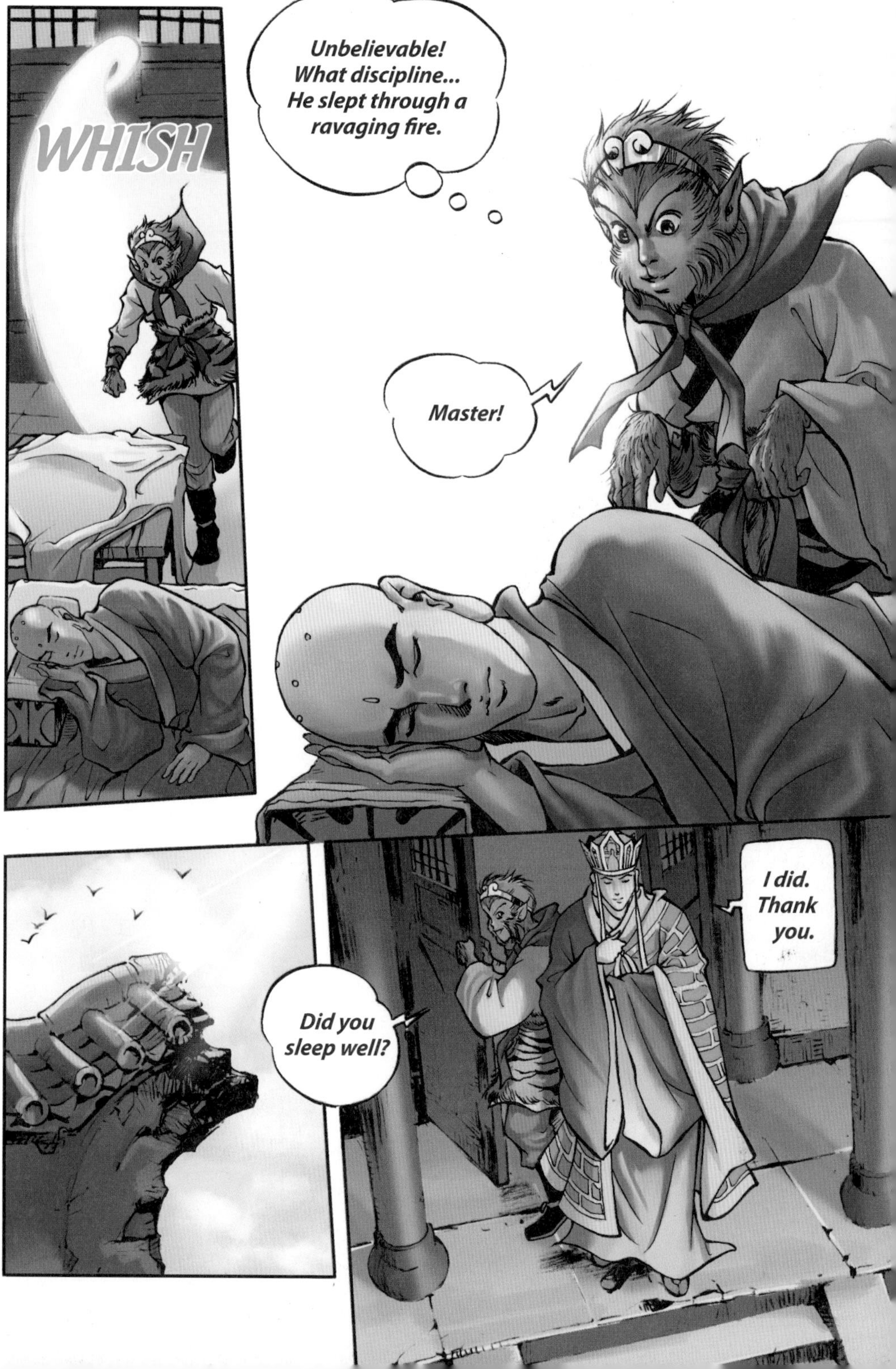
WHISH
Unbelievable! What discipline... He slept through a ravaging fire.
Master!
I did. Thank you.
Did you sleep well?

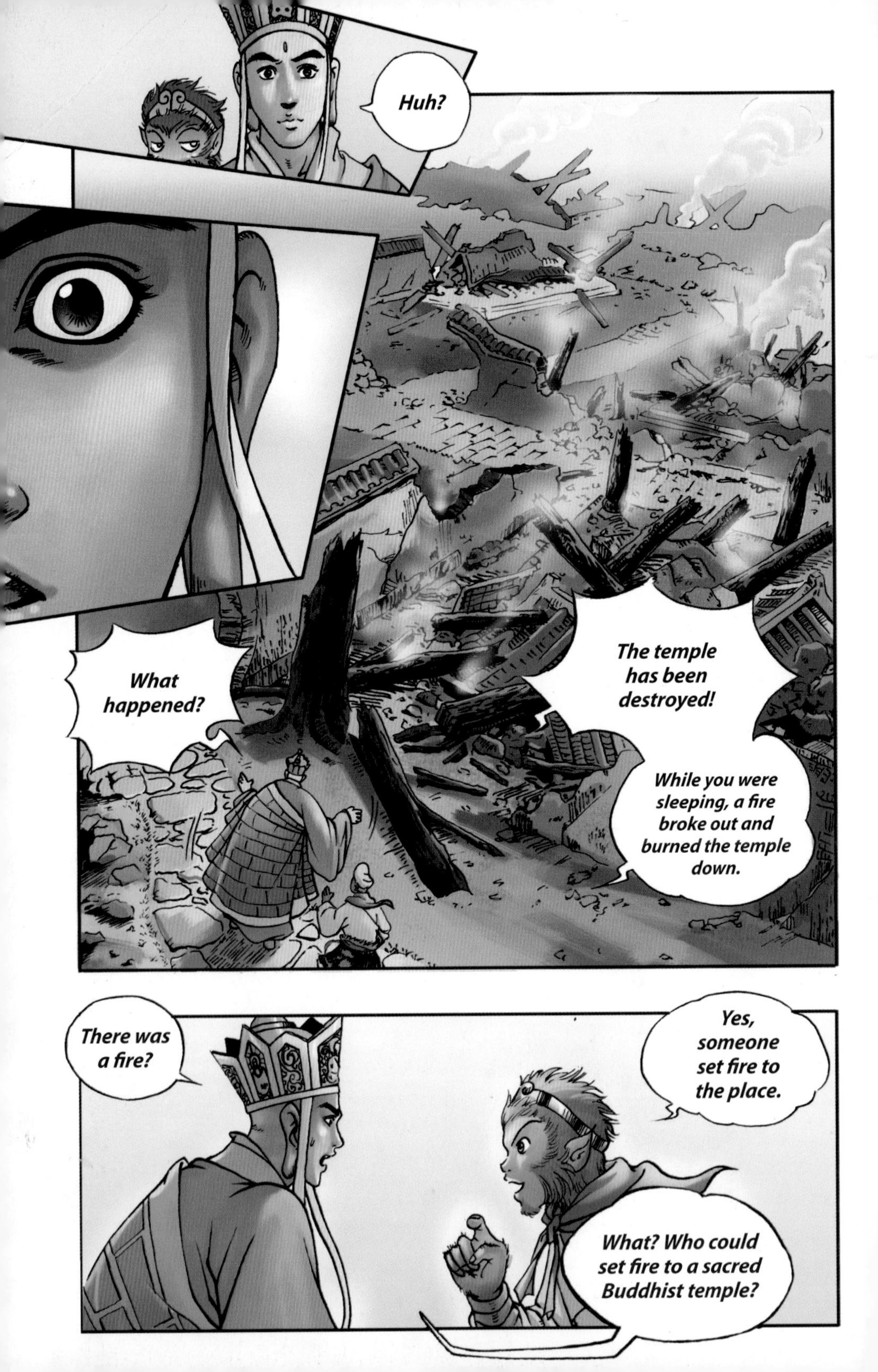
Huh?
What happened?
The temple has been destroyed!
While you were sleeping, a fire broke out and burned the temple down.
There was a fire?
Yes, someone set fire to the place.
What? Who could set fire to a sacred Buddhist temple?

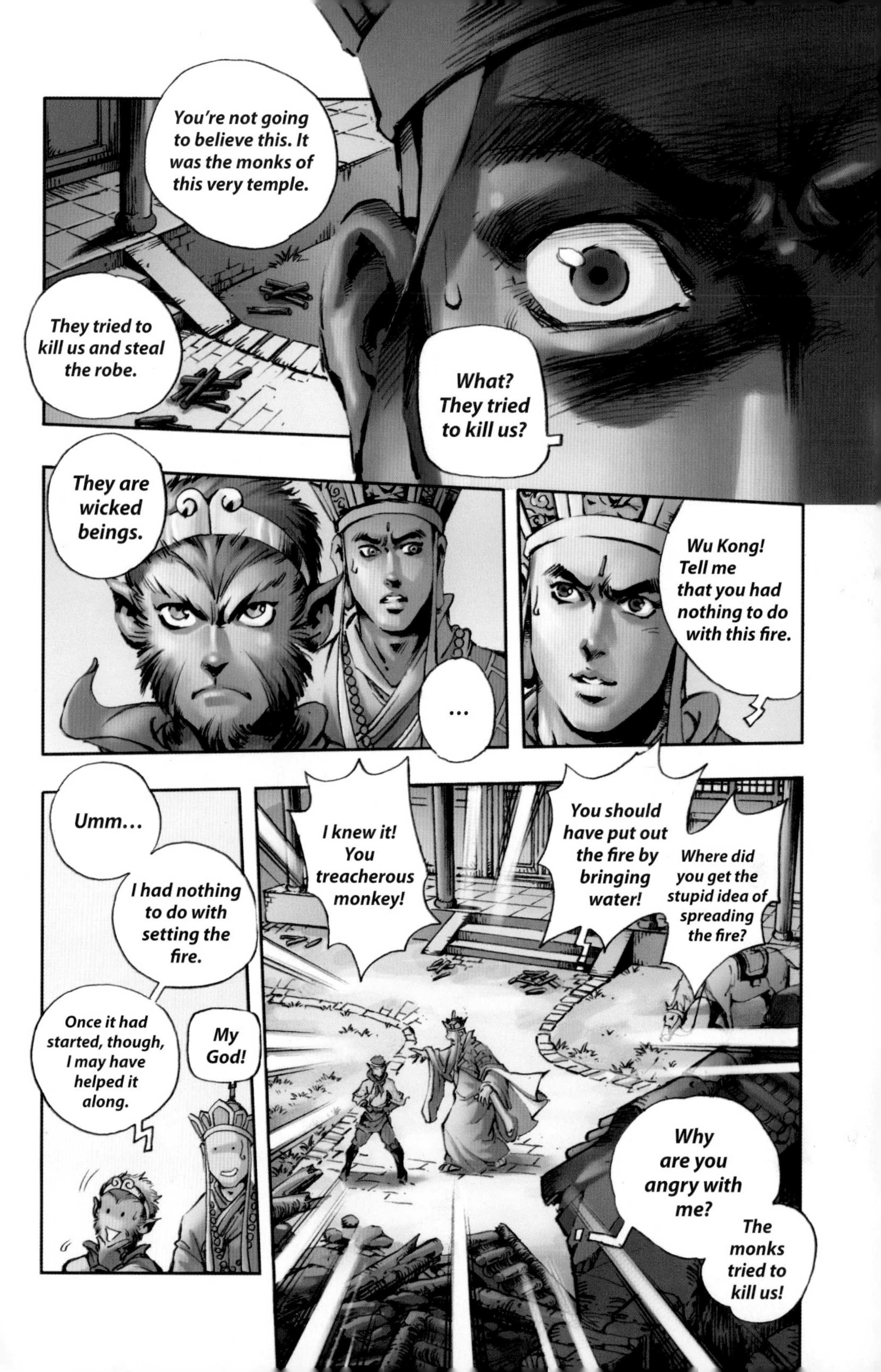
You're not going to believe this. It was the monks of this very temple.
They tried to kill us and steal the robe.
What? They tried to kill us?
They are wicked beings.
...
Wu Kong! Tell me that you had nothing to do with this fire.
Umm...
I had nothing to do with setting the fire.
Once it had started, though, I may have helped it along.
My God!
I knew it! You treacherous monkey!
You should have put out the fire by bringing water!
Where did you get the stupid idea of spreading the fire?
Why are you angry with me?
The monks tried to kill us!

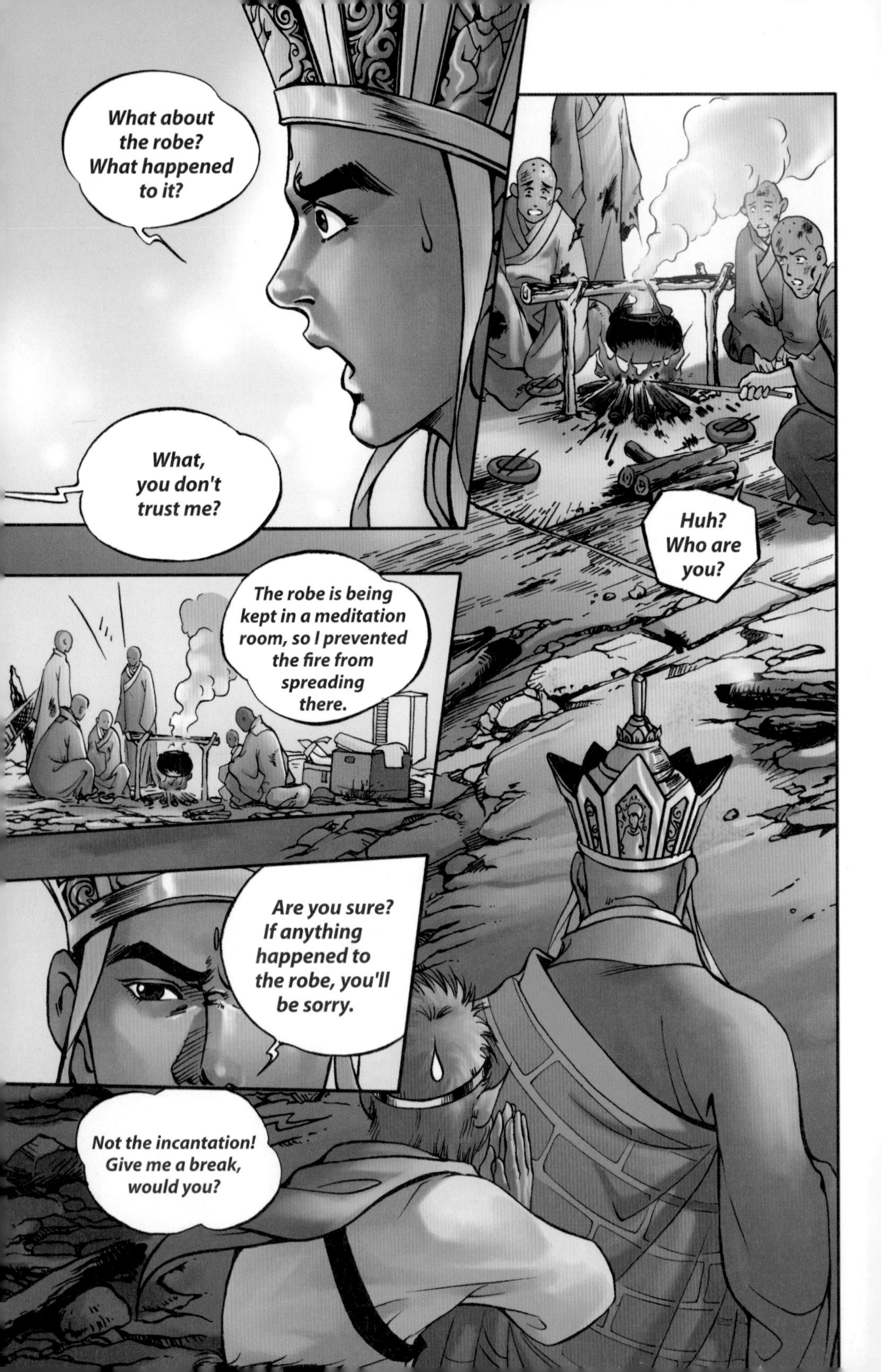
What about the robe? What happened to it?
What, you don't trust me?
Huh? Who are you?
The robe is being kept in a meditation room, so I prevented the fire from spreading there.
Are you sure? If anything happened to the robe, you'll be sorry.
Not the incantation! Give me a break, would you?

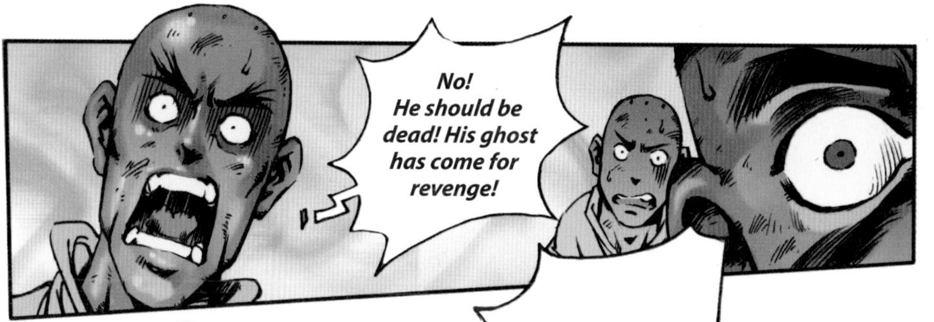
No!
He should be dead! His ghost has come for revenge!

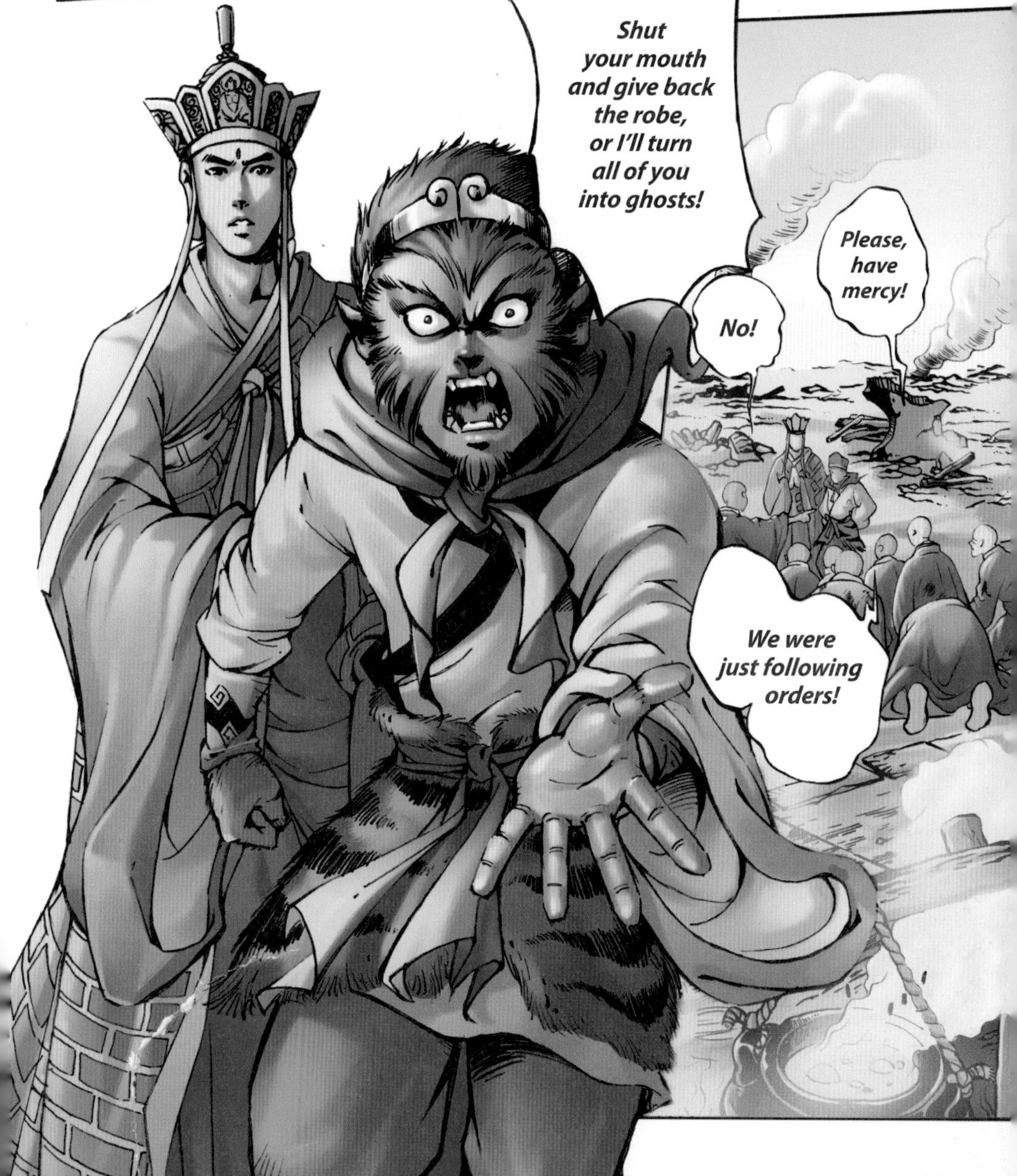
Shut your mouth and give back the robe, or I'll turn all of you into ghosts!
Please, have mercy!
No!
We were just following orders!

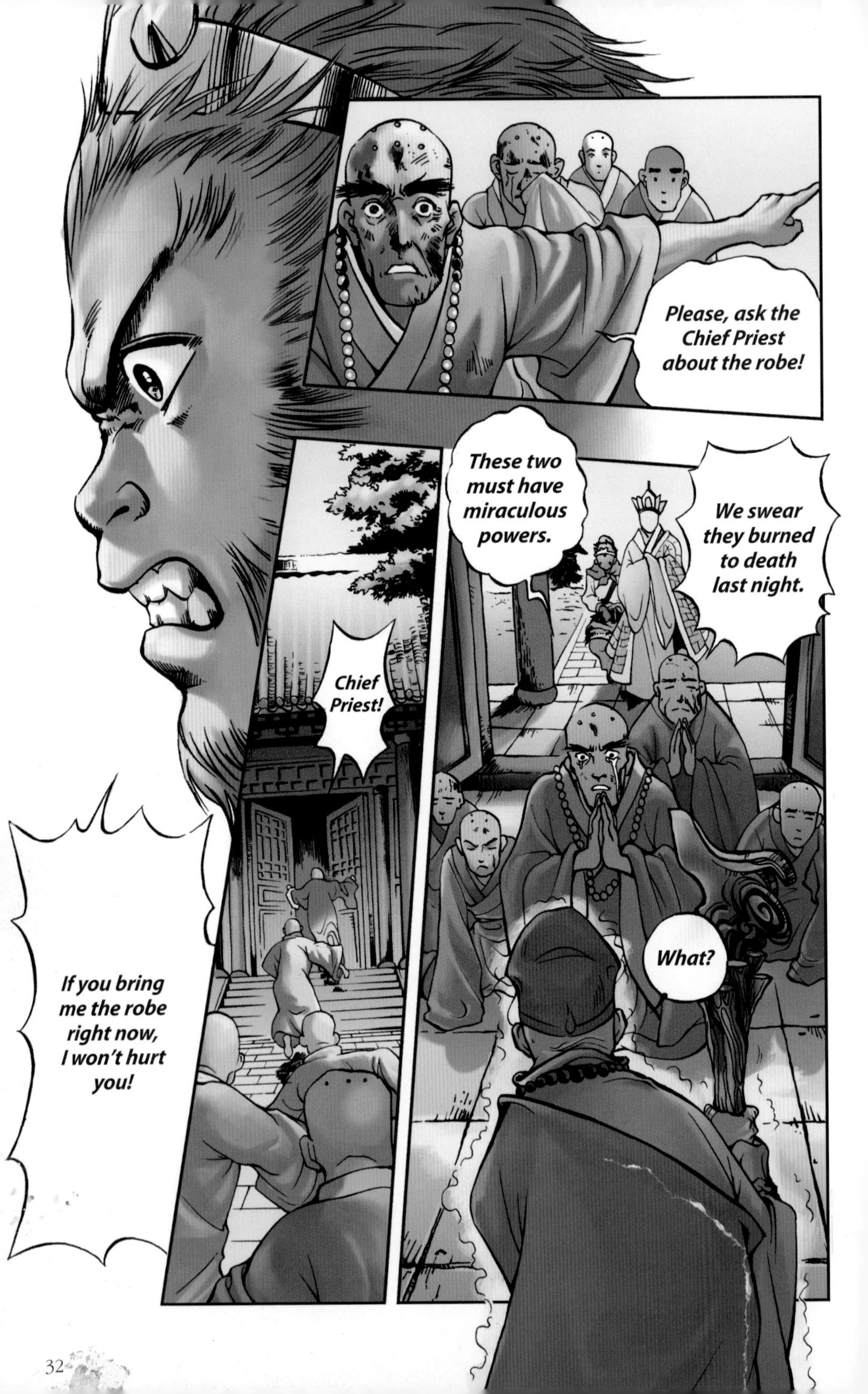
Please, ask the Chief Priest about the robe!
Chief Priest!
These two must have miraculous powers.
We swear they burned to death last night.
What?
If you bring me the robe right now, I won't hurt you!

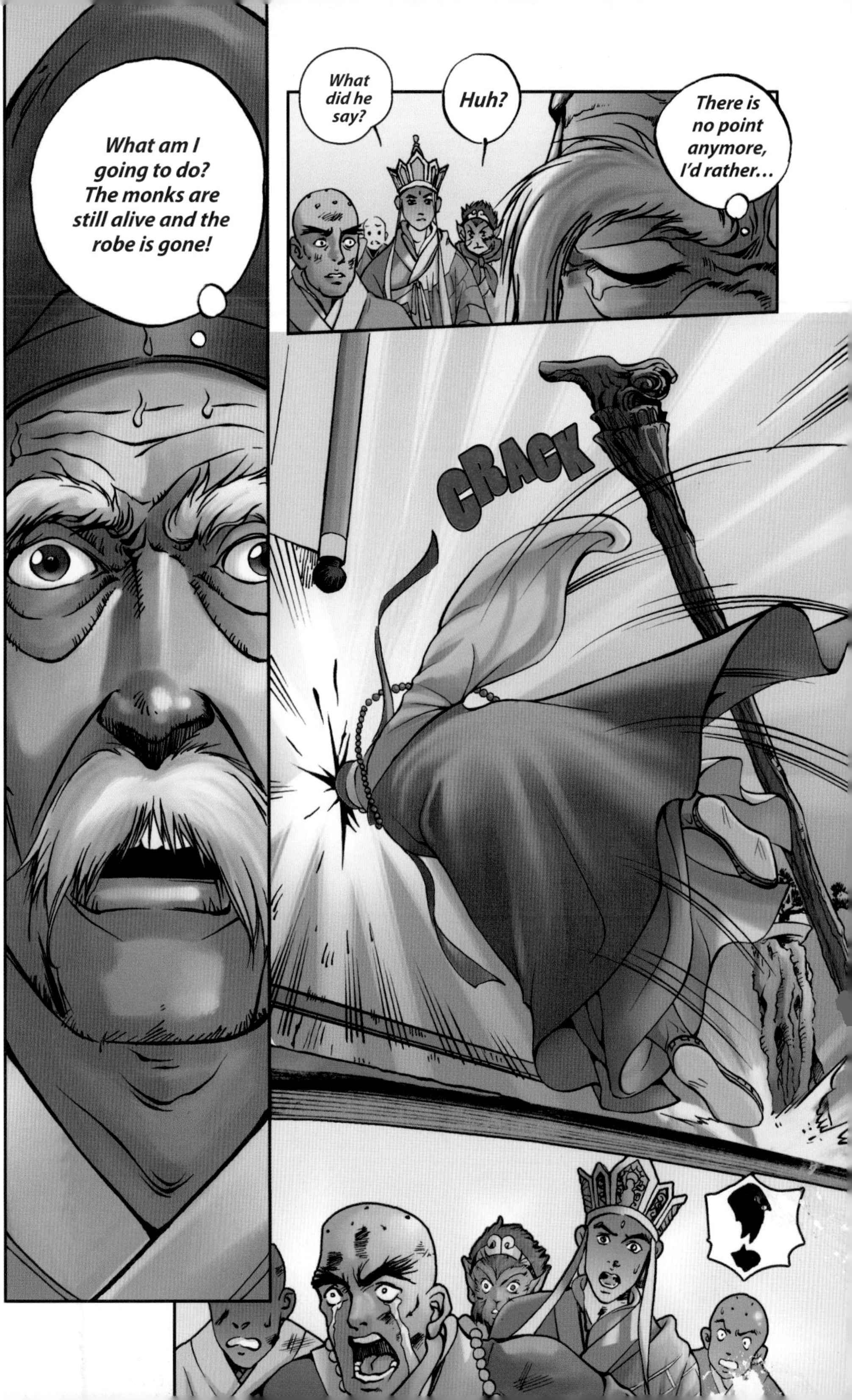
What am I going to do? The monks are still alive and the robe is gone!
What did he say?
Huh?
There is no point anymore, I'd rather…
CRACK
!

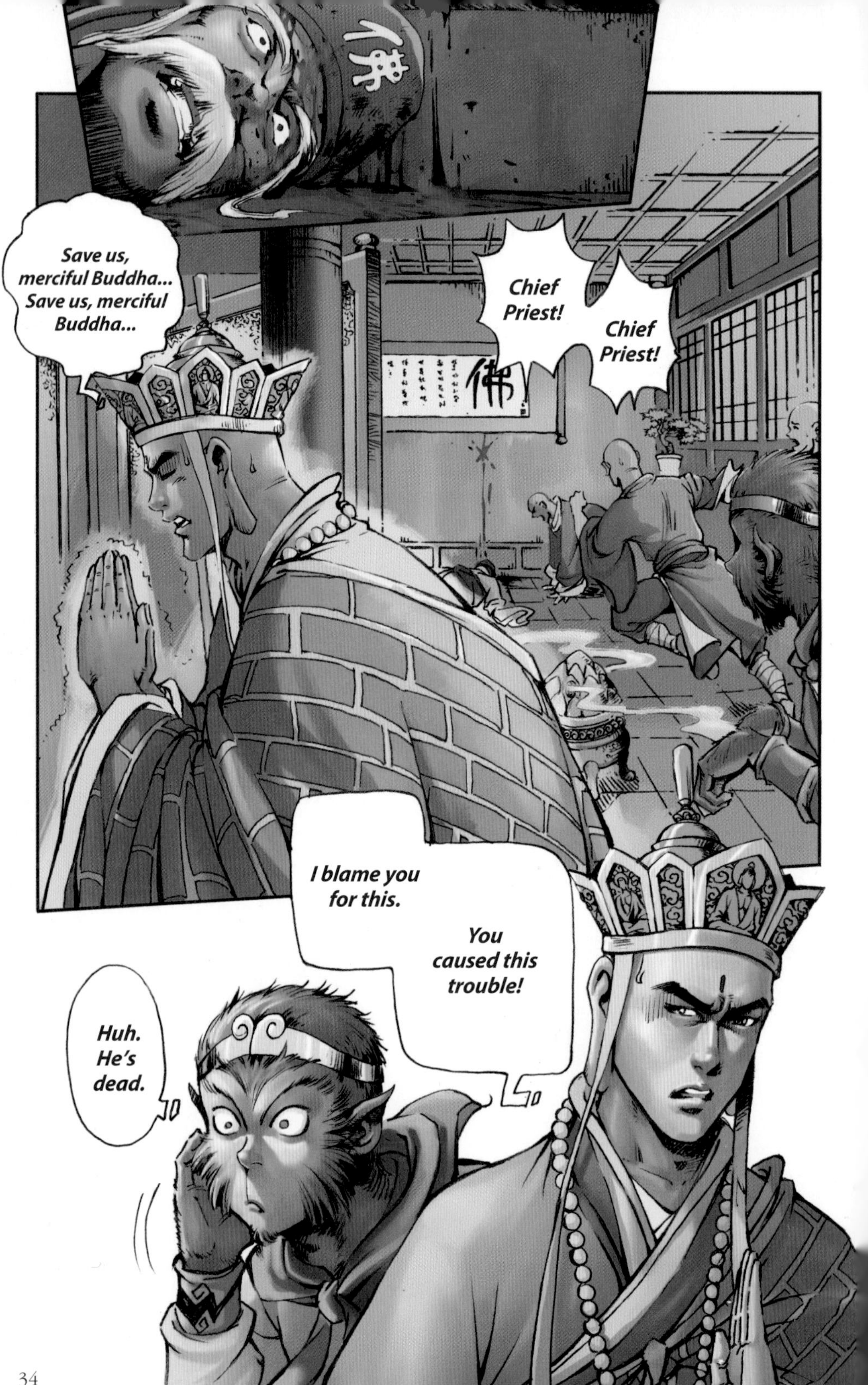
Save us, merciful Buddha... Save us, merciful Buddha...
Chief Priest!
Chief Priest!
I blame you for this.
You caused this trouble!
Huh. He's dead.

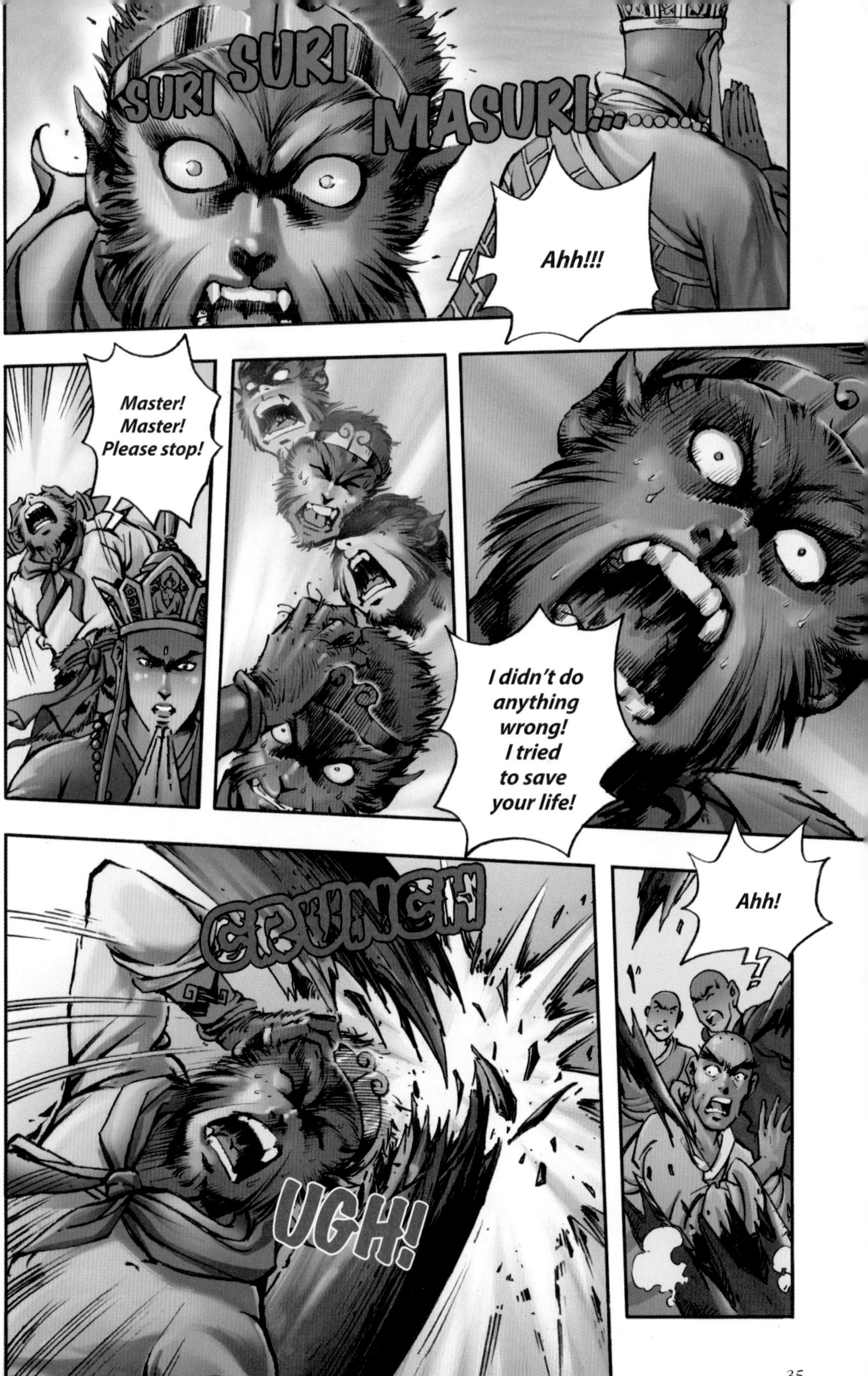
SURI SURI MASURI...
Ahh!!!
Master! Master! Please stop!
I didn't do anything wrong! I tried to save your life!
CRUNCH
UGH!
Ahh!

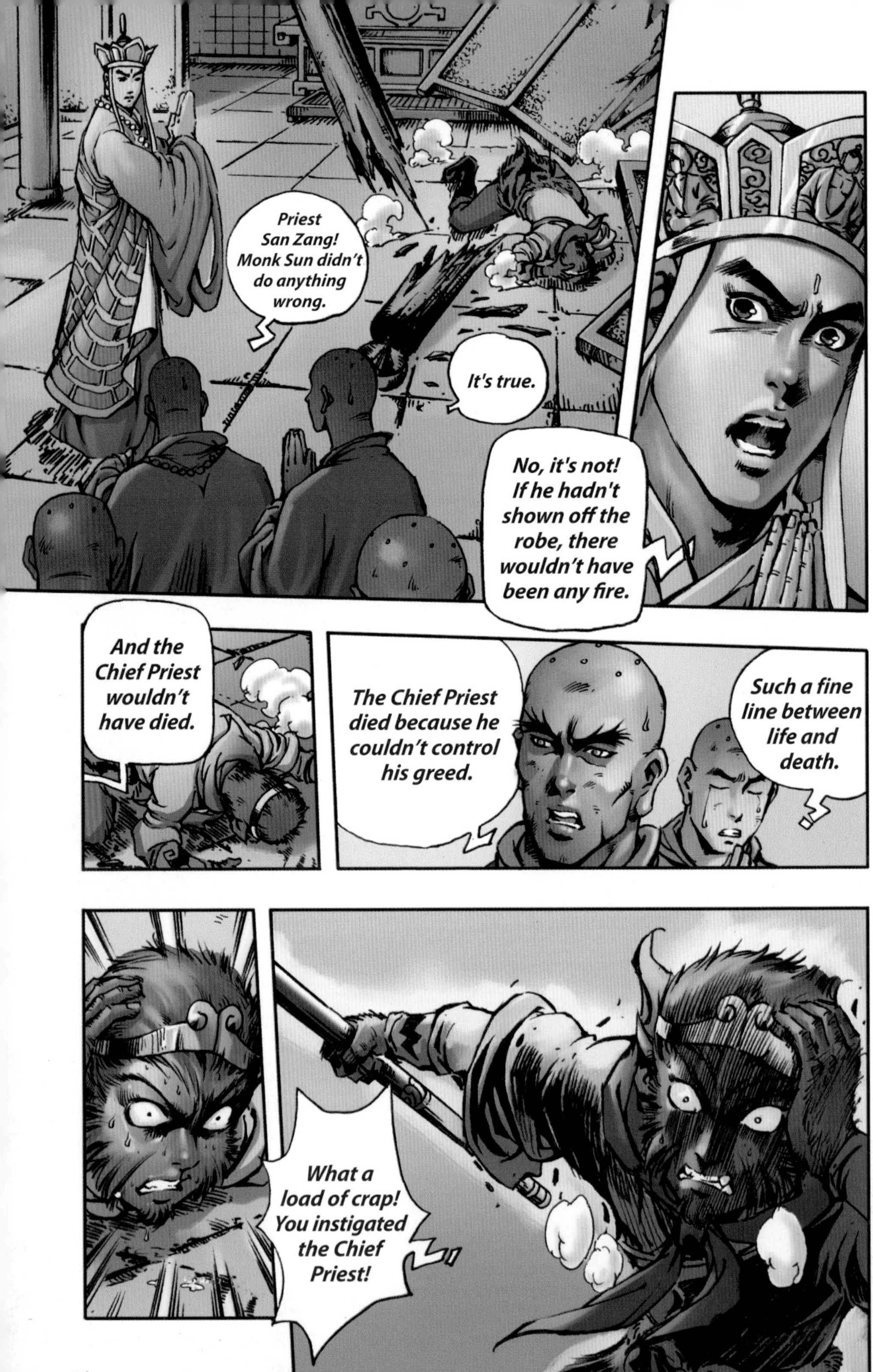
Priest San Zang! Monk Sun didn't do anything wrong.
It's true.
No, it's not! If he hadn't shown off the robe, there wouldn't have been any fire.
And the Chief Priest wouldn't have died.
The Chief Priest died because he couldn't control his greed.
Such a fine line between life and death.
What a load of crap! You instigated the Chief Priest!

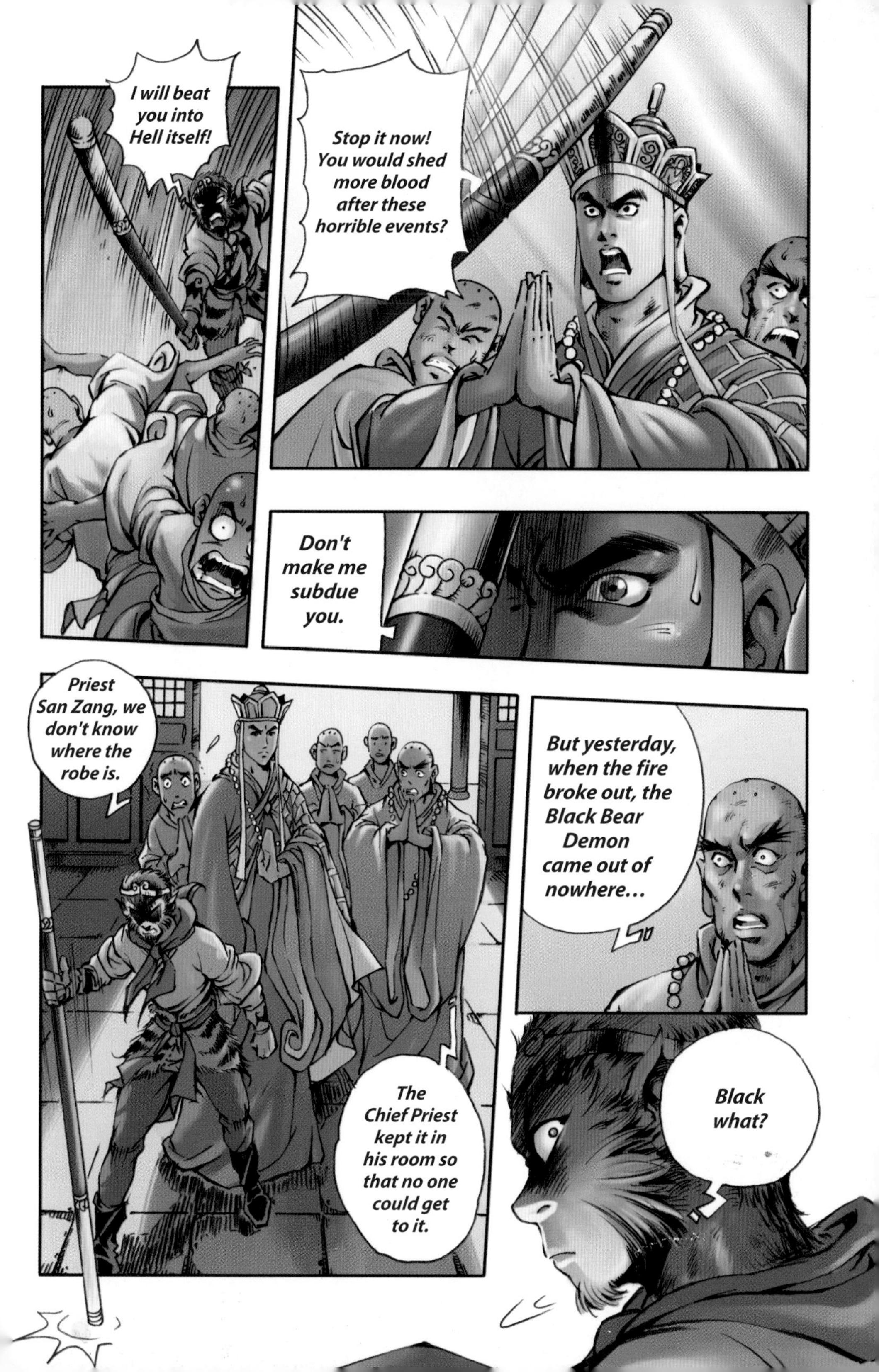

I will beat you into Hell itself!
Stop it now! You would shed more blood after these horrible events?
Don't make me subdue you.
Priest San Zang, we don't know where the robe is.
The Chief Priest kept it in his room so that no one could get to it.
But yesterday, when the fire broke out, the Black Bear Demon came out of nowhere…
Black what?

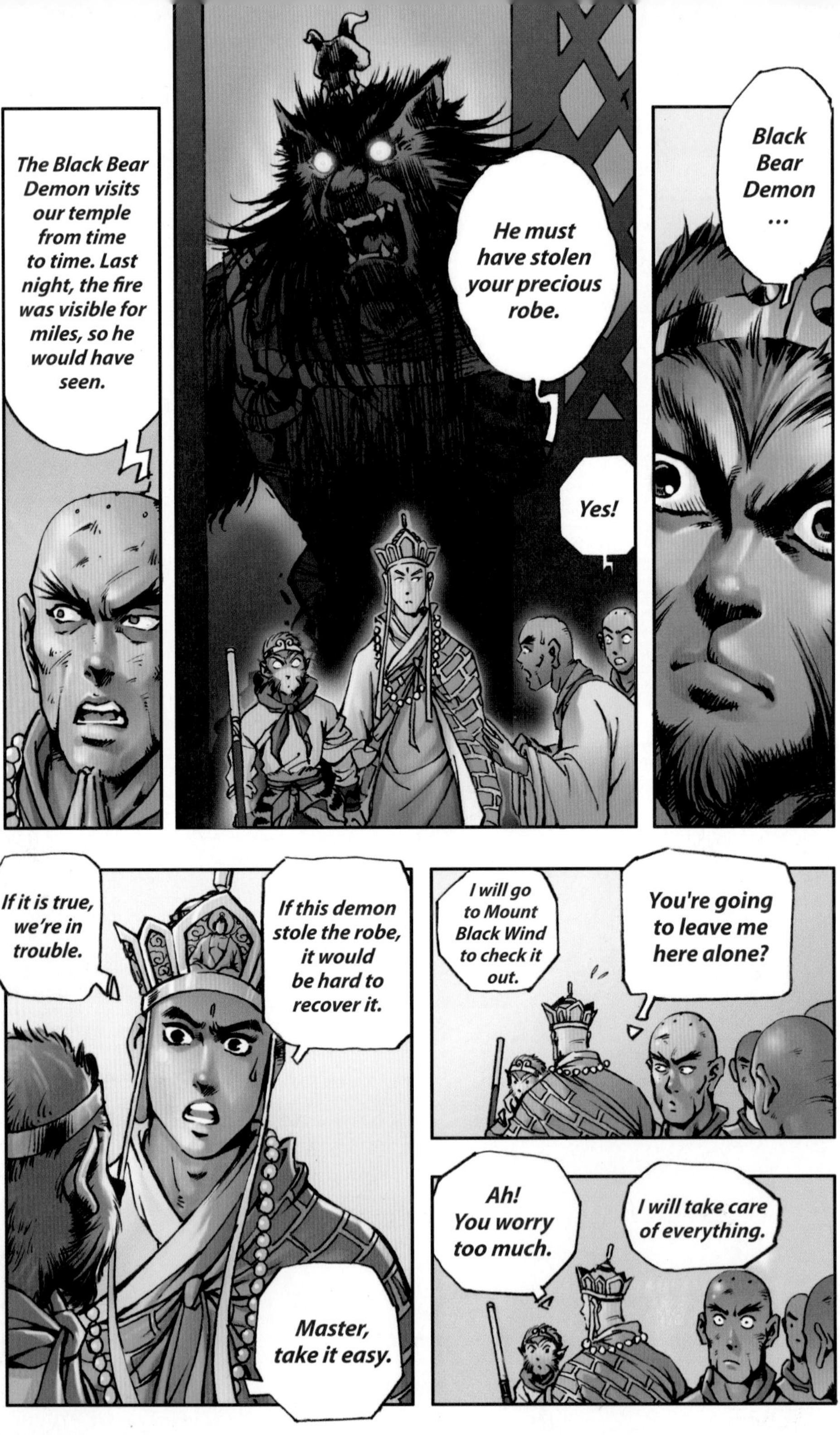
The Black Bear Demon visits our temple from time to time. Last night, the fire was visible for miles, so he would have seen.
He must have stolen your precious robe.
Yes!
Black Bear Demon …
If it is true, we're in trouble.
If this demon stole the robe, it would be hard to recover it.
Master, take it easy.
I will go to Mount Black Wind to check it out.
You're going to leave me here alone?
Ah! You worry too much.
I will take care of everything.

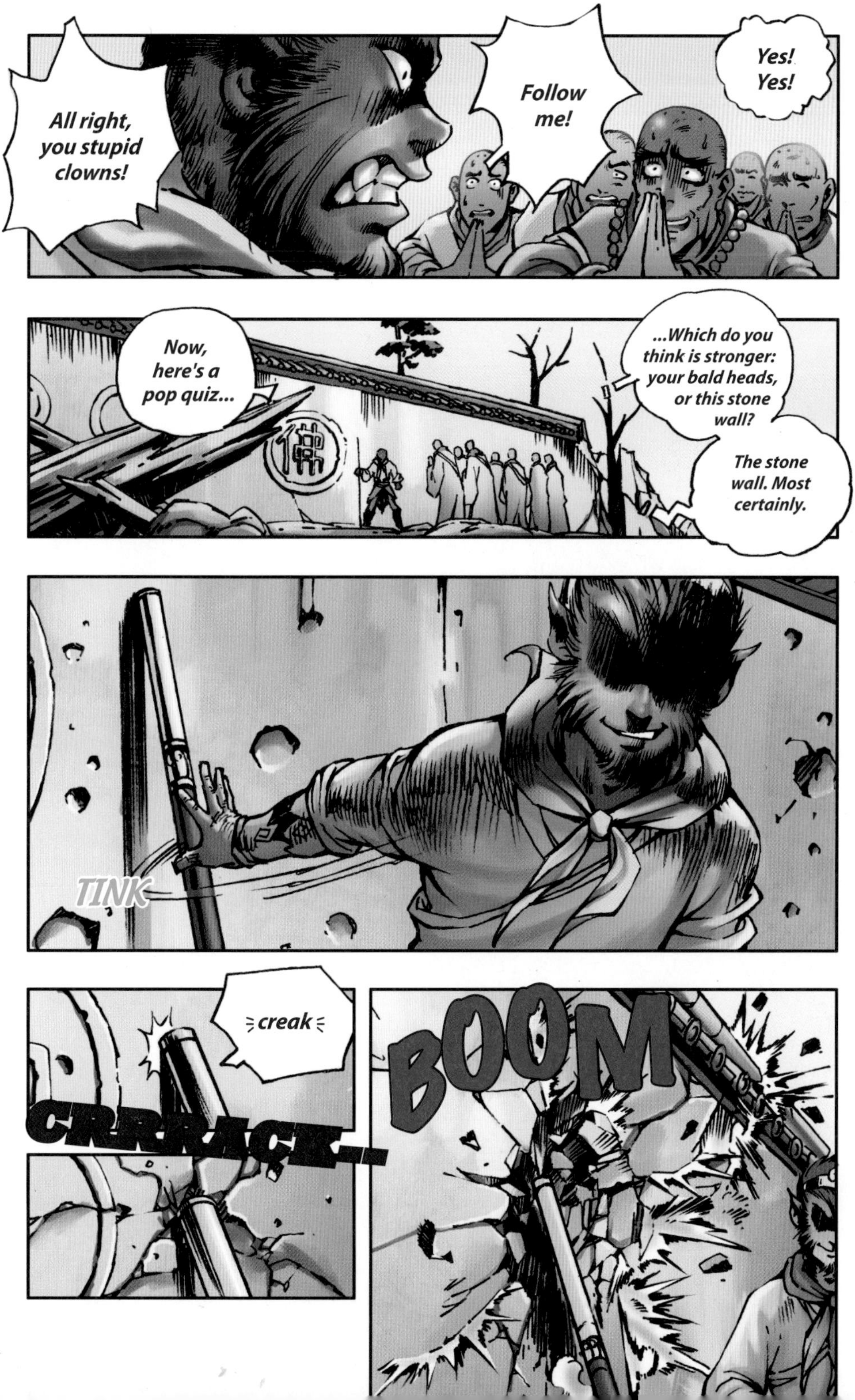
All right, you stupid clowns!
Follow me!
Yes! Yes!
Now, here's a pop quiz...
...Which do you think is stronger: your bald heads, or this stone wall?
The stone wall. Most certainly.
TINK
creak
CRRACK...
BOOM

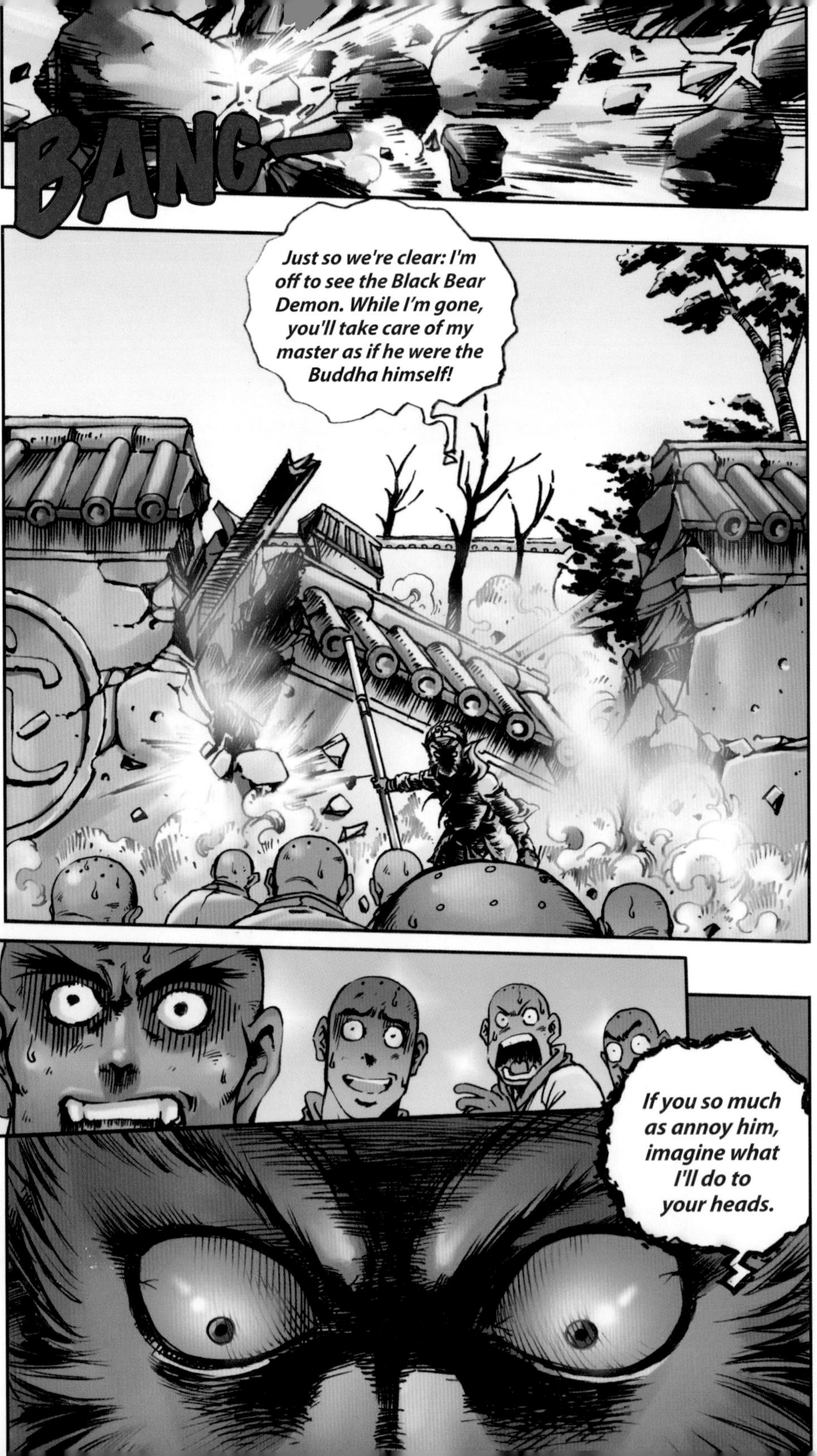
BANG—
Just so we're clear: I'm off to see the Black Bear Demon. While I'm gone, you'll take care of my master as if he were the Buddha himself!
If you so much as annoy him, imagine what I'll do to your heads.

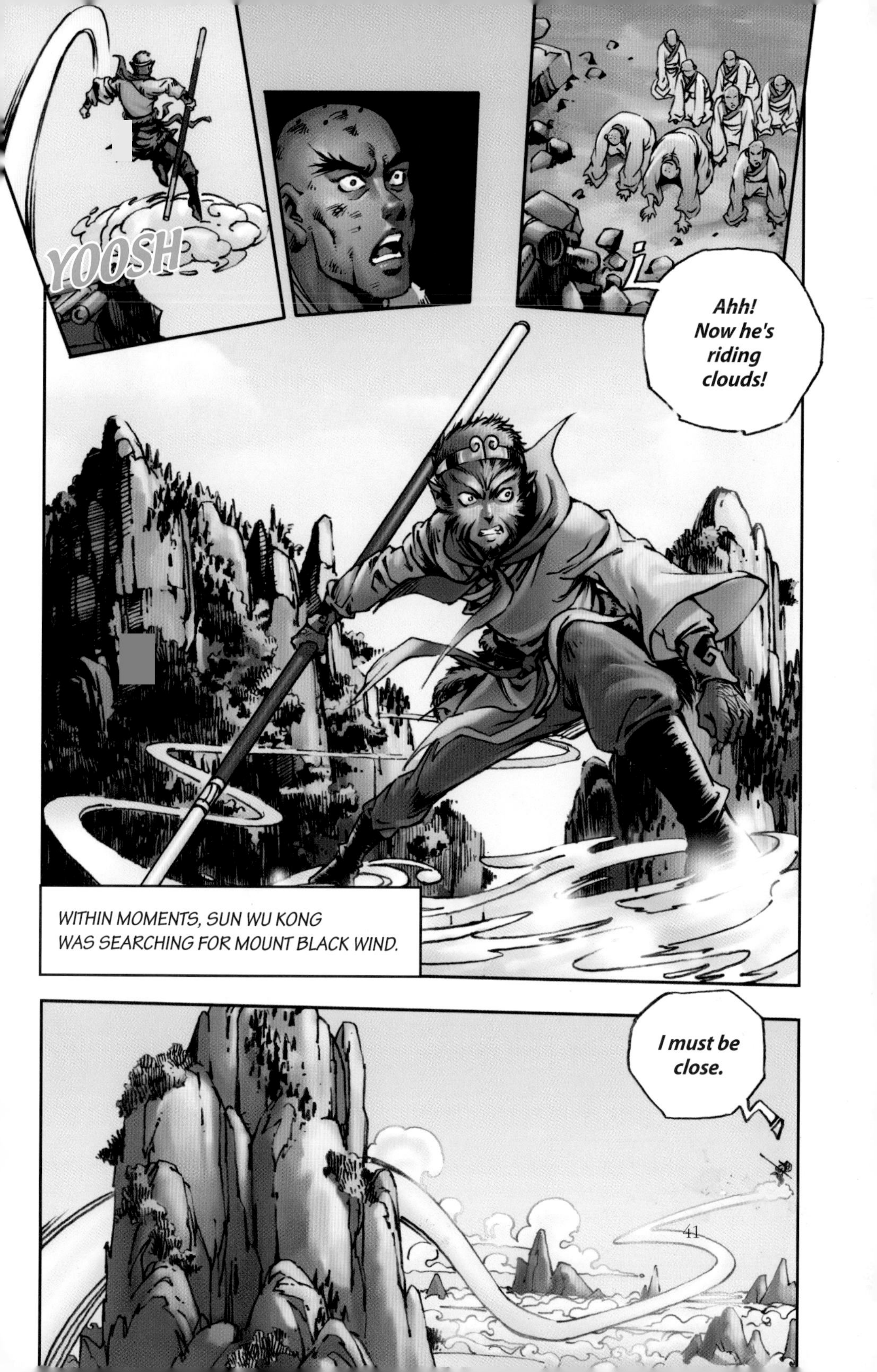
YOOSH
Ahh! Now he's riding clouds!
WITHIN MOMENTS, SUN WU KONG WAS SEARCHING FOR MOUNT BLACK WIND.
I must be close.

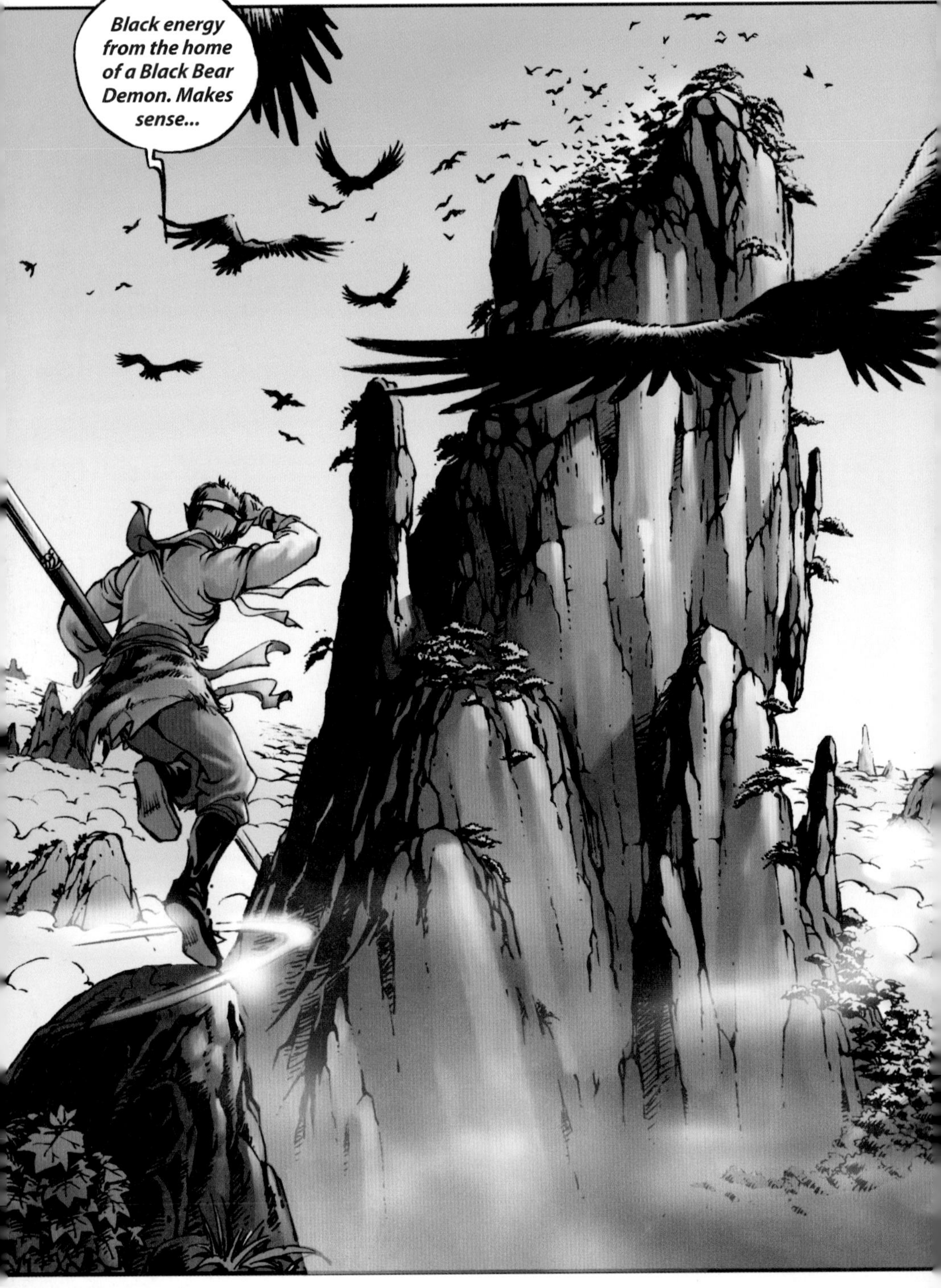
Black energy from the home of a Black Bear Demon. Makes sense...

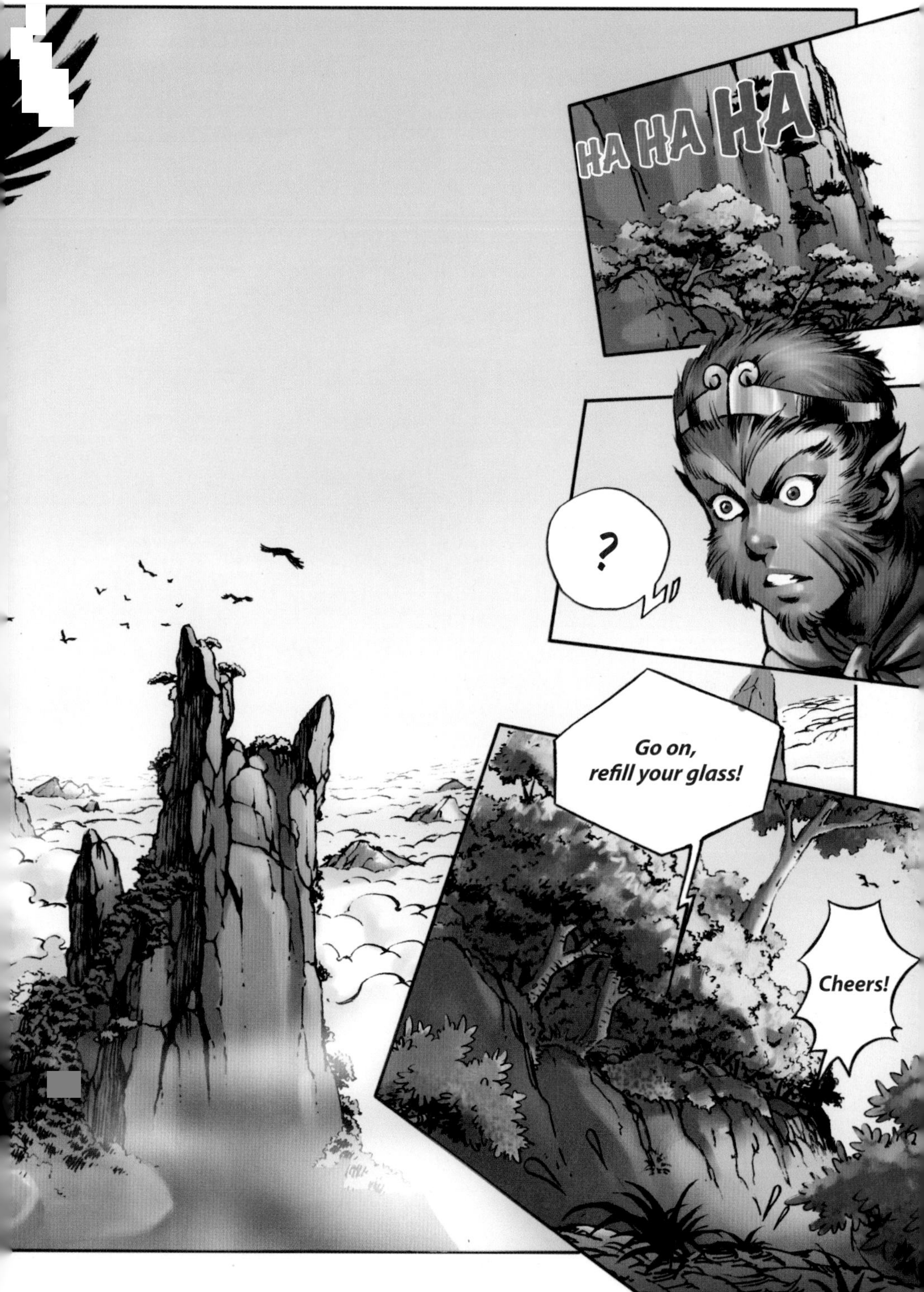
HA HA HA
?
Go on, refill your glass!
Cheers!

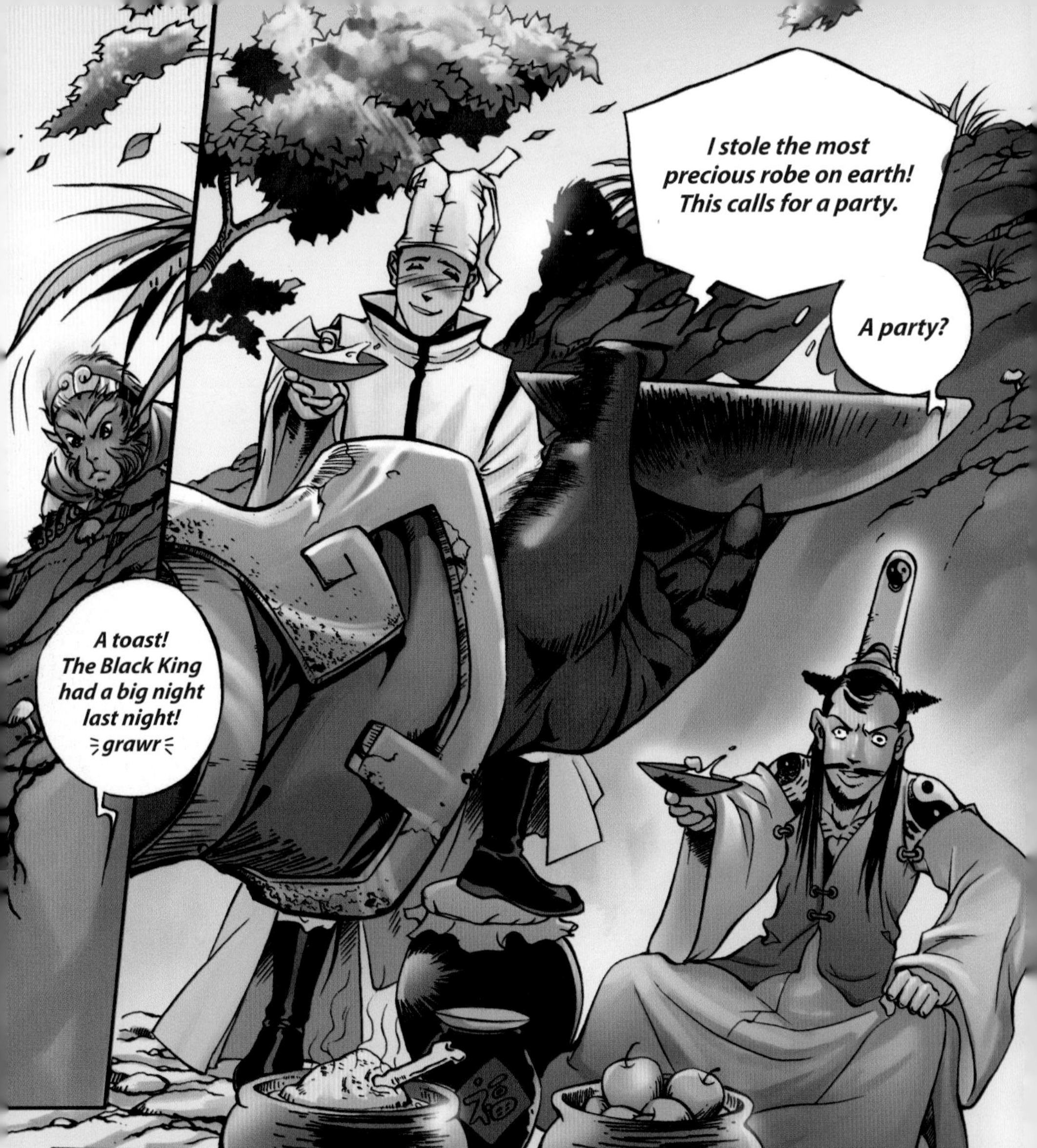
I stole the most precious robe on earth! This calls for a party.
A party?
A toast! The Black King had a big night last night!
grawr
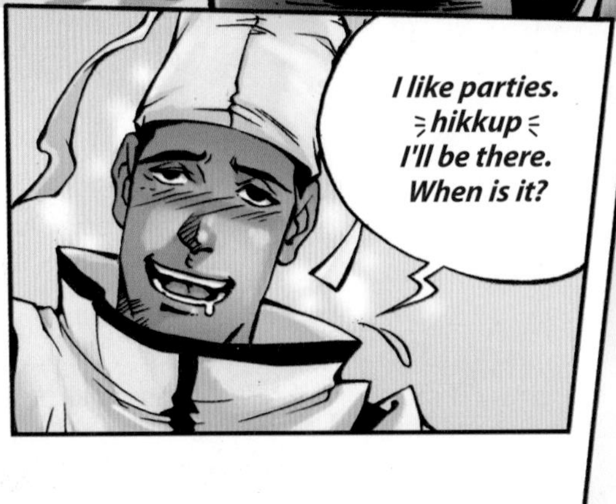
I like parties.
hikkup
I'll be there. When is it?
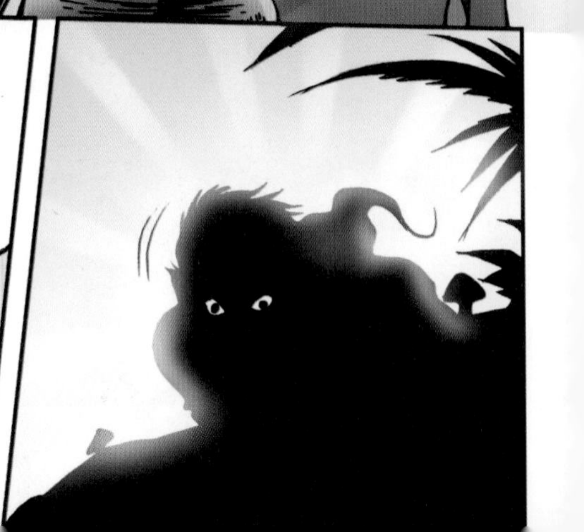

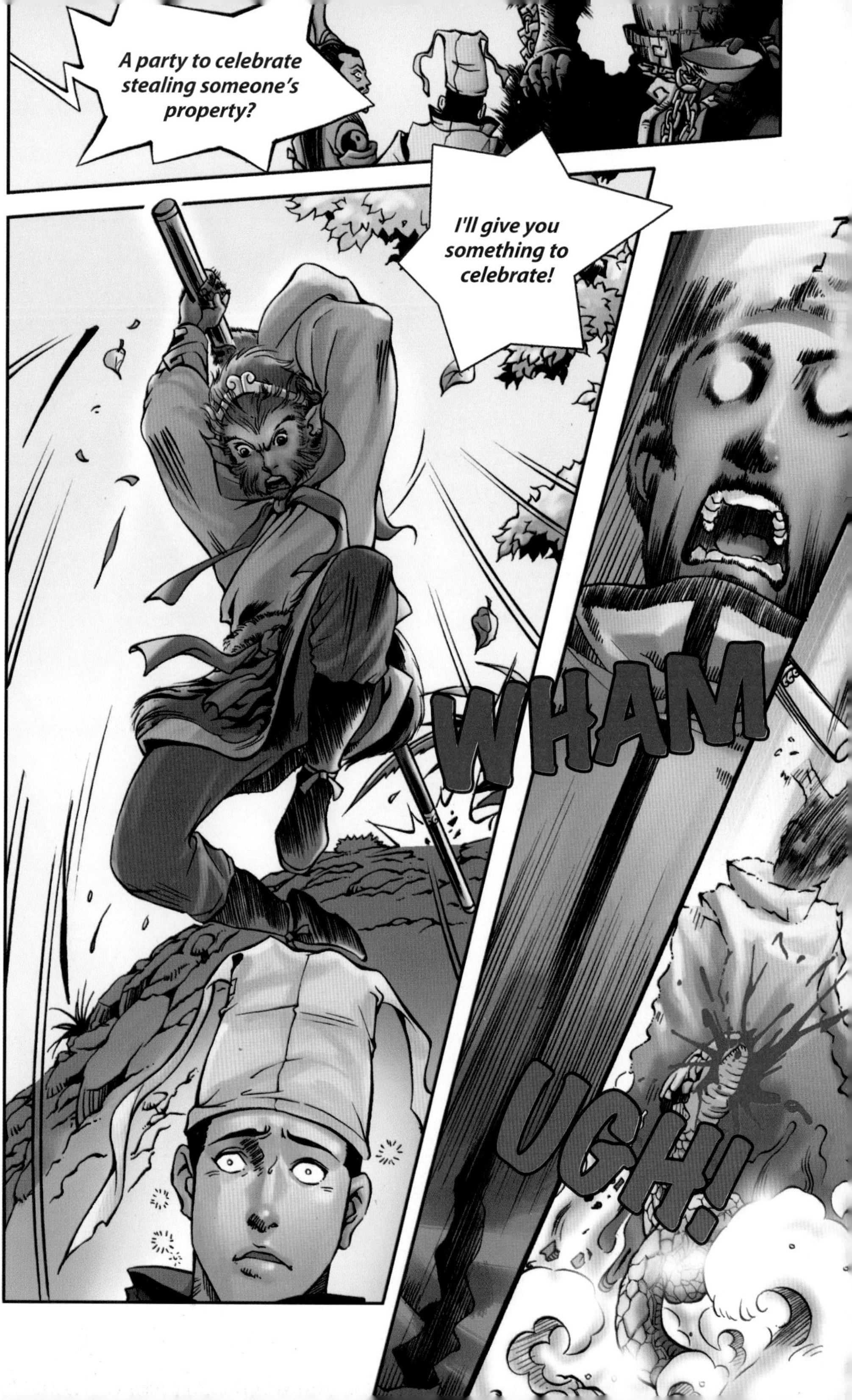
A party to celebrate stealing someone's property?
I'll give you something to celebrate!
WHAM
UGH!

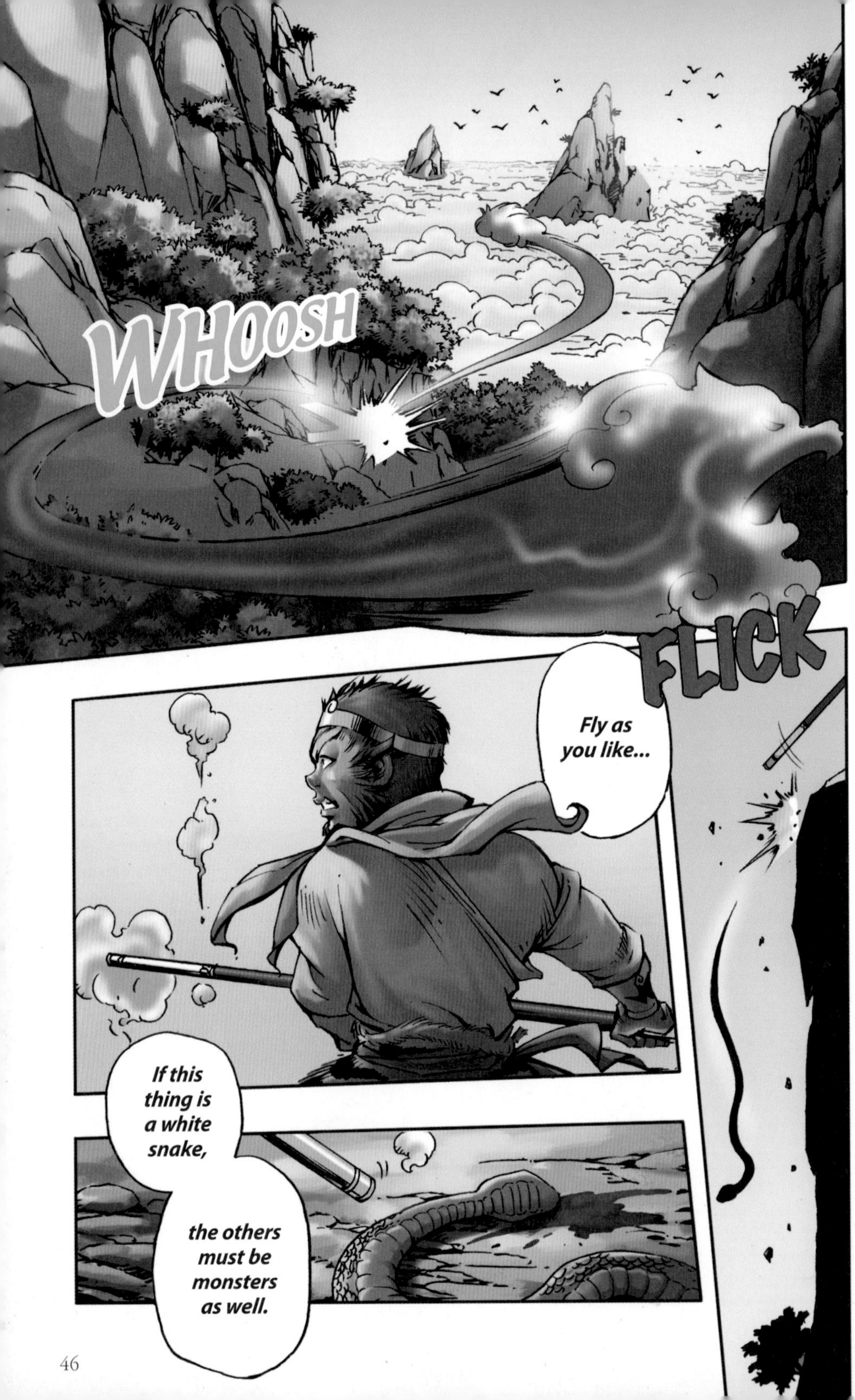
WHOOSH
FLICK
Fly as you like...
If this thing is a white snake,
the others must be monsters as well.

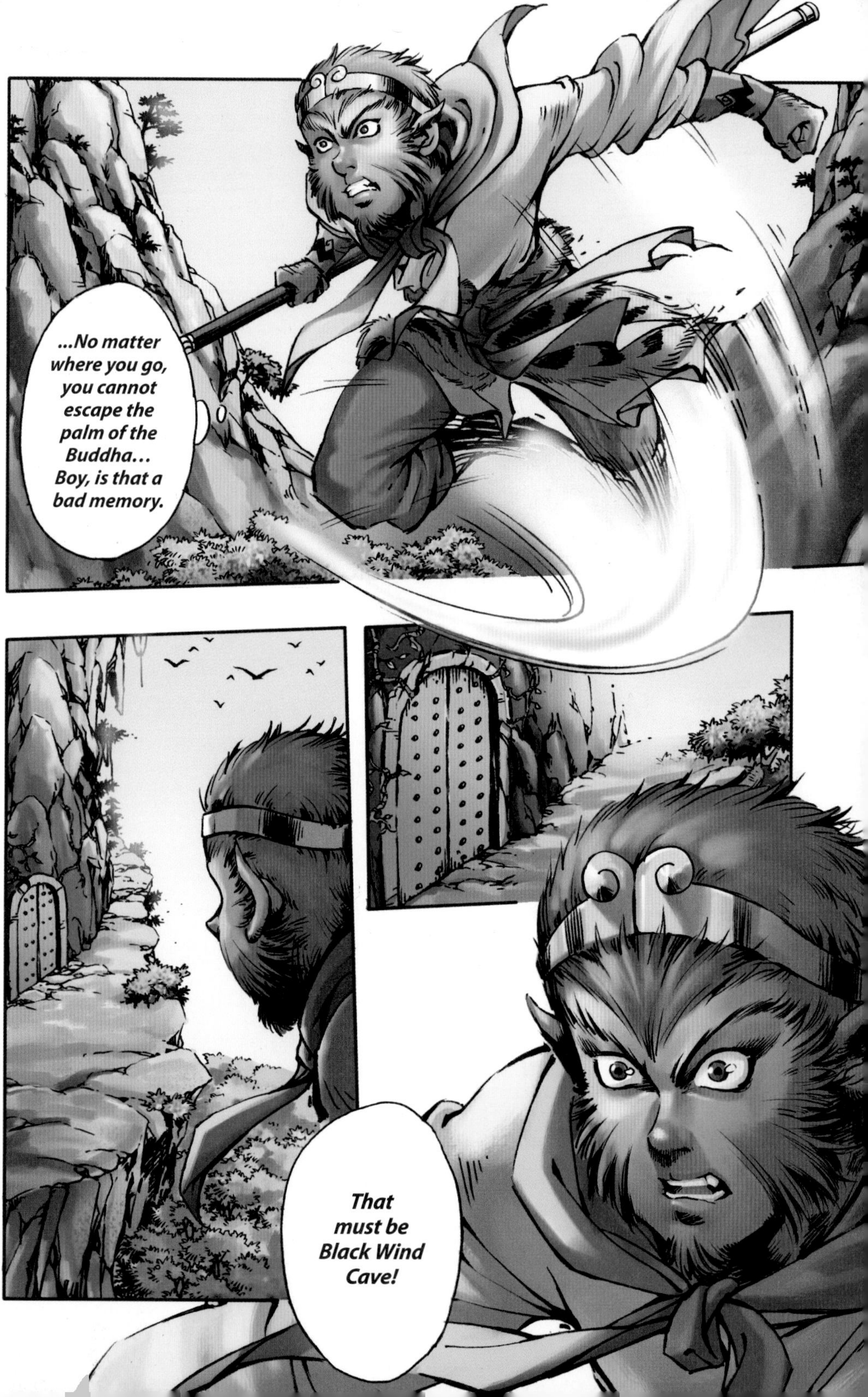
...No matter where you go, you cannot escape the palm of the Buddha... Boy, is that a bad memory.
That must be Black Wind Cave!

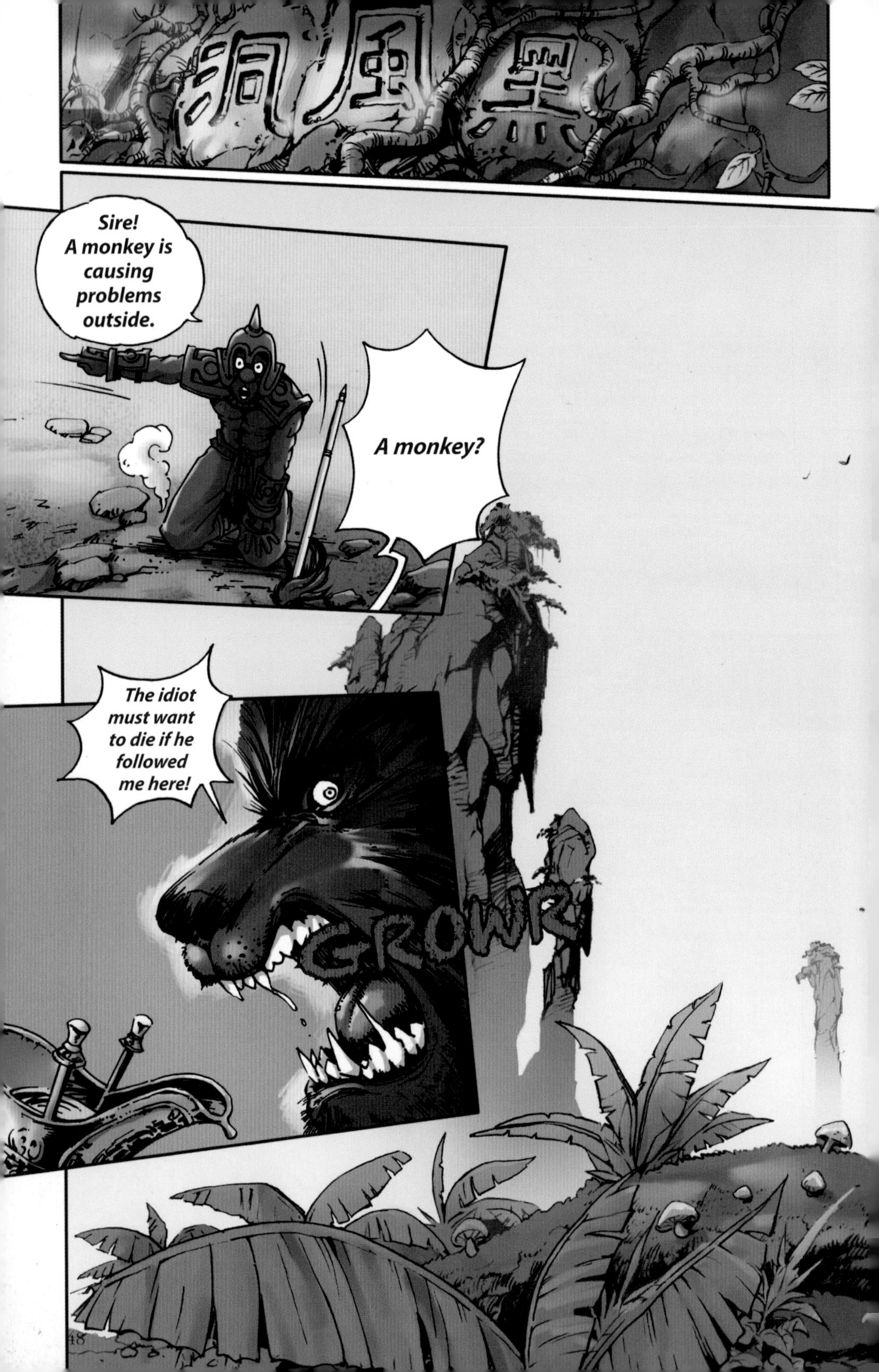
黑風洞
Sire!
A monkey is causing problems outside.
A monkey?
The idiot must want to die if he followed me here!
GROWR

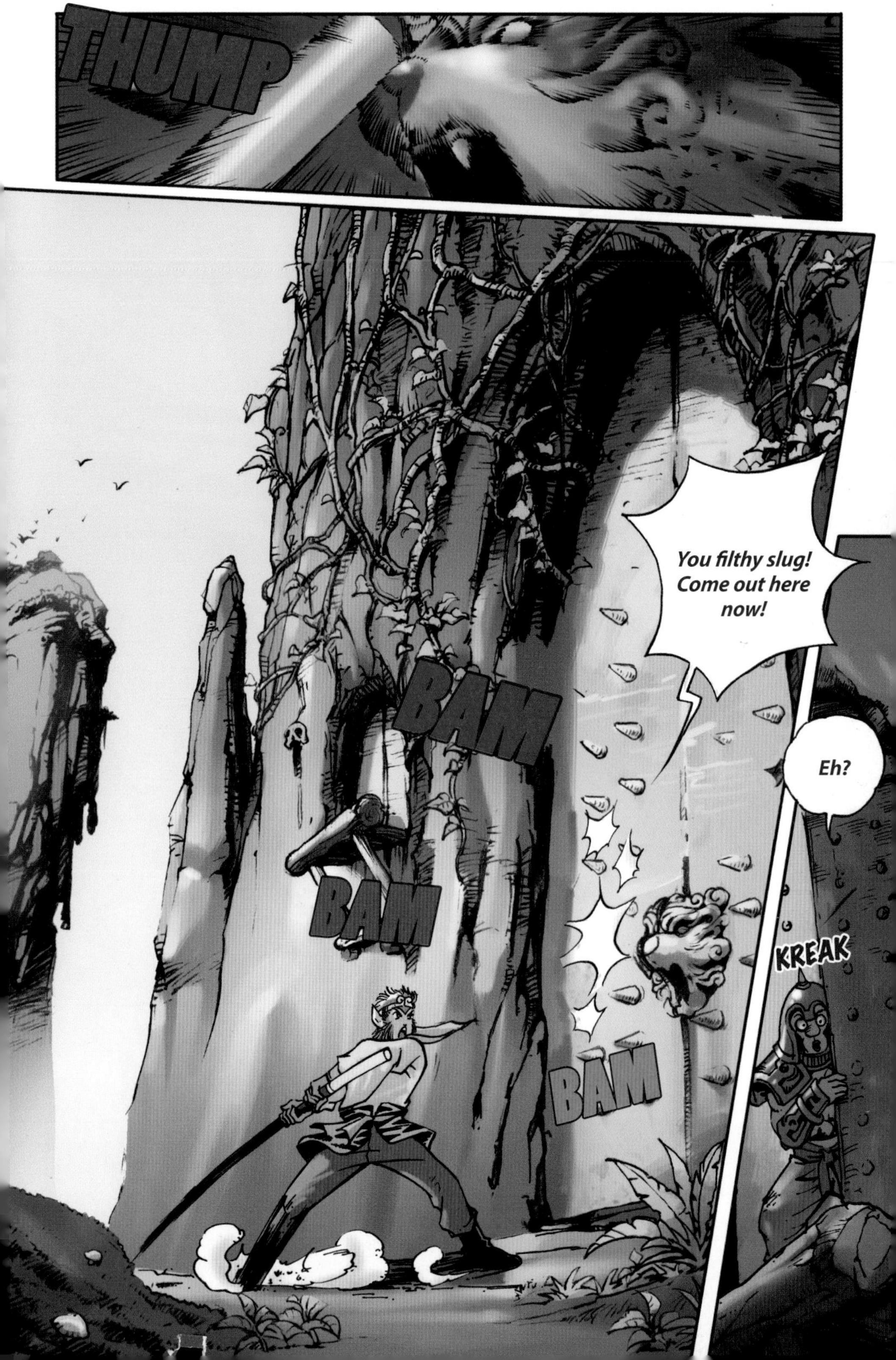
THUMP
You filthy slug! Come out here now!
BAM
BAM
BAM
Eh?
KREAK

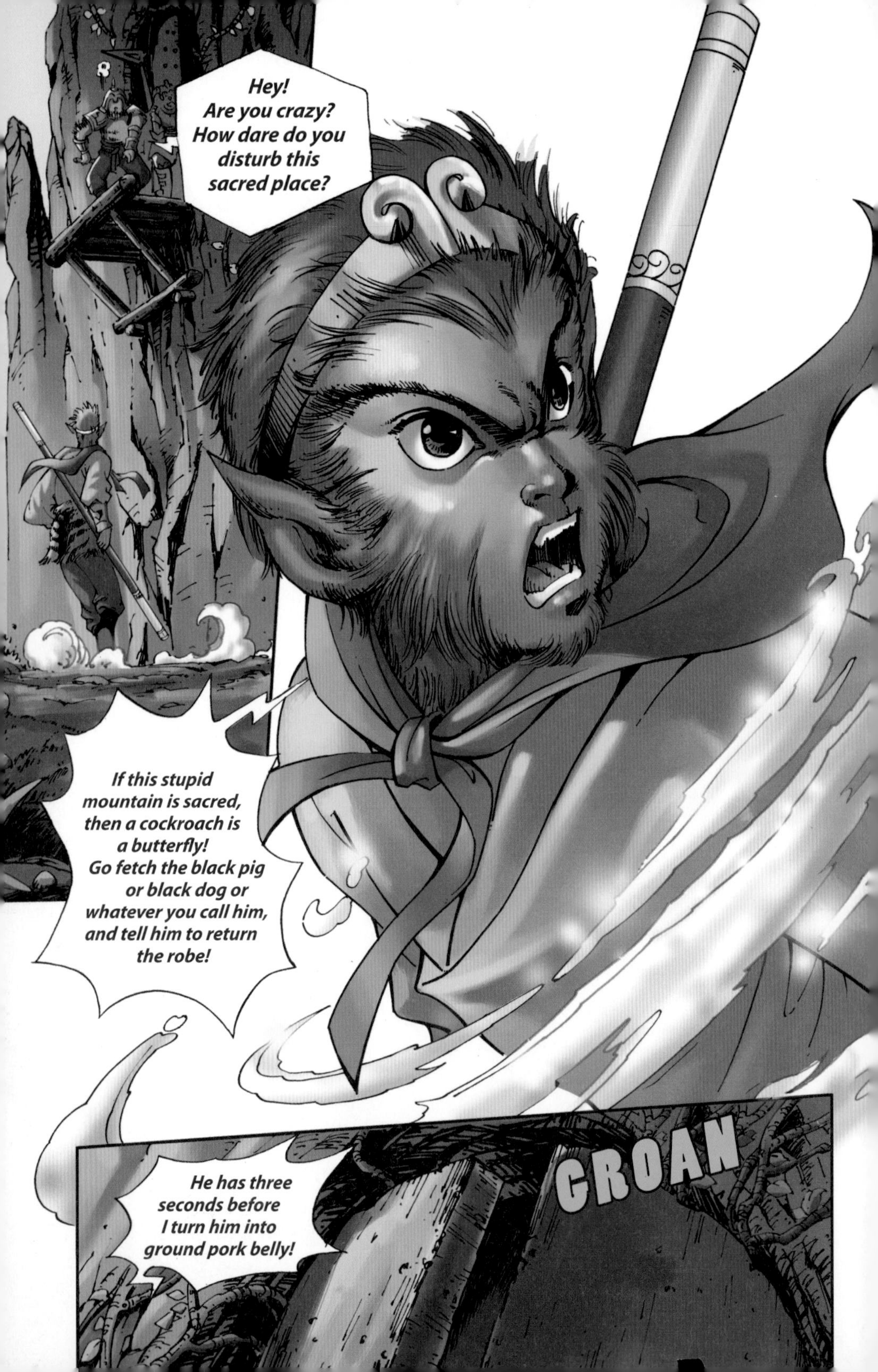
Hey! Are you crazy? How dare do you disturb this sacred place?
If this stupid mountain is sacred, then a cockroach is a butterfly! Go fetch the black pig or black dog or whatever you call him, and tell him to return the robe!
He has three seconds before I turn him into ground pork belly!
GROAN

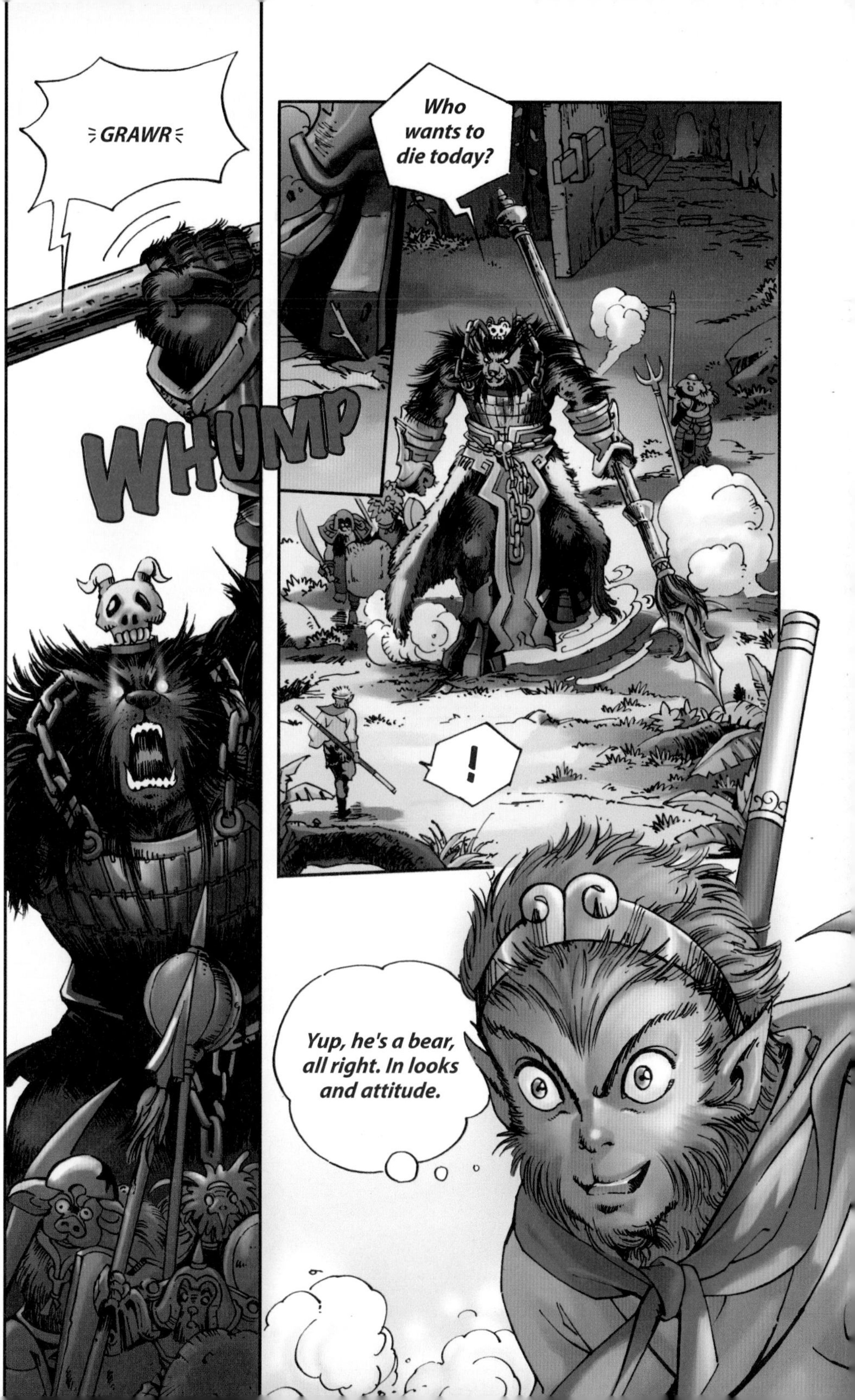
GRAWR
WHUMP
Who wants to die today?
!
Yup, he's a bear, all right. In looks and attitude.

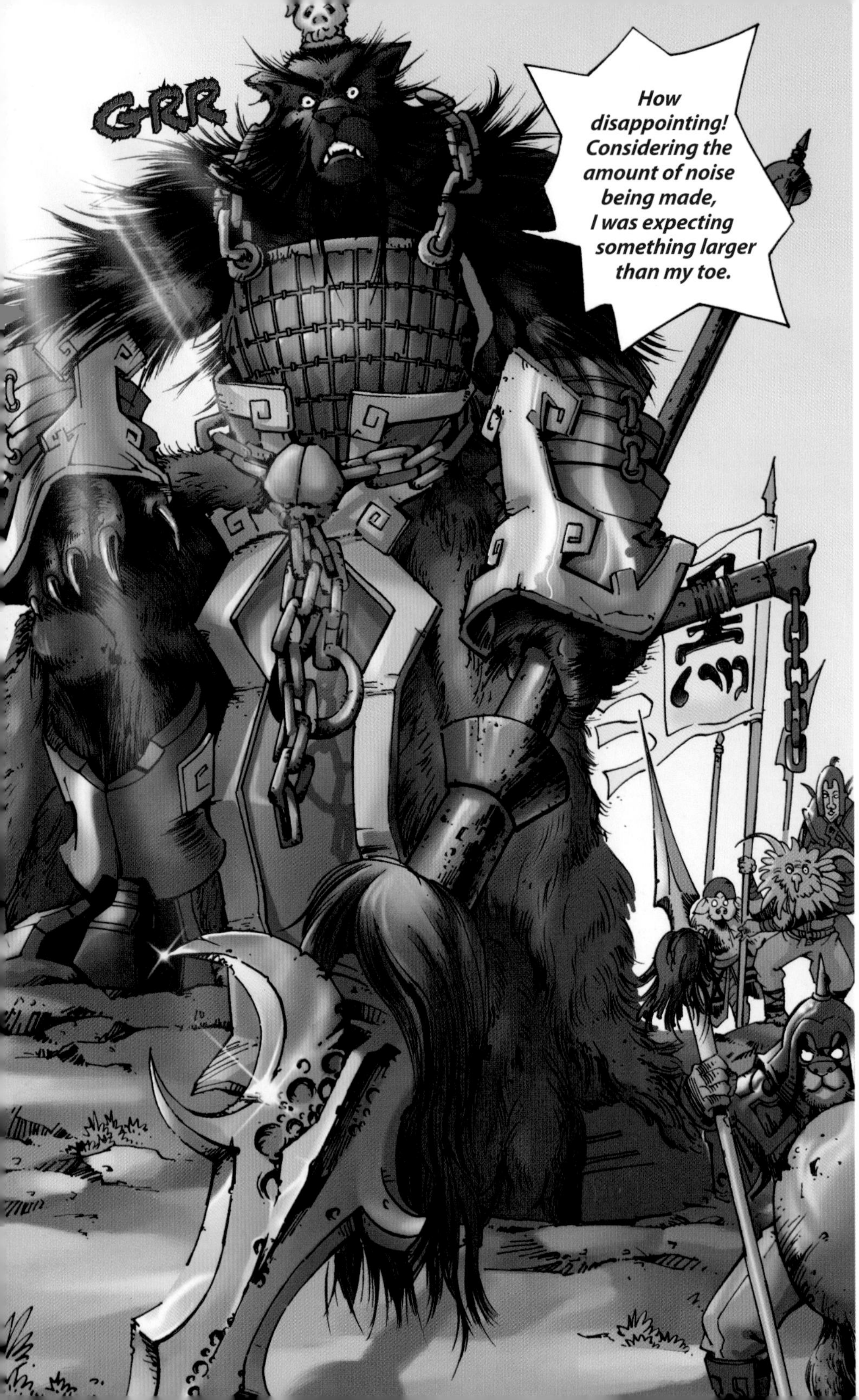
GRR
How disappointing! Considering the amount of noise being made, I was expecting something larger than my toe.

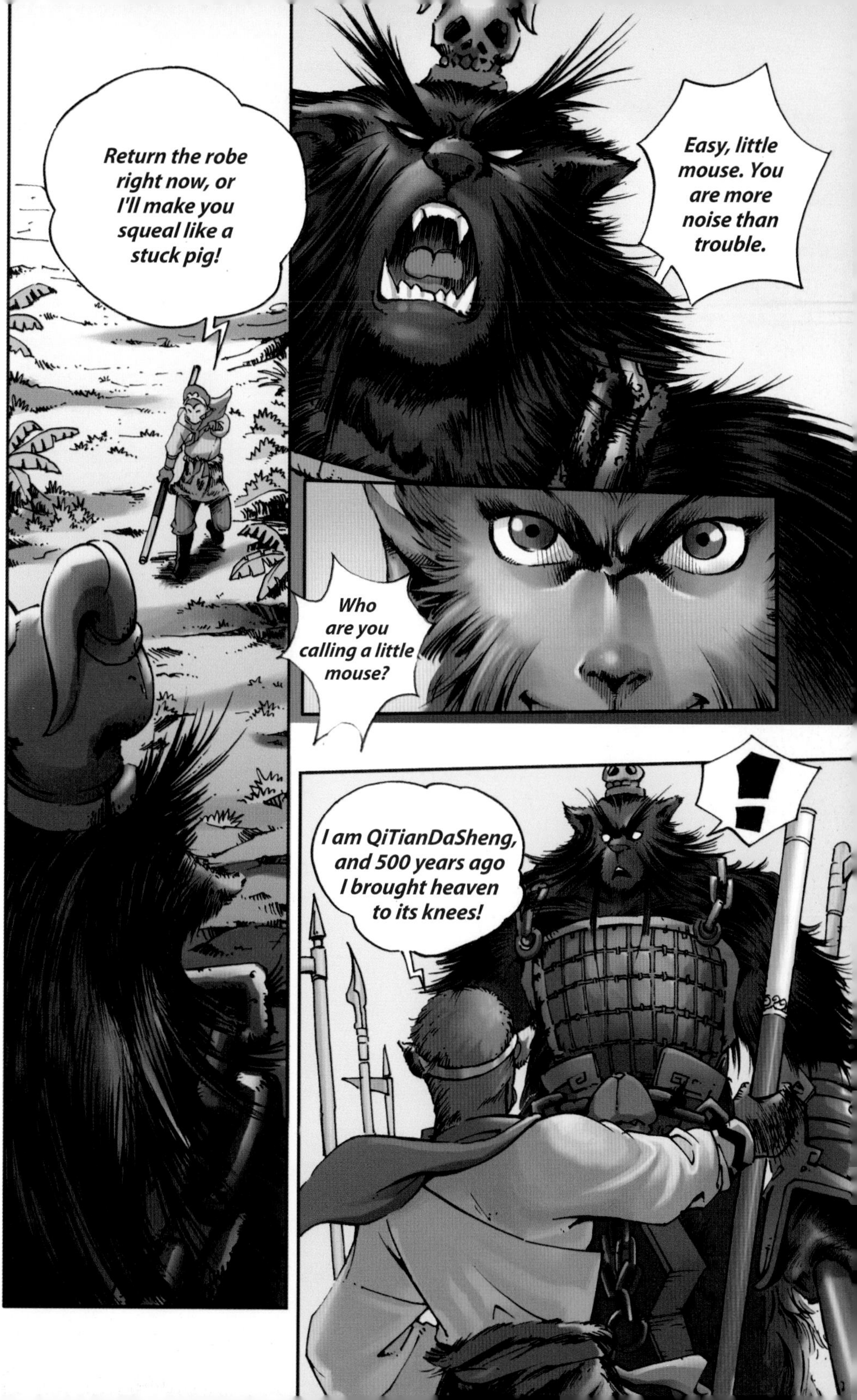
Return the robe right now, or I'll make you squeal like a stuck pig!
Easy, little mouse. You are more noise than trouble.
Who are you calling a little mouse?
!
I am QiTianDaSheng, and 500 years ago I brought heaven to its knees!

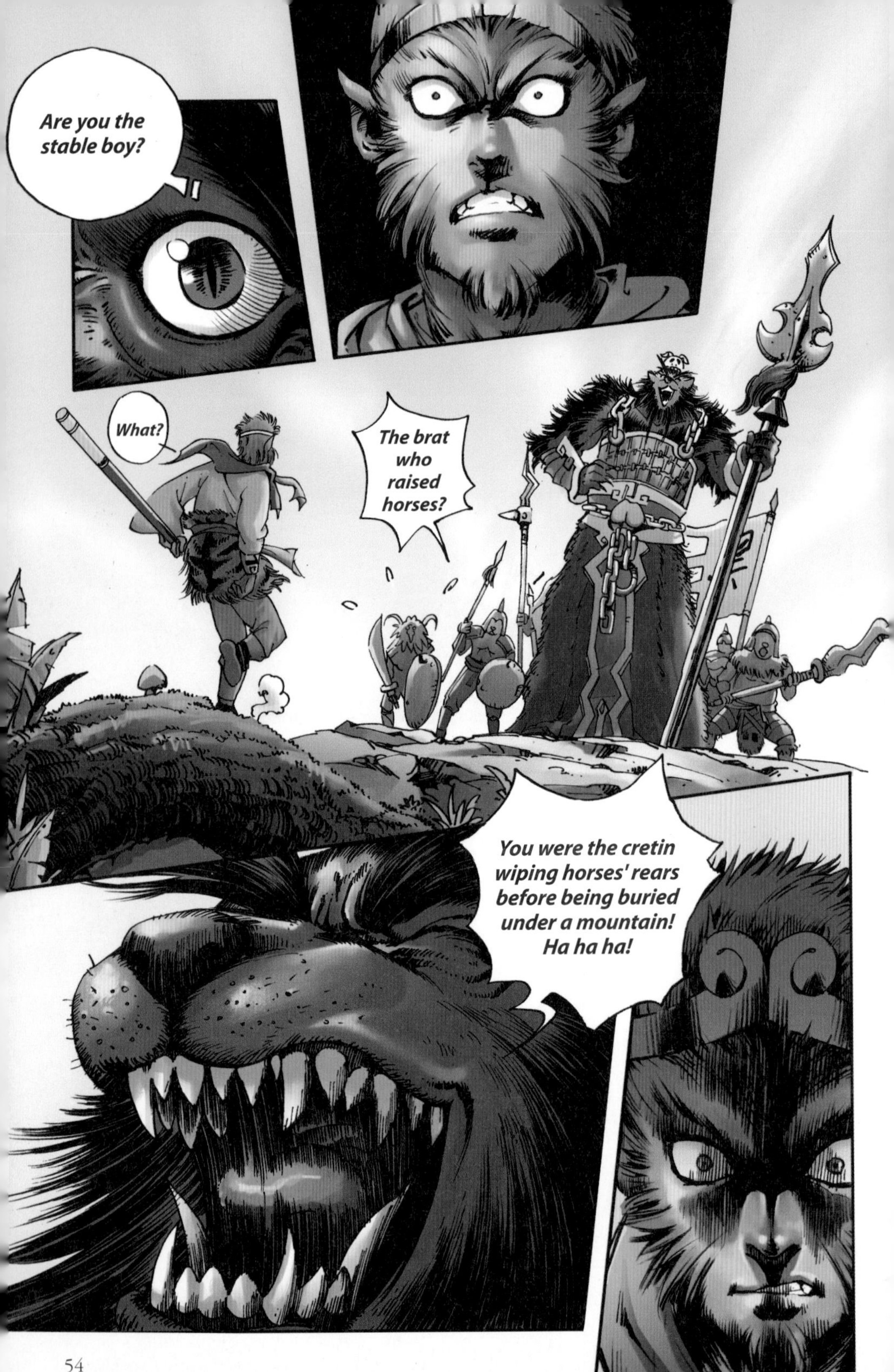
Are you the stable boy?
What?
The brat who raised horses?
You were the cretin wiping horses' rears before being buried under a mountain! Ha ha ha!

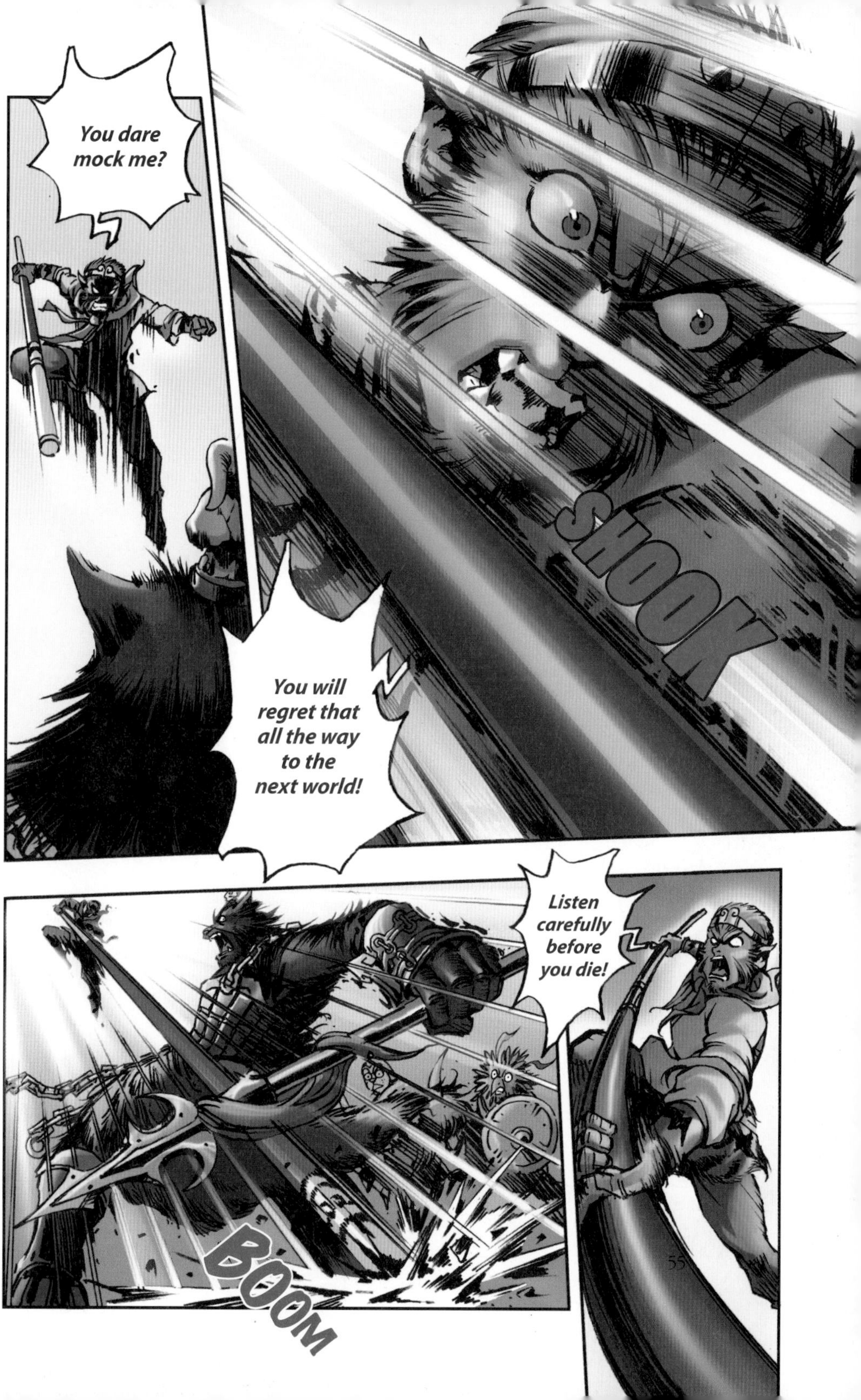
You dare mock me?
SHOOK
You will regret that all the way to the next world!
Listen carefully before you die!
BOOM
55

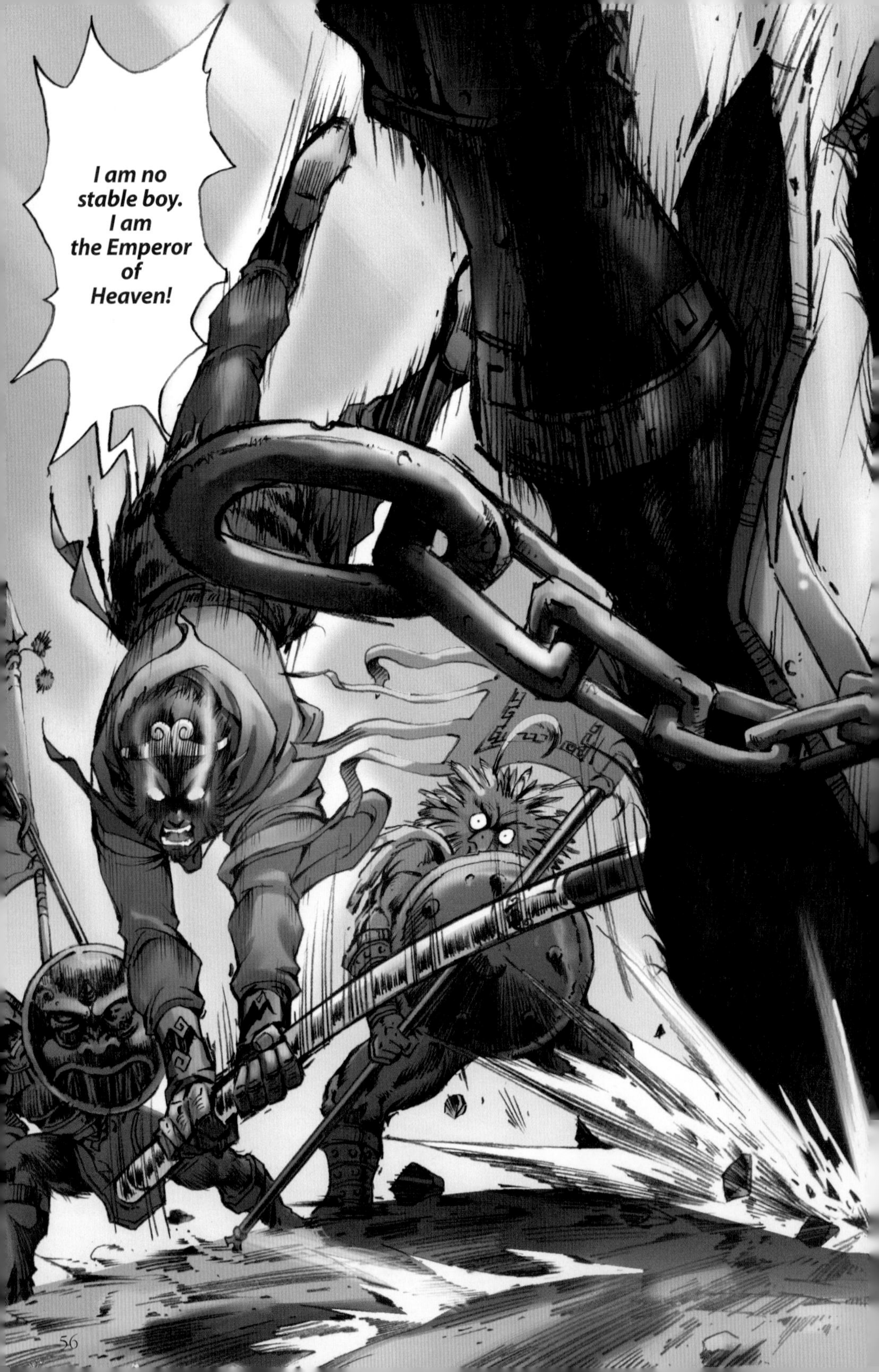
I am no stable boy. I am the Emperor of Heaven!

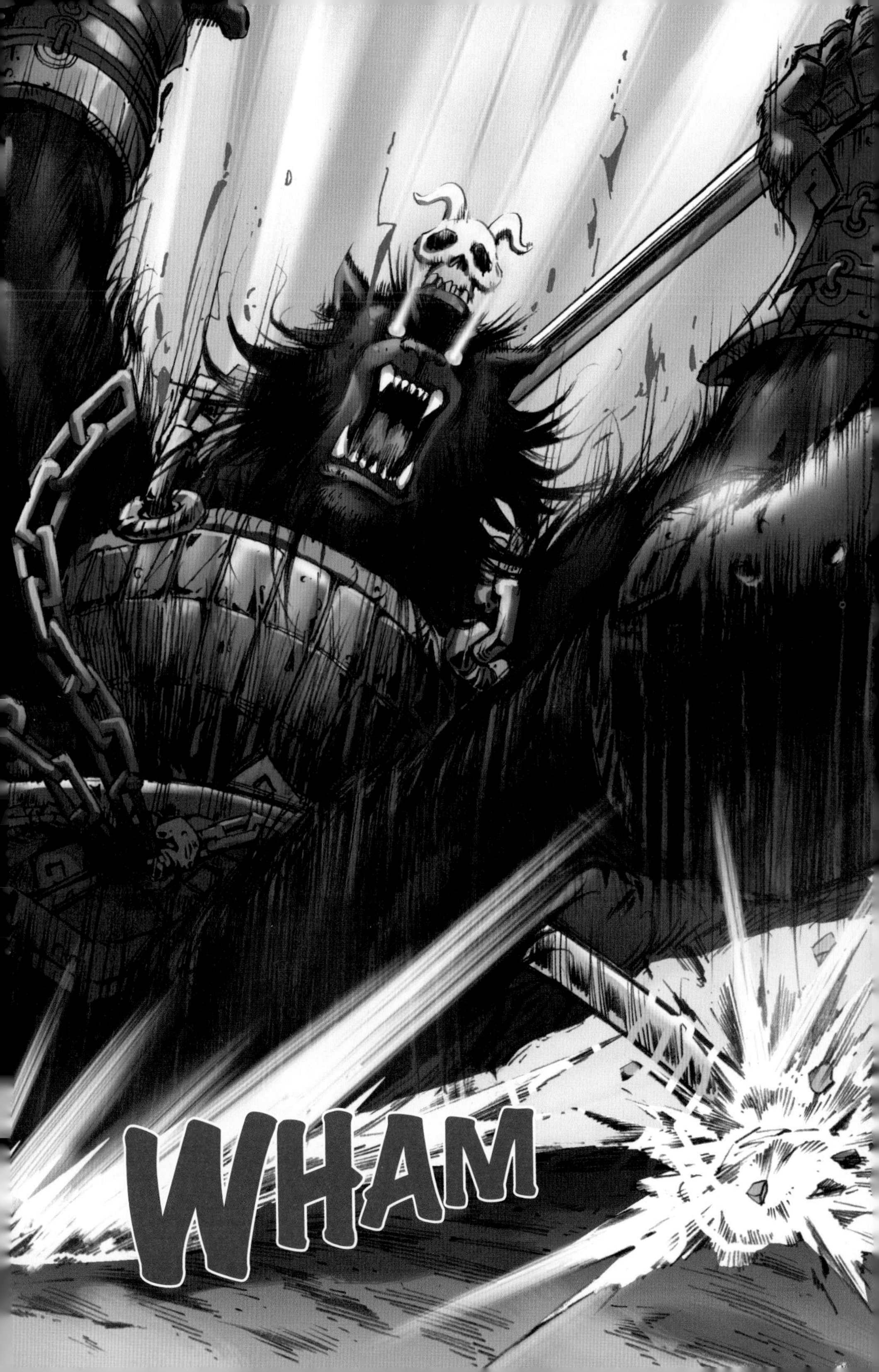
WHAM

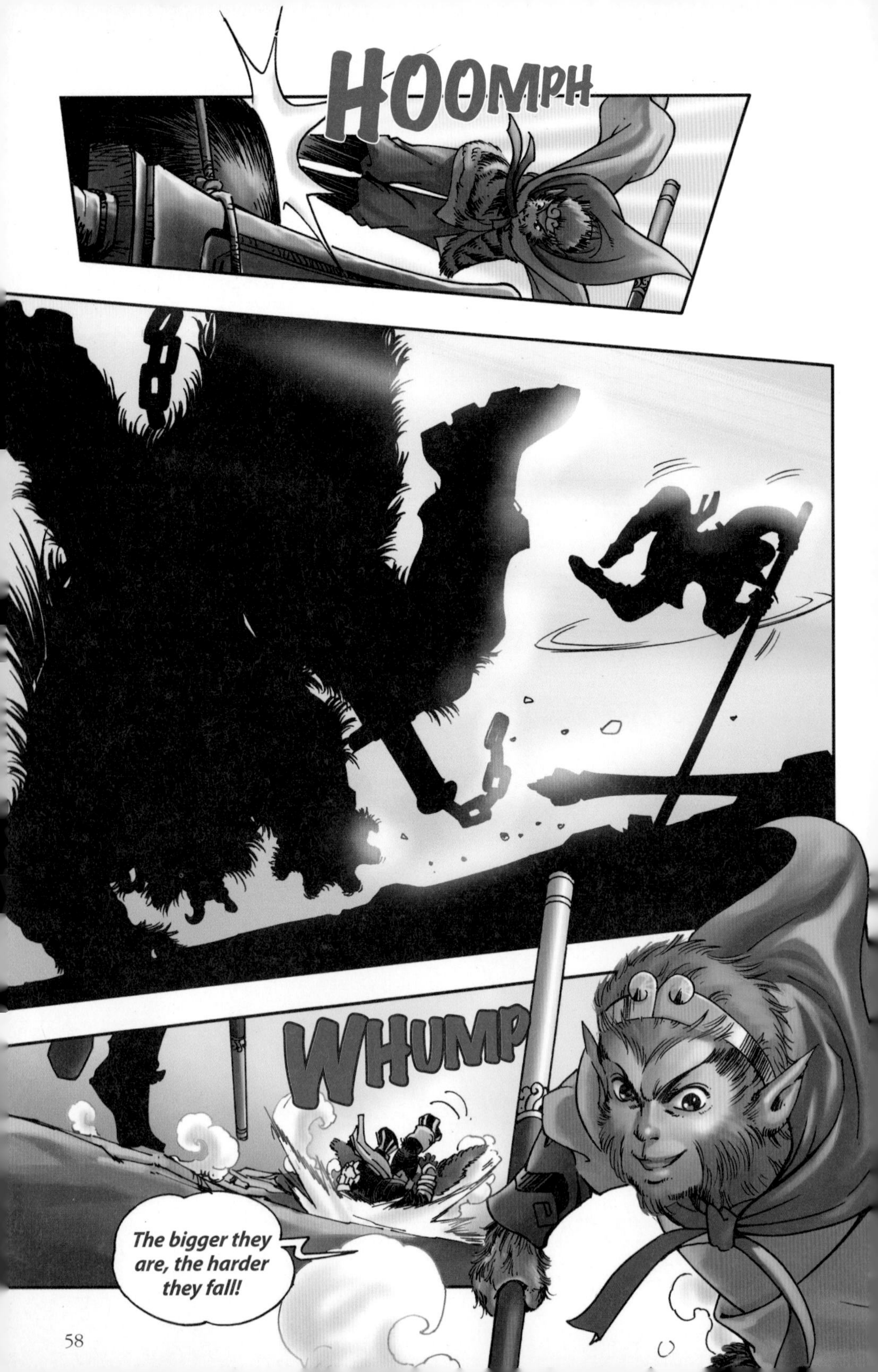
HOOMPH
WHUMP
The bigger they are, the harder they fall!

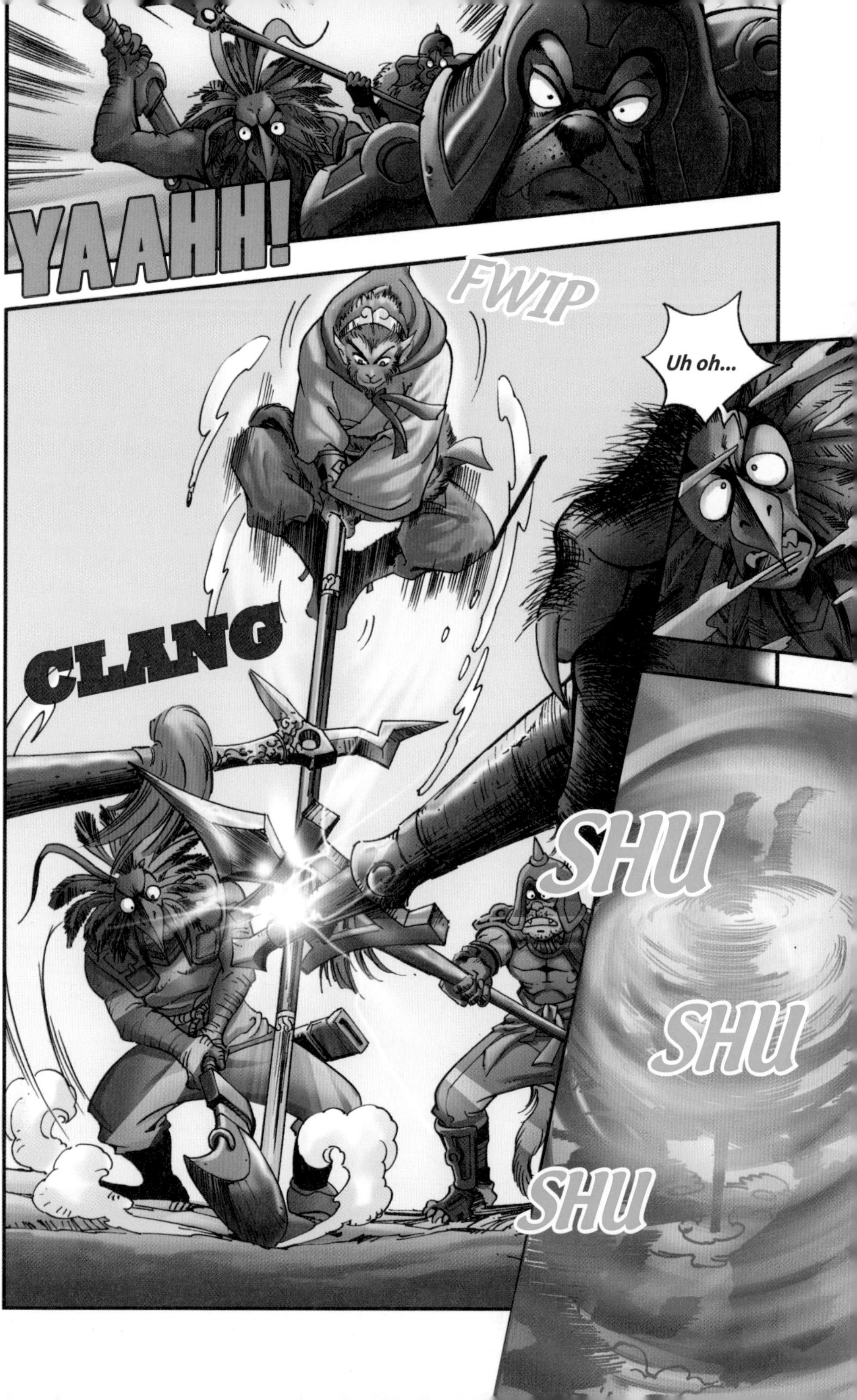
YAAHH!
FWIP
Uh oh...
CLANG
SHU
SHU
SHU

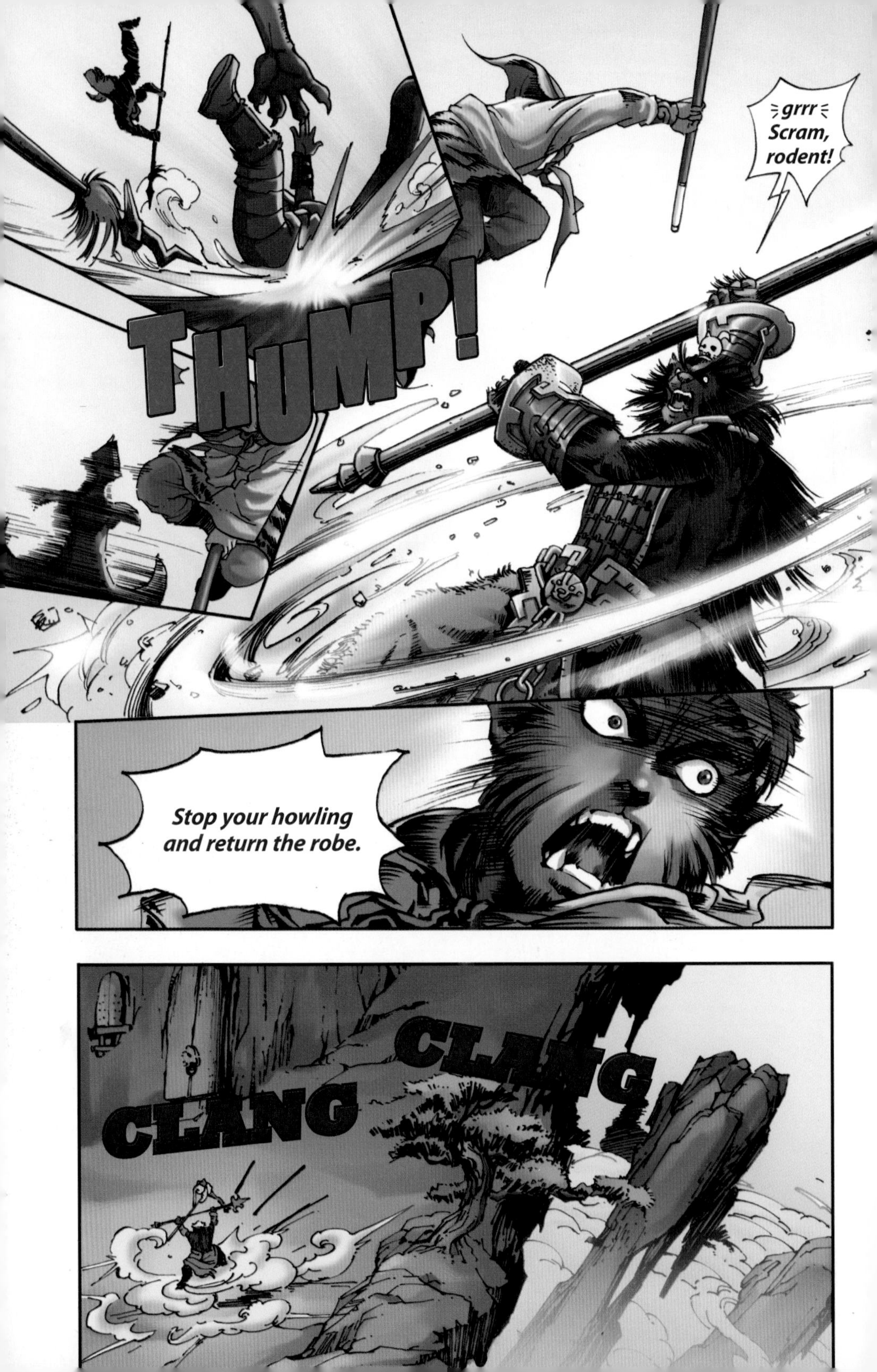
grrr Scram, rodent!
THUMP!
Stop your howling and return the robe.
CLANG
CLANG

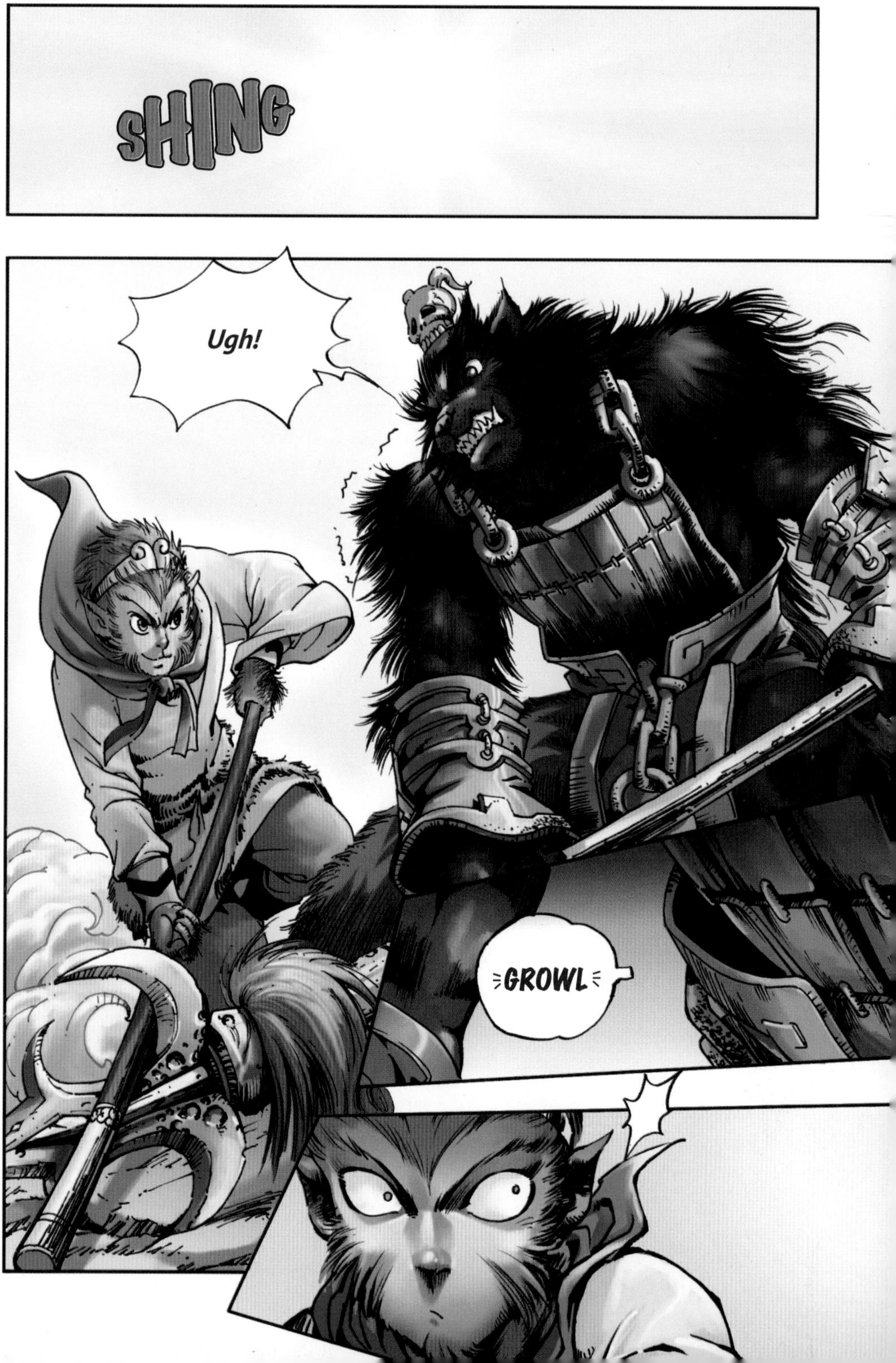
SHING
Ugh!
GROWL

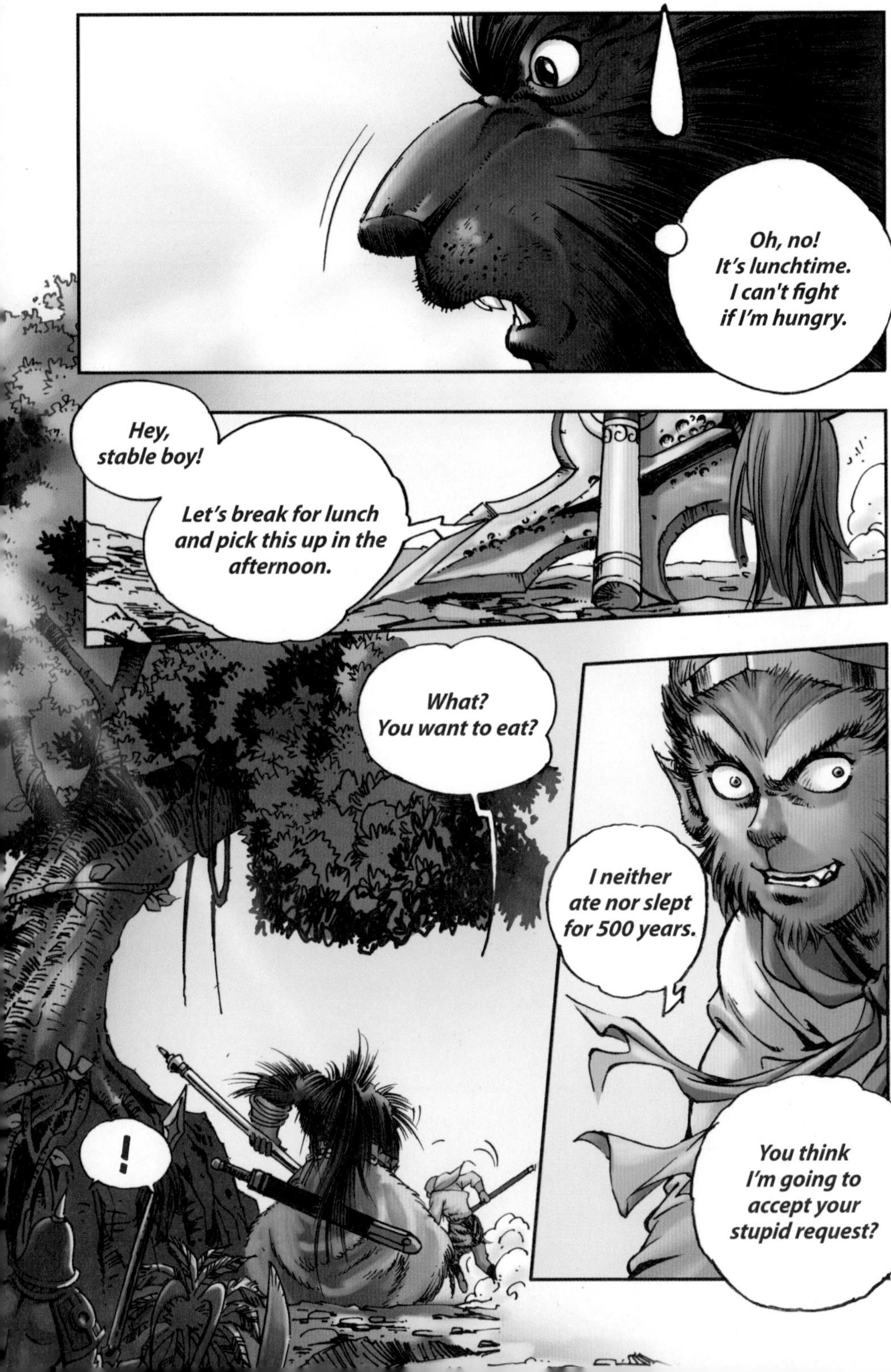
Oh, no! It's lunchtime. I can't fight if I'm hungry.
Hey, stable boy!
Let's break for lunch and pick this up in the afternoon.
What? You want to eat?
I neither ate nor slept for 500 years.
You think I'm going to accept your stupid request?
!

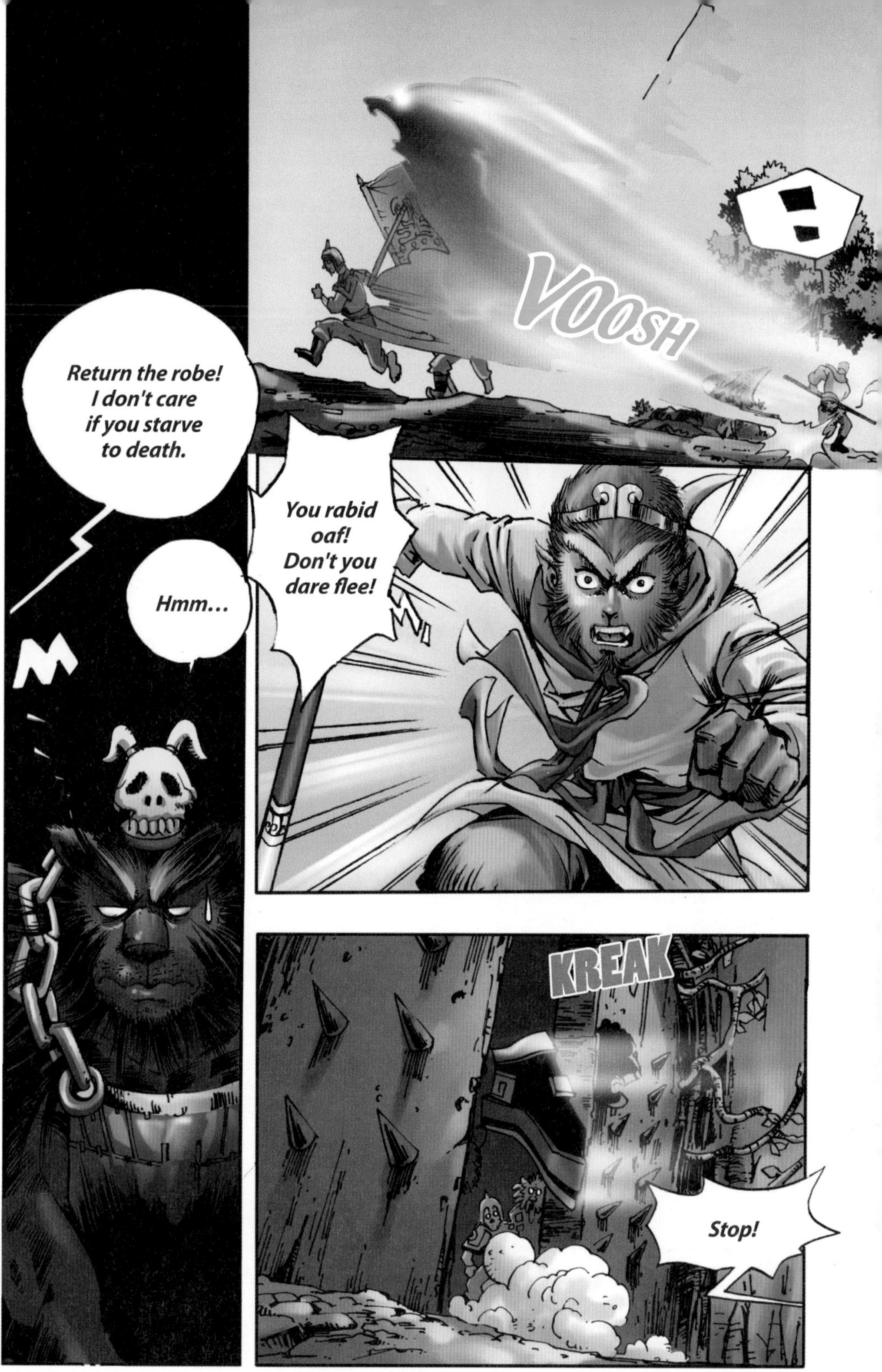

VOOSH
!
Return the robe! I don't care if you starve to death.
Hmm...
You rabid oaf! Don't you dare flee!
KREAK
Stop!

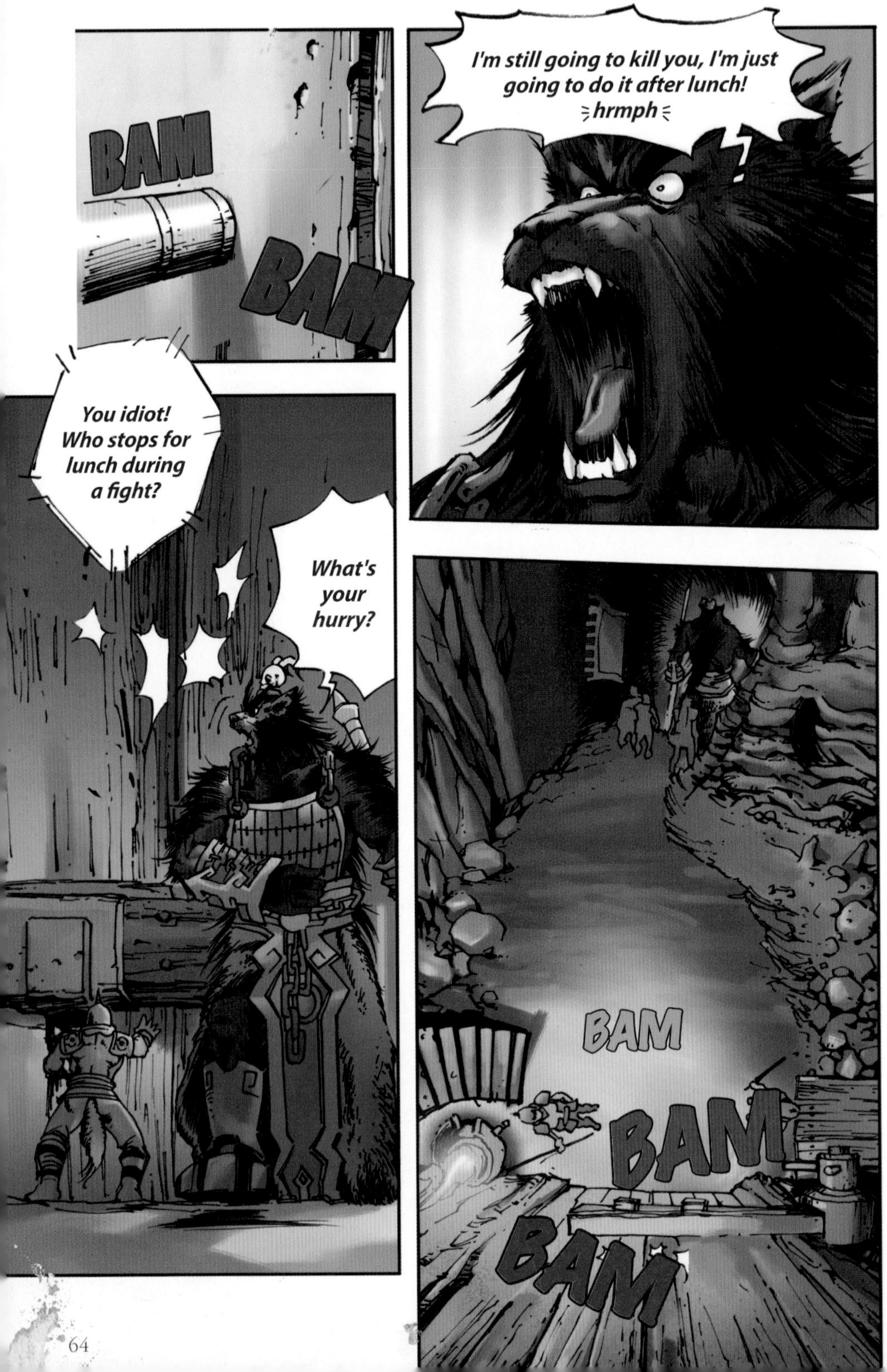
BAM
BAM
I'm still going to kill you, I'm just going to do it after lunch!
hrmph
You idiot! Who stops for lunch during a fight?
What's your hurry?
BAM
BAM
BAM

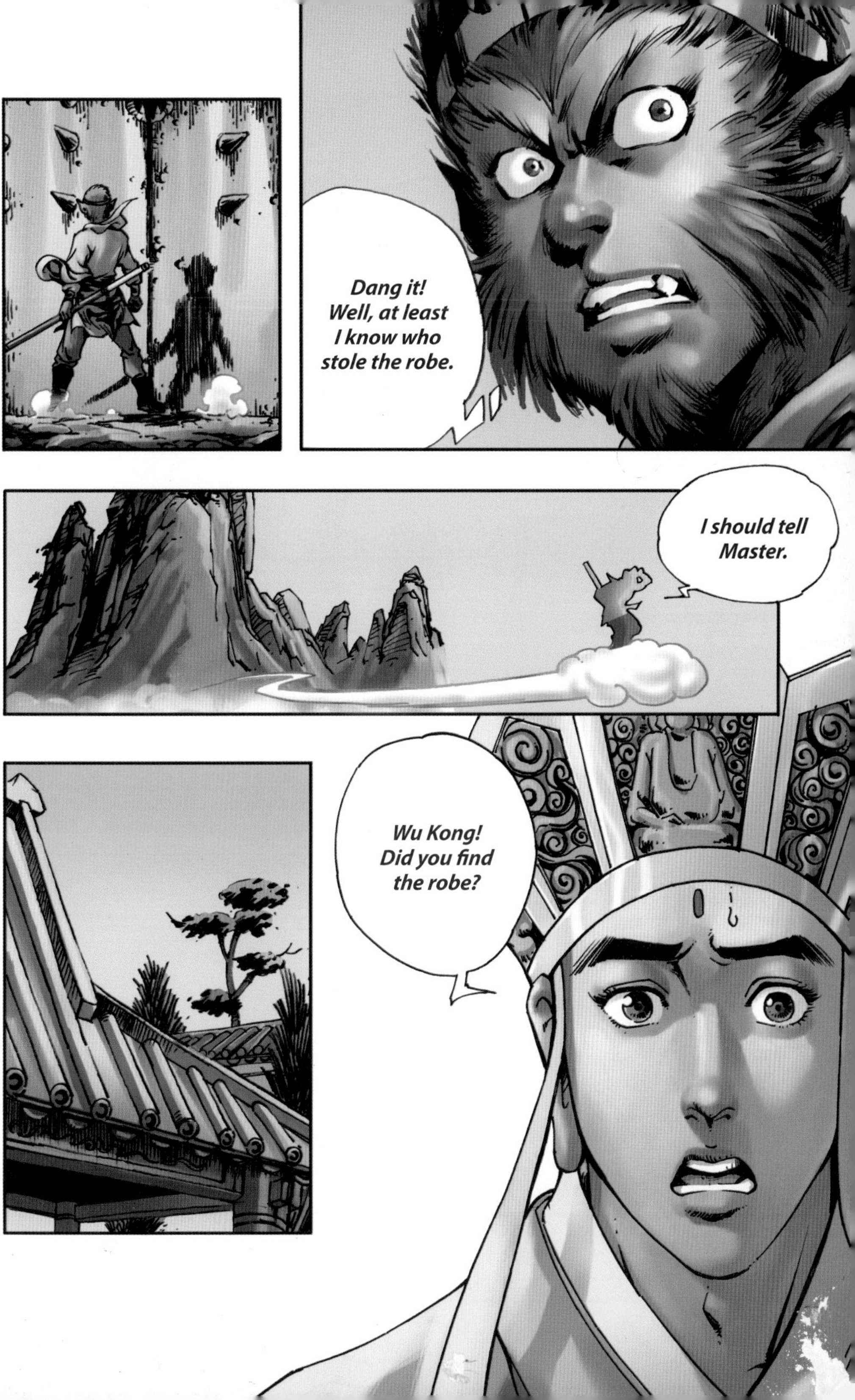
Dang it! Well, at least I know who stole the robe.
I should tell Master.
Wu Kong! Did you find the robe?

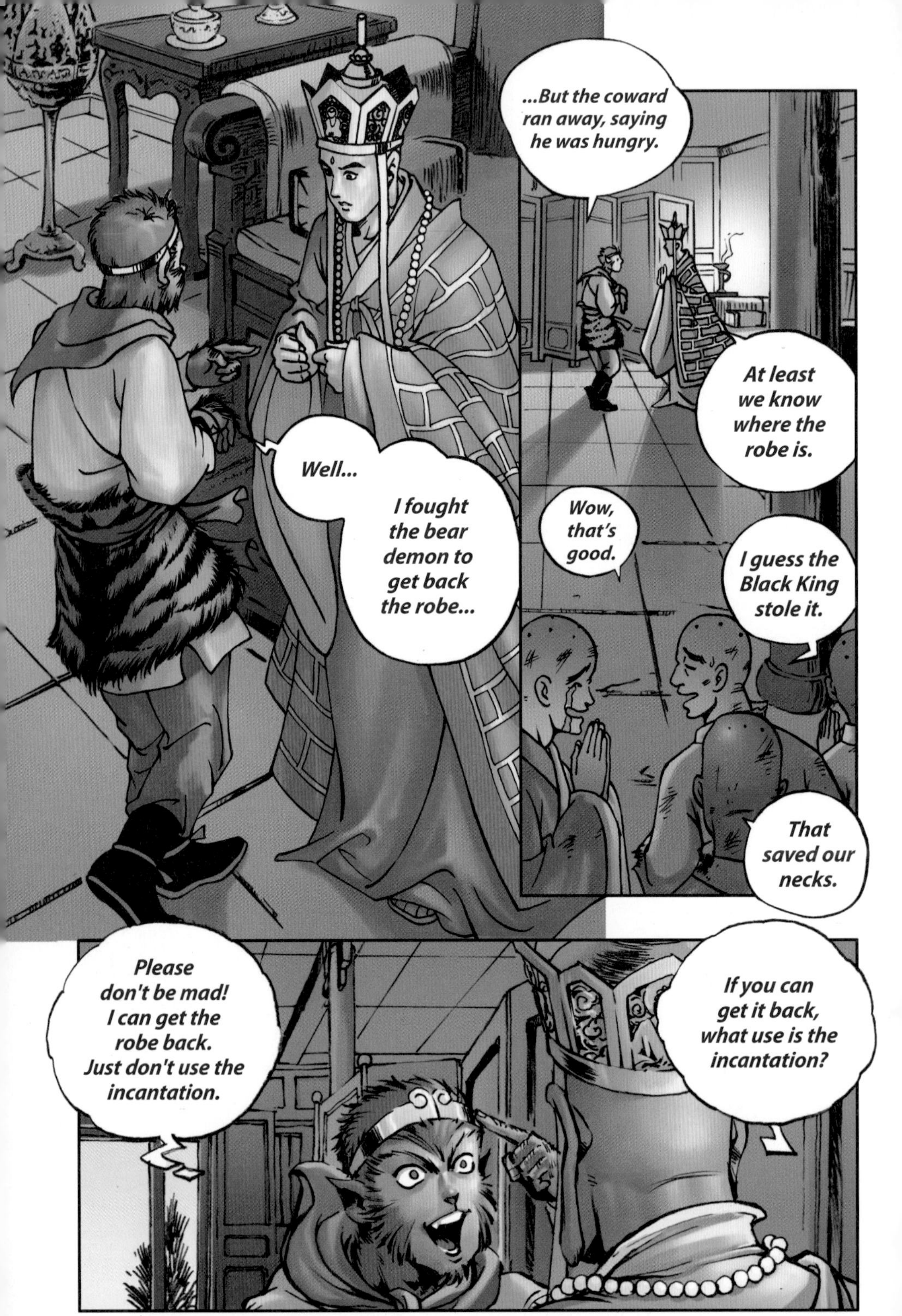
Well...
I fought the bear demon to get back the robe...
...But the coward ran away, saying he was hungry.
At least we know where the robe is.
Wow, that's good.
I guess the Black King stole it.
That saved our necks.
Please don't be mad! I can get the robe back. Just don't use the incantation.
If you can get it back, what use is the incantation?

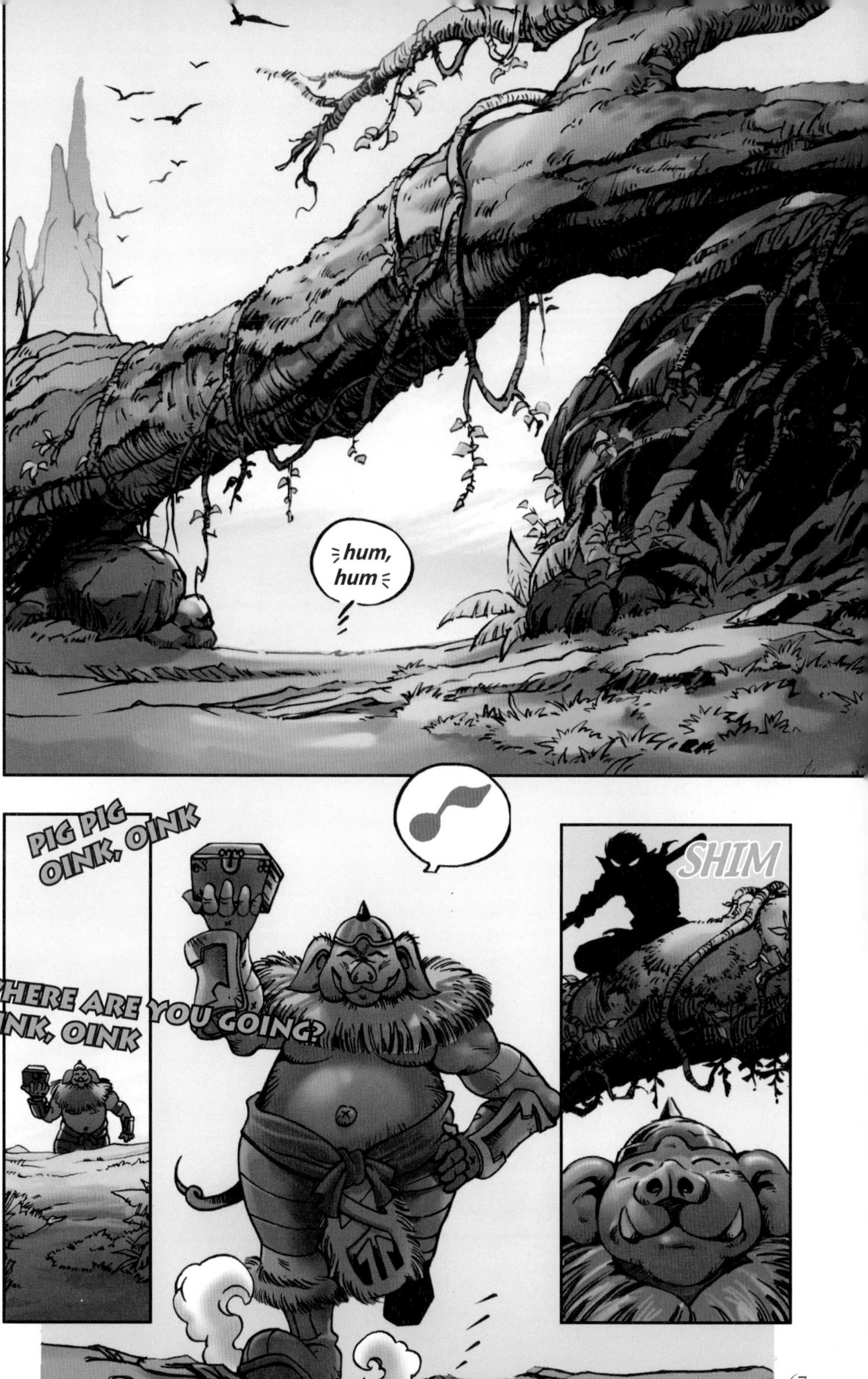
hum,
hum
PIG PIG
OINK, OINK
WHERE ARE YOU GOING?
OINK, OINK
SHIM

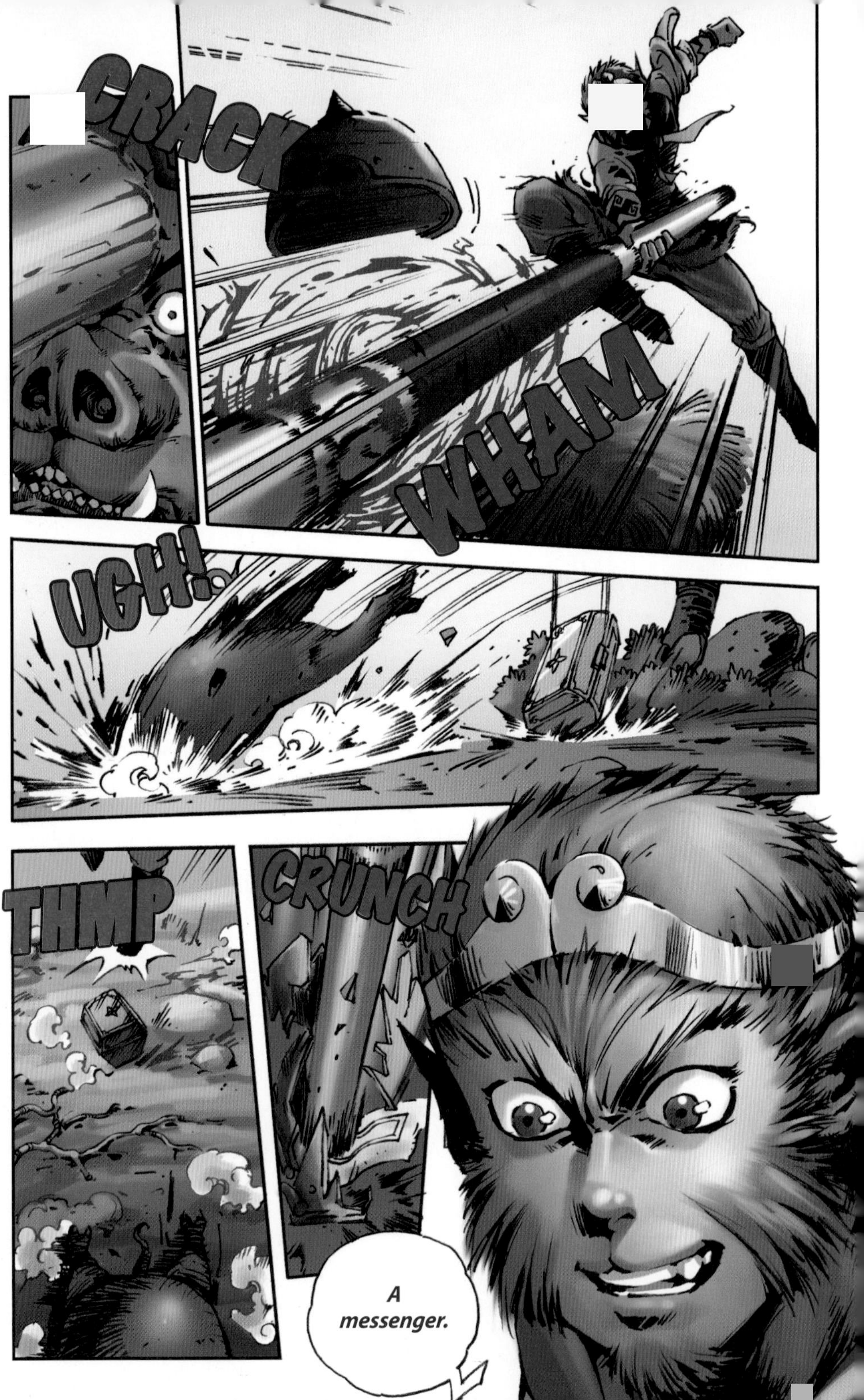
CRACK
WHAM
UGH!
THMP
CRUNCH
A messenger.

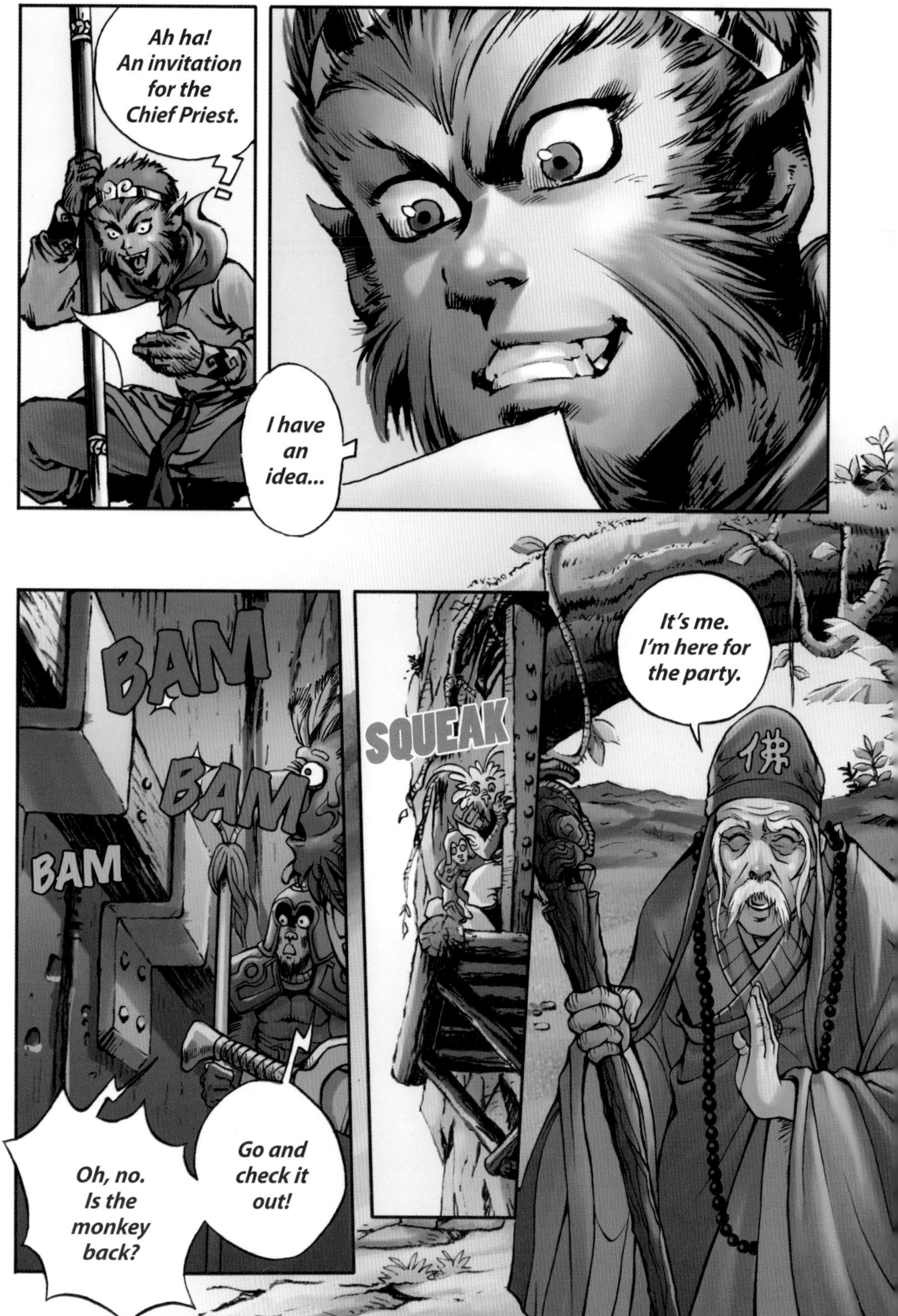
Ah ha! An invitation for the Chief Priest.
I have an idea...
BAM
BAM
BAM
Go and check it out!
Oh, no. Is the monkey back?
SQUEAK
It's me. I'm here for the party.

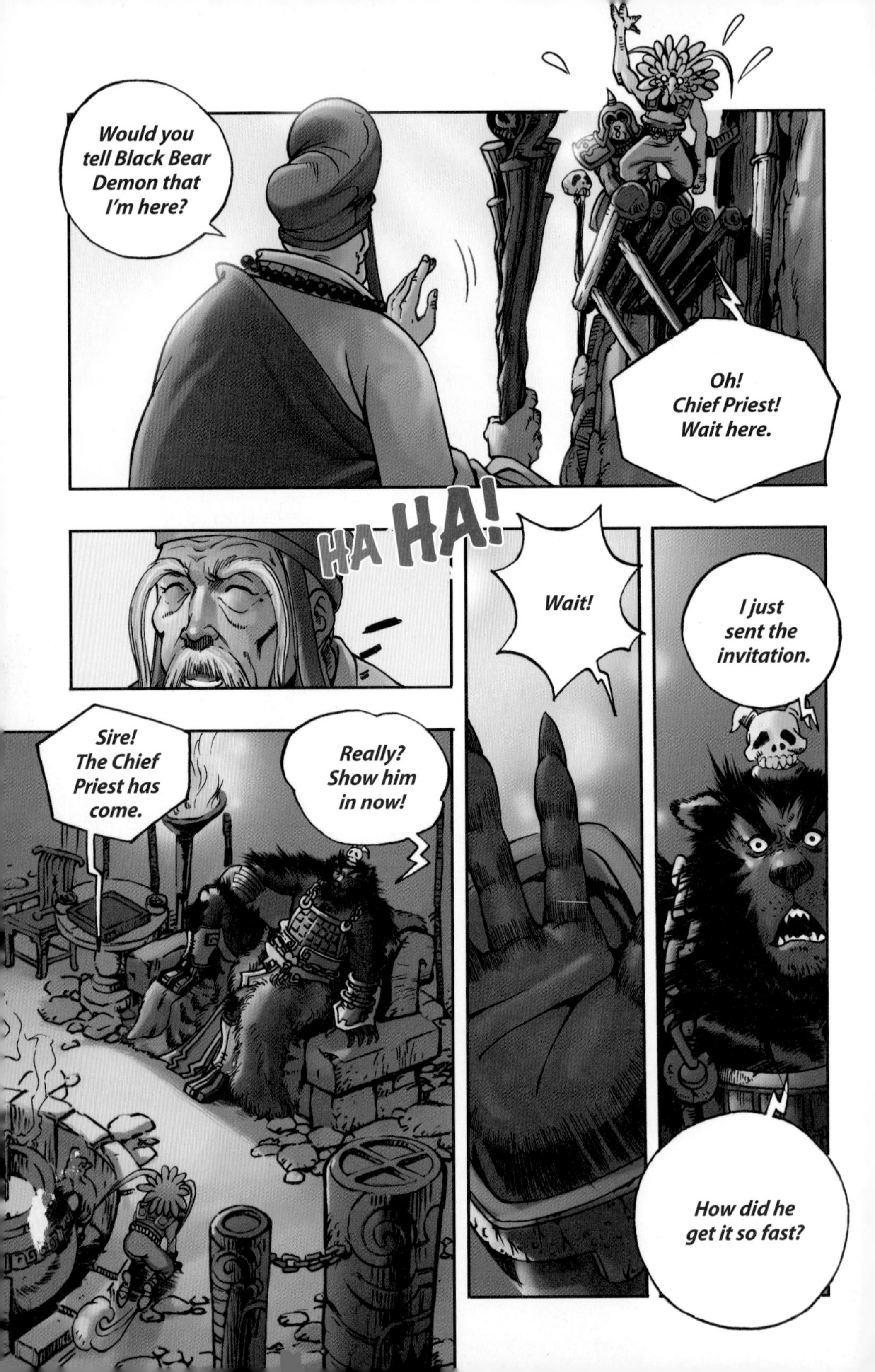
Would you tell Black Bear Demon that I'm here?
Oh! Chief Priest! Wait here.
HA HA!
Wait!
I just sent the invitation.
Sire! The Chief Priest has come.
Really? Show him in now!
How did he get it so fast?

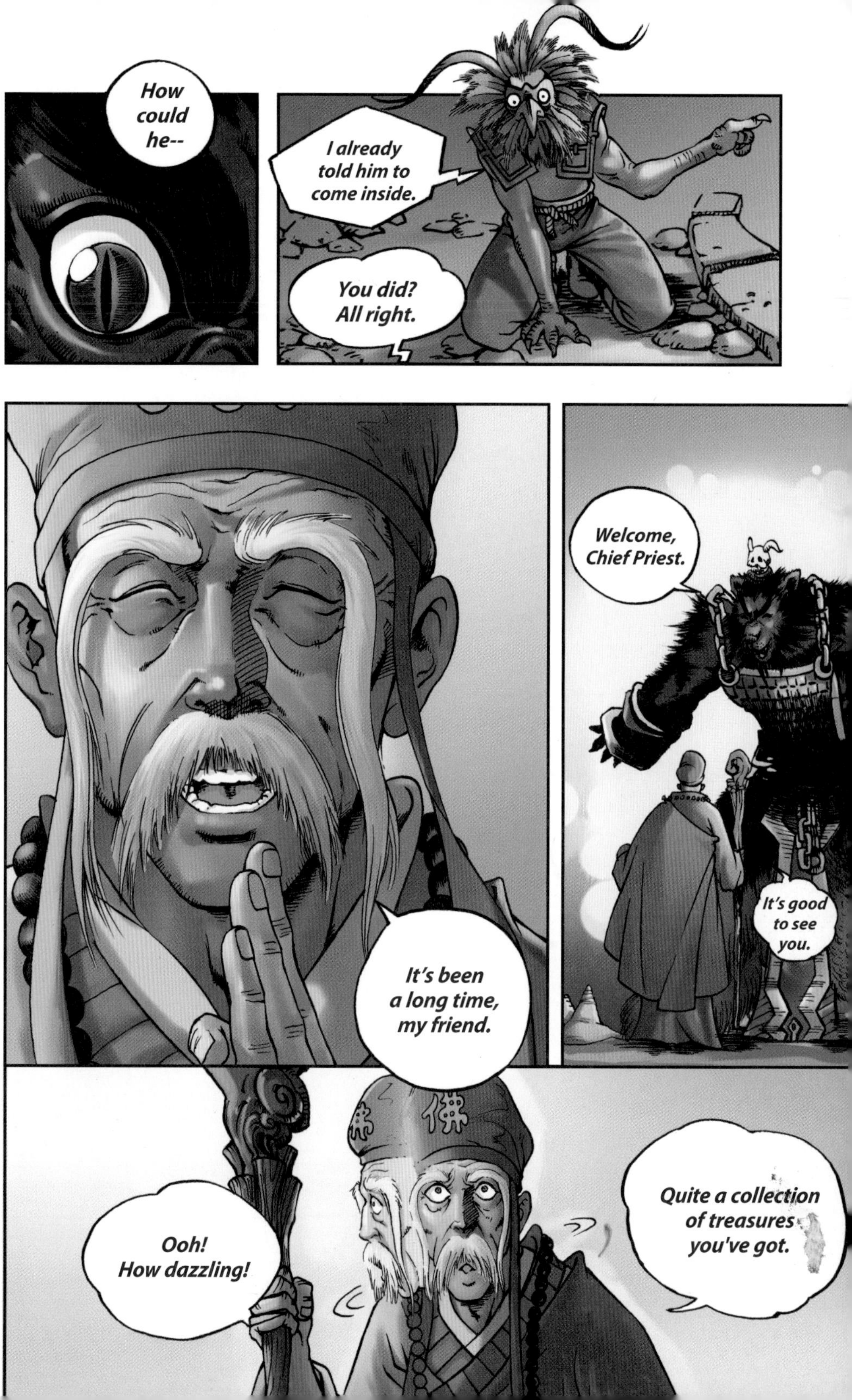
How could he--
I already told him to come inside.
You did? All right.
It's been a long time, my friend.
Welcome, Chief Priest.
It's good to see you.
Ooh! How dazzling!
Quite a collection of treasures you've got.

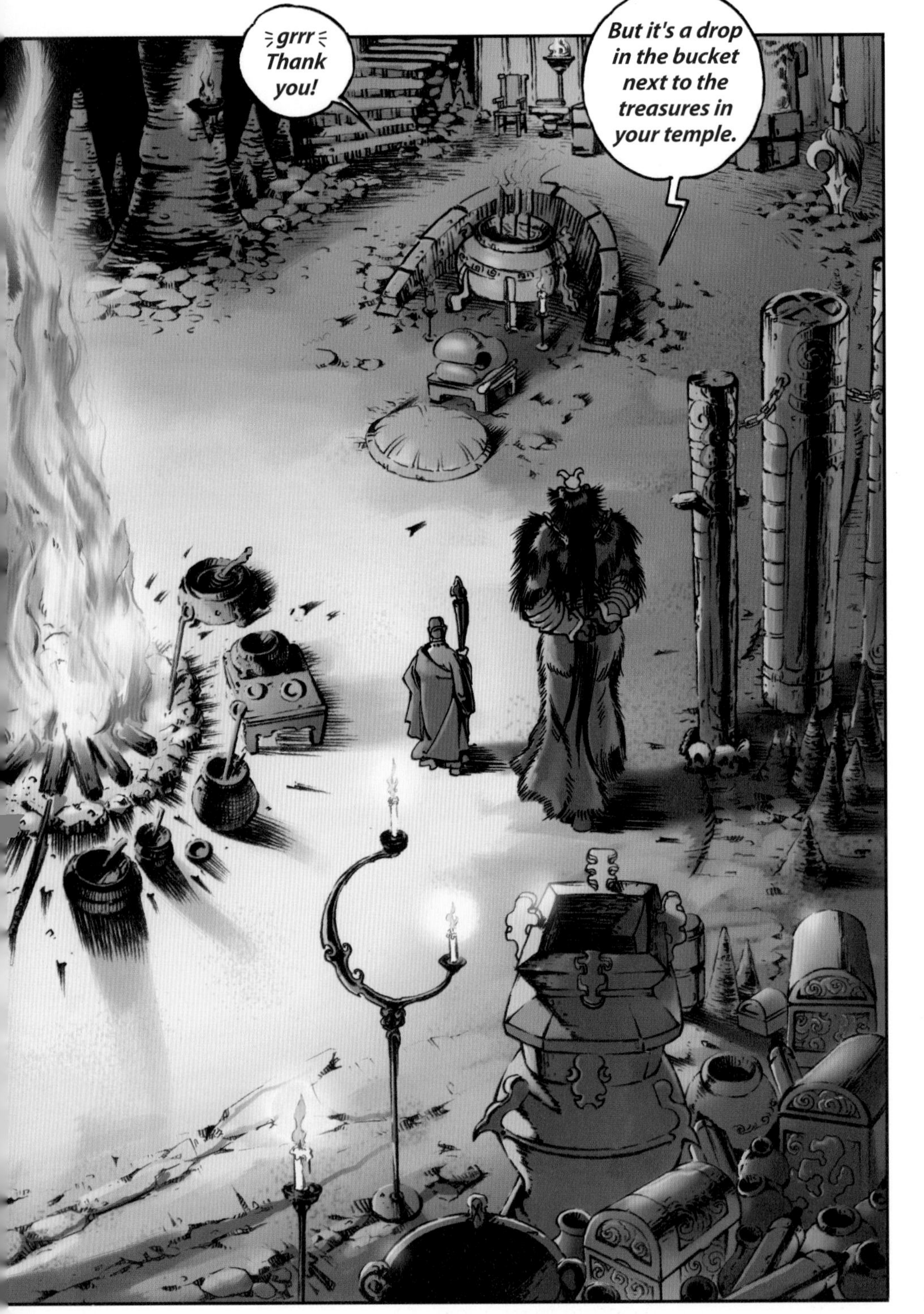
grrr
Thank you!
But it's a drop in the bucket next to the treasures in your temple.

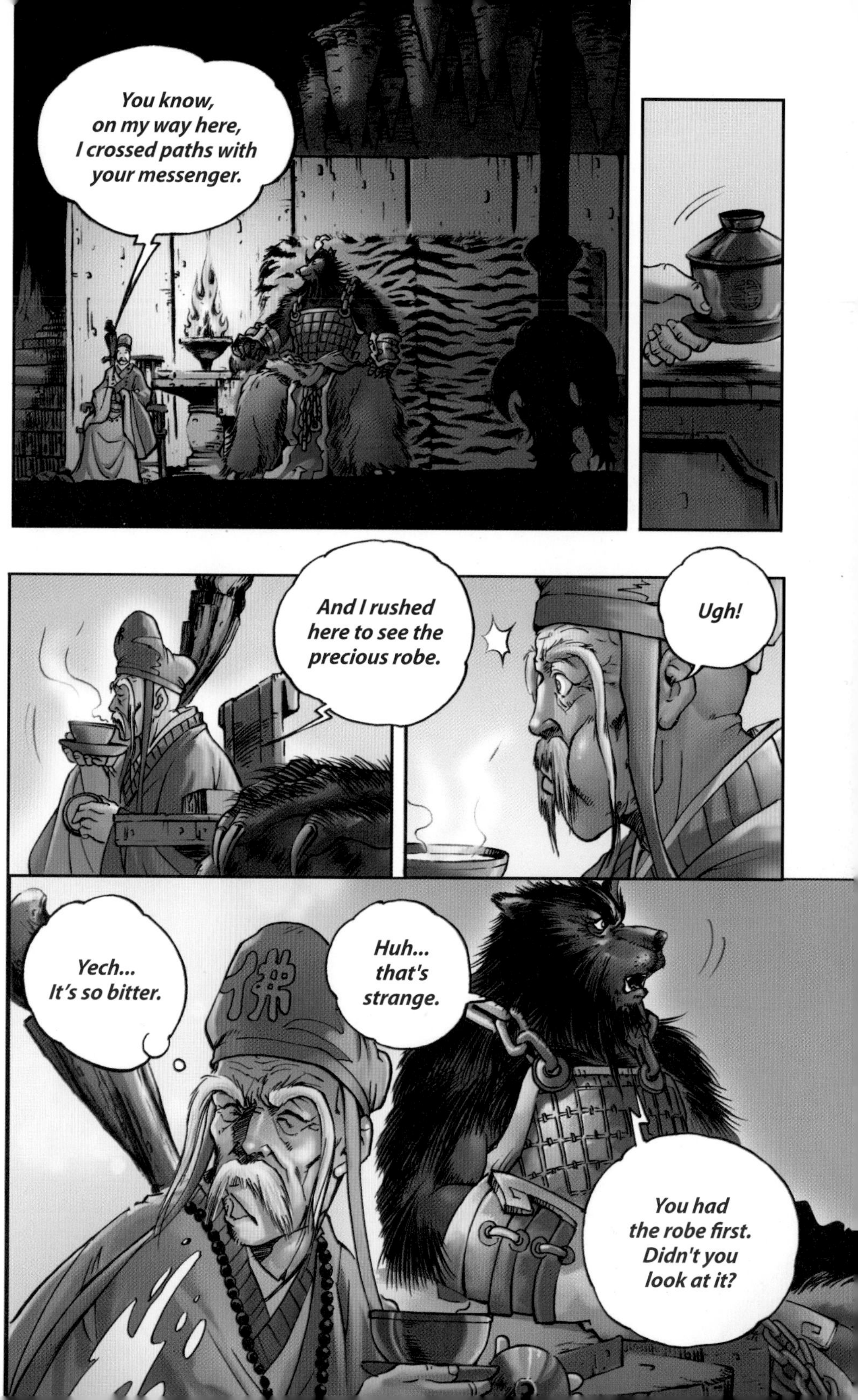
You know, on my way here, I crossed paths with your messenger.
And I rushed here to see the precious robe.
Ugh!
Yech... It's so bitter.
Huh... that's strange.
You had the robe first. Didn't you look at it?

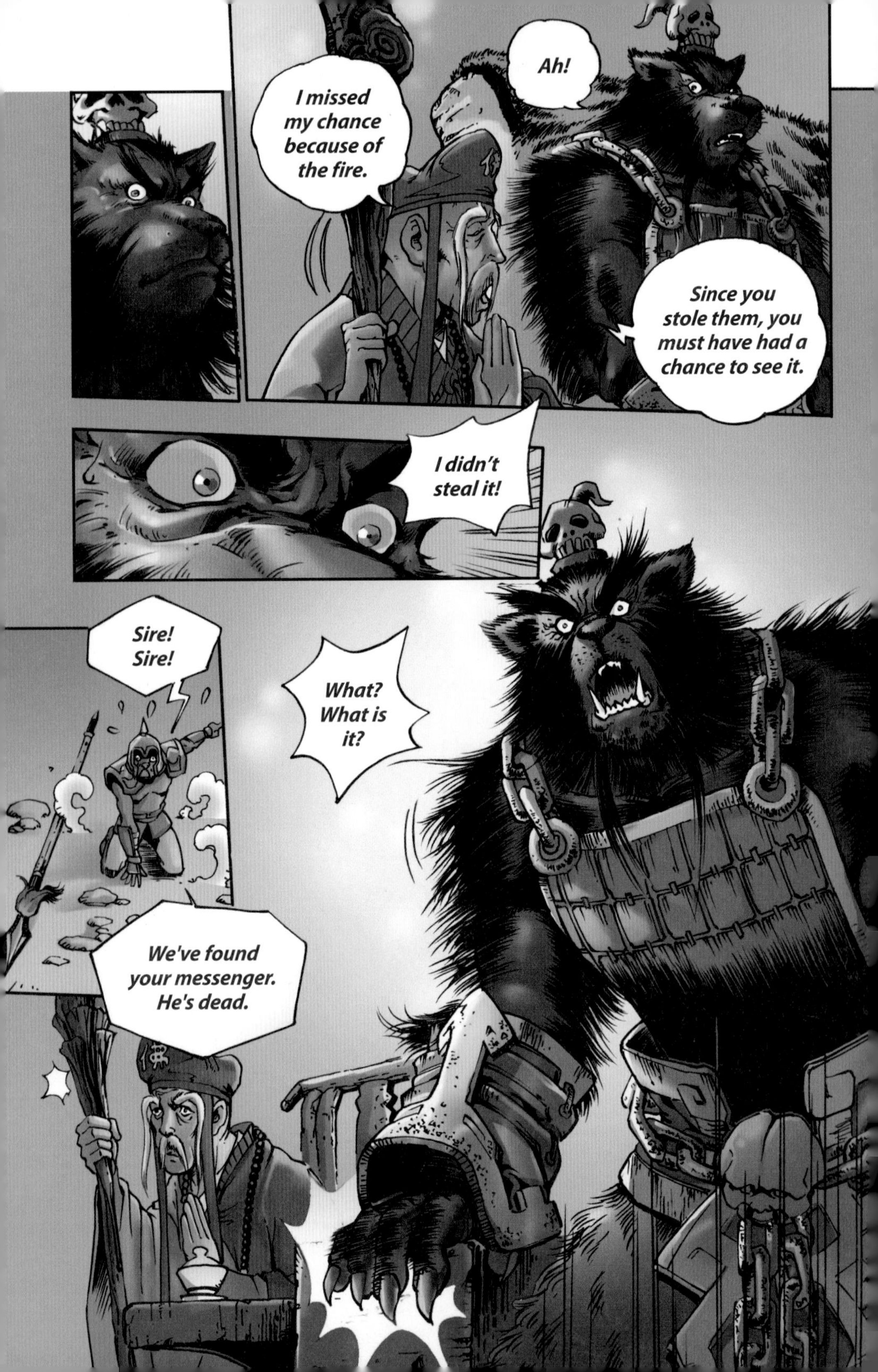
I missed my chance because of the fire.
Ah!
Since you stole them, you must have had a chance to see it.
I didn't steal it!
Sire! Sire!
What? What is it?
We've found your messenger. He's dead.

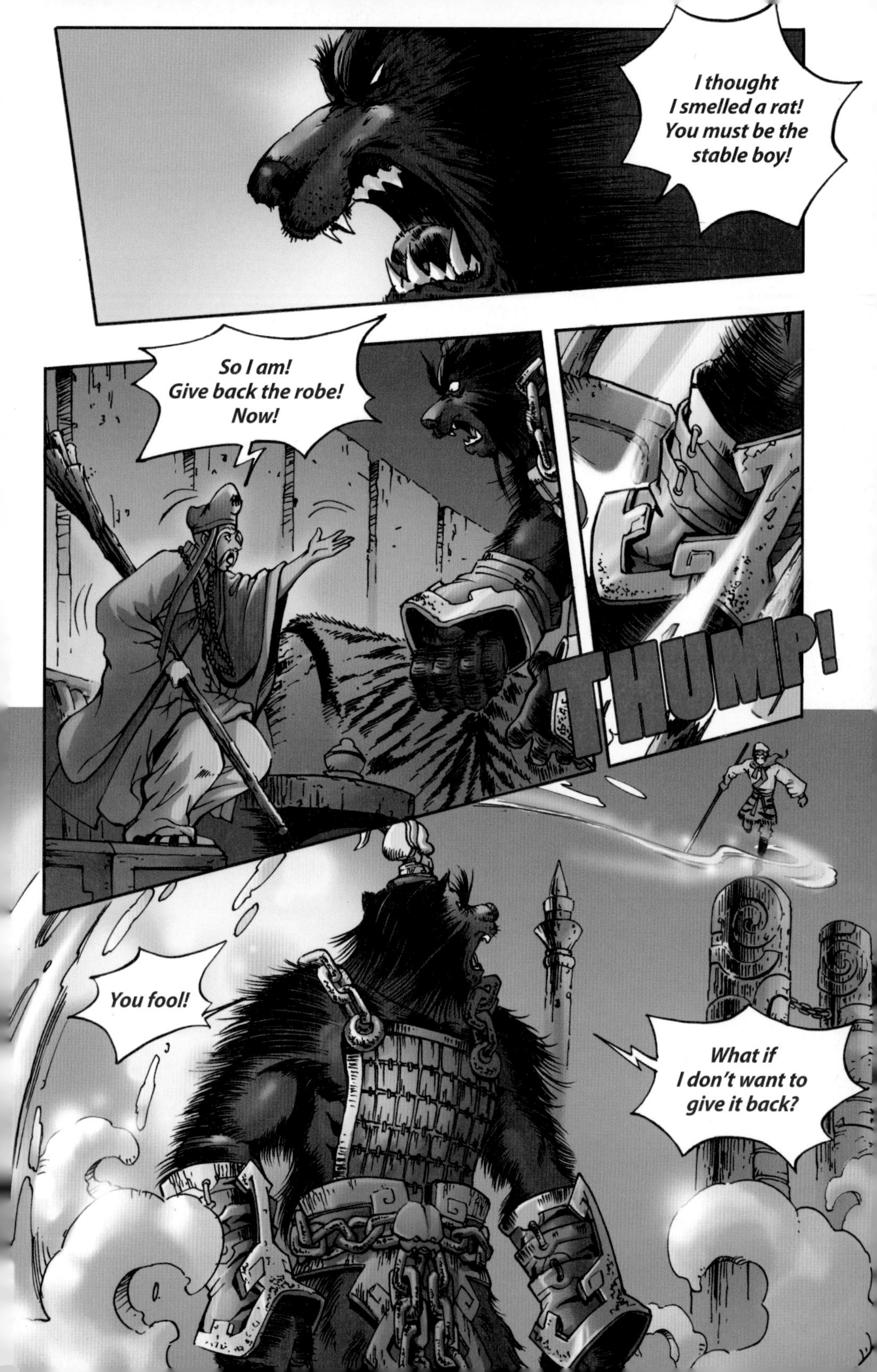
I thought I smelled a rat! You must be the stable boy!
So I am! Give back the robe! Now!
THUMP!
You fool!
What if I don't want to give it back?

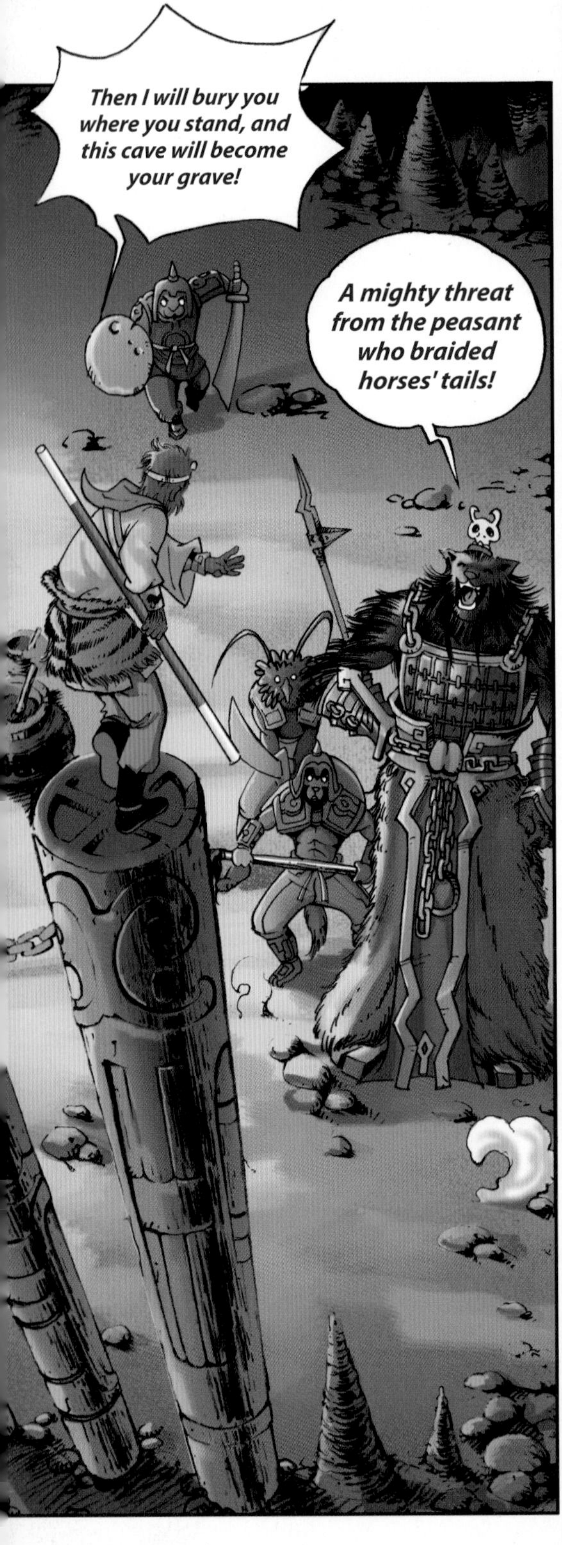
Then I will bury you where you stand, and this cave will become your grave!
A mighty threat from the peasant who braided horses' tails!

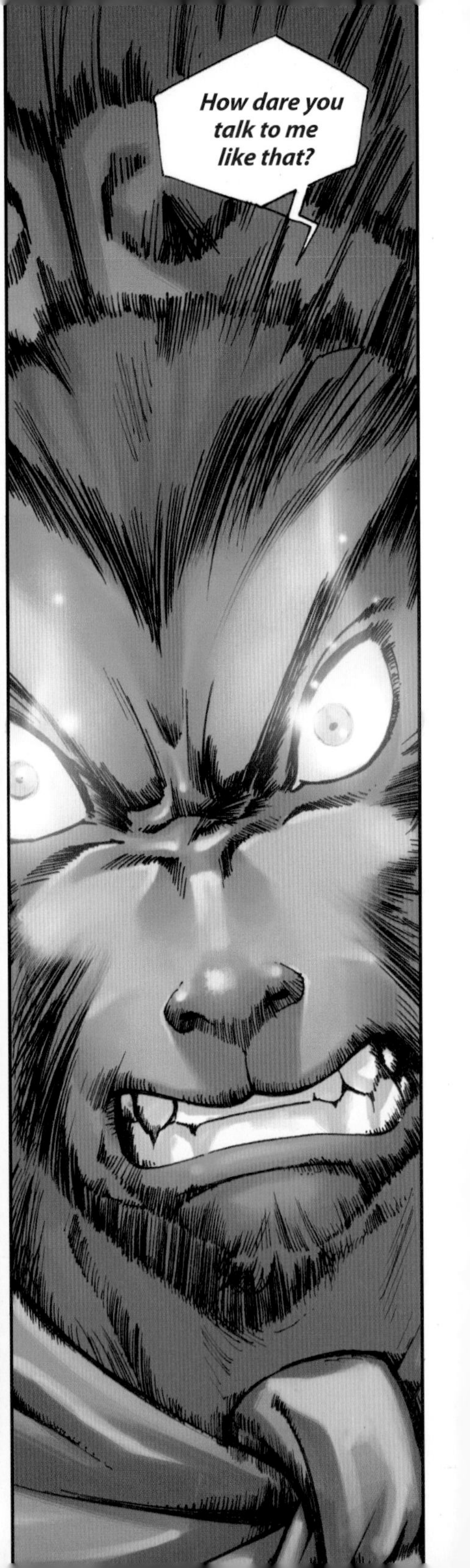
How dare you talk to me like that?

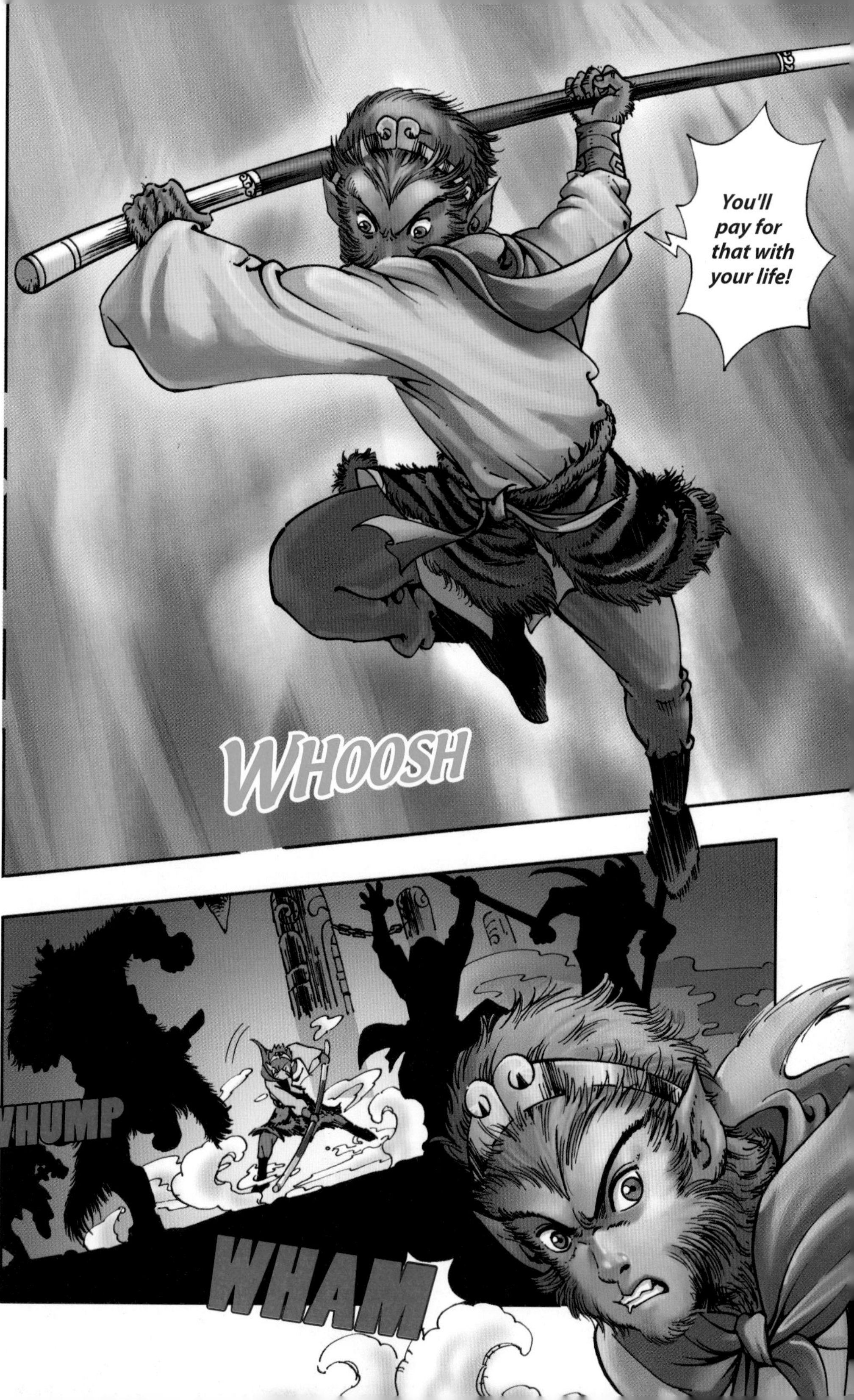
You'll pay for that with your life!
WHOOSH
WHUMP
WHAM

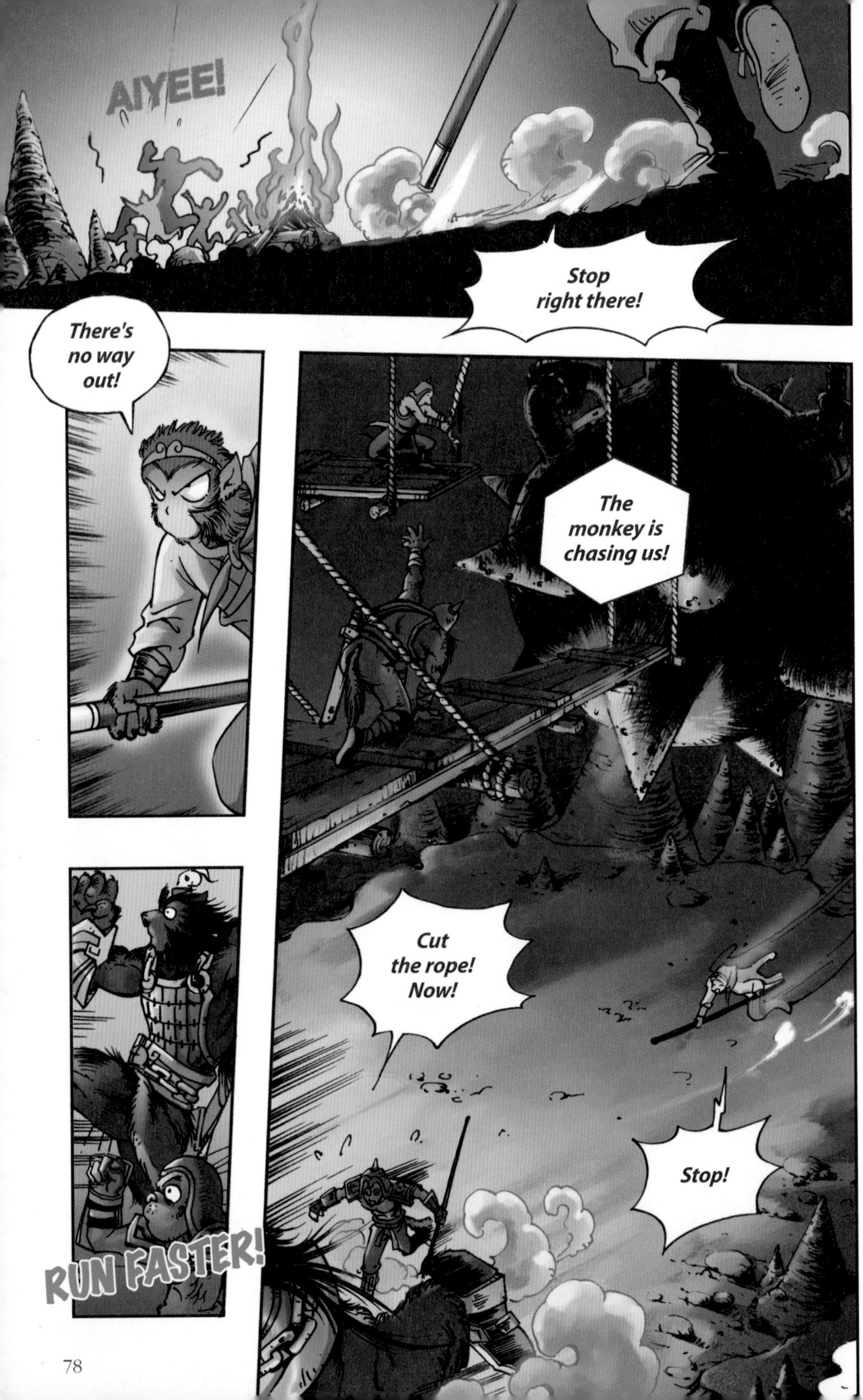
AIYEE!
Stop right there!
There's no way out!
The monkey is chasing us!
RUN FASTER!
Cut the rope! Now!
Stop!

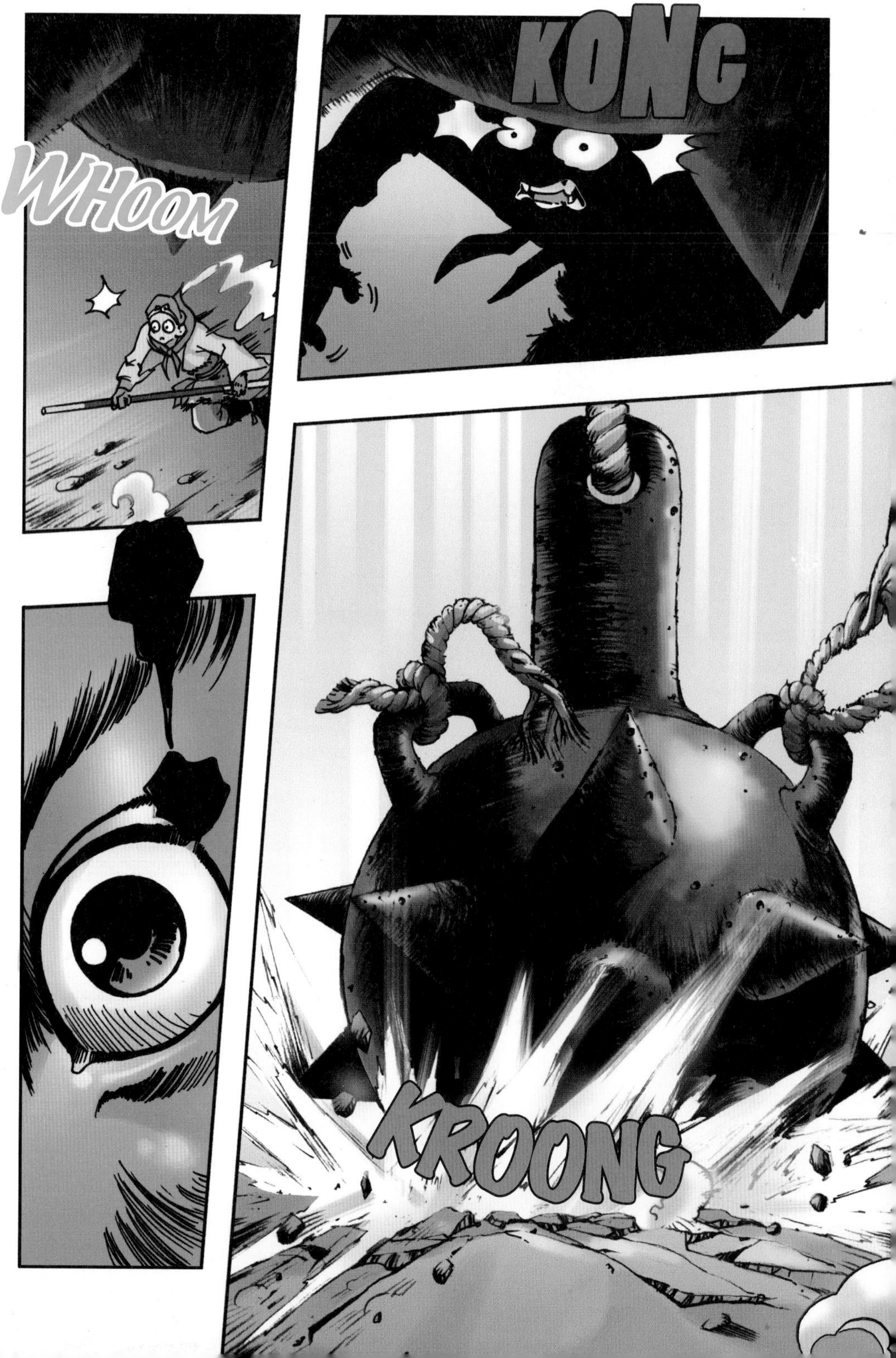
KONG
WHOOM
KROONG

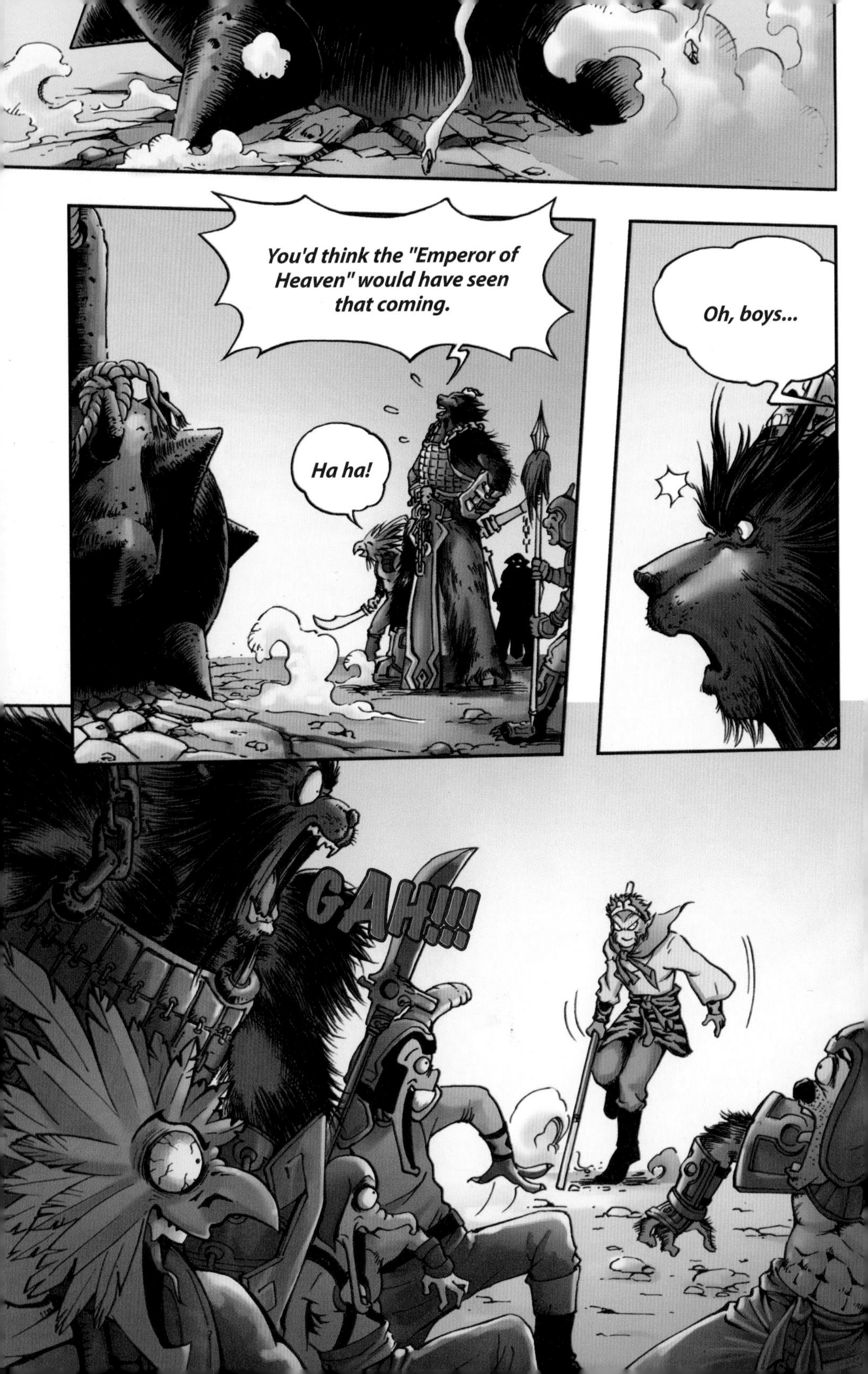
You'd think the "Emperor of Heaven" would have seen that coming.
Ha ha!
Oh, boys...
GAH!!!

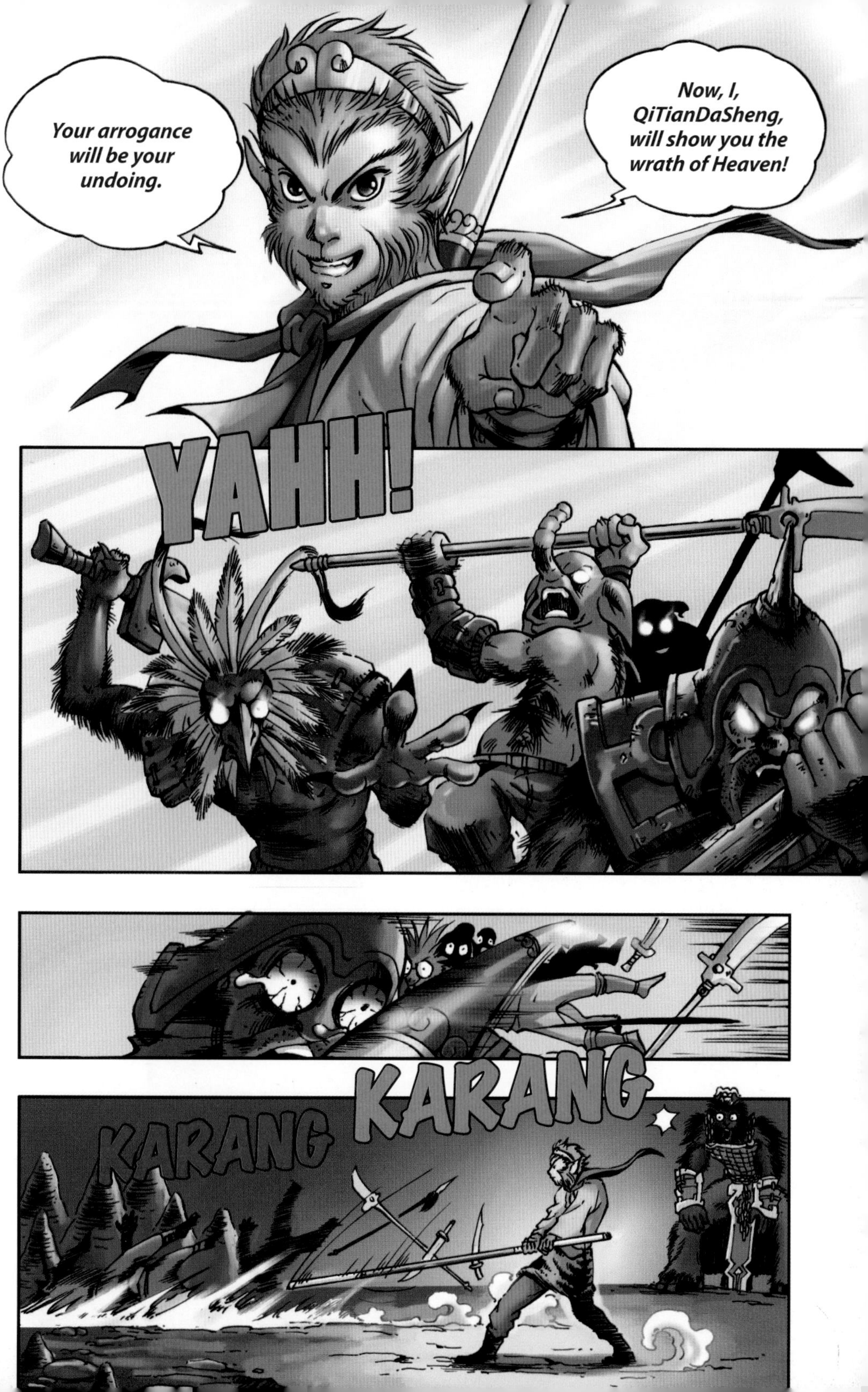
Your arrogance will be your undoing.
Now, I, QiTianDaSheng, will show you the wrath of Heaven!
YAHH!
KARANG KARANG

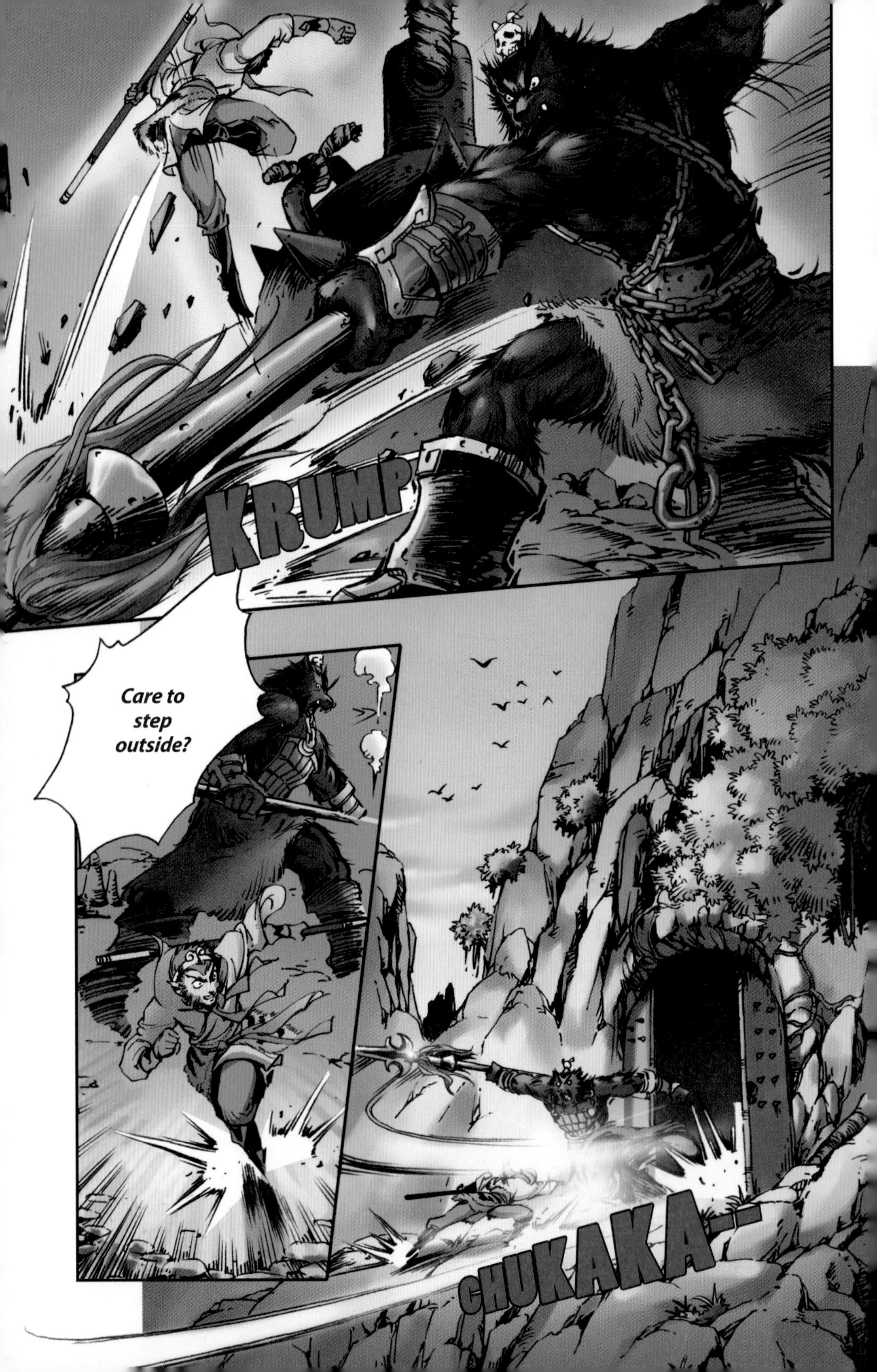
KRUMP
Care to step outside?
CHUKAKA--

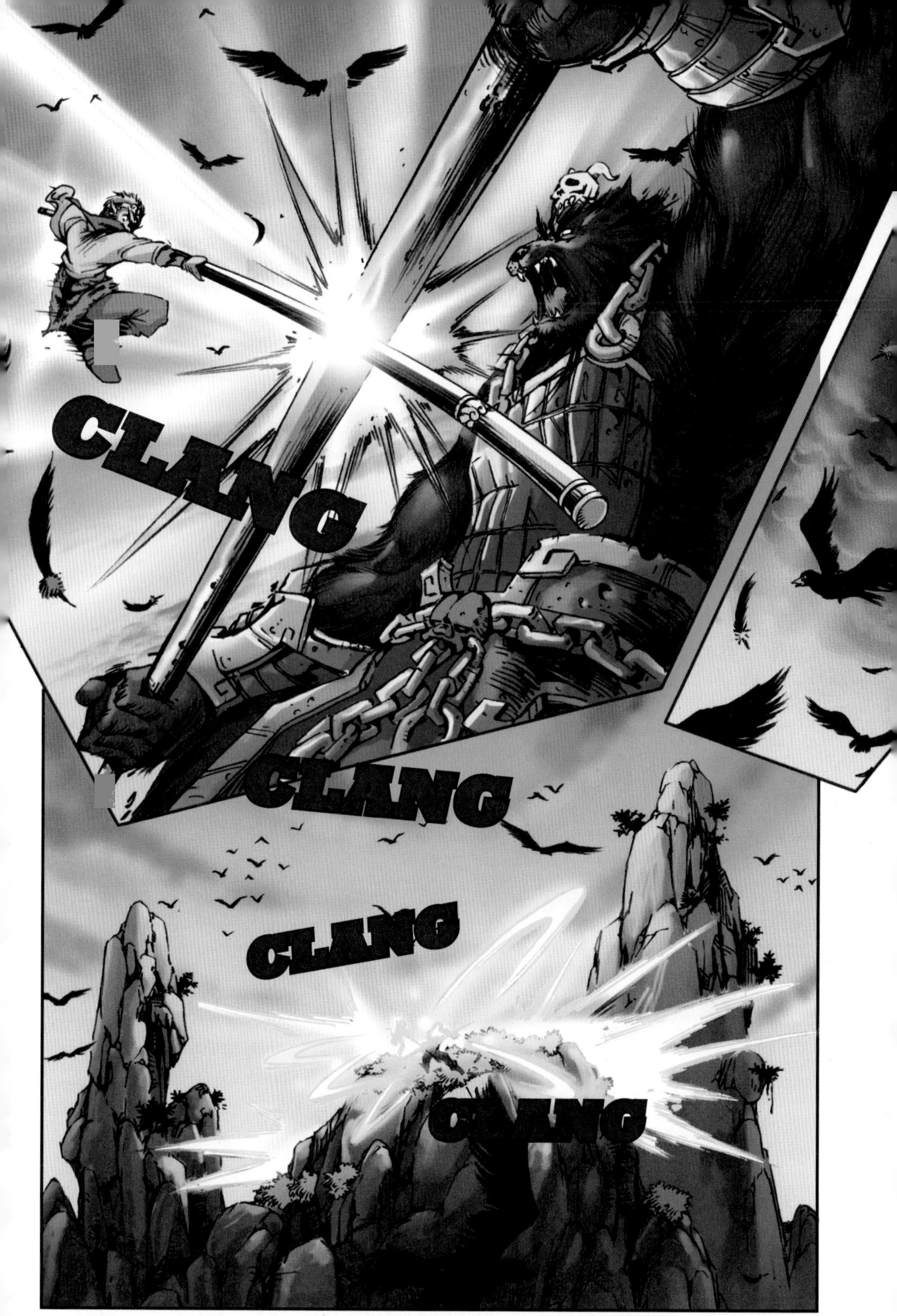
CLANG
CLANG
CLANG

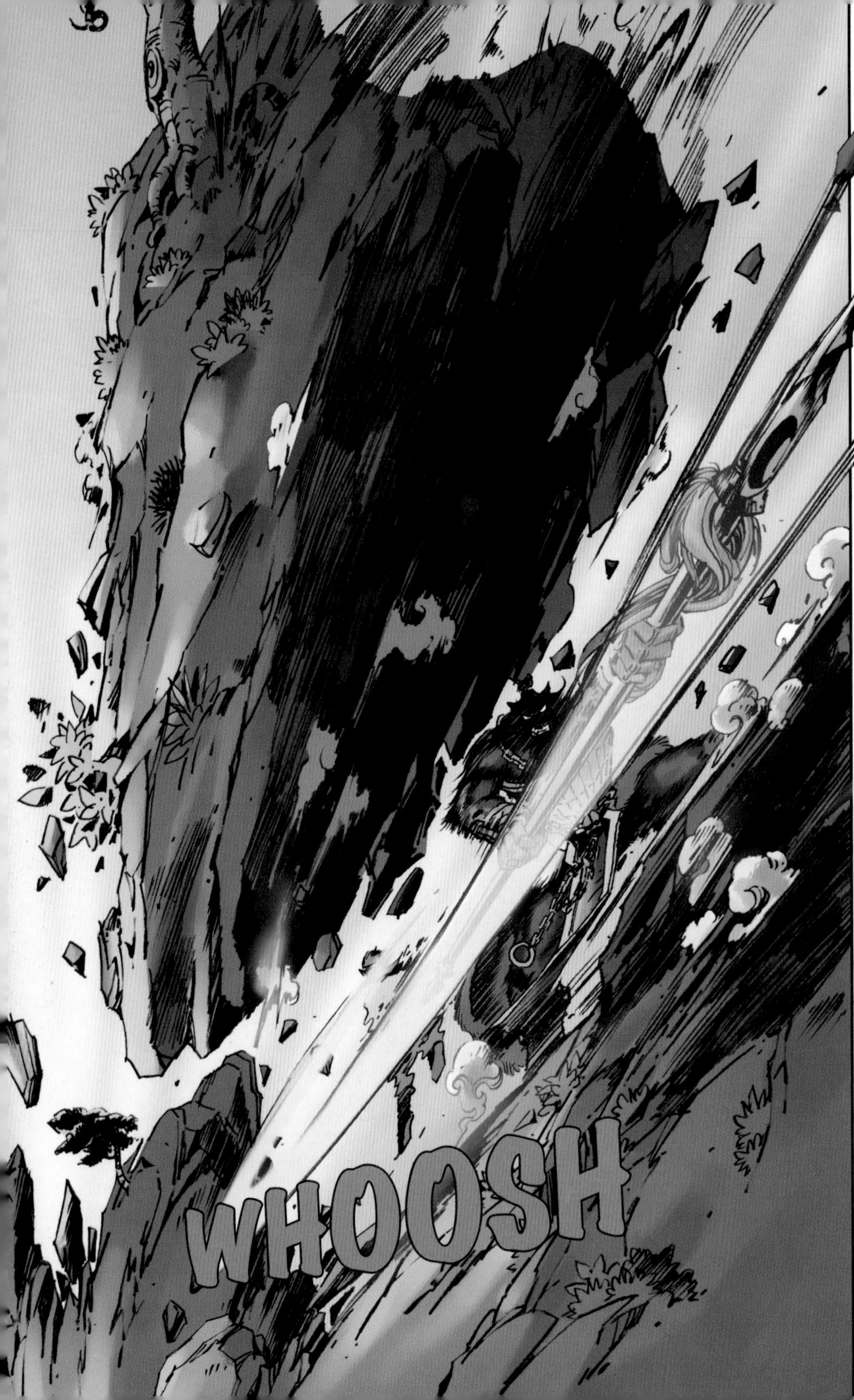
WHOOSH

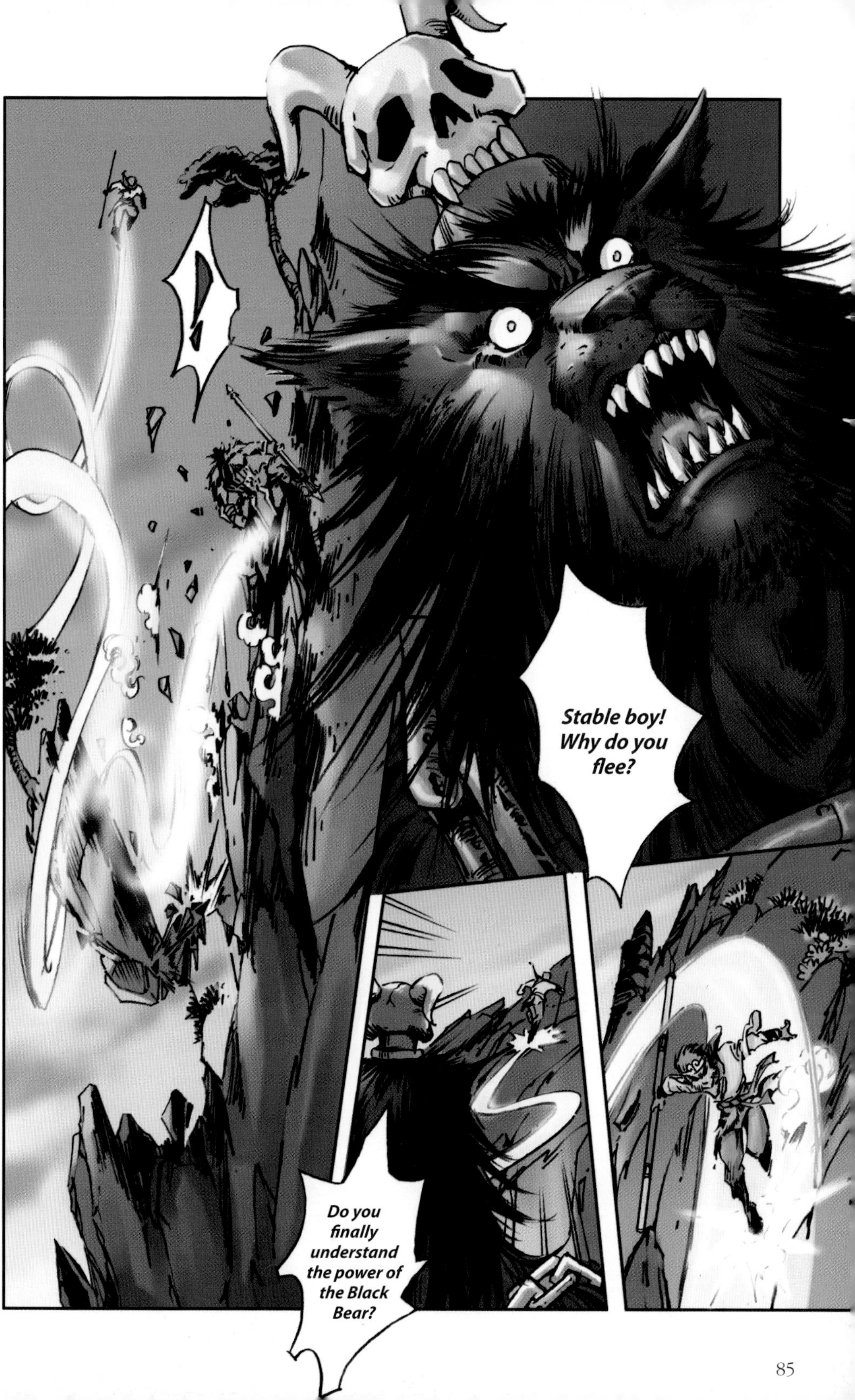
Stable boy! Why do you flee?
Do you finally understand the power of the Black Bear?

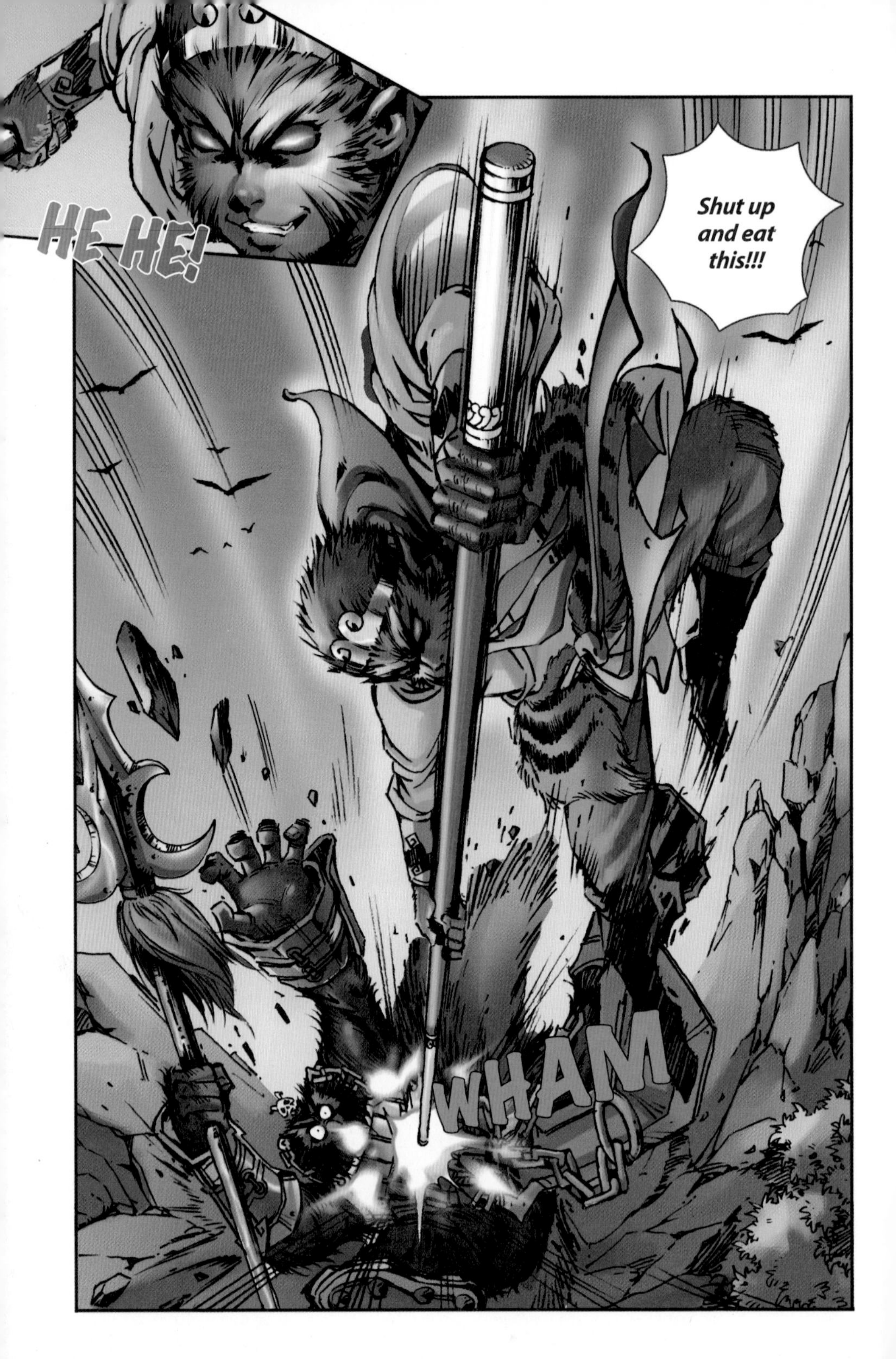
HE HE!
Shut up and eat this!!!
WHAM

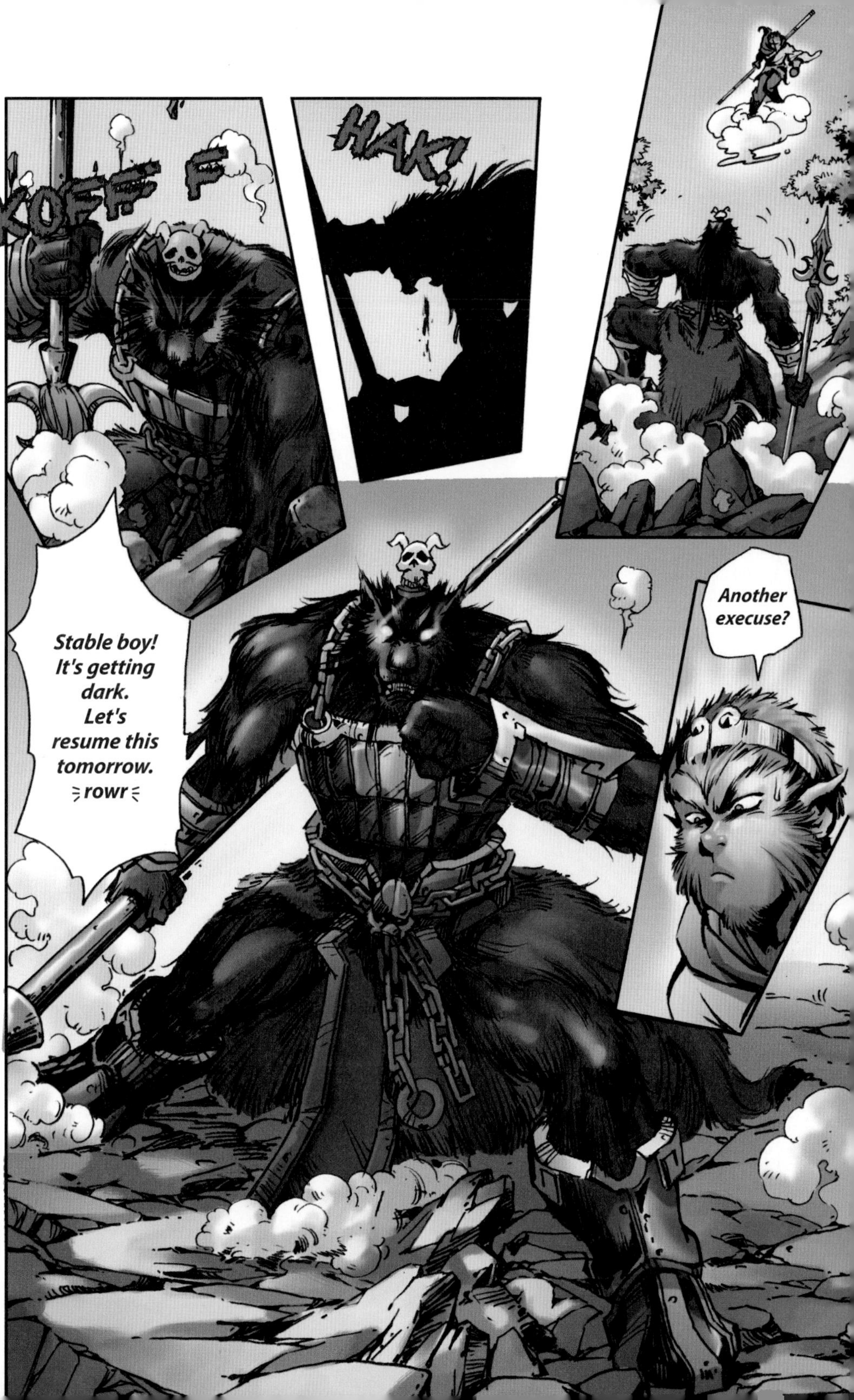
KOFFF F
HAK!
Stable boy! It's getting dark. Let's resume this tomorrow.
rowr
Another execuse?

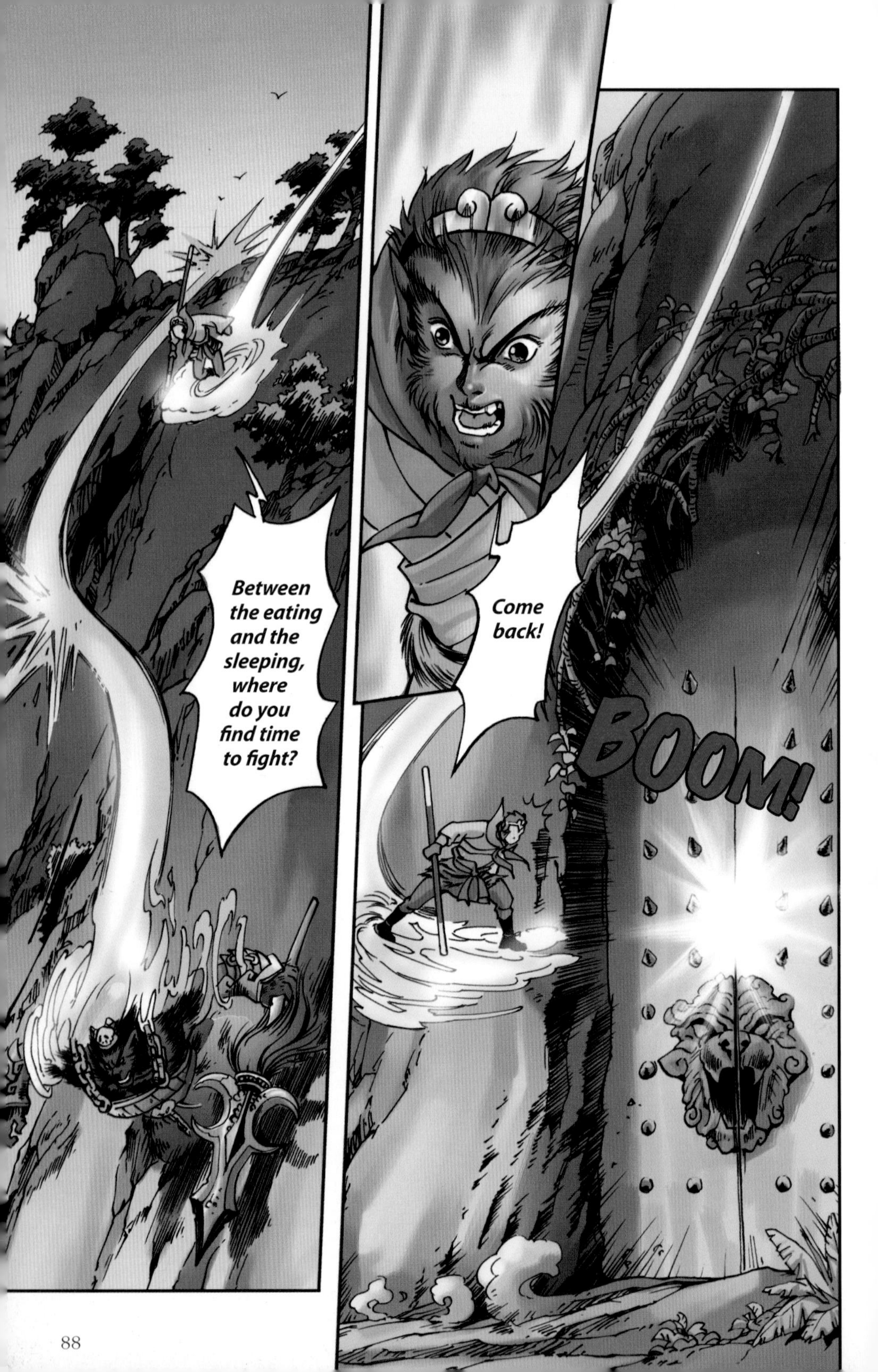
Between the eating and the sleeping, where do you find time to fight?
Come back!
BOOM!

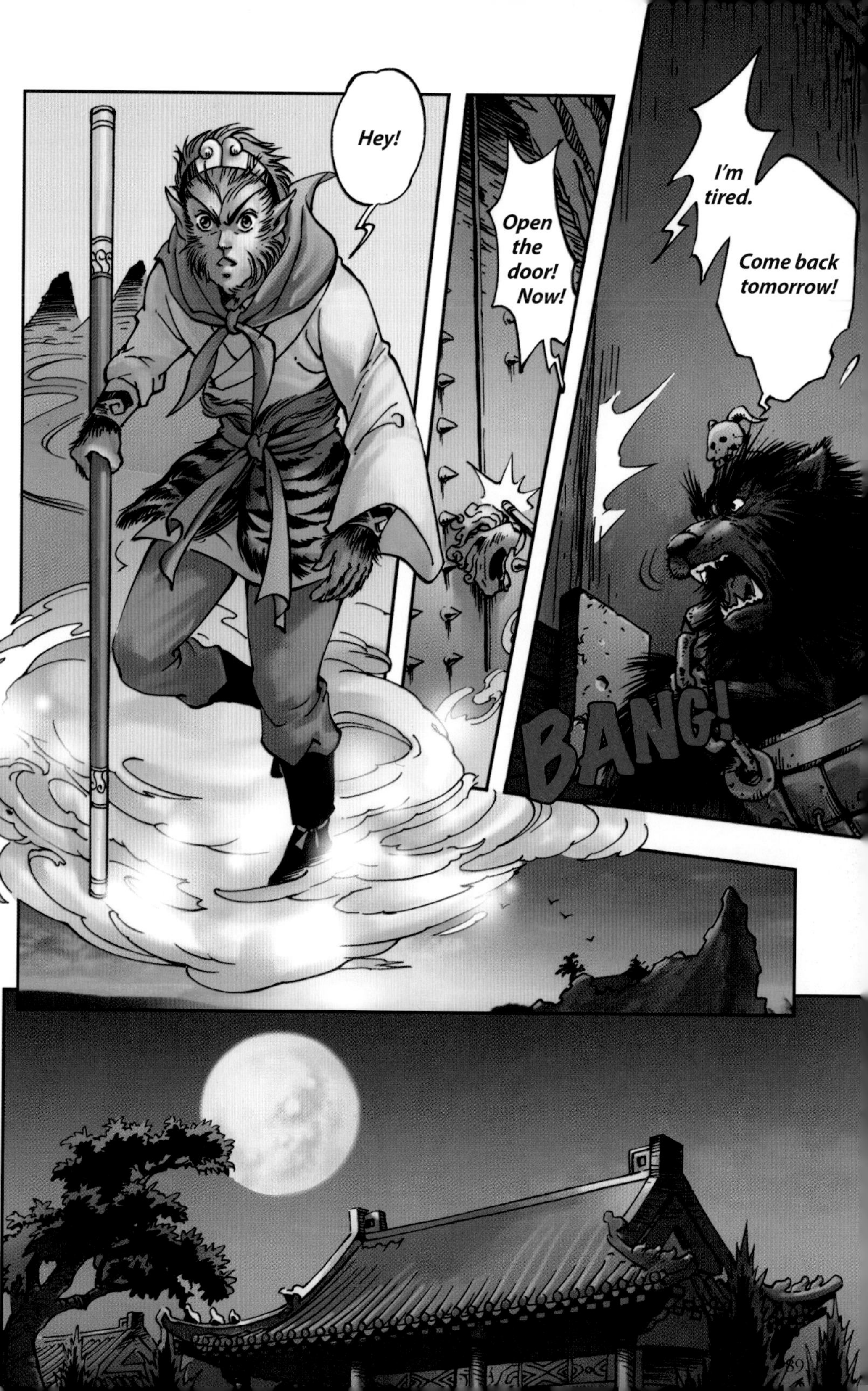
Hey!
Open the door! Now!
I'm tired.
Come back tomorrow!
BANG!

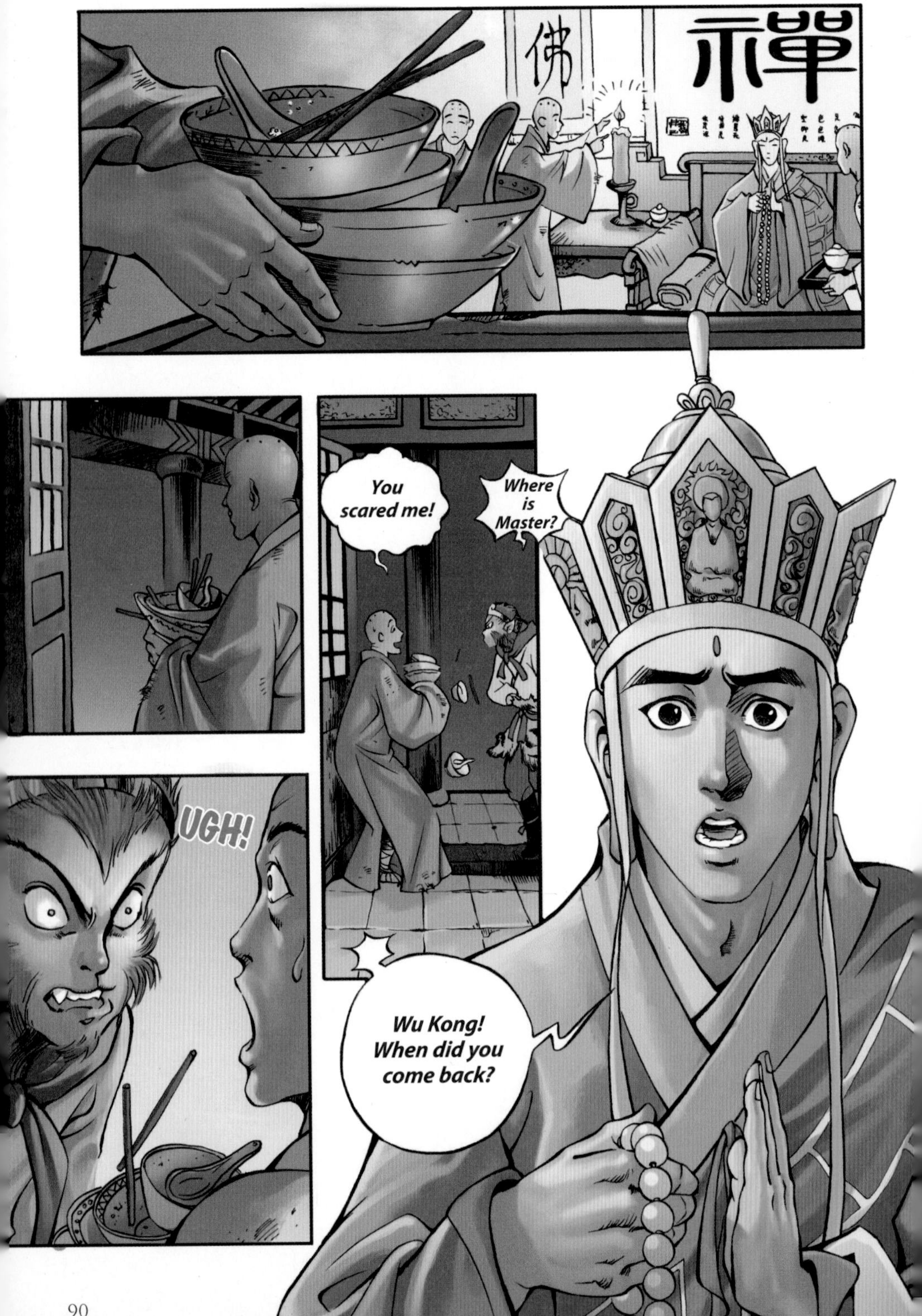
佛
禪
UGH!
You scared me!
Where is Master?
Wu Kong! When did you come back?

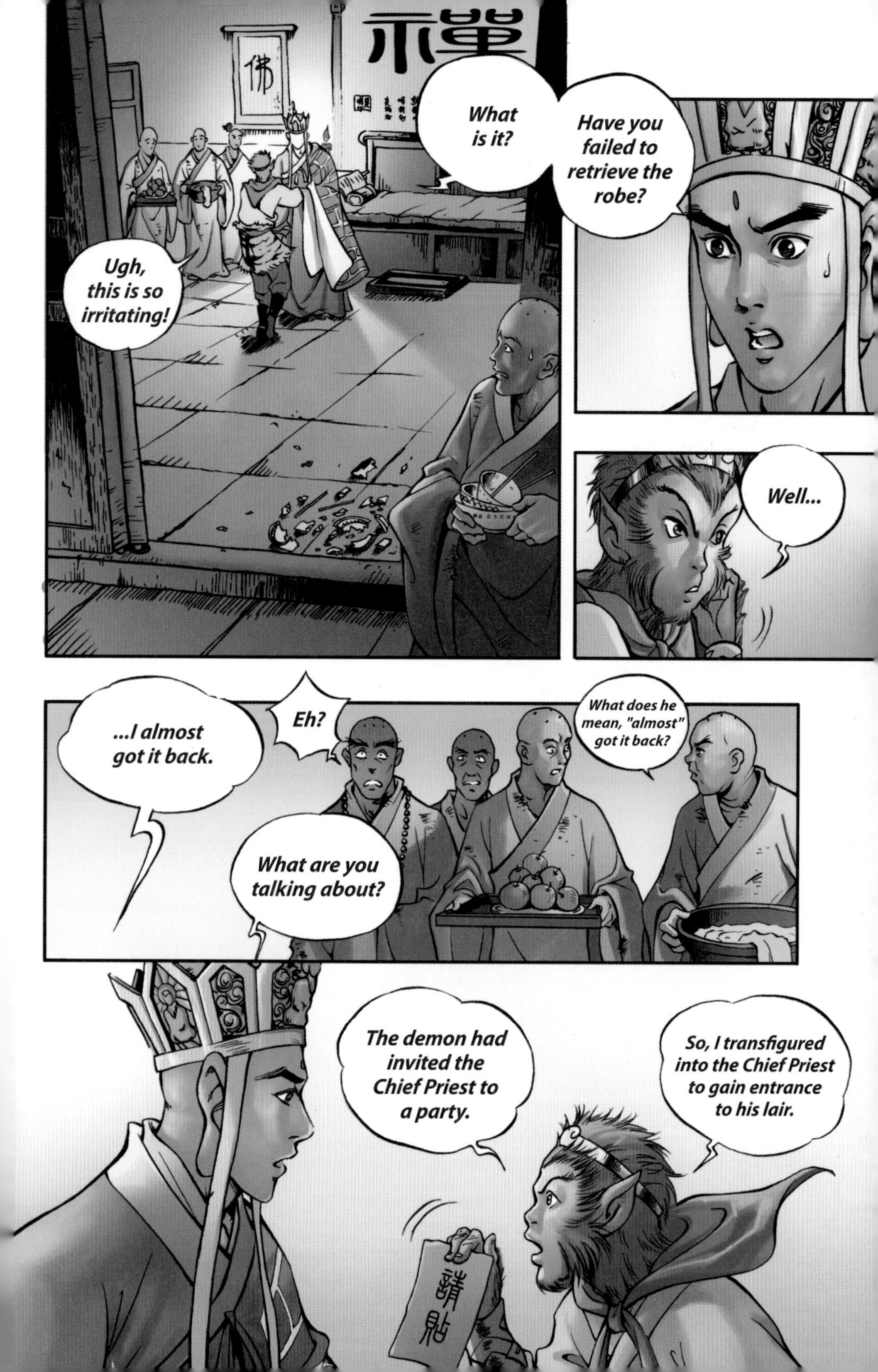

禪
佛
Ugh, this is so irritating!
What is it?
Have you failed to retrieve the robe?
Well...
...I almost got it back.
Eh?
What does he mean, "almost" got it back?
What are you talking about?
The demon had invited the Chief Priest to a party.
So, I transfigured into the Chief Priest to gain entrance to his lair.
請貼

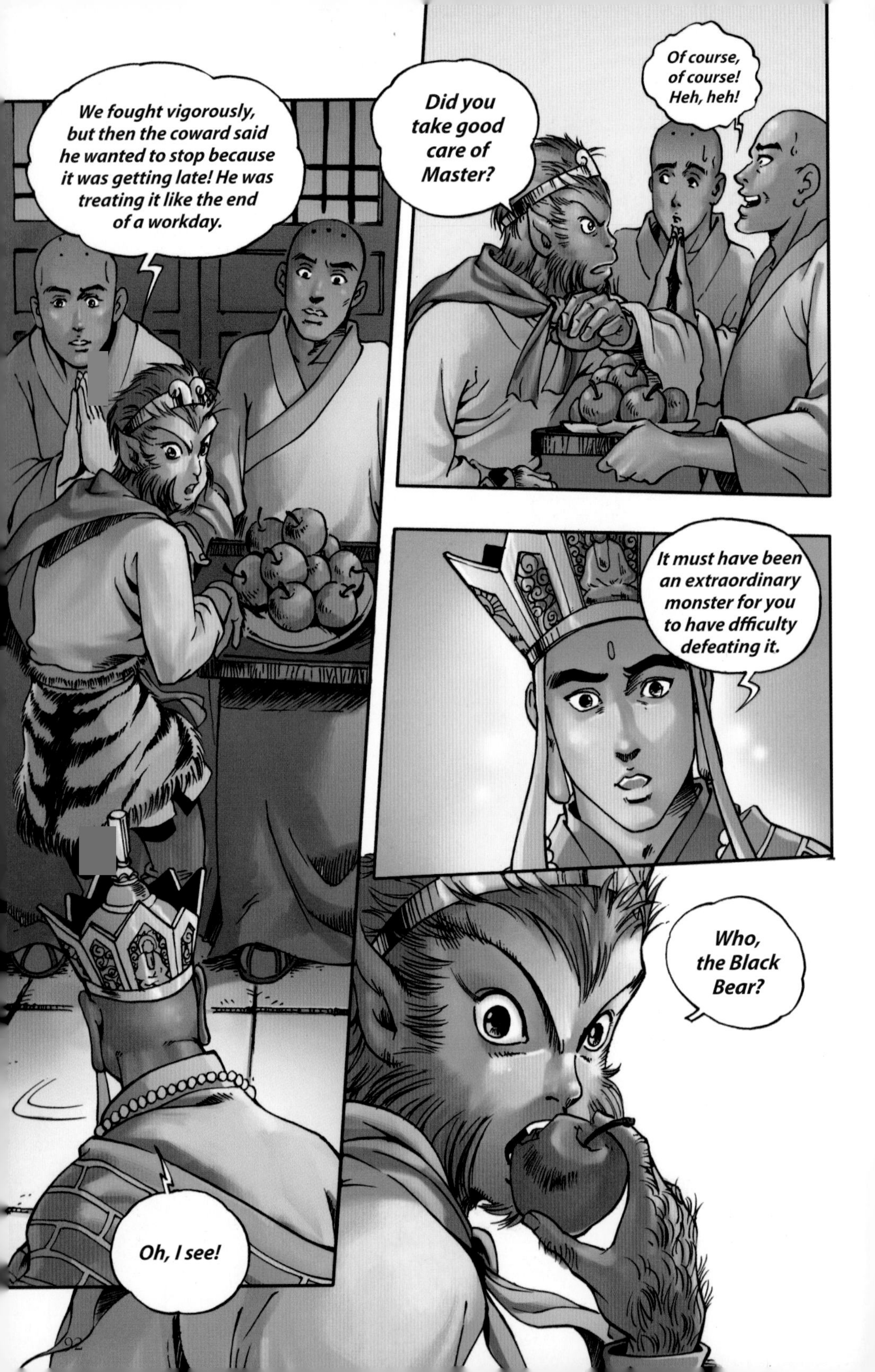

Did you take good care of Master?
Of course, of course! Heh, heh!
It must have been an extraordinary monster for you to have dfficulty defeating it.
Who, the Black Bear?
We fought vigorously, but then the coward said he wanted to stop because it was getting late! He was treating it like the end of a workday.
Oh, I see!

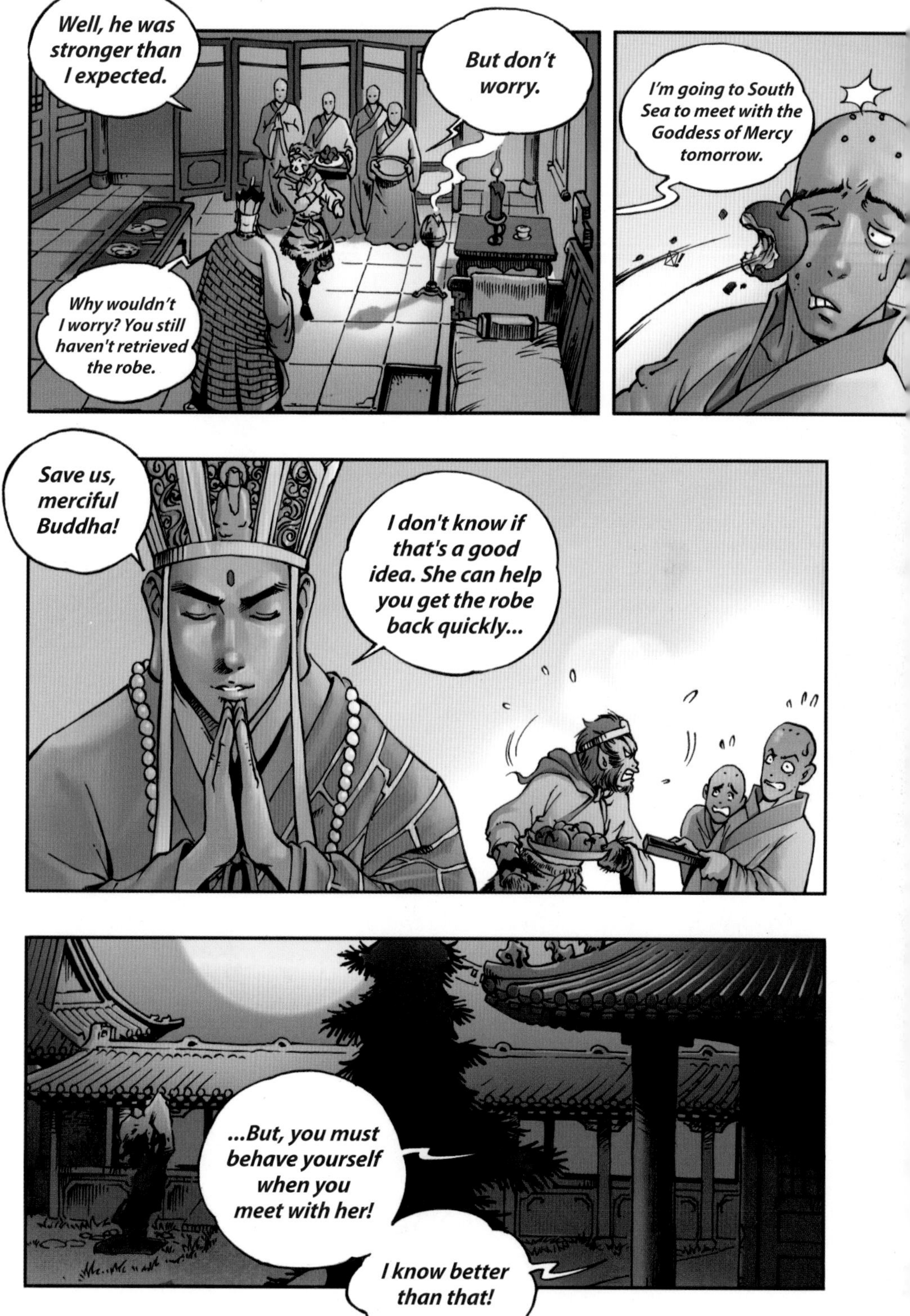
Well, he was stronger than I expected.
But don't worry.
Why wouldn't I worry? You still haven't retrieved the robe.
I'm going to South Sea to meet with the Goddess of Mercy tomorrow.
Save us, merciful Buddha!
I don't know if that's a good idea. She can help you get the robe back quickly...
...But, you must behave yourself when you meet with her!
I know better than that!

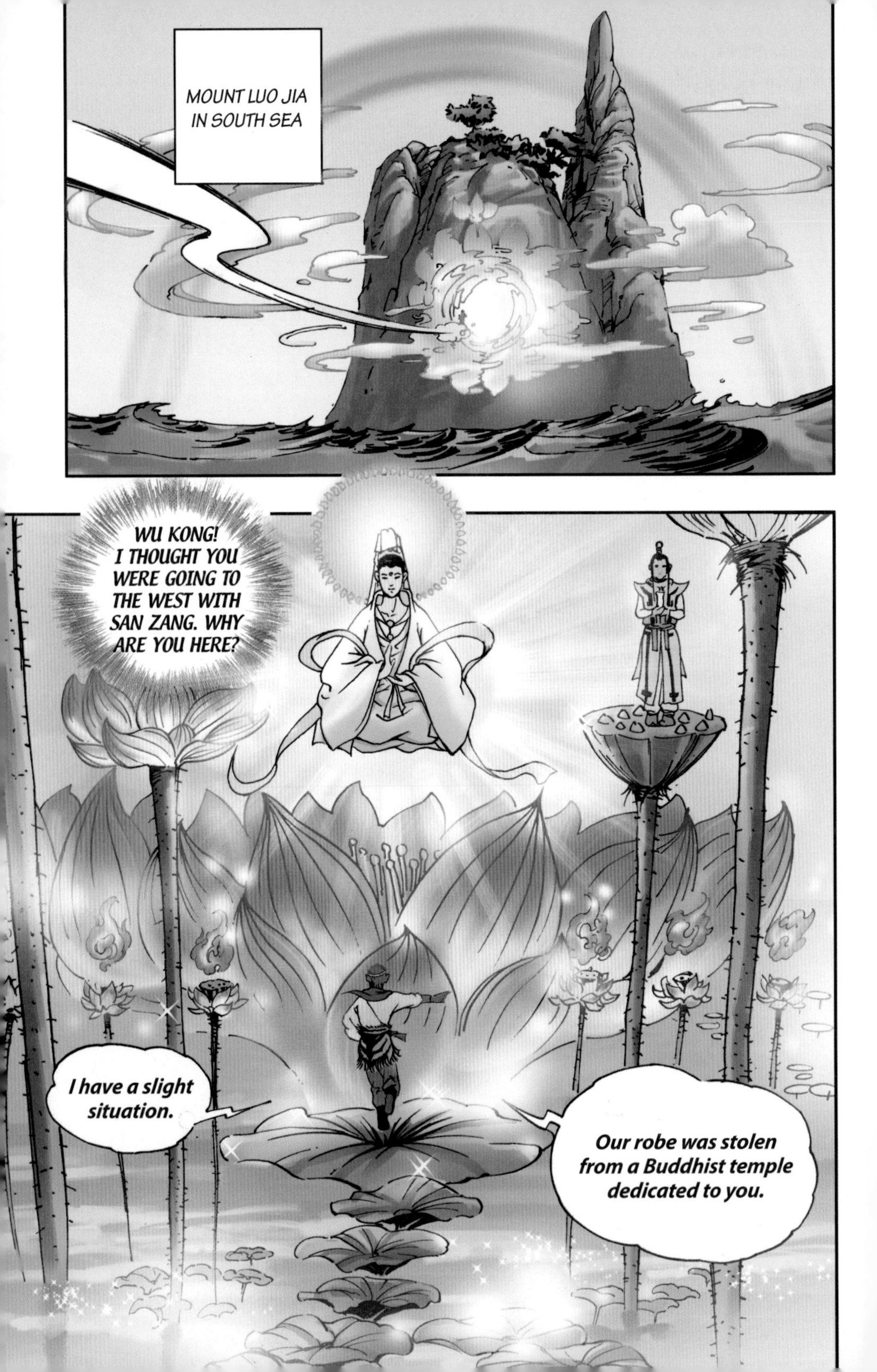
MOUNT LUO JIA IN SOUTH SEA
WU KONG! I THOUGHT YOU WERE GOING TO THE WEST WITH SAN ZANG. WHY ARE YOU HERE?
I have a slight situation.
Our robe was stolen from a Buddhist temple dedicated to you.

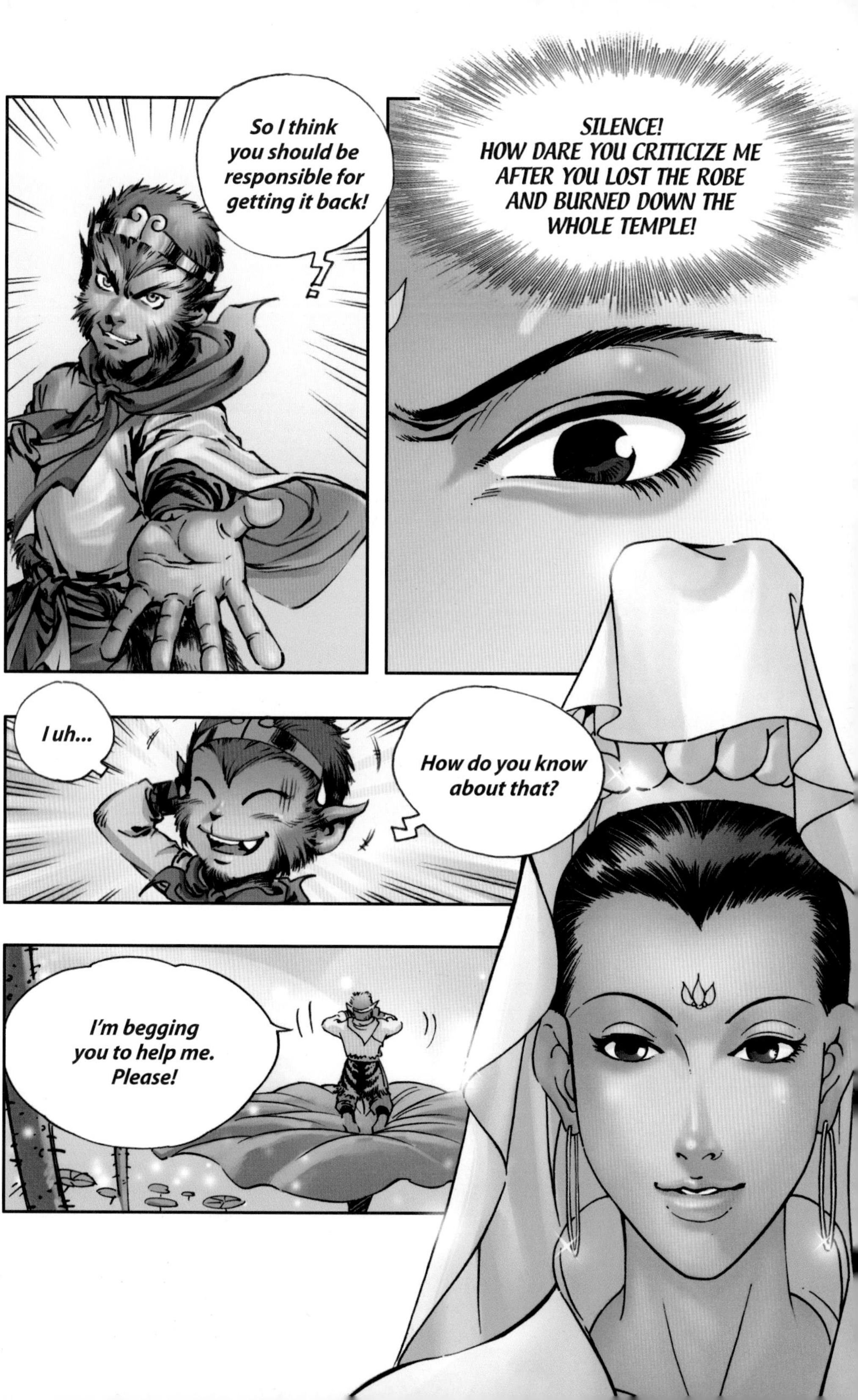
So I think you should be responsible for getting it back!
SILENCE! HOW DARE YOU CRITICIZE ME AFTER YOU LOST THE ROBE AND BURNED DOWN THE WHOLE TEMPLE!
I uh...
How do you know about that?
I'm begging you to help me. Please!

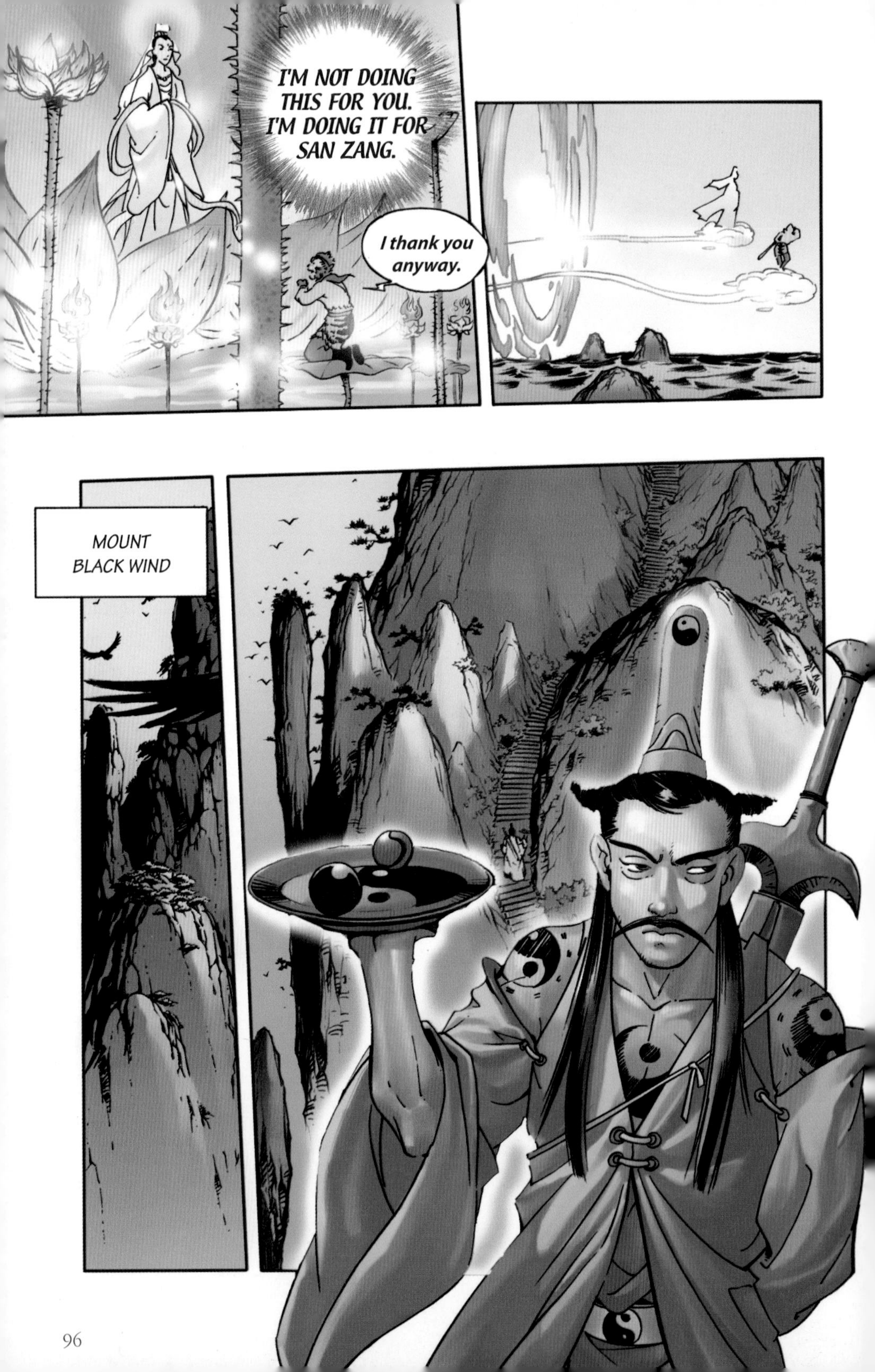

I'M NOT DOING THIS FOR YOU. I'M DOING IT FOR SAN ZANG.
I thank you anyway.
MOUNT BLACK WIND

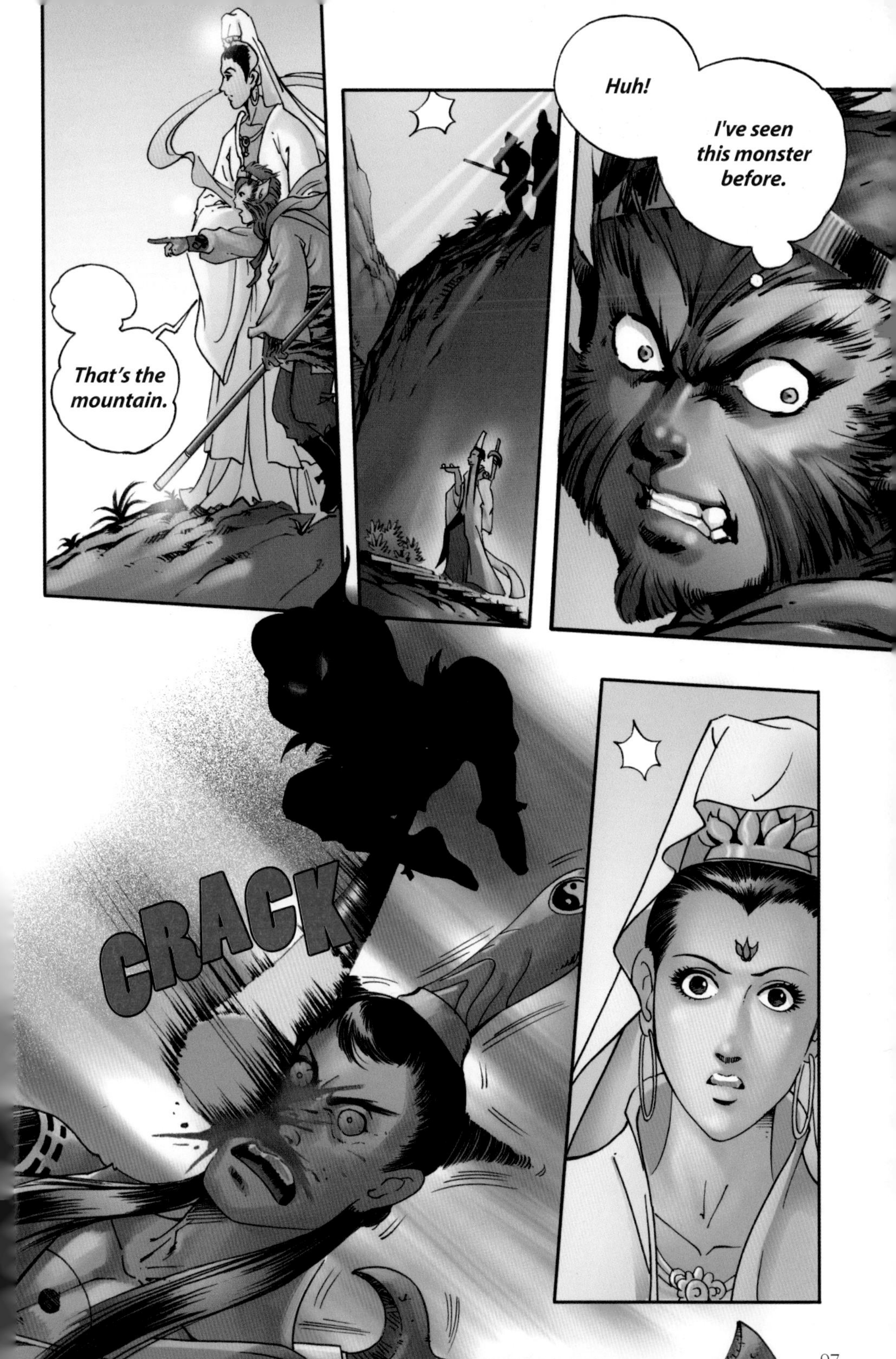
That's the mountain.
Huh!
I've seen this monster before.
CRACK

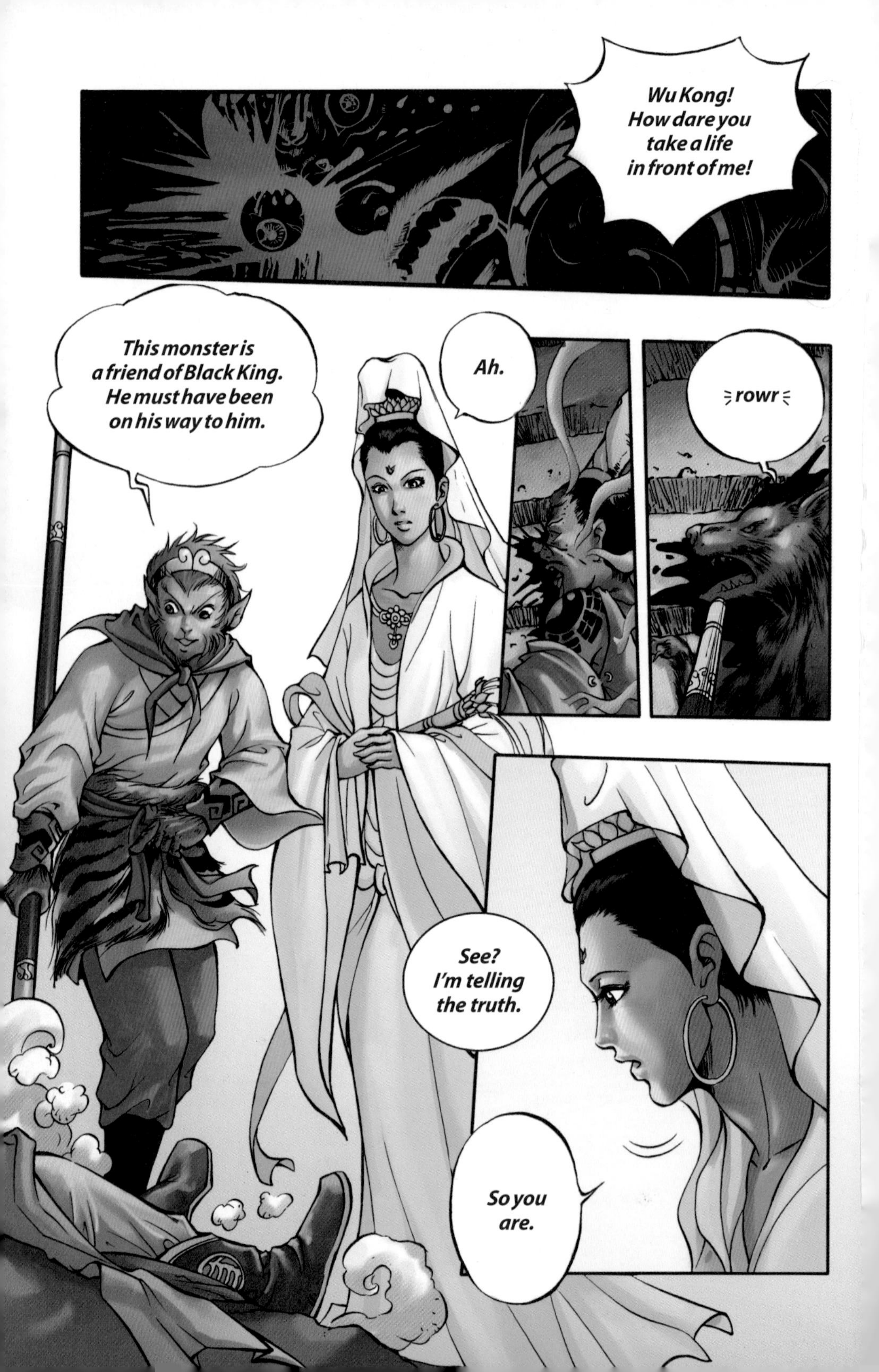
Wu Kong! How dare you take a life in front of me!
This monster is a friend of Black King. He must have been on his way to him.
Ah.
rowr
See? I'm telling the truth.
So you are.

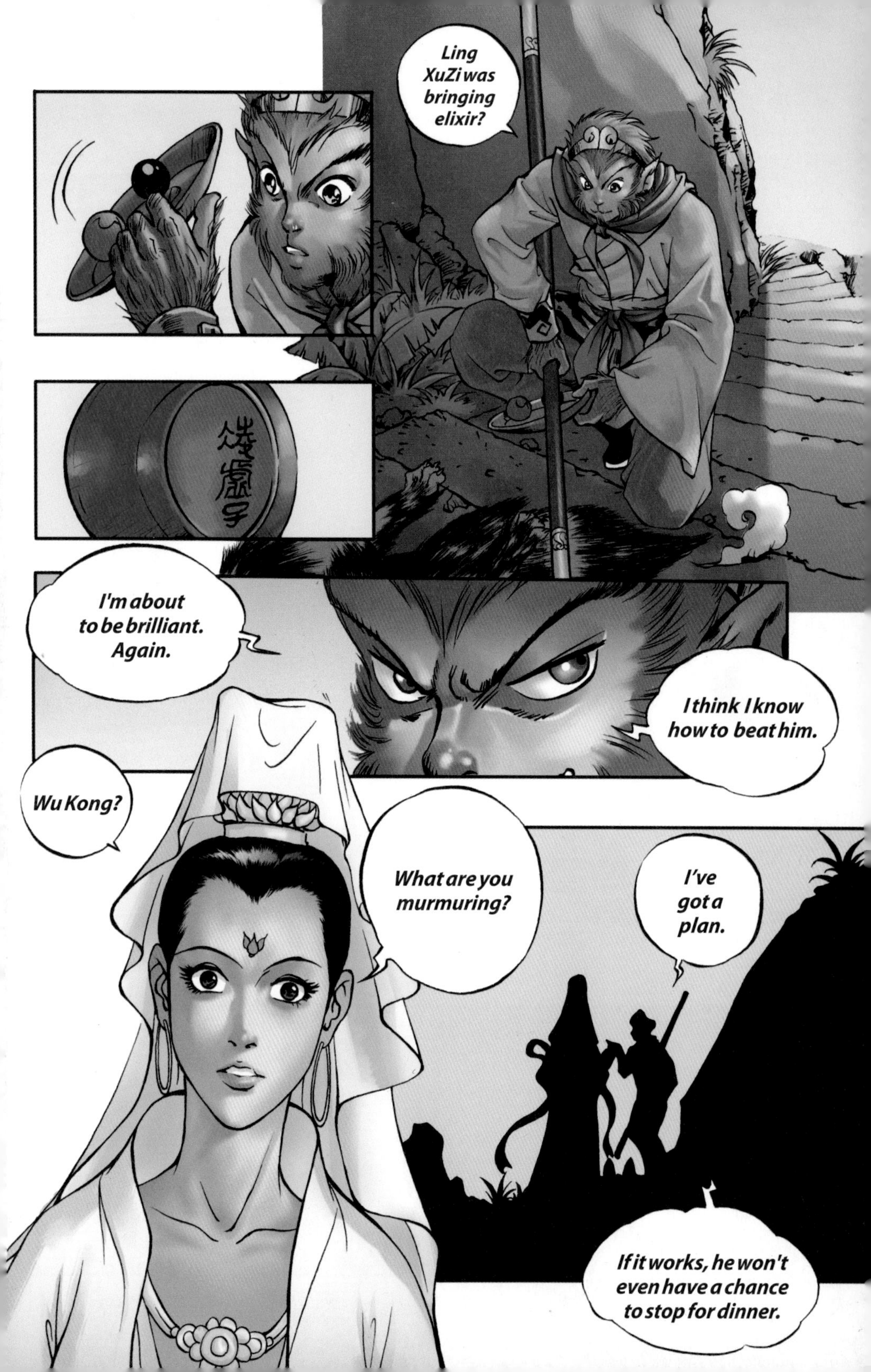

Ling XuZi was bringing elixir?
I'm about to be brilliant. Again.
I think I know how to beat him.
Wu Kong?
What are you murmuring?
I've got a plan.
If it works, he won't even have a chance to stop for dinner.

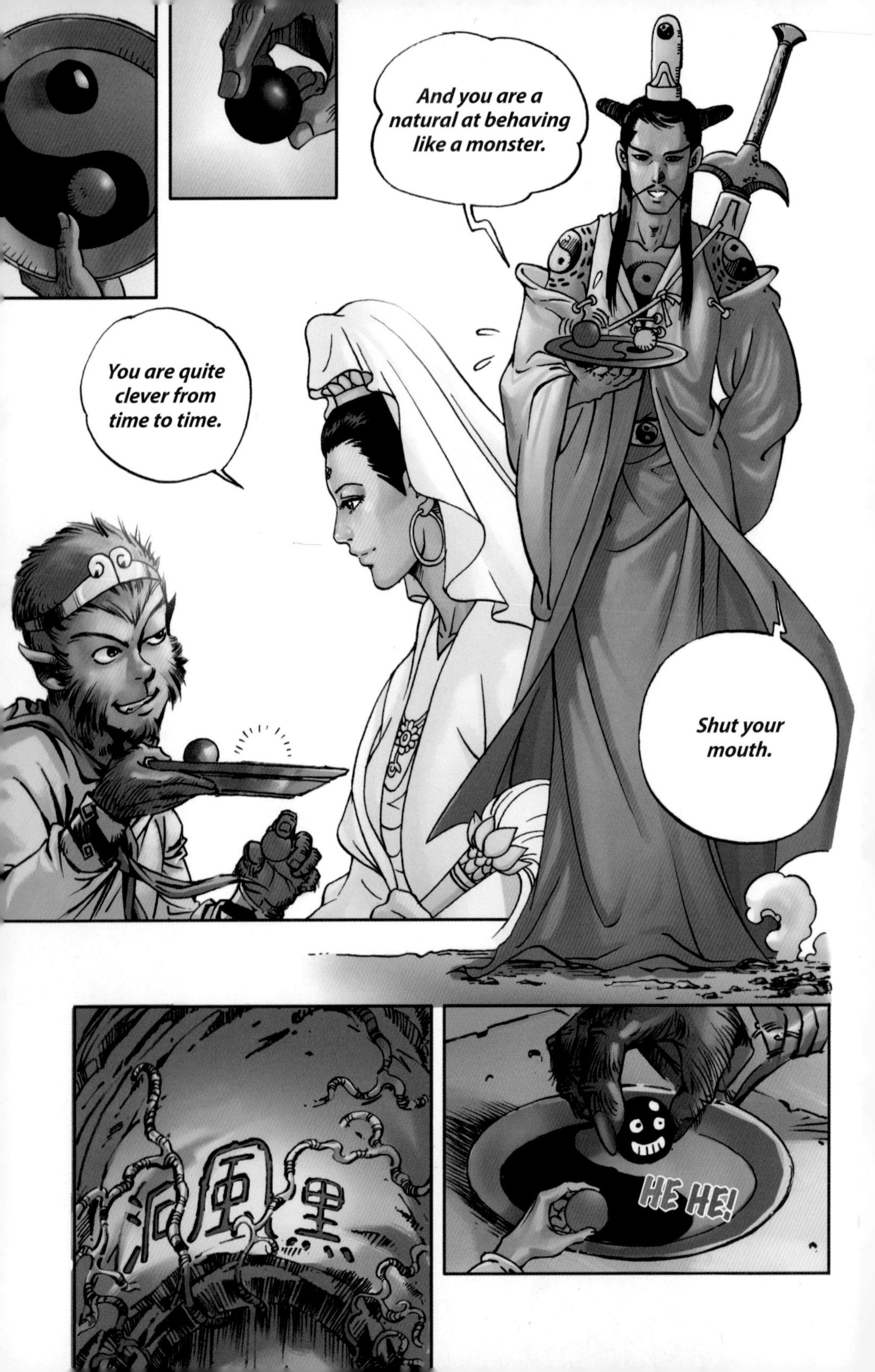
And you are a natural at behaving like a monster.
You are quite clever from time to time.
Shut your mouth.
HE HE!

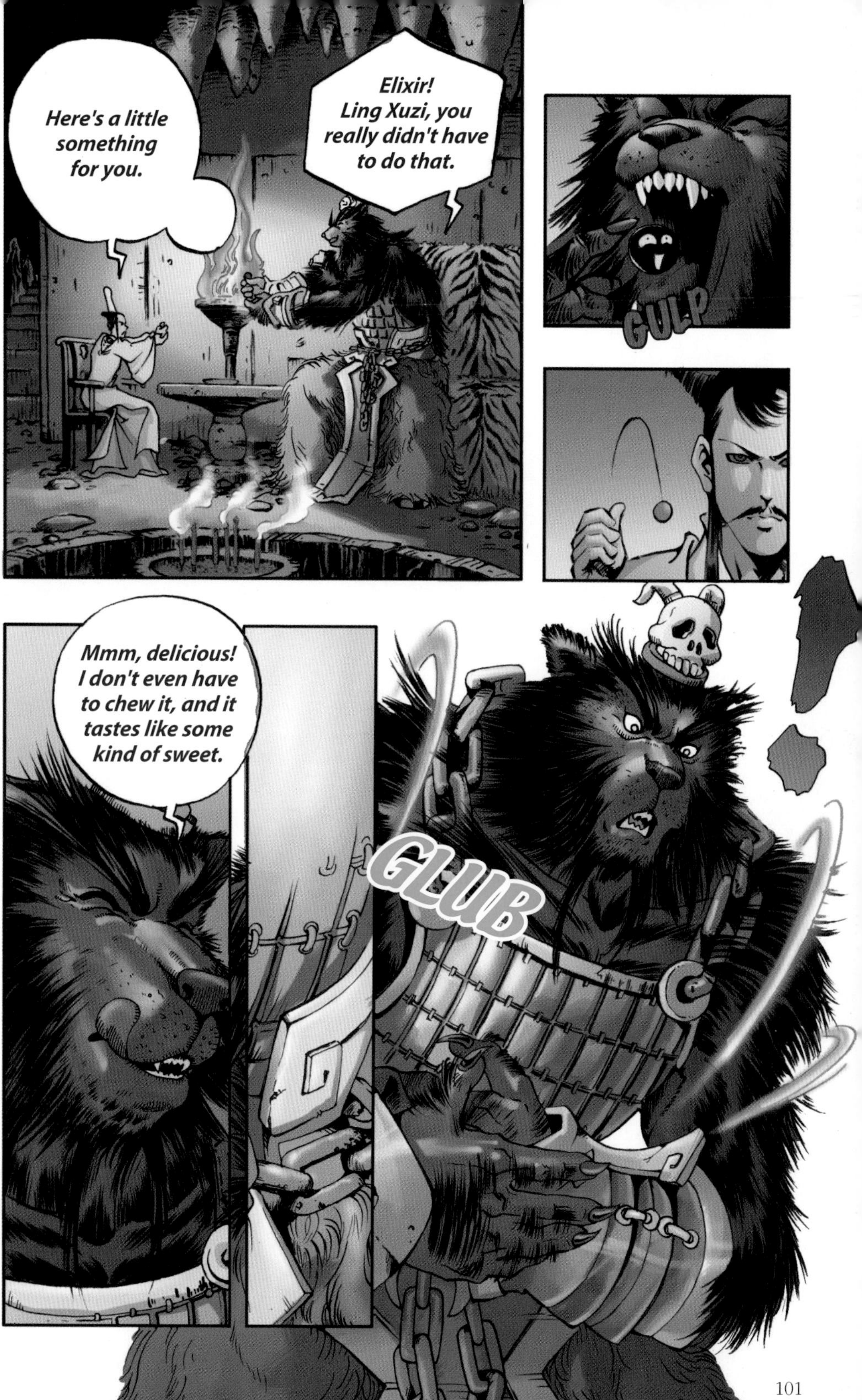
Here's a little something for you.
Elixir! Ling Xuzi, you really didn't have to do that.
GULP
Mmm, delicious! I don't even have to chew it, and it tastes like some kind of sweet.
GLUB

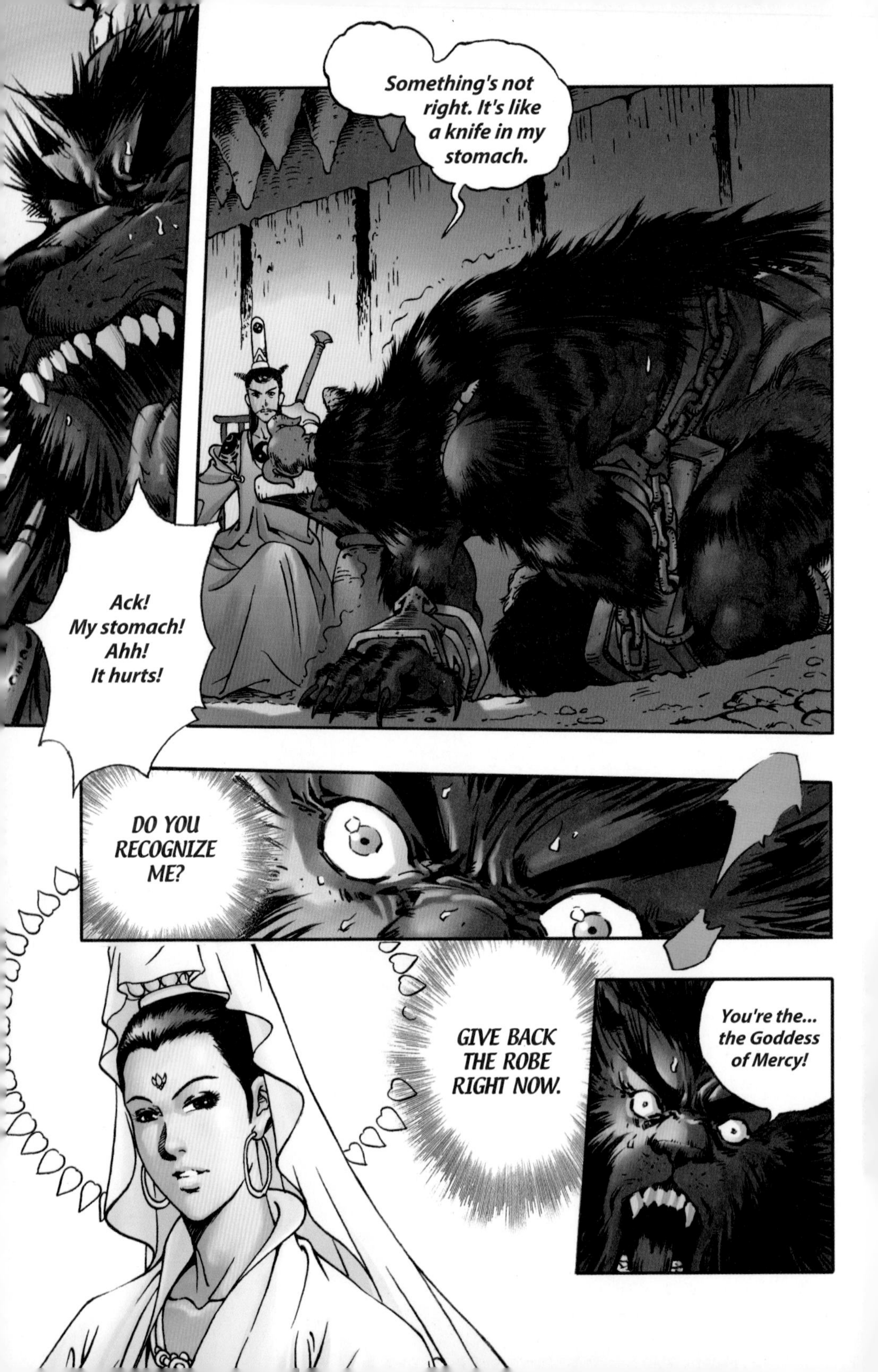
Something's not right. It's like a knife in my stomach.
Ack! My stomach! Ahh! It hurts!
DO YOU RECOGNIZE ME?
GIVE BACK THE ROBE RIGHT NOW.
You're the... the Goddess of Mercy!

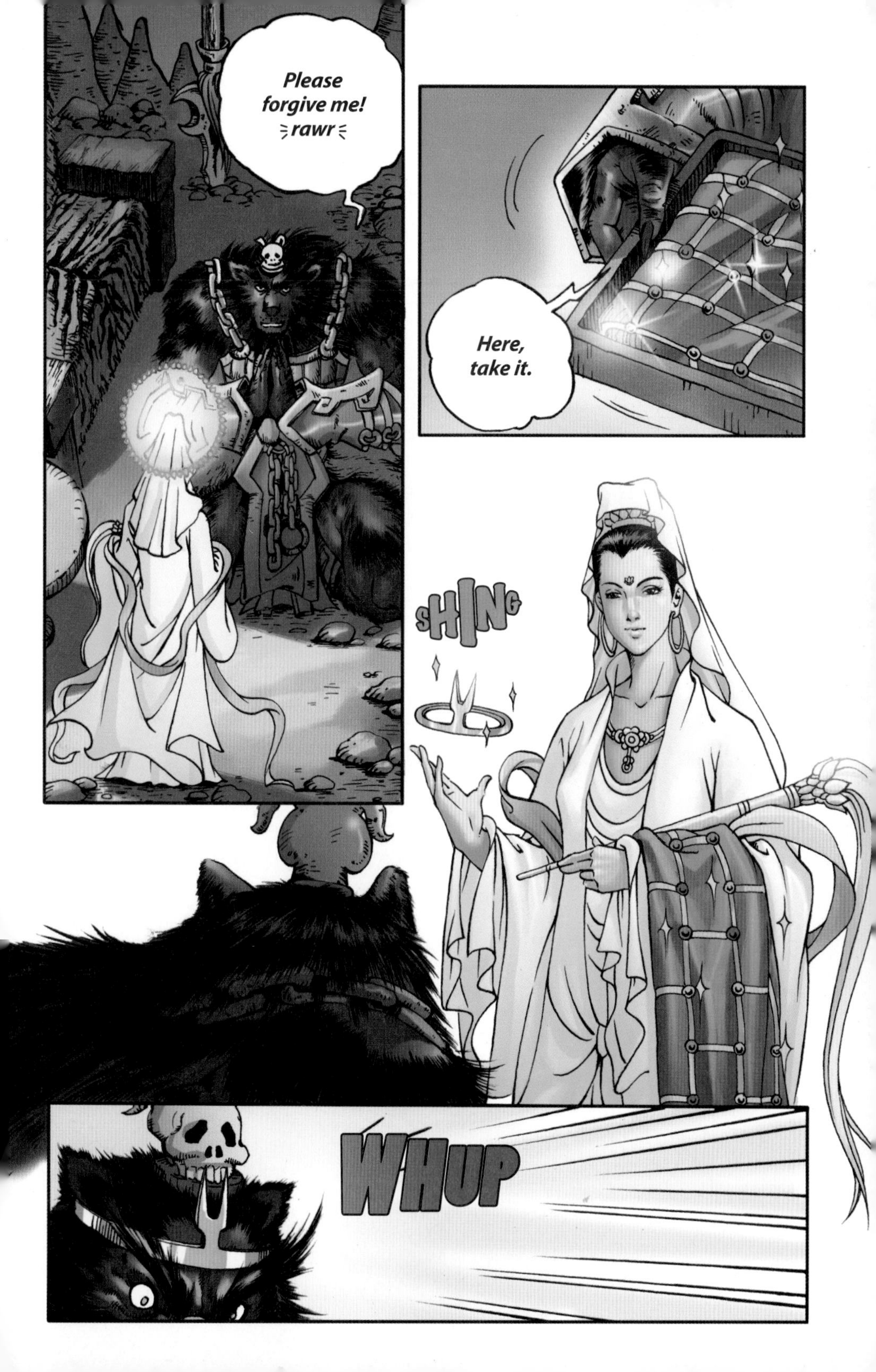
Please forgive me! rawr
Here, take it.
SHING
WHUP

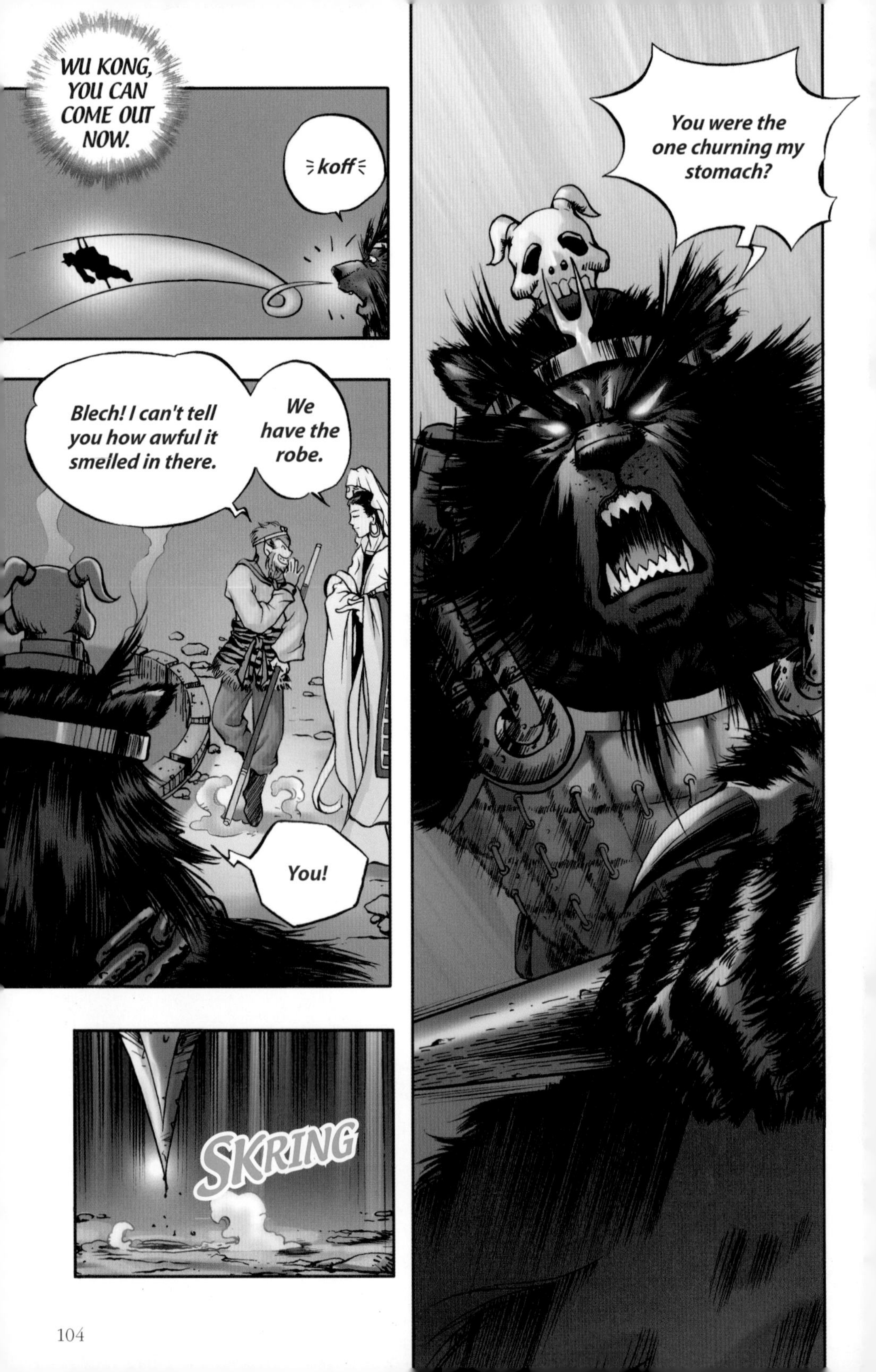
WU KONG, YOU CAN COME OUT NOW.
koff
Blech! I can't tell you how awful it smelled in there.
We have the robe.
You!
SKRING
You were the one churning my stomach?

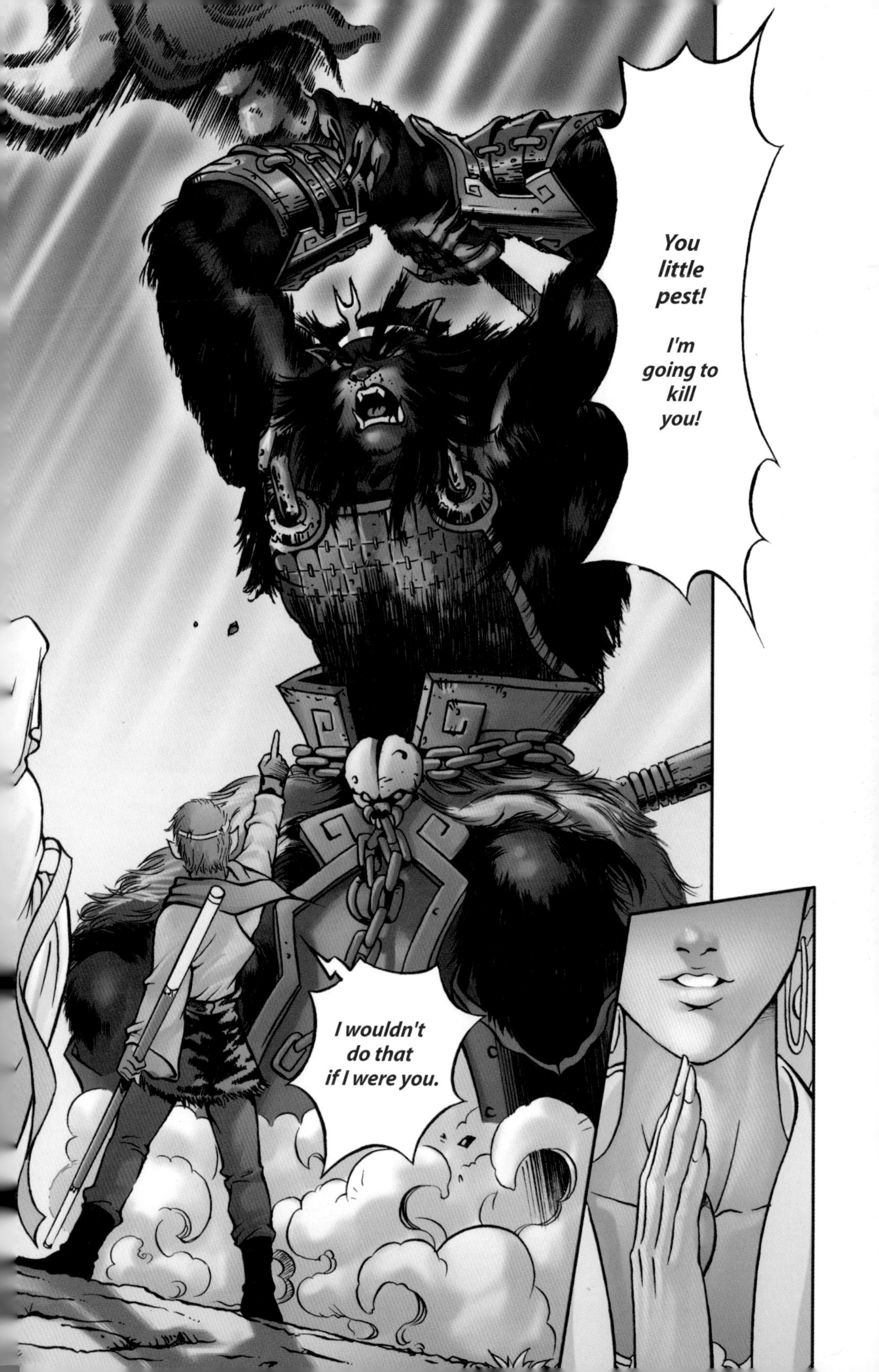
You little pest!
I'm going to kill you!
I wouldn't do that if I were you.

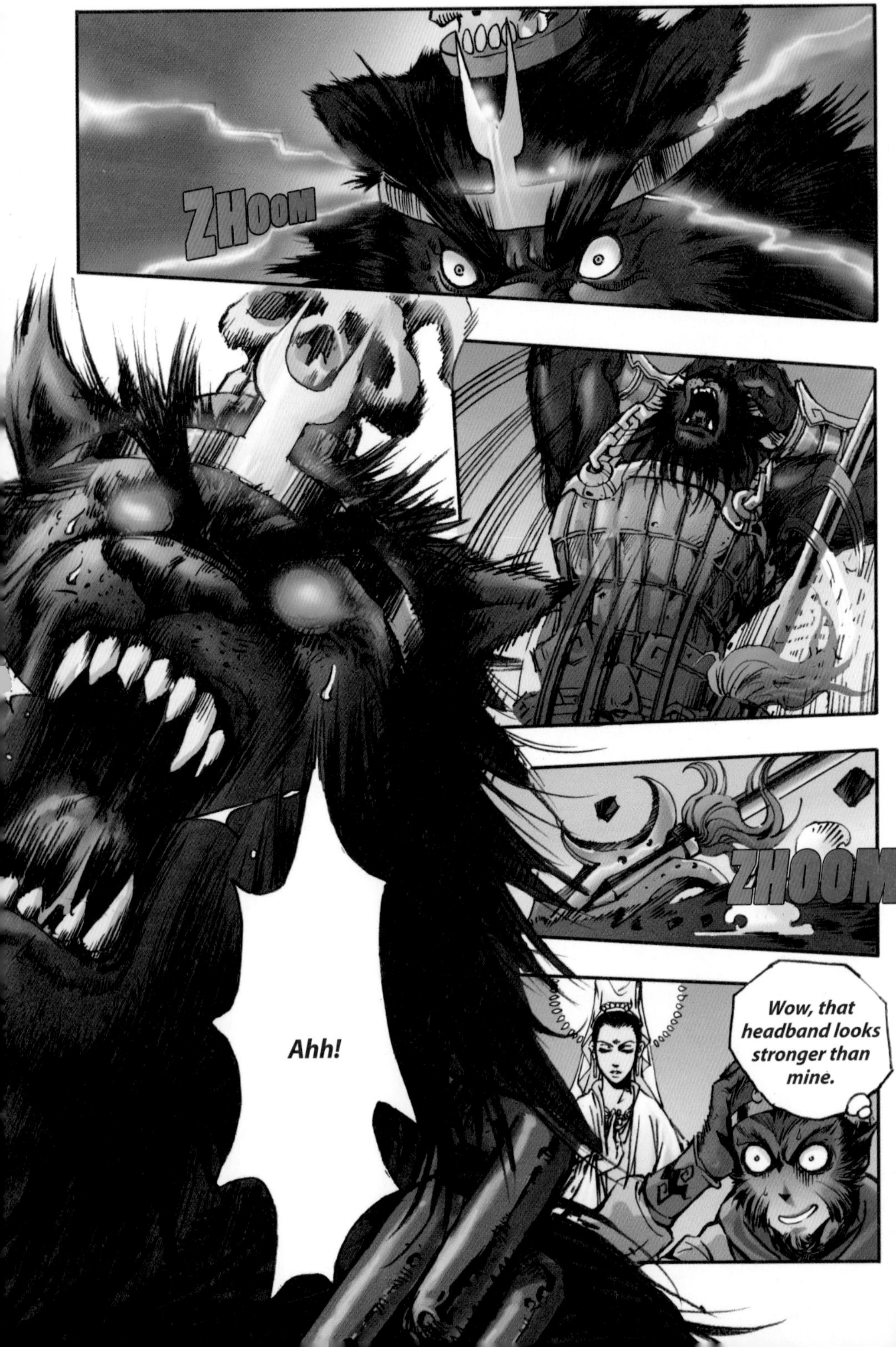
ZHOOM
ZHOOM
Ahh!
Wow, that headband looks stronger than mine.

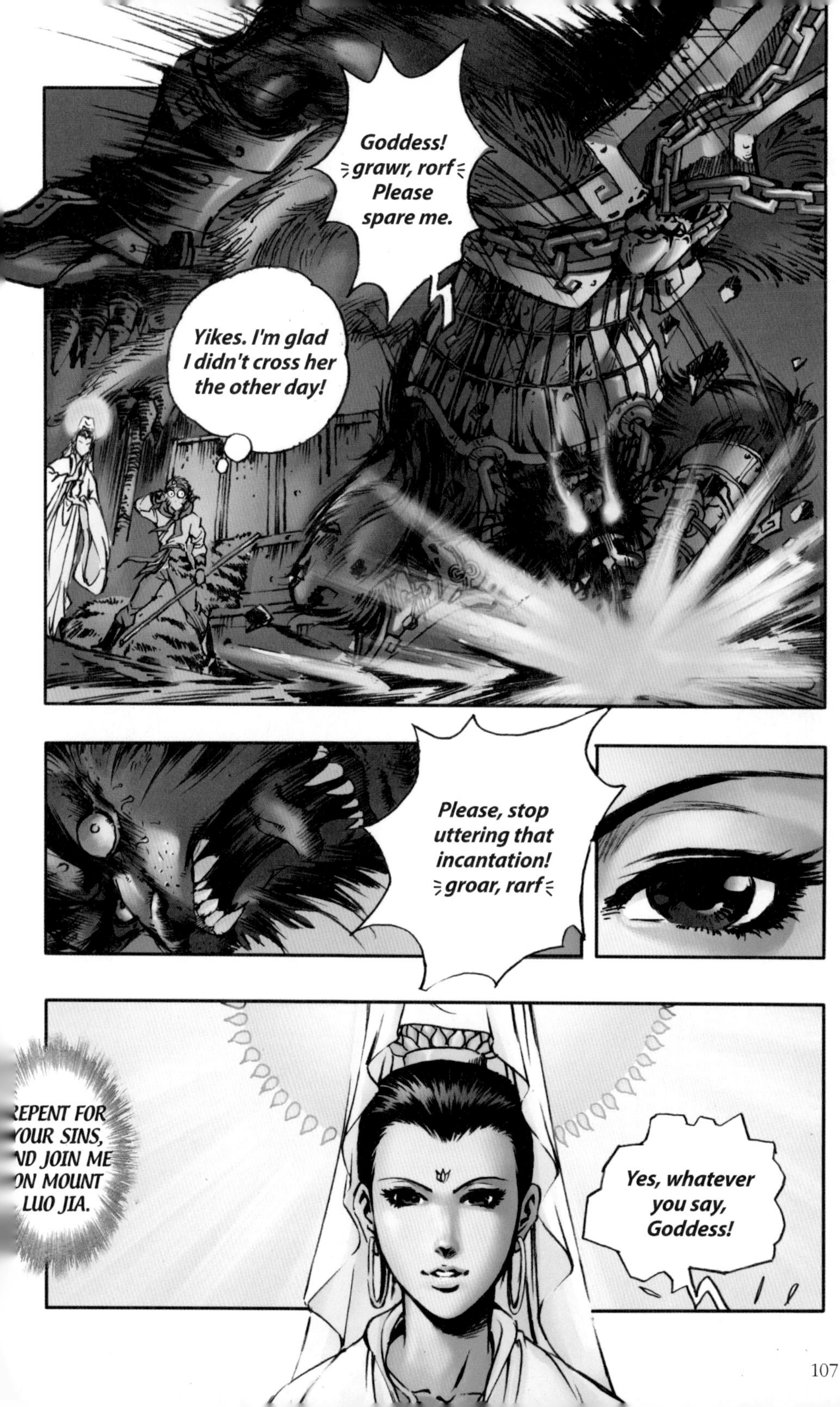
Goddess! grawr, rorf Please spare me.
Yikes. I'm glad I didn't cross her the other day!
Please, stop uttering that incantation! groar, rarf
REPENT FOR YOUR SINS, AND JOIN ME ON MOUNT LUO JIA.
Yes, whatever you say, Goddess!

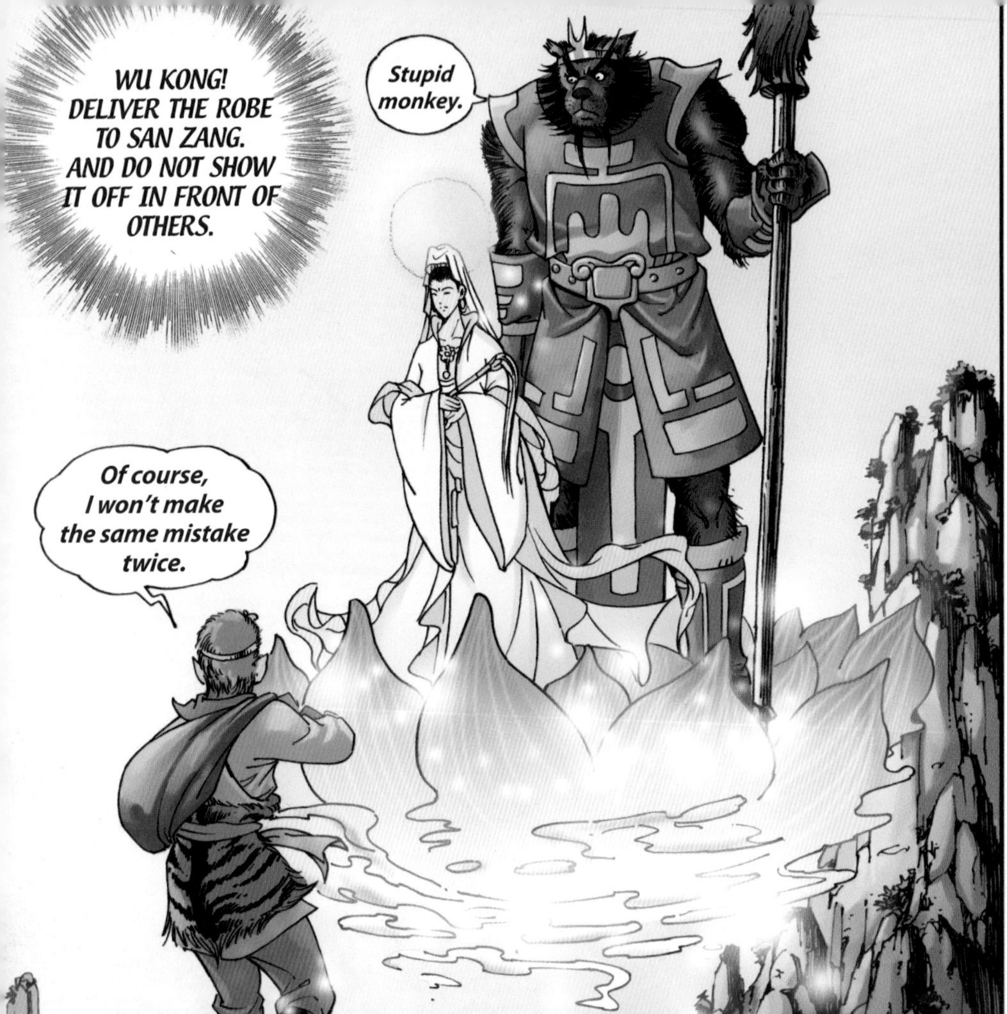
WU KONG! DELIVER THE ROBE TO SAN ZANG. AND DO NOT SHOW IT OFF IN FRONT OF OTHERS.
Stupid monkey.
Of course, I won't make the same mistake twice.

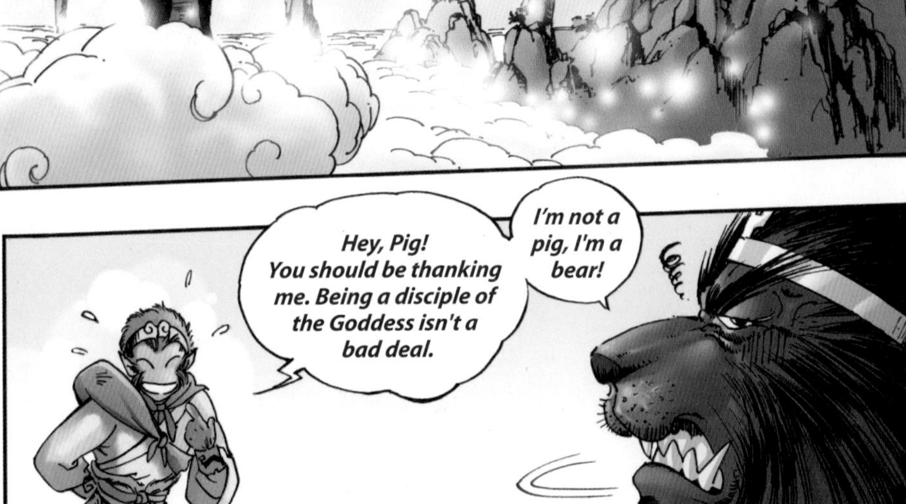
Hey, Pig! You should be thanking me. Being a disciple of the Goddess isn't a bad deal.
I'm not a pig, I'm a bear!

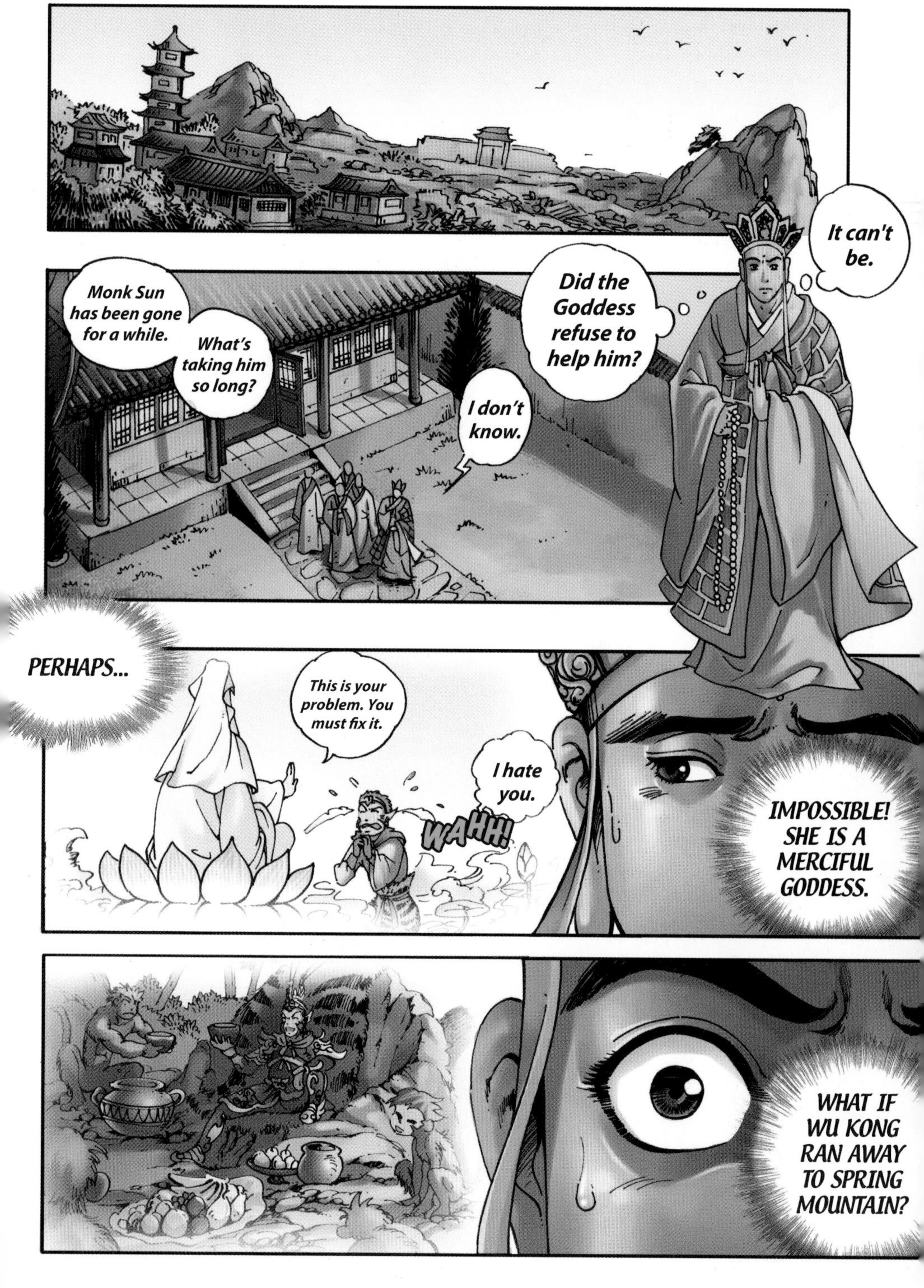
Monk Sun has been gone for a while.
What's taking him so long?
I don't know.
Did the Goddess refuse to help him?
It can't be.
PERHAPS...
This is your problem. You must fix it.
I hate you.
WAHH!
IMPOSSIBLE! SHE IS A MERCIFUL GODDESS.
WHAT IF WU KONG RAN AWAY TO SPRING MOUNTAIN?

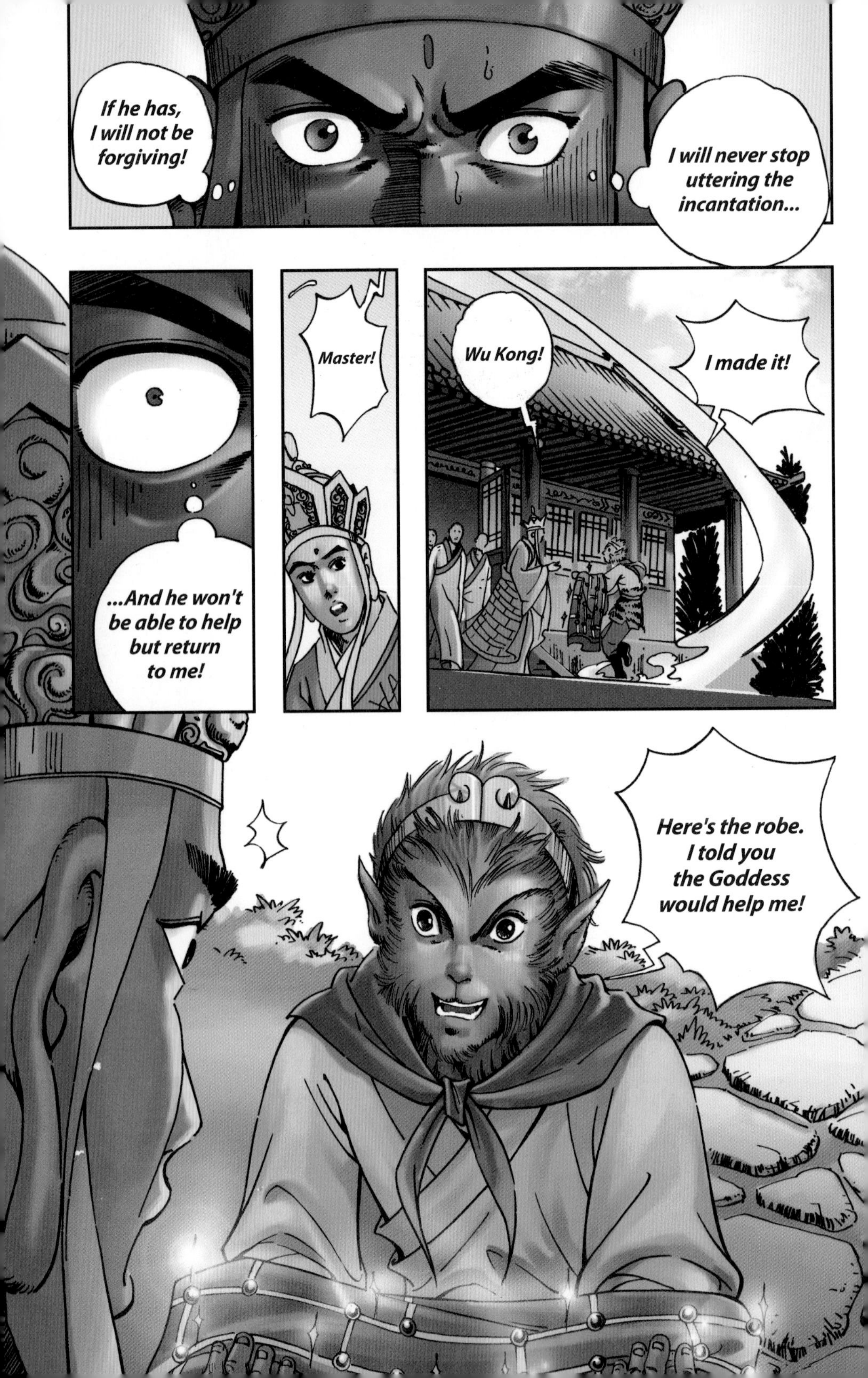
If he has, I will not be forgiving!
I will never stop uttering the incantation...
...And he won't be able to help but return to me!
Master!
Wu Kong!
I made it!
Here's the robe. I told you the Goddess would help me!

It's a miracle.

I thank the Goddess for her secret act of virtue.

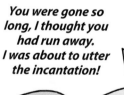

You were gone so long, I thought you had run away. I was about to utter the incantation!

Oh, come on! Don't say that! The thought alone hurts my head.

Monk San Zang! Since everything is all right, you'd better sleep tonight and leave tomorrow.

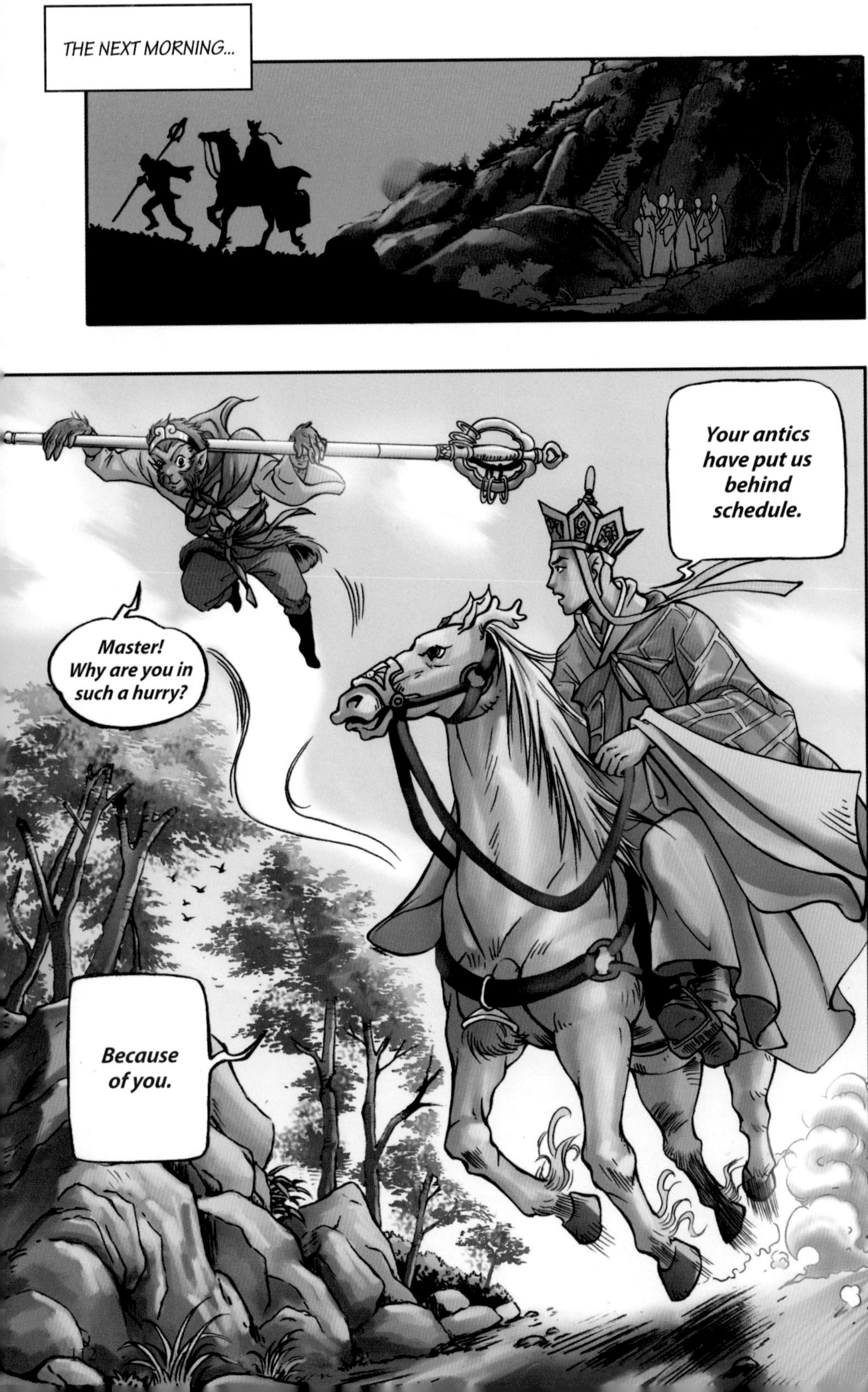
THE NEXT MORNING...
Your antics have put us behind schedule.
Master! Why are you in such a hurry?
Because of you.

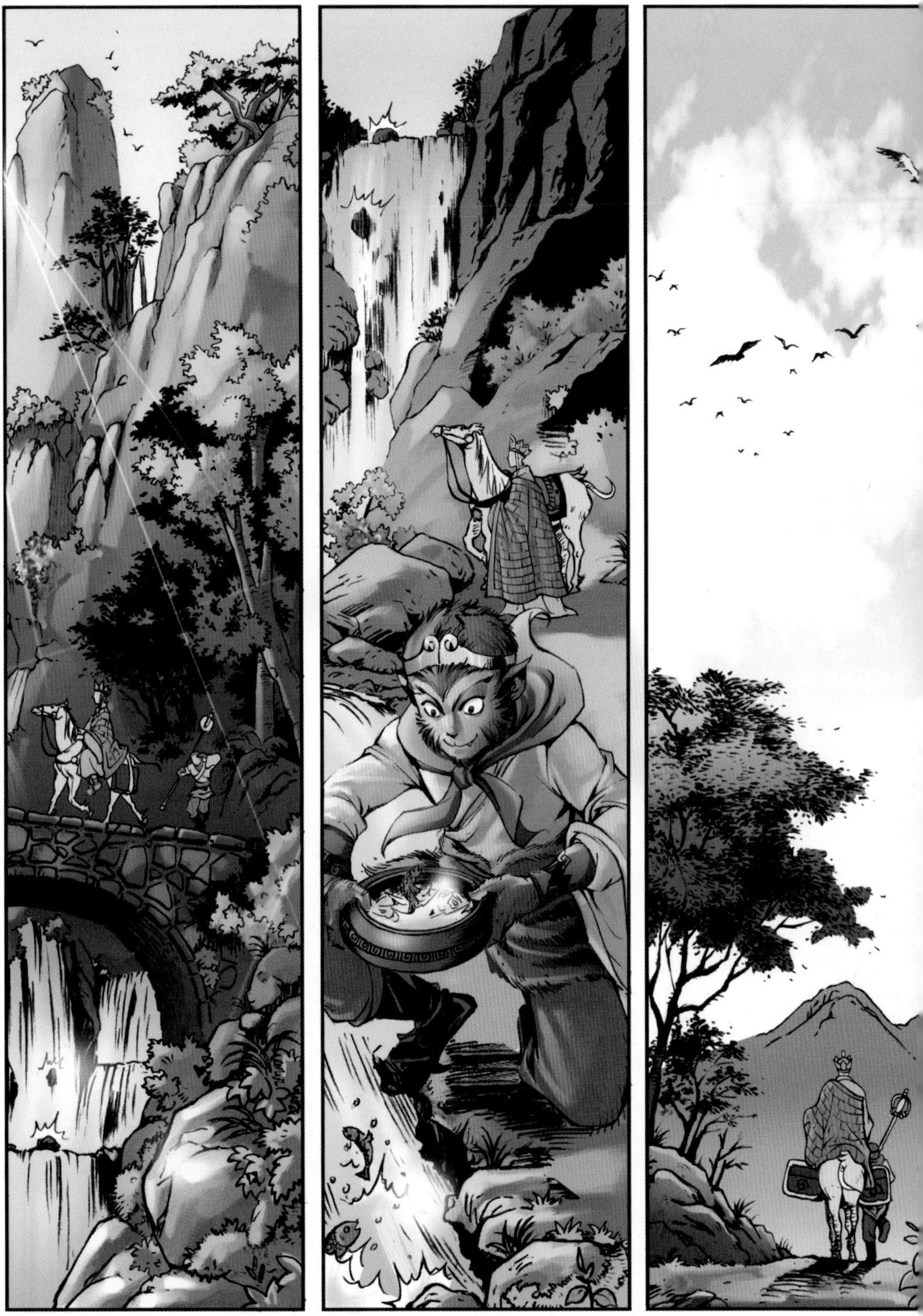

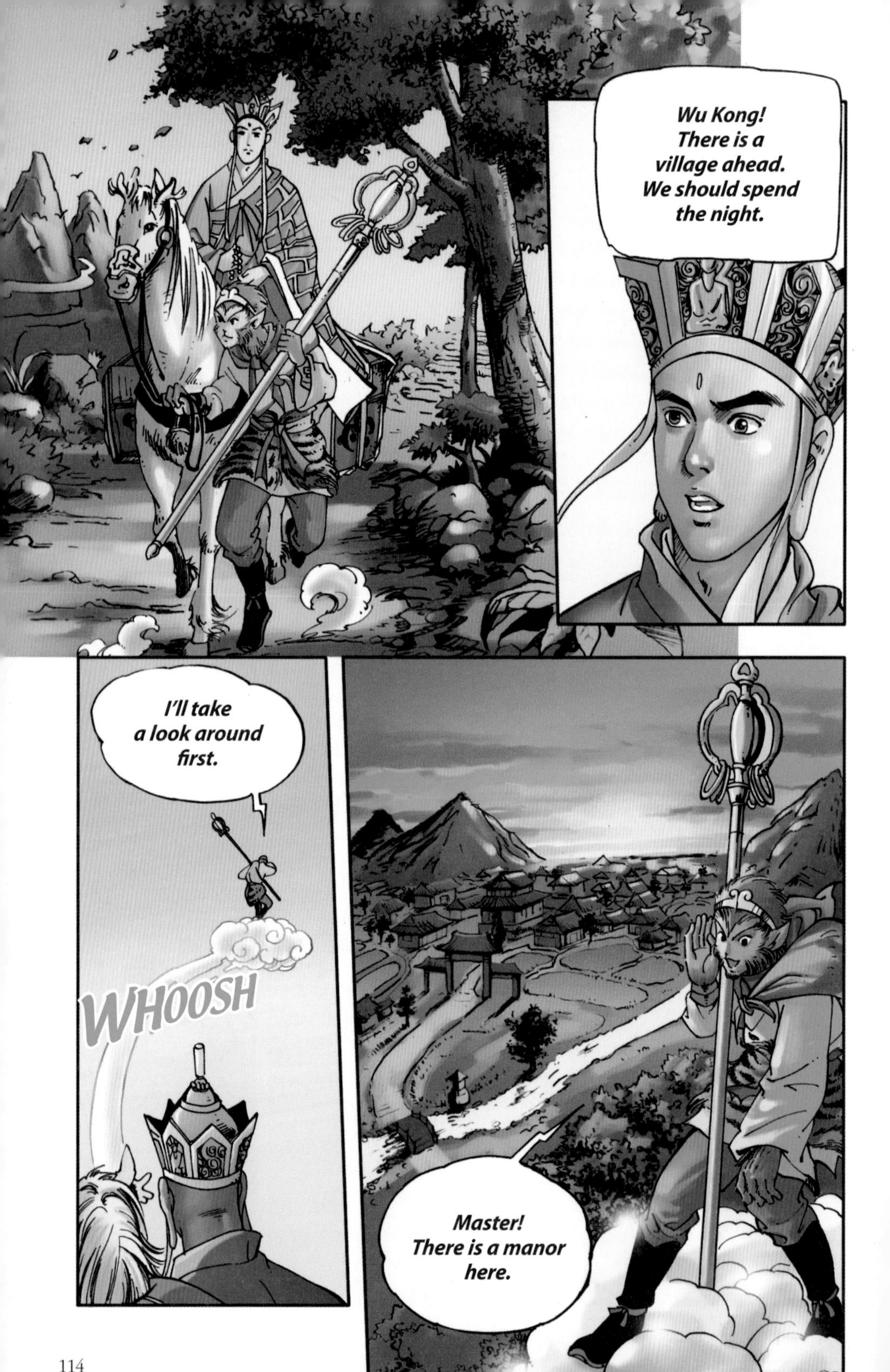
Wu Kong! There is a village ahead. We should spend the night.
I'll take a look around first.
WHOOSH
Master! There is a manor here.

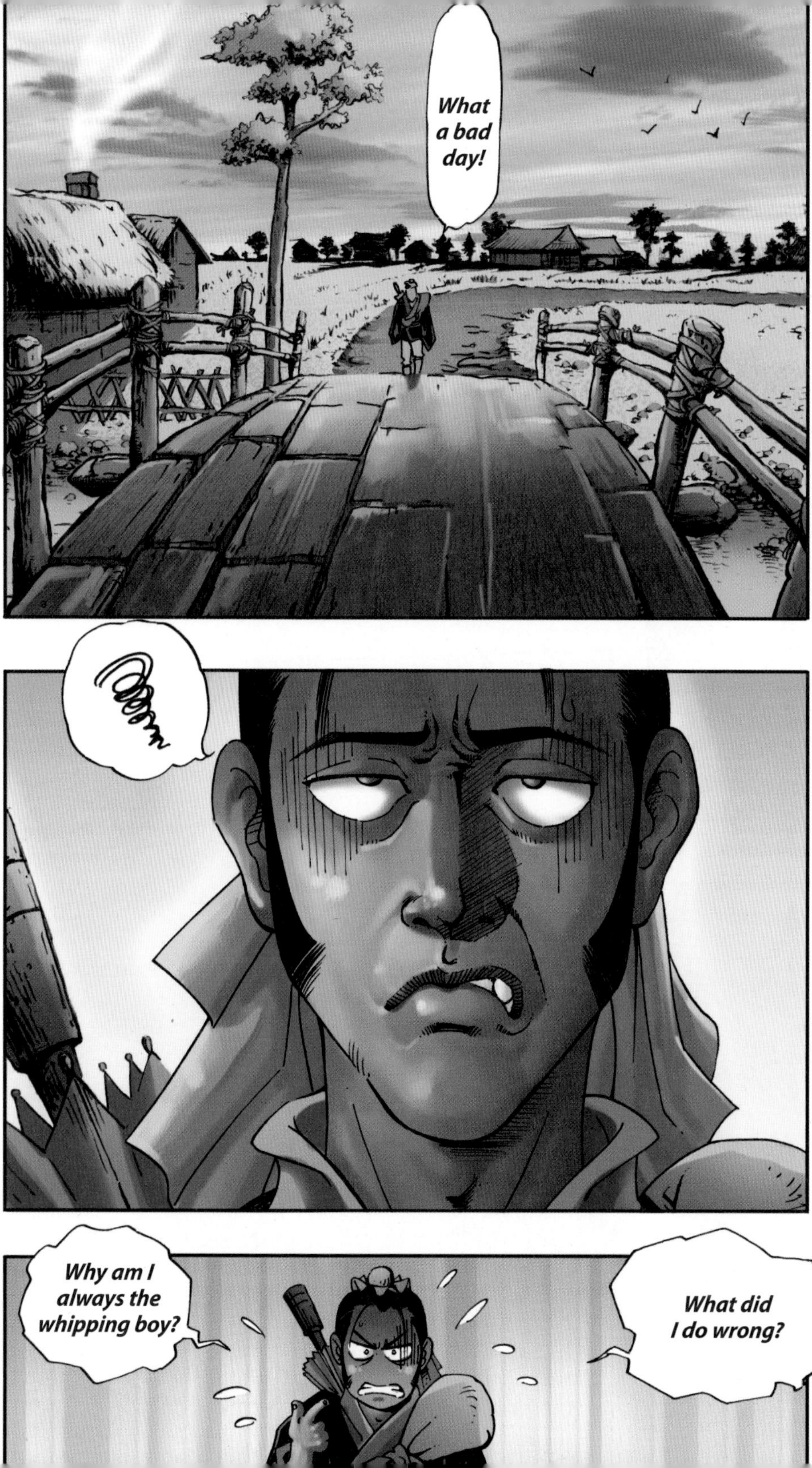
What a bad day!
Why am I always the whipping boy?
What did I do wrong?

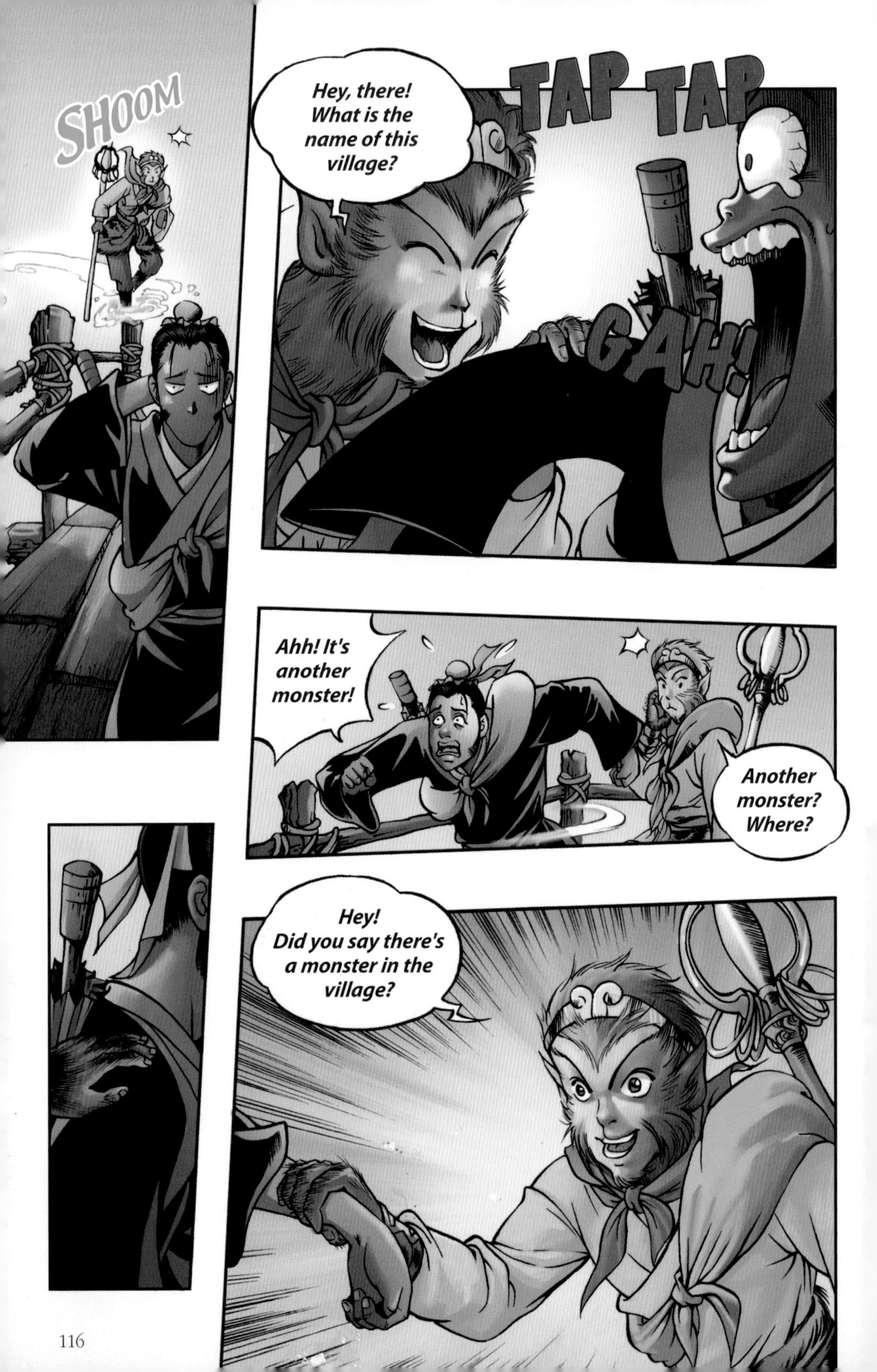
SHOOM
Hey, there! What is the name of this village?
TAP TAP
GAH!
Ahh! It's another monster!
Another monster? Where?
Hey! Did you say there's a monster in the village?

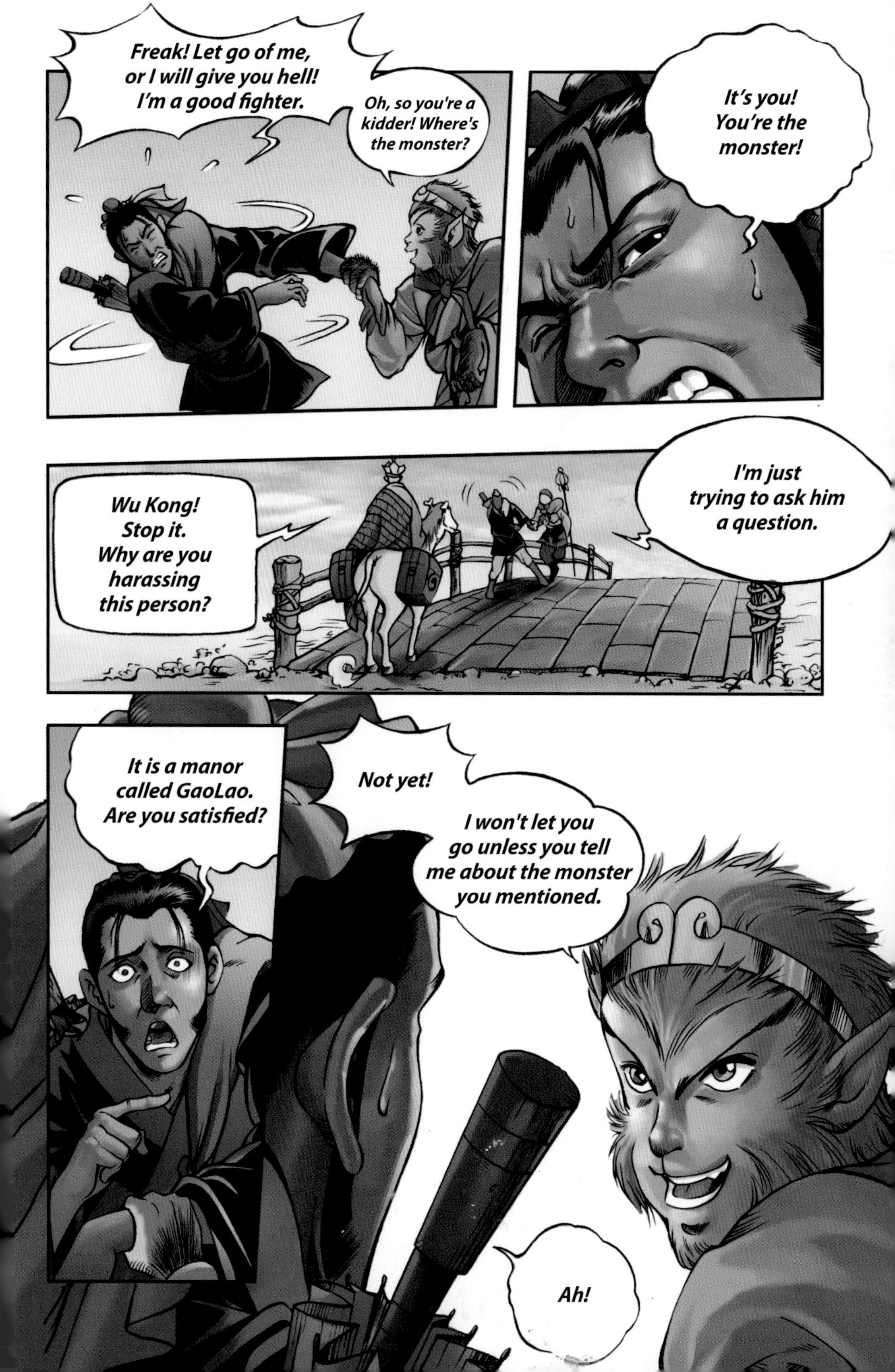

Freak! Let go of me, or I will give you hell! I'm a good fighter.
Oh, so you're a kidder! Where's the monster?
It's you! You're the monster!
Wu Kong! Stop it. Why are you harassing this person?
I'm just trying to ask him a question.
It is a manor called GaoLao. Are you satisfied?
Not yet!
I won't let you go unless you tell me about the monster you mentioned.
Ah!

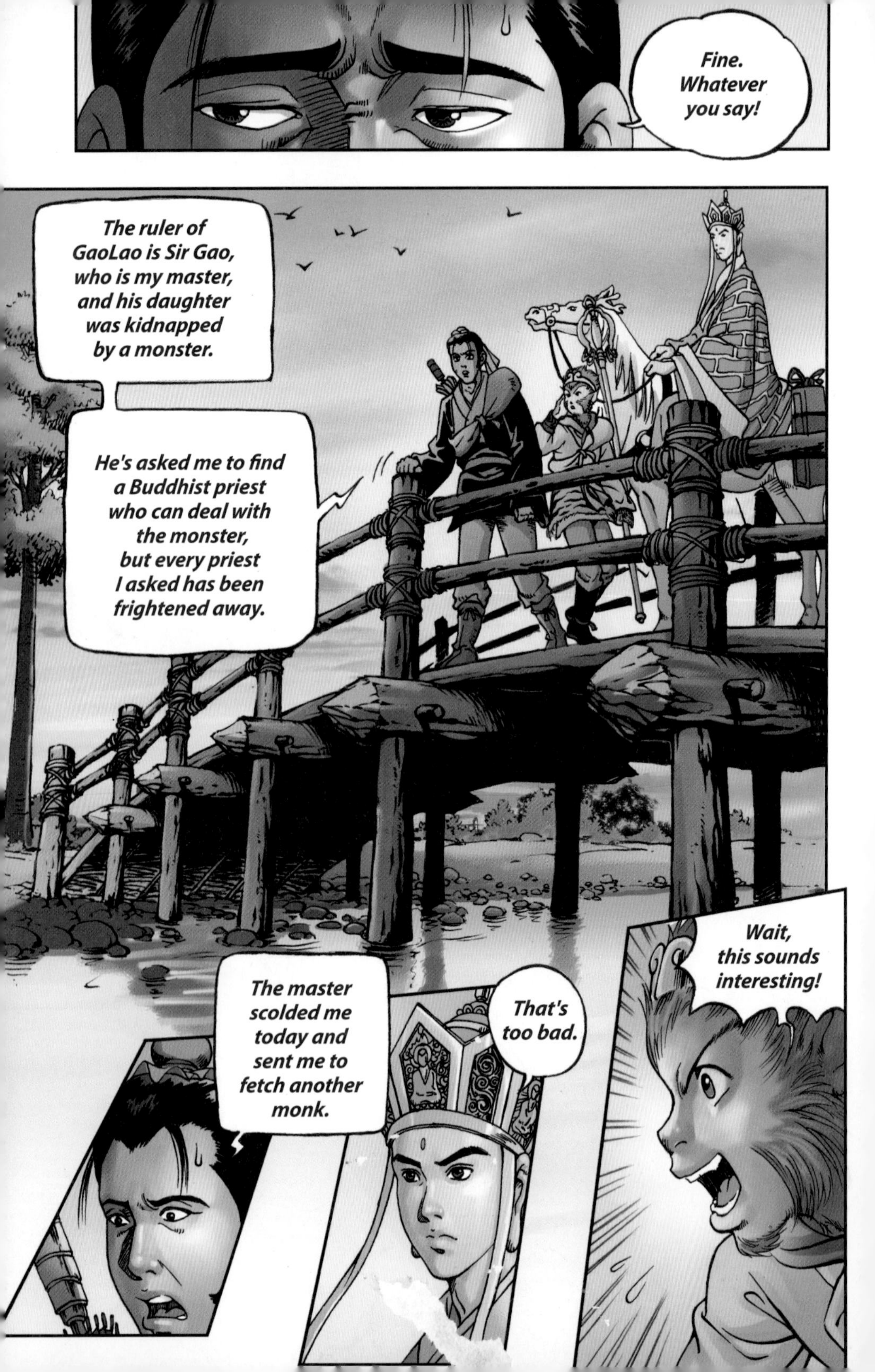
Fine. Whatever you say!
The ruler of GaoLao is Sir Gao, who is my master, and his daughter was kidnapped by a monster.
He's asked me to find a Buddhist priest who can deal with the monster, but every priest I asked has been frightened away.
The master scolded me today and sent me to fetch another monk.
That's too bad.
Wait, this sounds interesting!

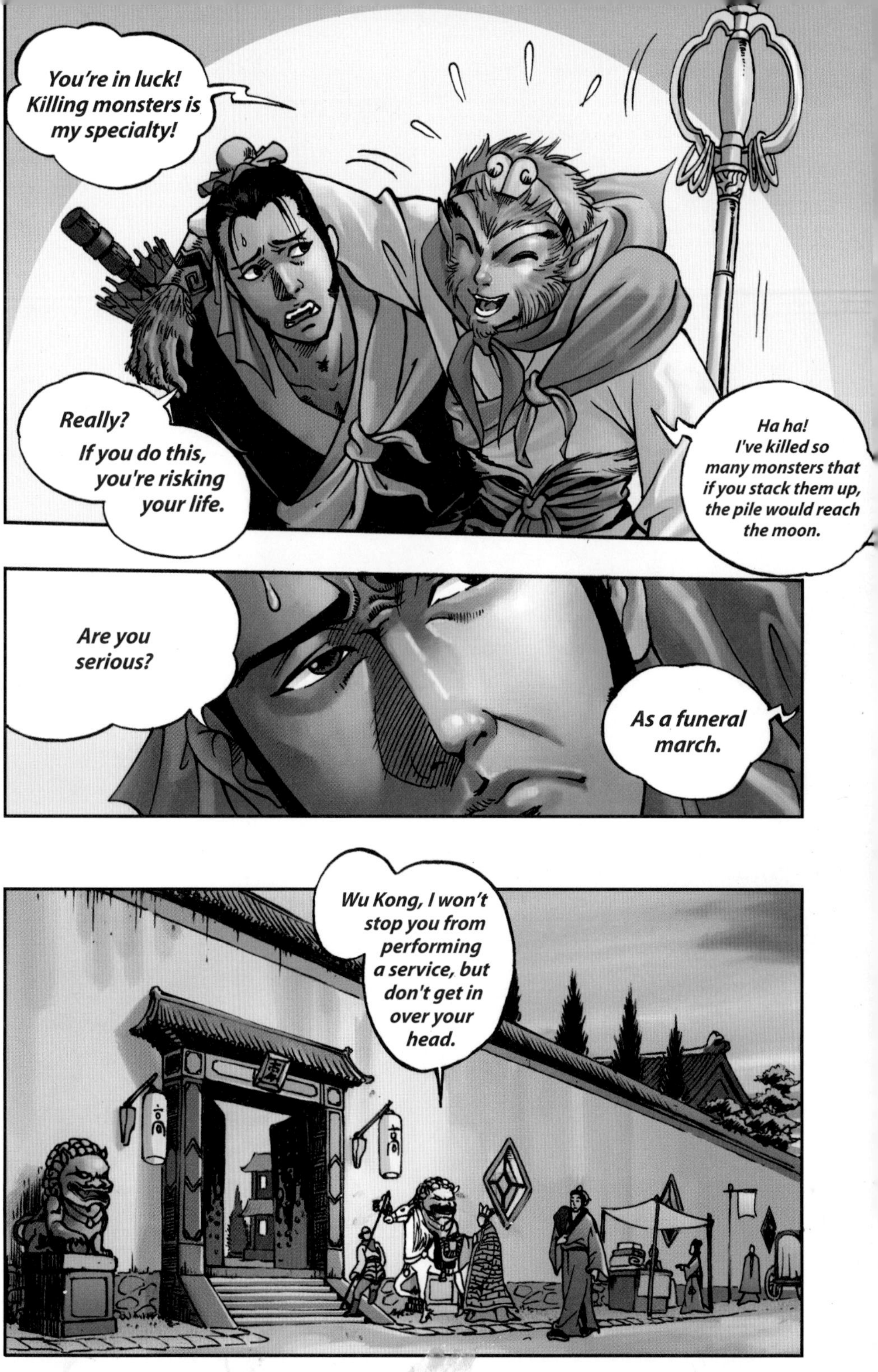
You're in luck! Killing monsters is my specialty!
Really? If you do this, you're risking your life.
Ha ha! I've killed so many monsters that if you stack them up, the pile would reach the moon.
Are you serious?
As a funeral march.
Wu Kong, I won't stop you from performing a service, but don't get in over your head.

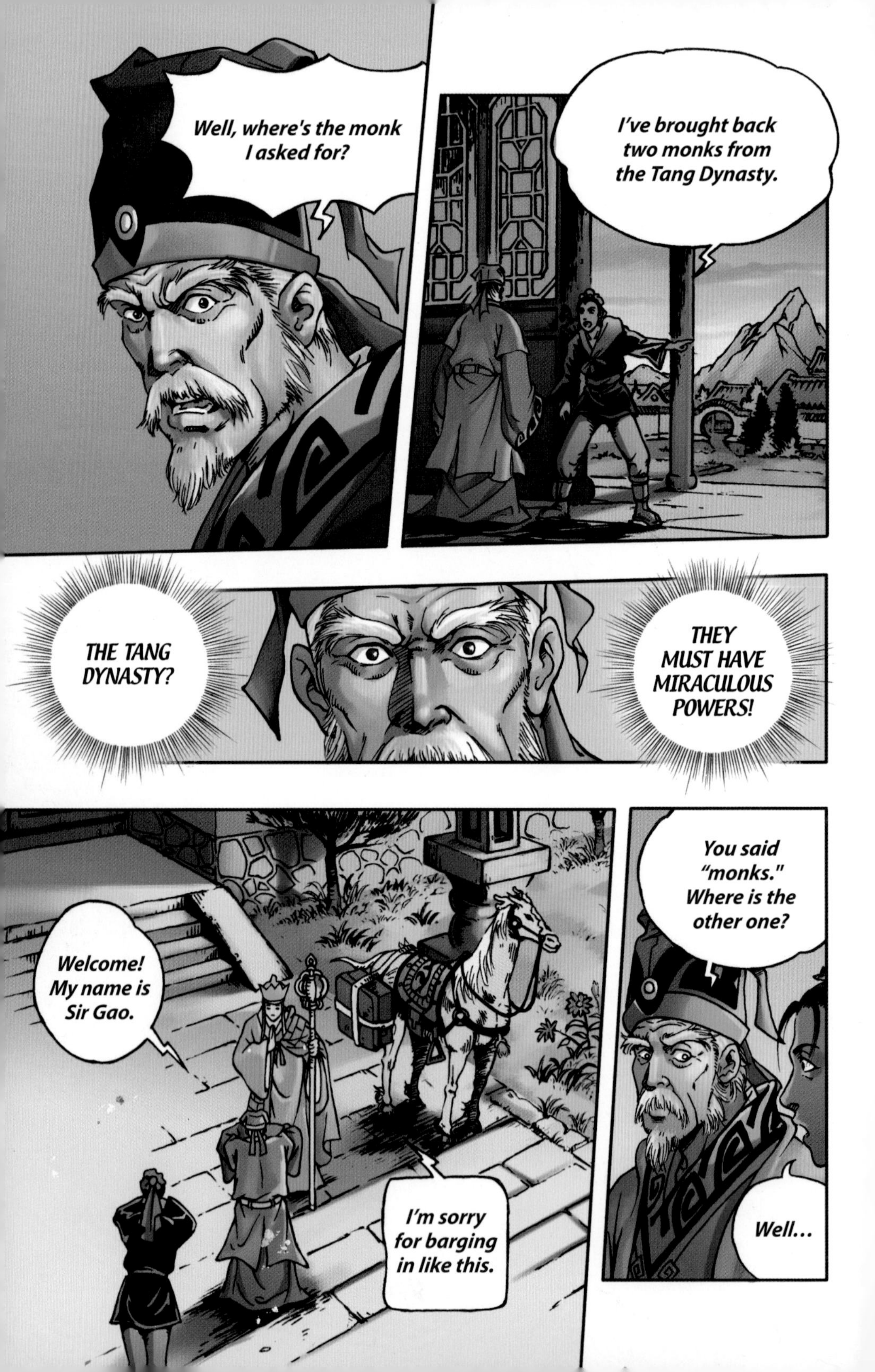
Well, where's the monk I asked for?
I've brought back two monks from the Tang Dynasty.
THE TANG DYNASTY?
THEY MUST HAVE MIRACULOUS POWERS!
Welcome! My name is Sir Gao.
I'm sorry for barging in like this.
You said "monks." Where is the other one?
Well…

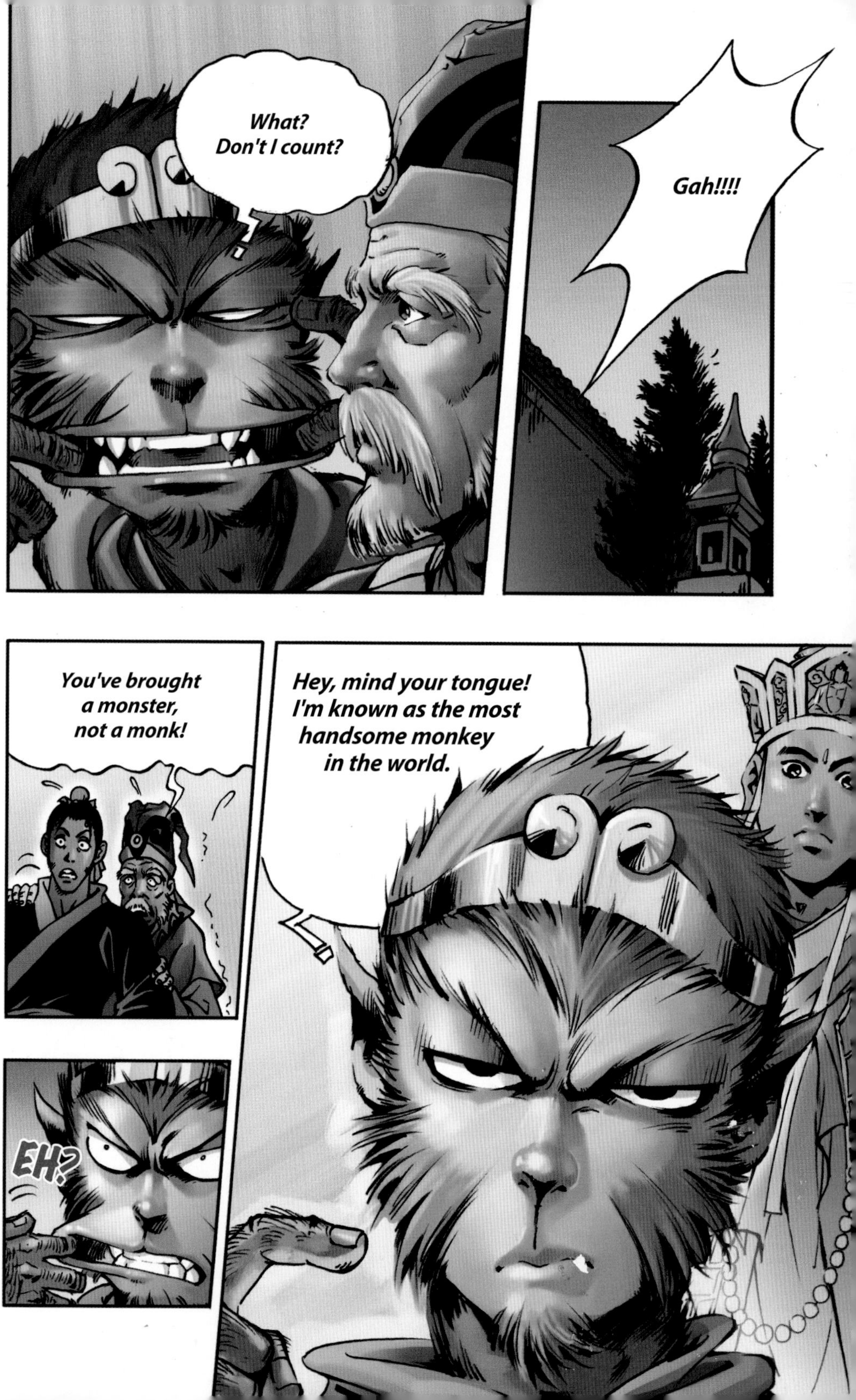
What?
Don't I count?
Gah!!!!
You've brought a monster, not a monk!
Hey, mind your tongue! I'm known as the most handsome monkey in the world.
EH?

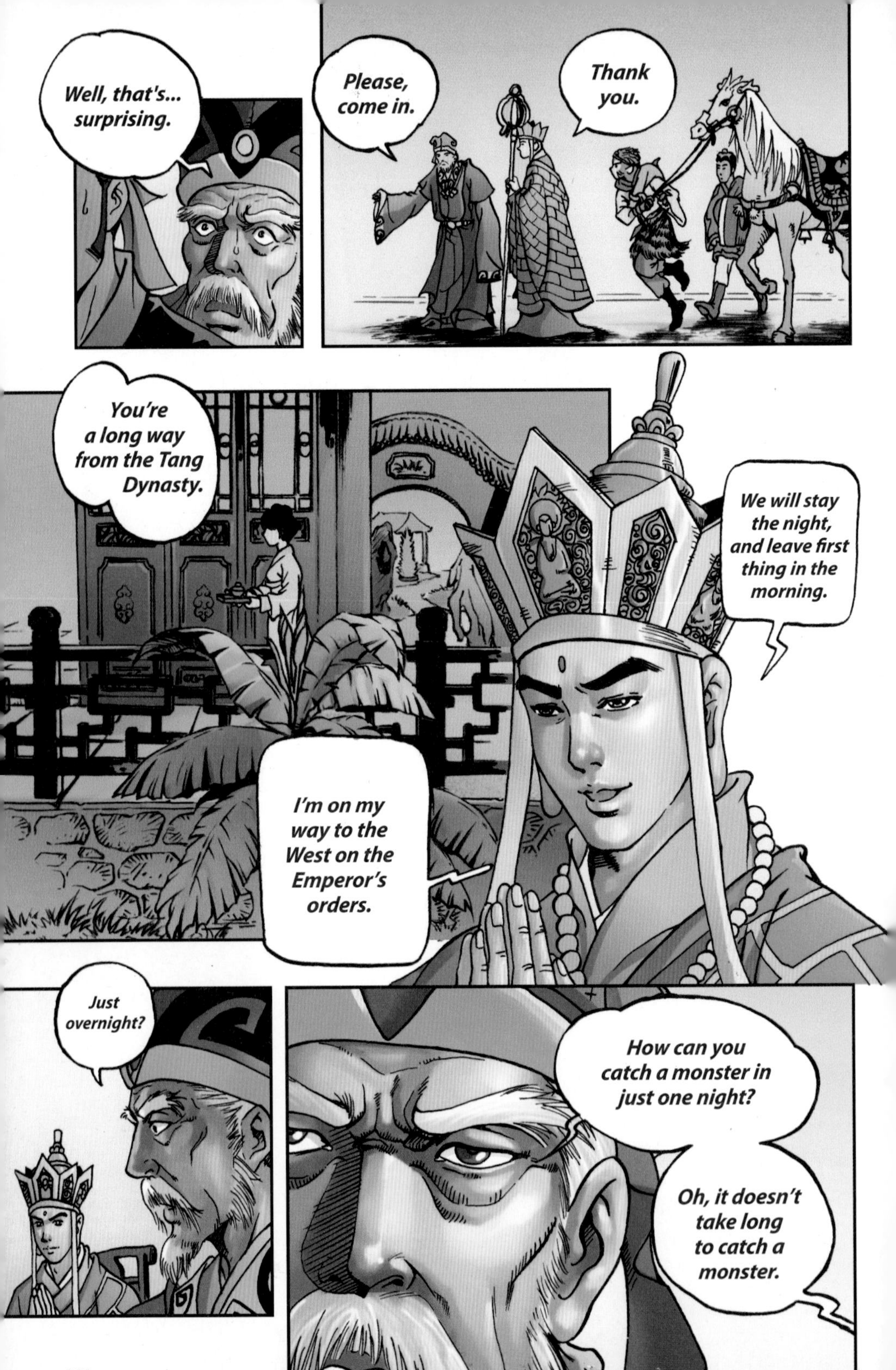
Well, that's... surprising.
Please, come in.
Thank you.
You're a long way from the Tang Dynasty.
We will stay the night, and leave first thing in the morning.
I'm on my way to the West on the Emperor's orders.
Just overnight?
How can you catch a monster in just one night?
Oh, it doesn't take long to catch a monster.

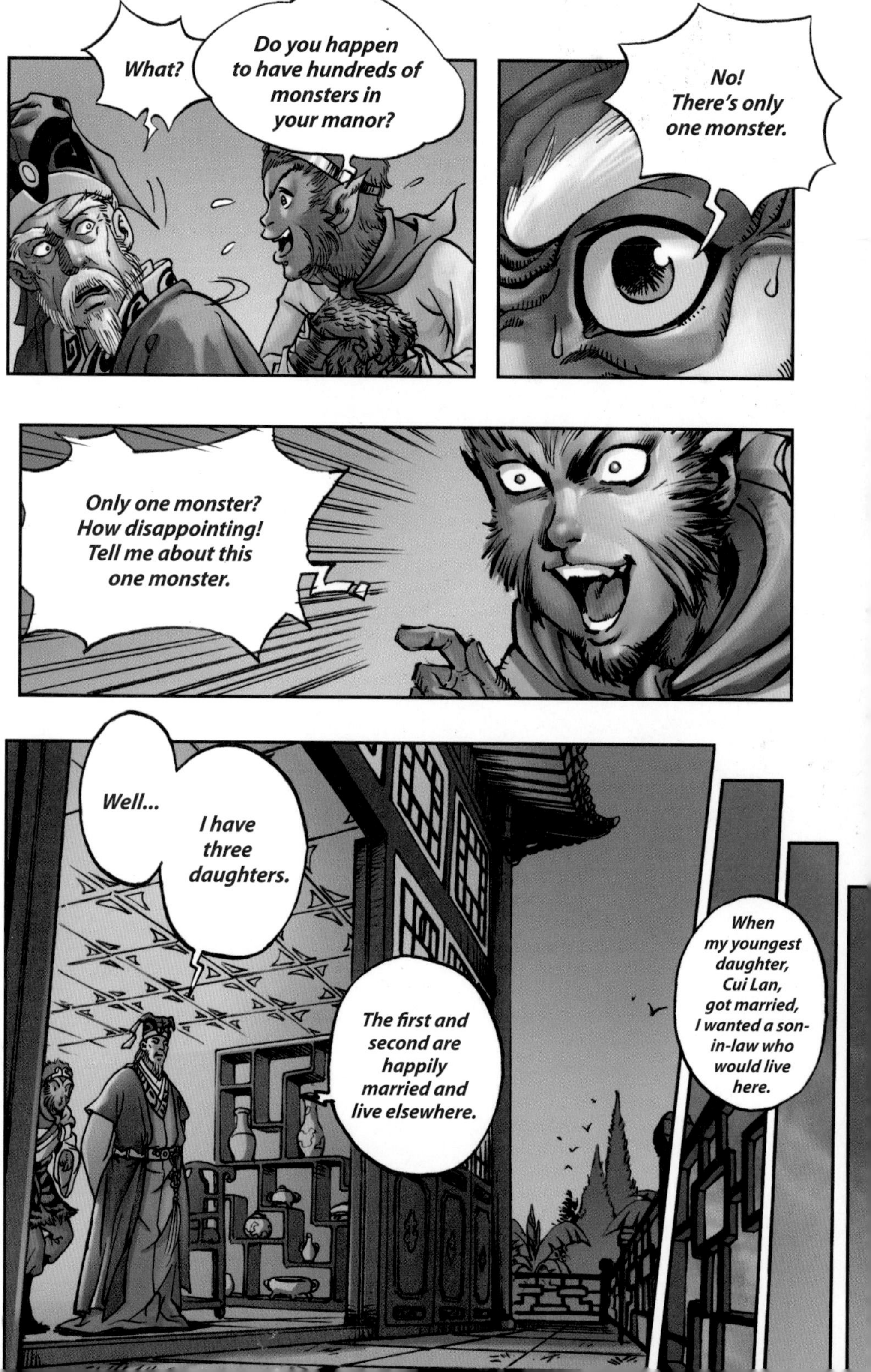
What?
Do you happen to have hundreds of monsters in your manor?
No! There's only one monster.
Only one monster? How disappointing! Tell me about this one monster.
Well...
I have three daughters.
The first and second are happily married and live elsewhere.
When my youngest daughter, Cui Lan, got married, I wanted a son-in-law who would live here.

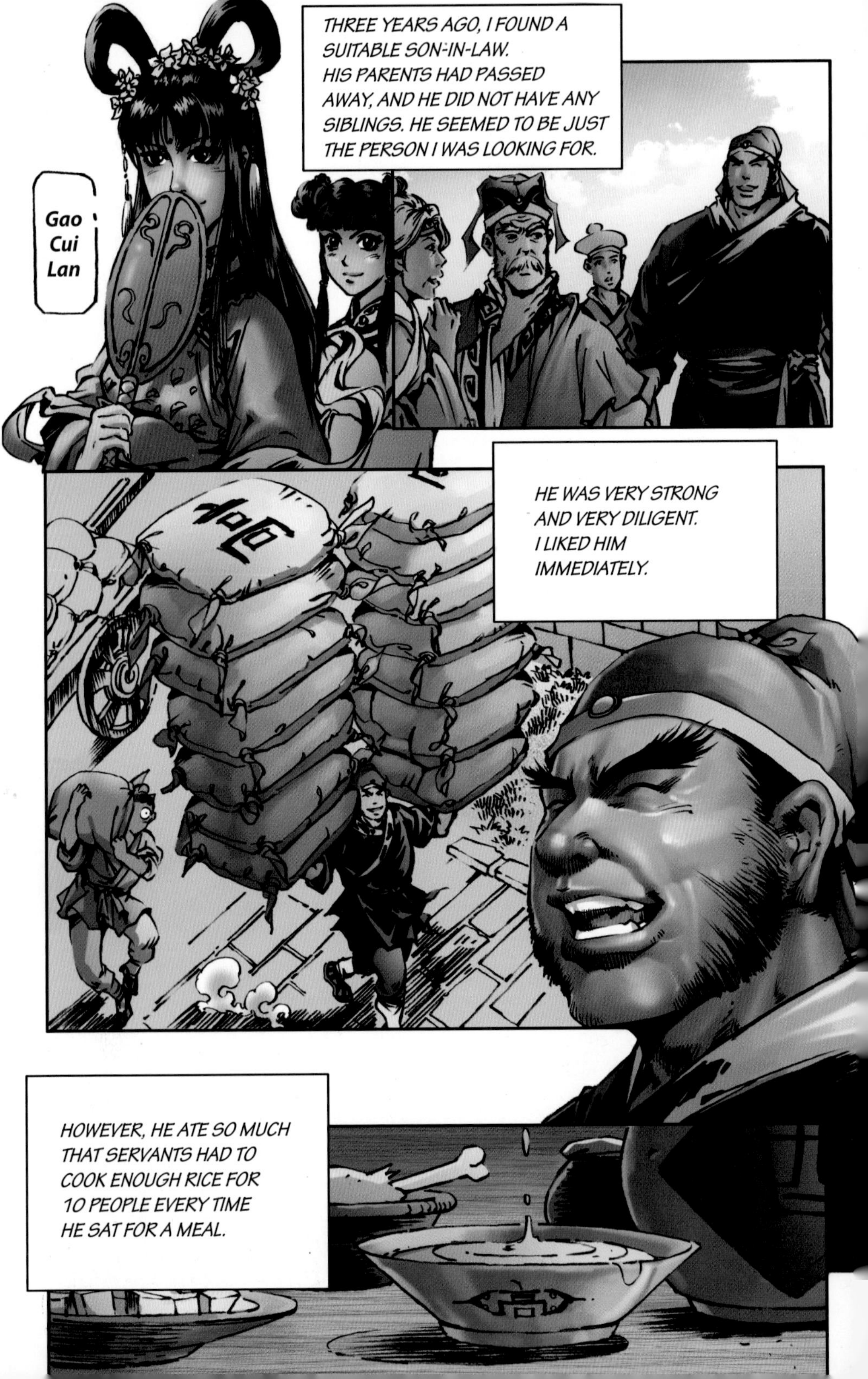
THREE YEARS AGO, I FOUND A SUITABLE SON-IN-LAW. HIS PARENTS HAD PASSED AWAY, AND HE DID NOT HAVE ANY SIBLINGS. HE SEEMED TO BE JUST THE PERSON I WAS LOOKING FOR.
Gao Cui Lan
HE WAS VERY STRONG AND VERY DILIGENT. I LIKED HIM IMMEDIATELY.
HOWEVER, HE ATE SO MUCH THAT SERVANTS HAD TO COOK ENOUGH RICE FOR 10 PEOPLE EVERY TIME HE SAT FOR A MEAL.

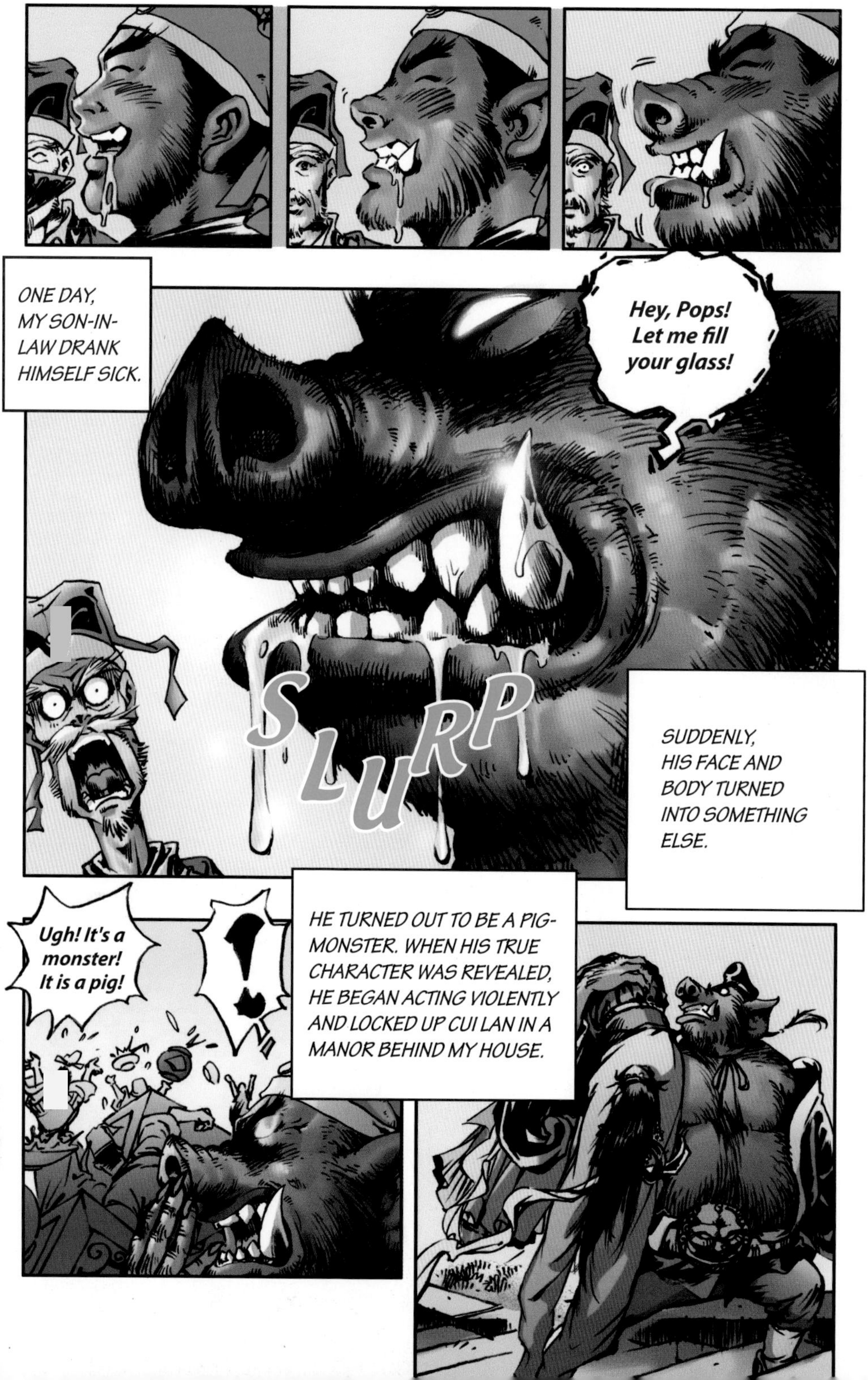
ONE DAY, MY SON-IN-LAW DRANK HIMSELF SICK.
Hey, Pops! Let me fill your glass!
SLURP
SUDDENLY, HIS FACE AND BODY TURNED INTO SOMETHING ELSE.
Ugh! It's a monster! It is a pig!
!
HE TURNED OUT TO BE A PIG-MONSTER. WHEN HIS TRUE CHARACTER WAS REVEALED, HE BEGAN ACTING VIOLENTLY AND LOCKED UP CUI LAN IN A MANOR BEHIND MY HOUSE.

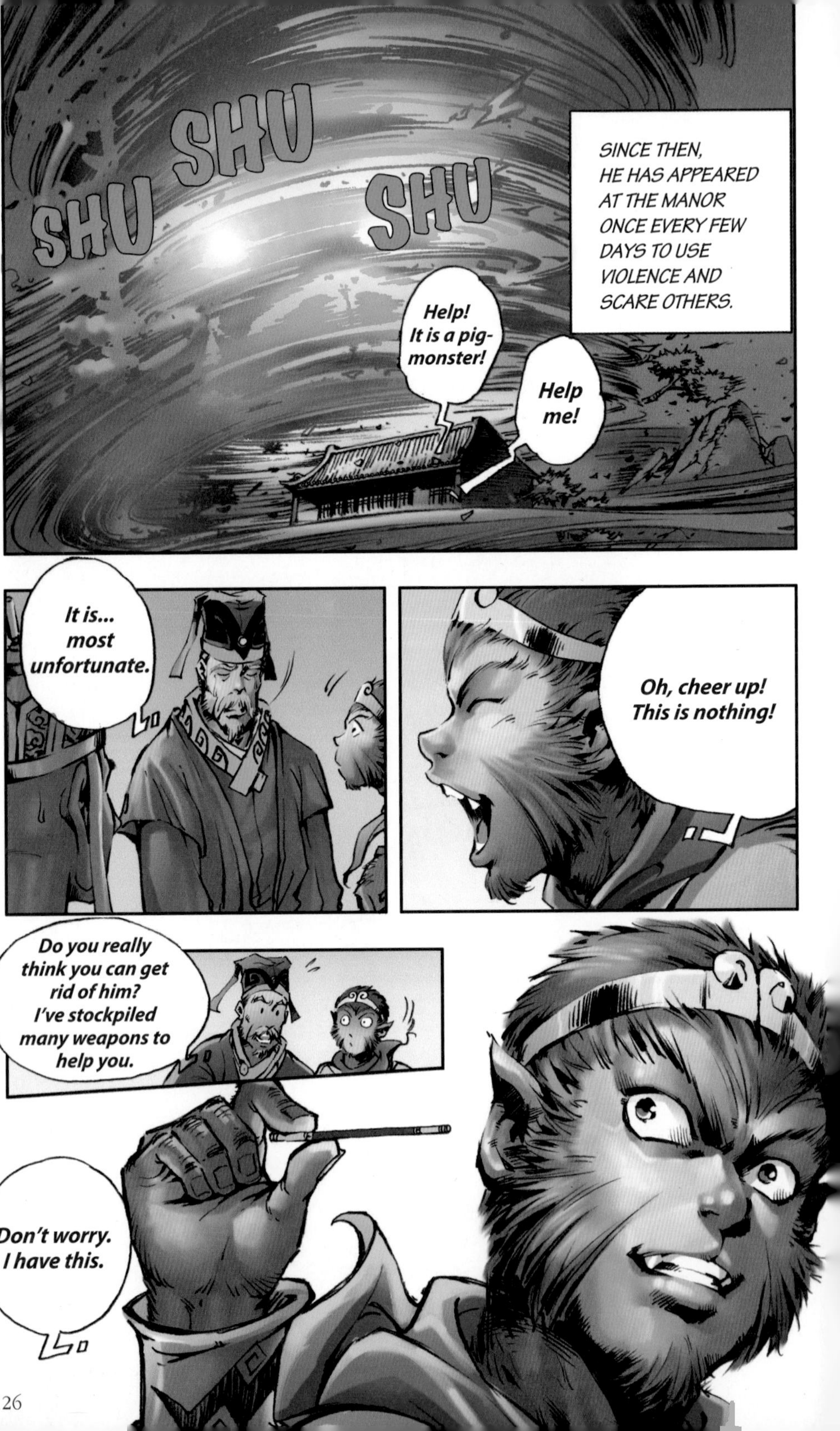
SHU SHU SHU
SINCE THEN, HE HAS APPEARED AT THE MANOR ONCE EVERY FEW DAYS TO USE VIOLENCE AND SCARE OTHERS.
Help! It is a pig-monster!
Help me!
It is... most unfortunate.
Oh, cheer up! This is nothing!
Do you really think you can get rid of him? I've stockpiled many weapons to help you.
Don't worry. I have this.

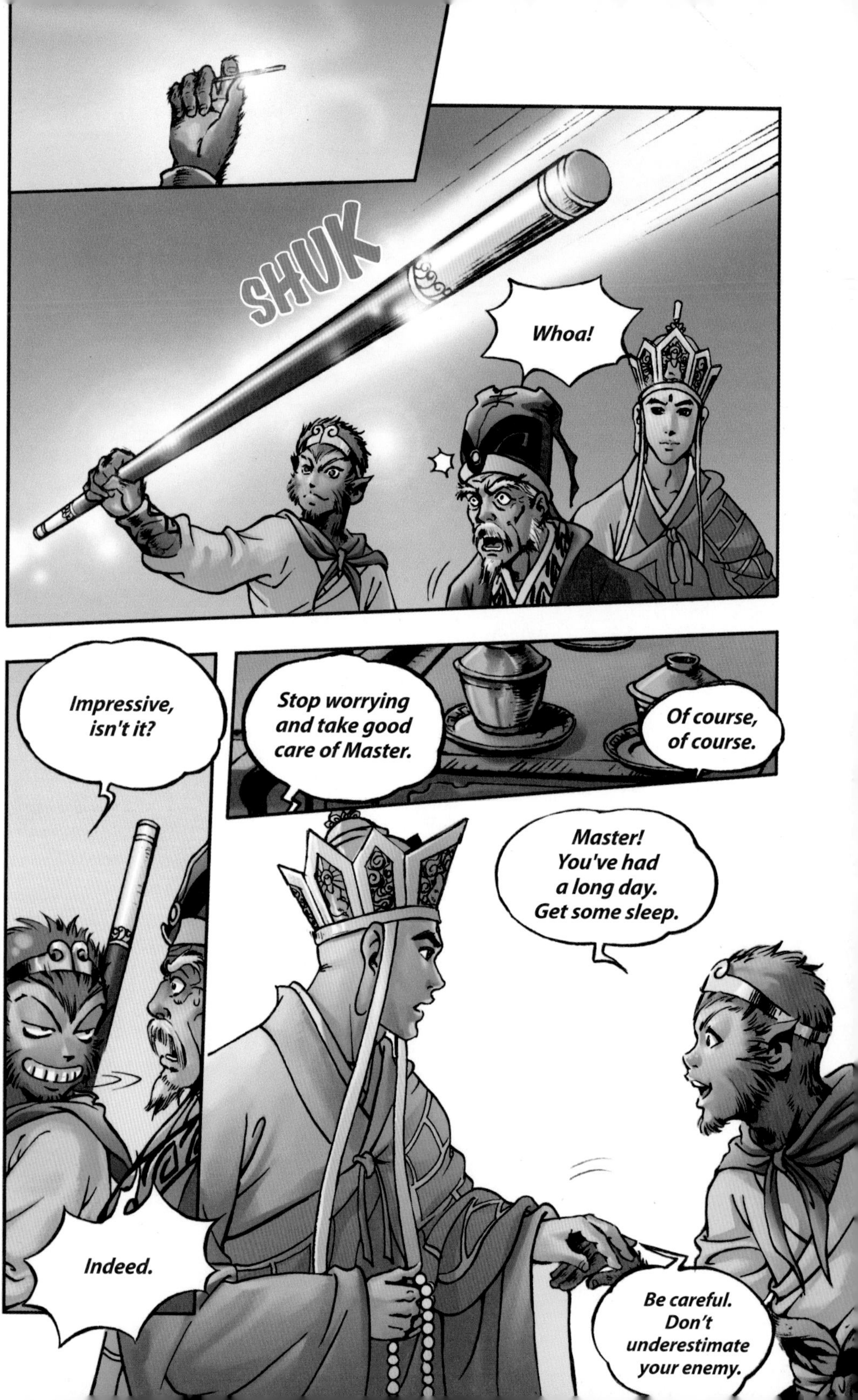
SHUK
Whoa!
Impressive, isn't it?
Indeed.
Stop worrying and take good care of Master.
Of course, of course.
Master! You've had a long day. Get some sleep.
Be careful. Don't underestimate your enemy.

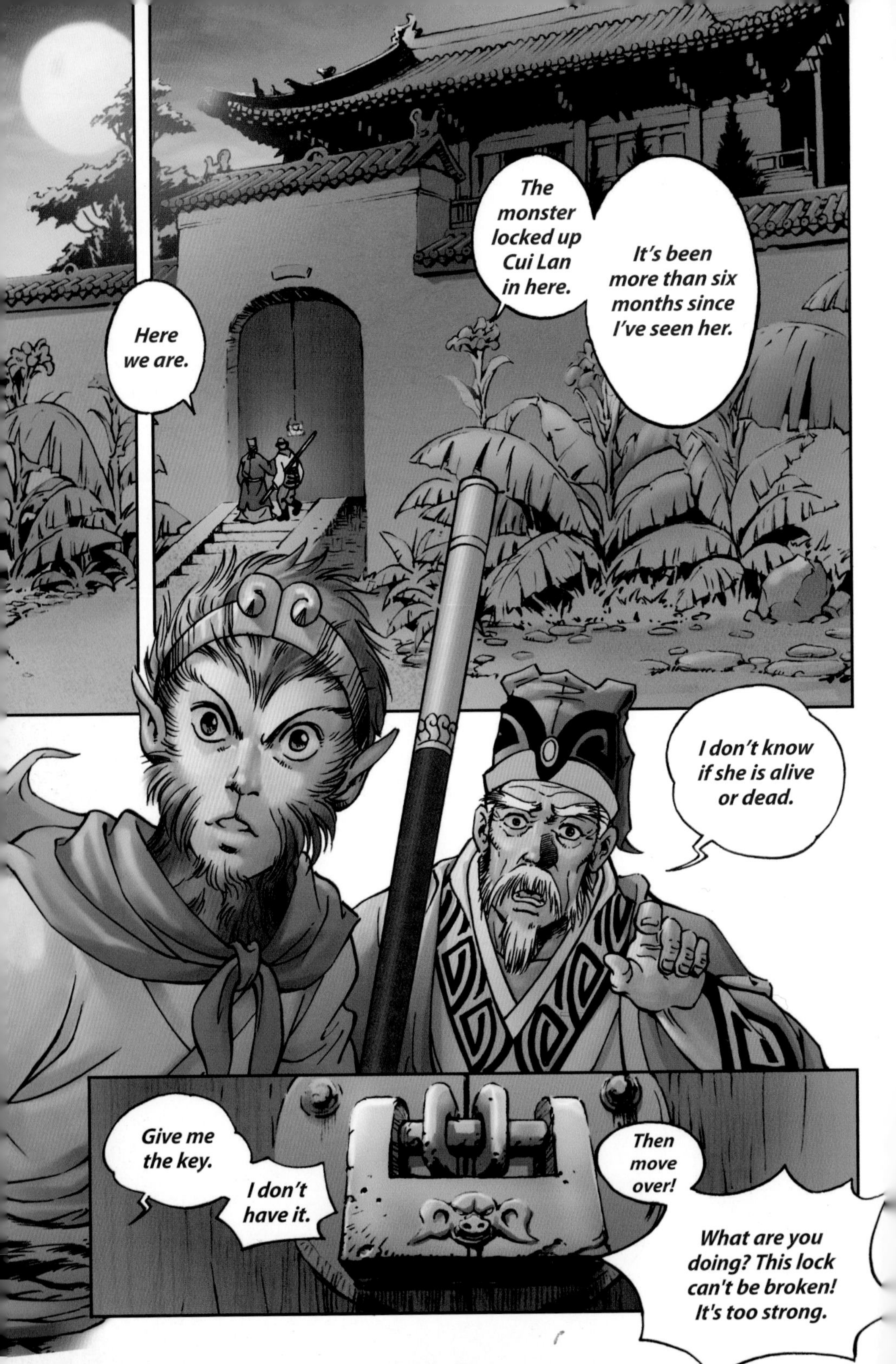
Here we are.
The monster locked up Cui Lan in here.
It's been more than six months since I've seen her.
I don't know if she is alive or dead.
Give me the key.
I don't have it.
Then move over!
What are you doing? This lock can't be broken! It's too strong.

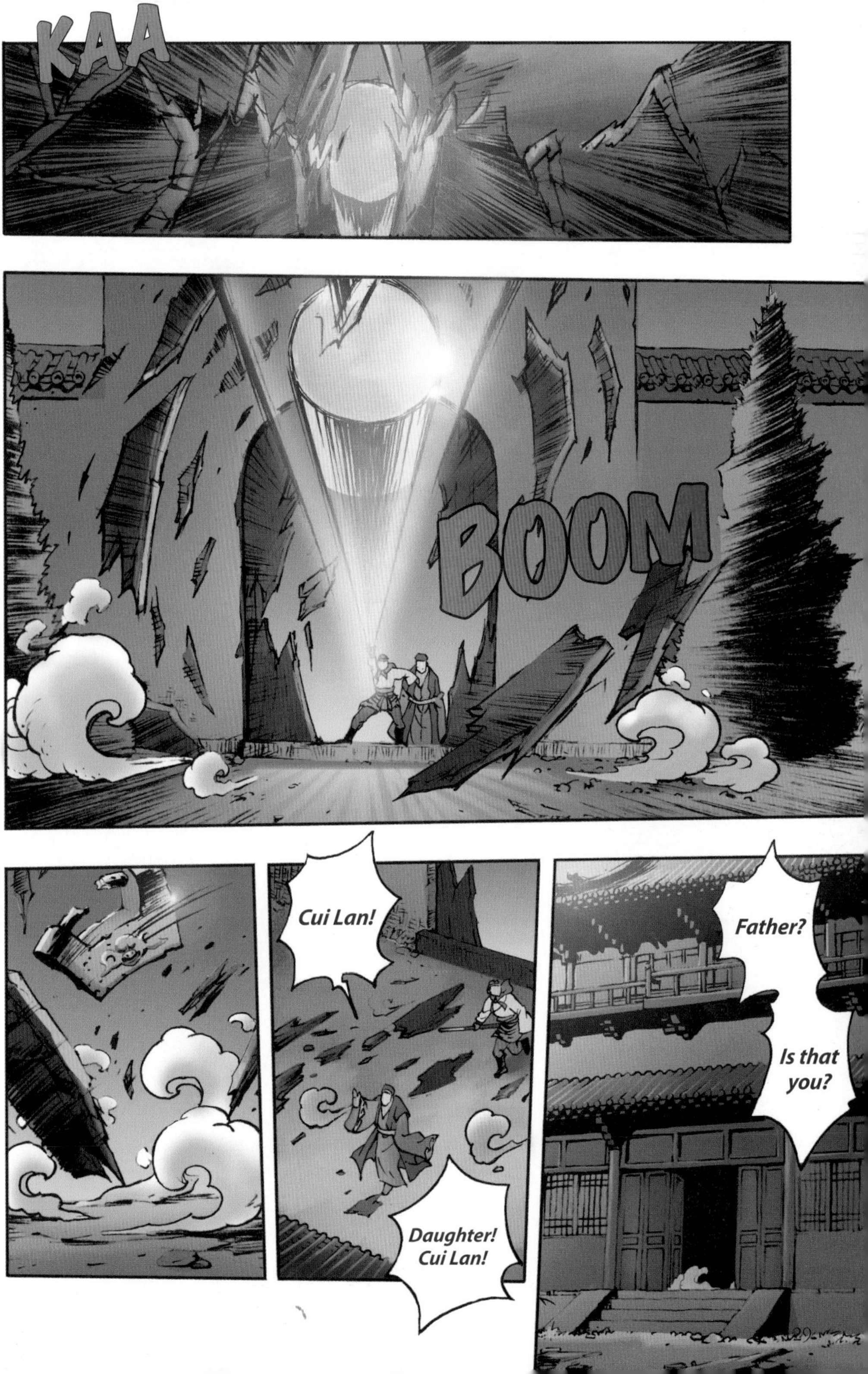
KAA
BOOM
Cui Lan!
Daughter! Cui Lan!
Father?
Is that you?

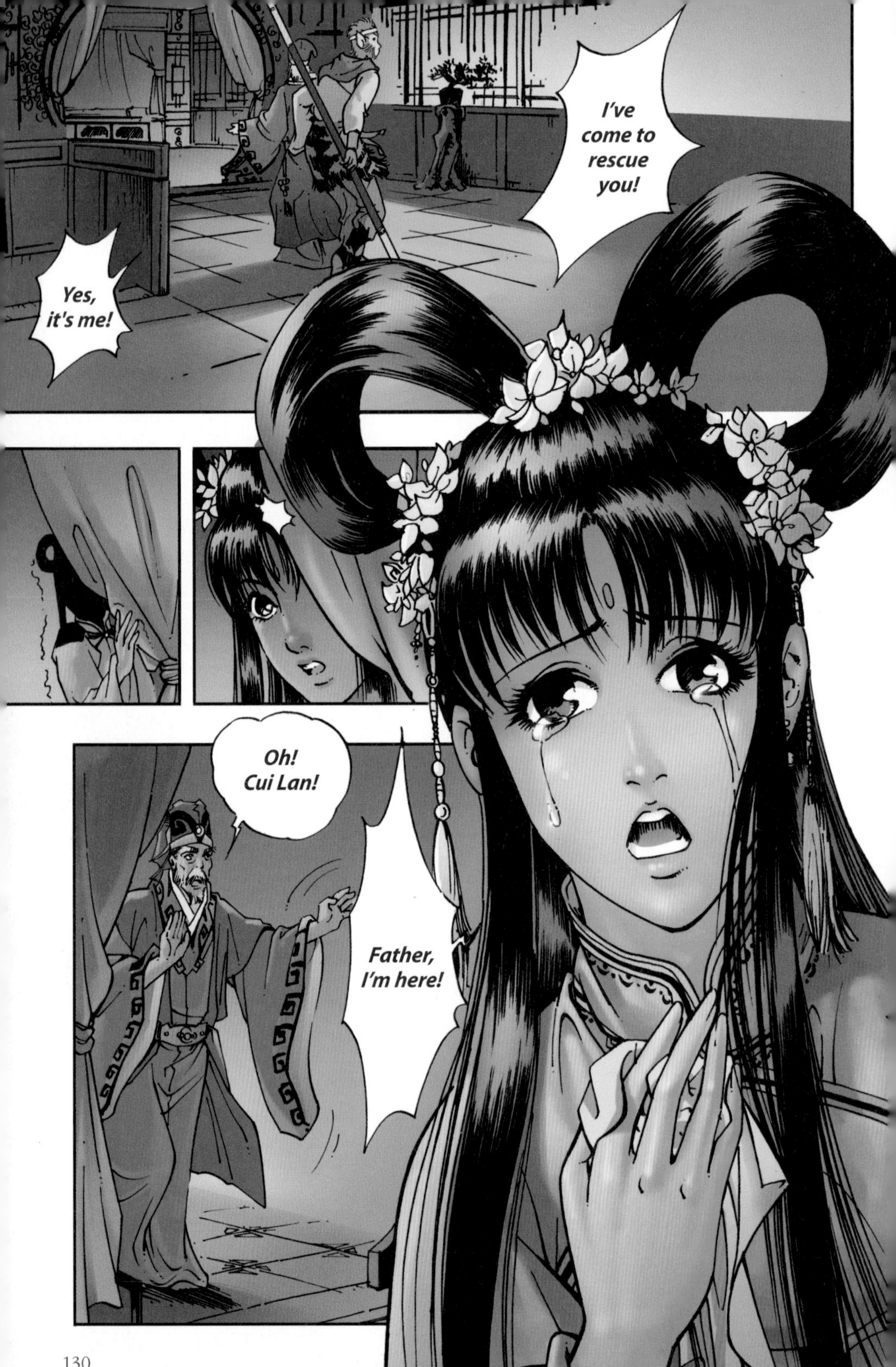
I've come to rescue you!
Yes, it's me!
Oh! Cui Lan!
Father, I'm here!

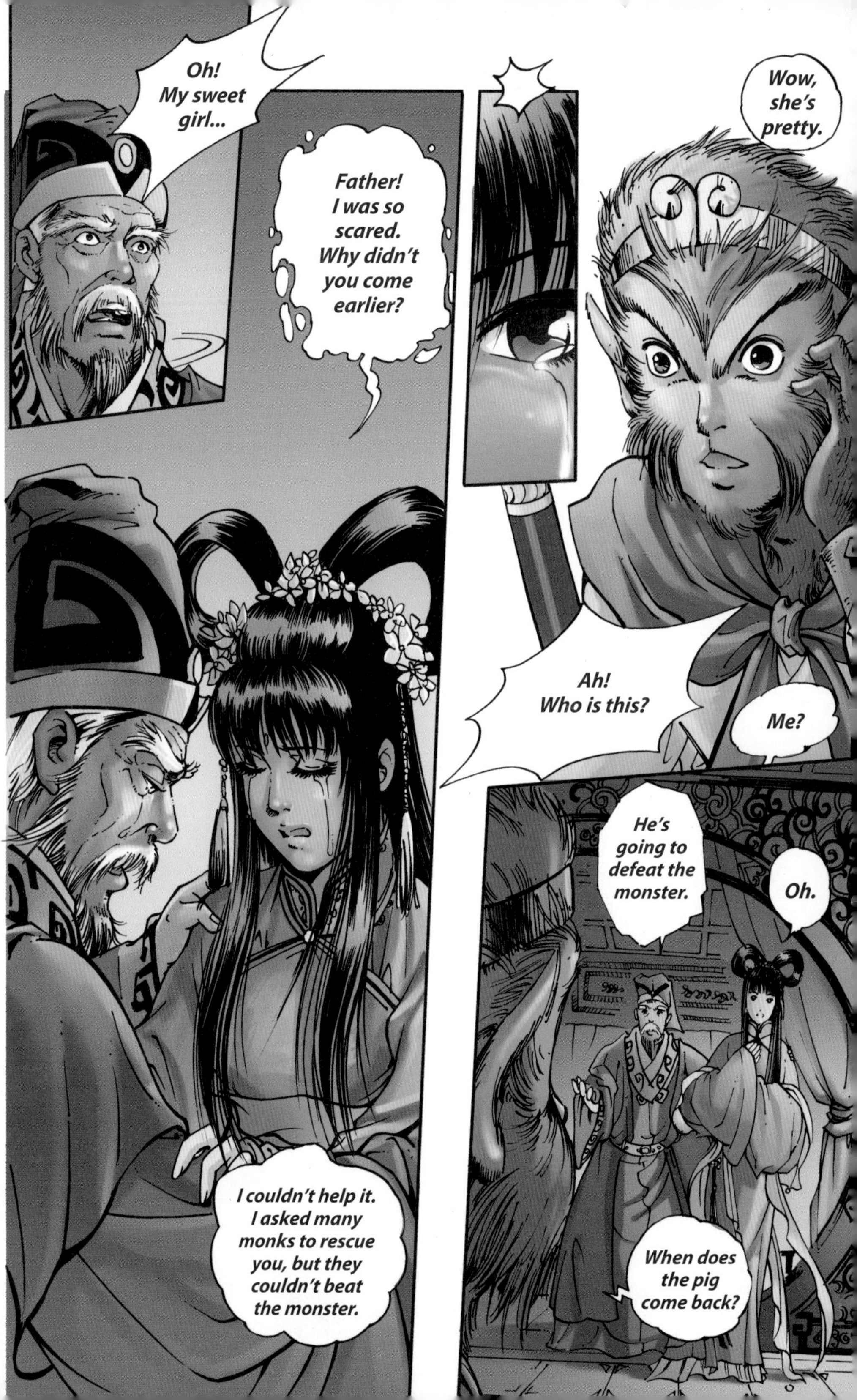
Oh! My sweet girl...
Father! I was so scared. Why didn't you come earlier?
I couldn't help it. I asked many monks to rescue you, but they couldn't beat the monster.
Wow, she's pretty.
Ah! Who is this?
Me?
He's going to defeat the monster.
Oh.
When does the pig come back?

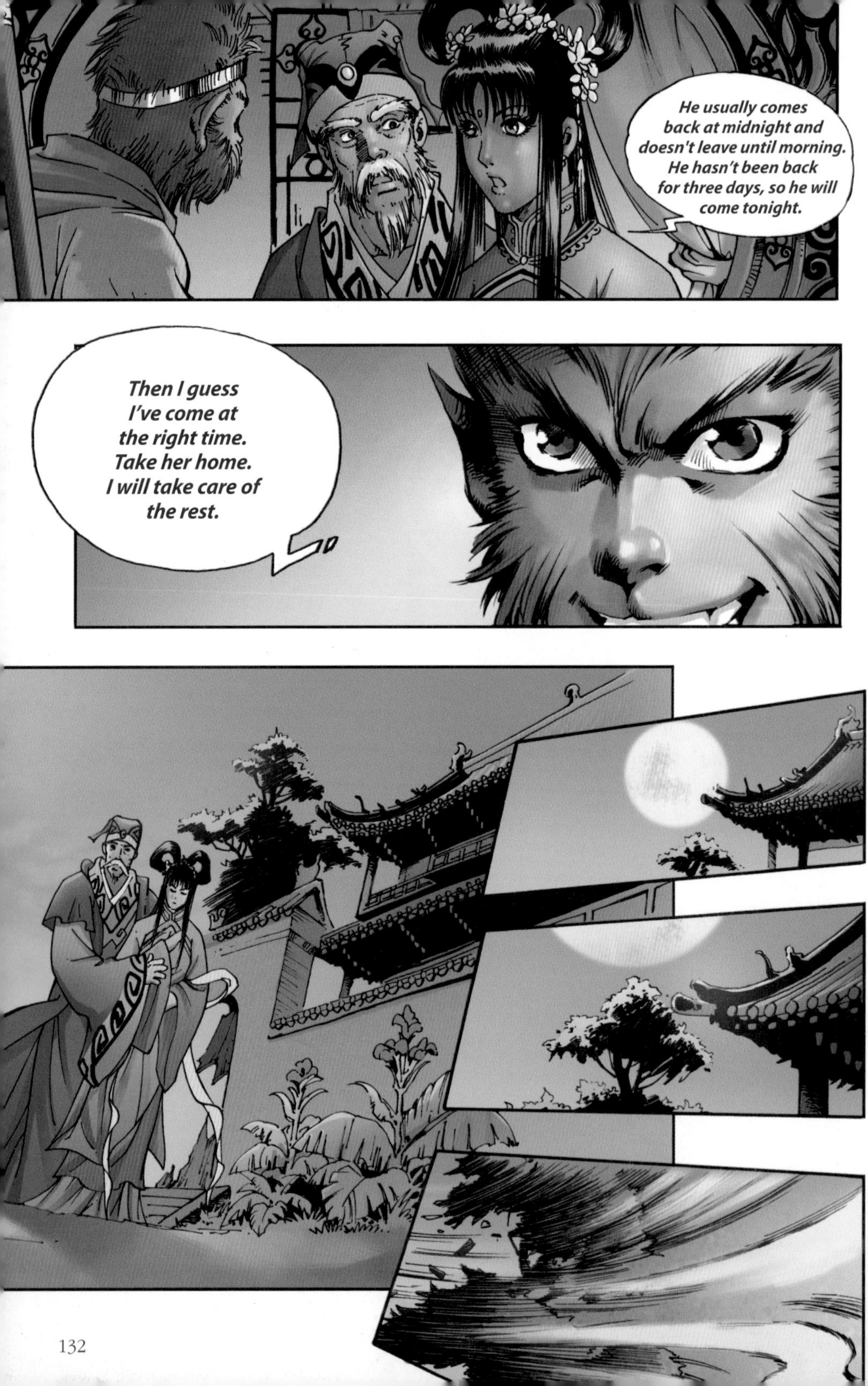
He usually comes back at midnight and doesn't leave until morning. He hasn't been back for three days, so he will come tonight.
Then I guess I've come at the right time. Take her home. I will take care of the rest.

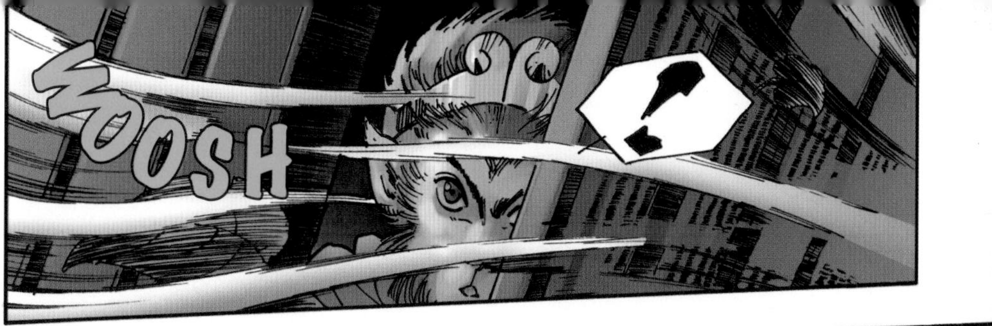
WOOSH
!
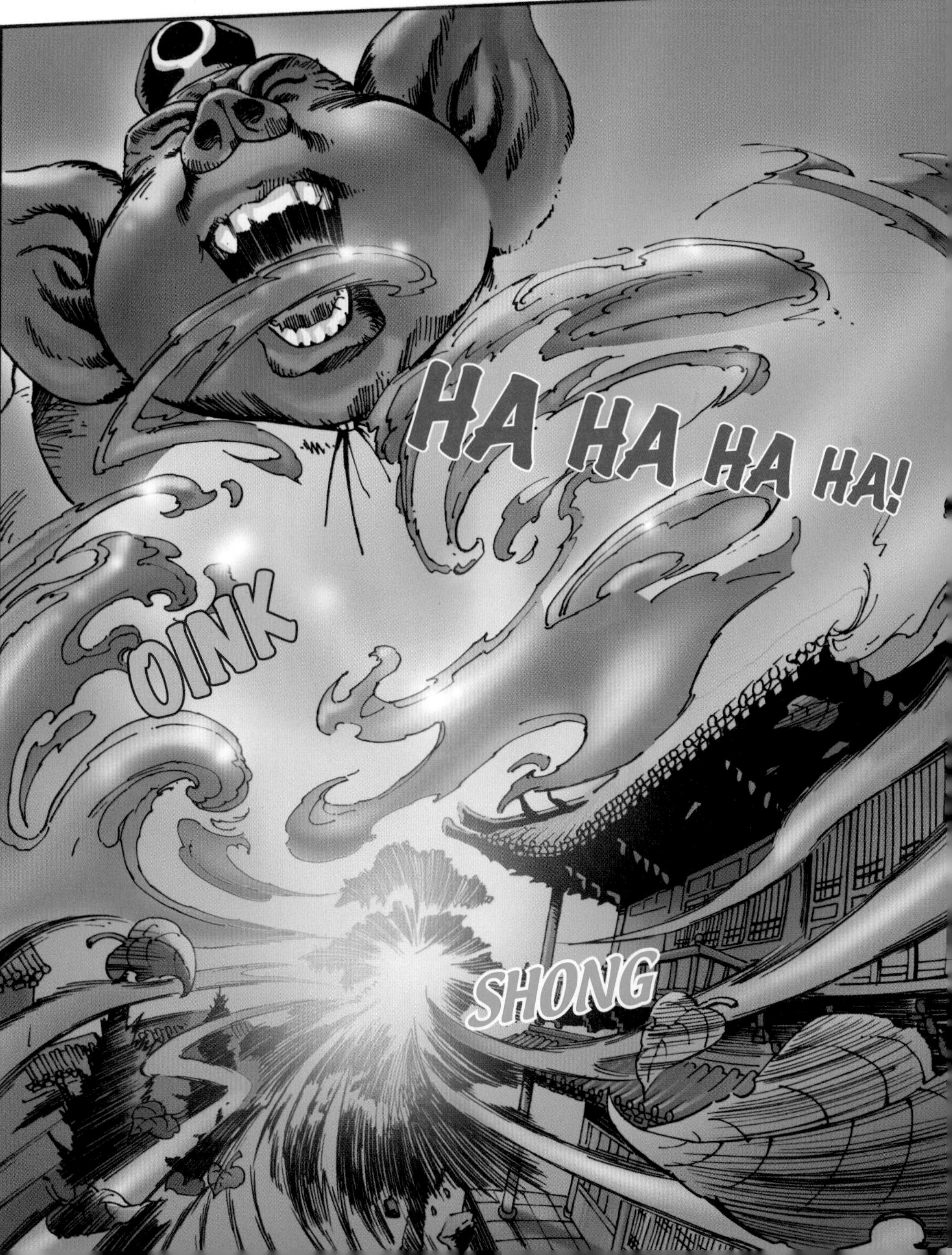
HA HA HA HA!
OINK
SHONG

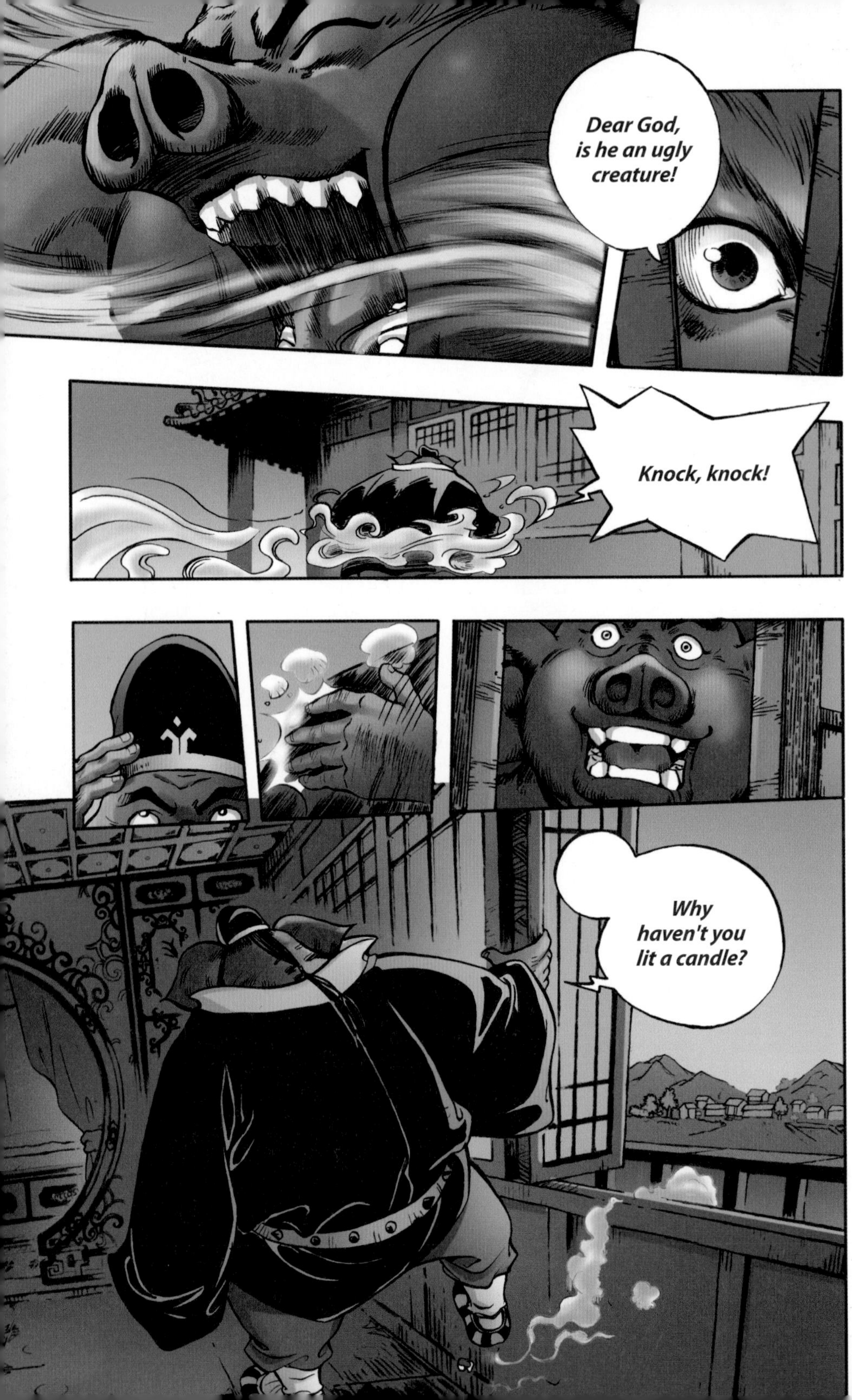
Dear God, is he an ugly creature!
Knock, knock!
Why haven't you lit a candle?

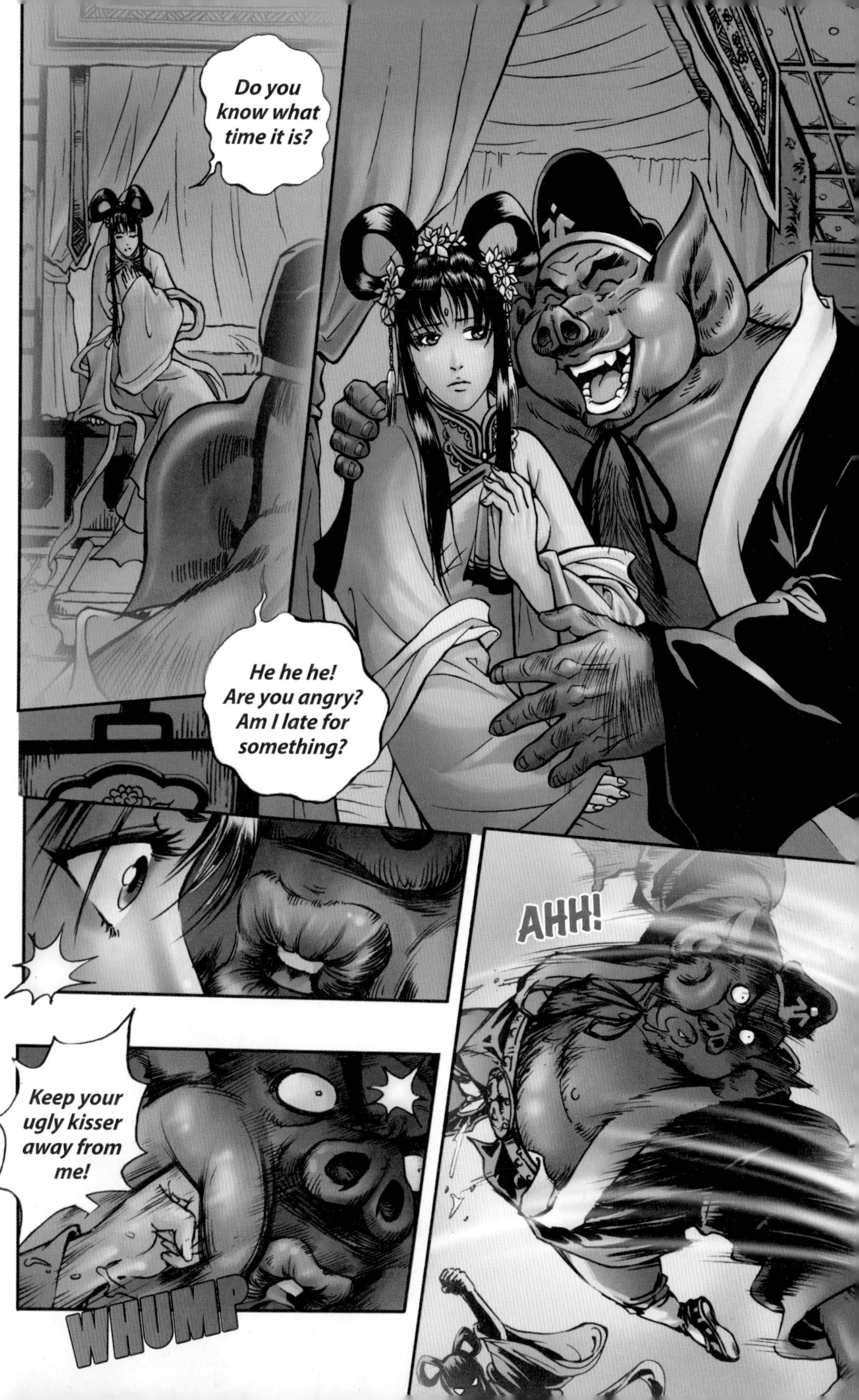
Do you know what time it is?
He he he! Are you angry? Am I late for something?
AHH!
Keep your ugly kisser away from me!
WHUMP

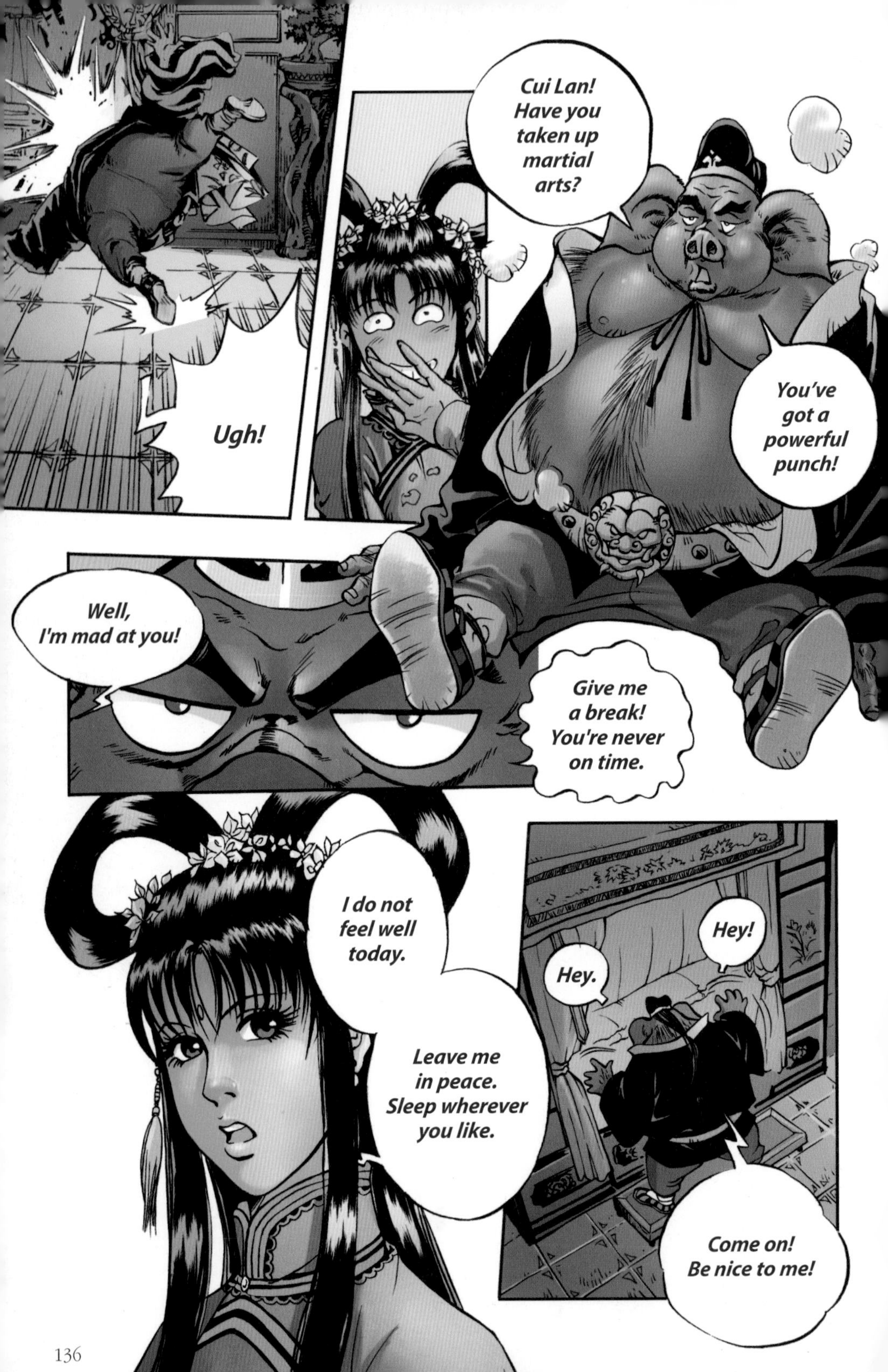
Ugh!
Cui Lan! Have you taken up martial arts?
You've got a powerful punch!
Well, I'm mad at you!
Give me a break! You're never on time.
I do not feel well today.
Leave me in peace. Sleep wherever you like.
Hey!
Hey.
Come on! Be nice to me!

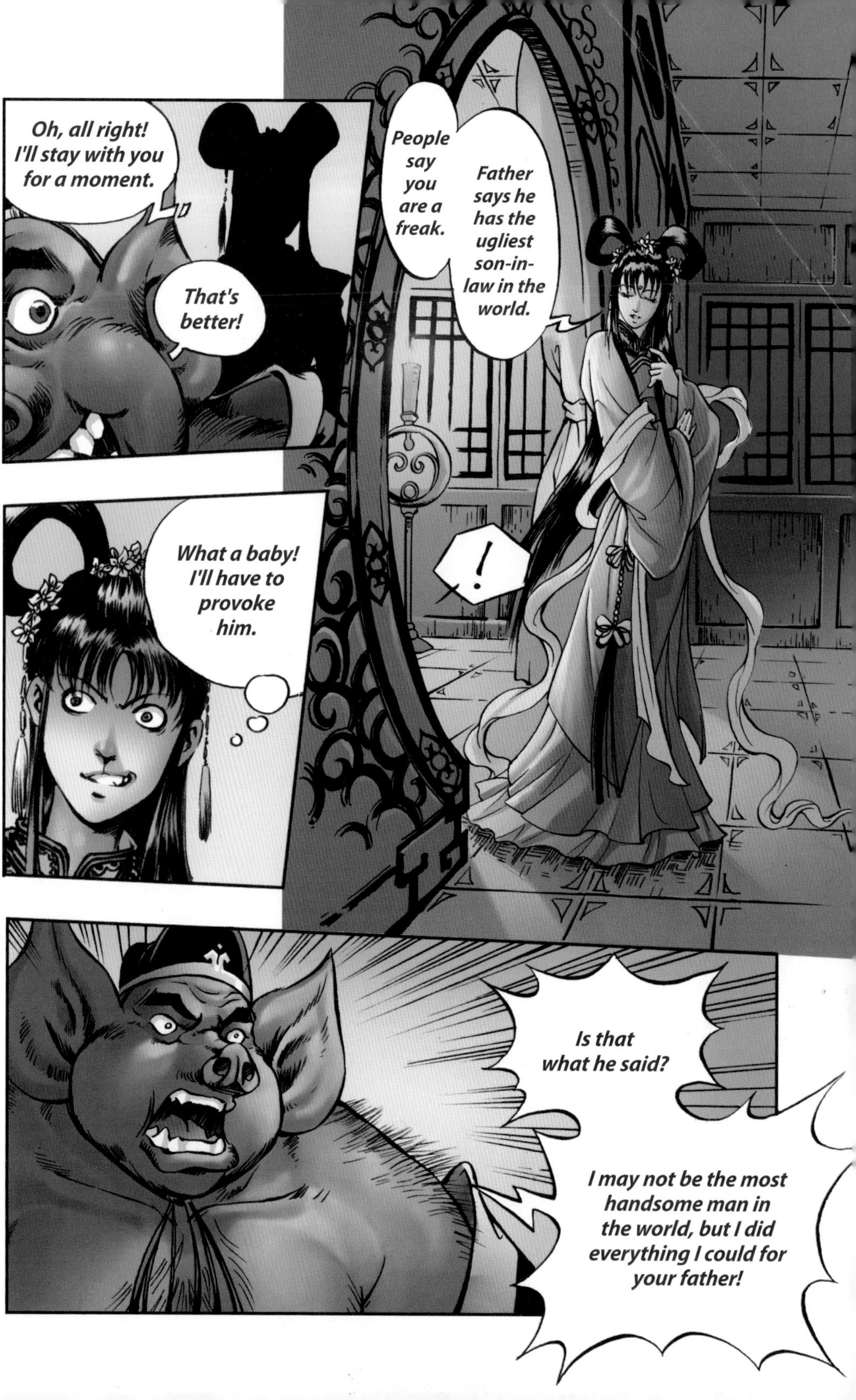
Oh, all right! I'll stay with you for a moment.
That's better!
People say you are a freak.
Father says he has the ugliest son-in-law in the world.
!
What a baby! I'll have to provoke him.
Is that what he said?
I may not be the most handsome man in the world, but I did everything I could for your father!

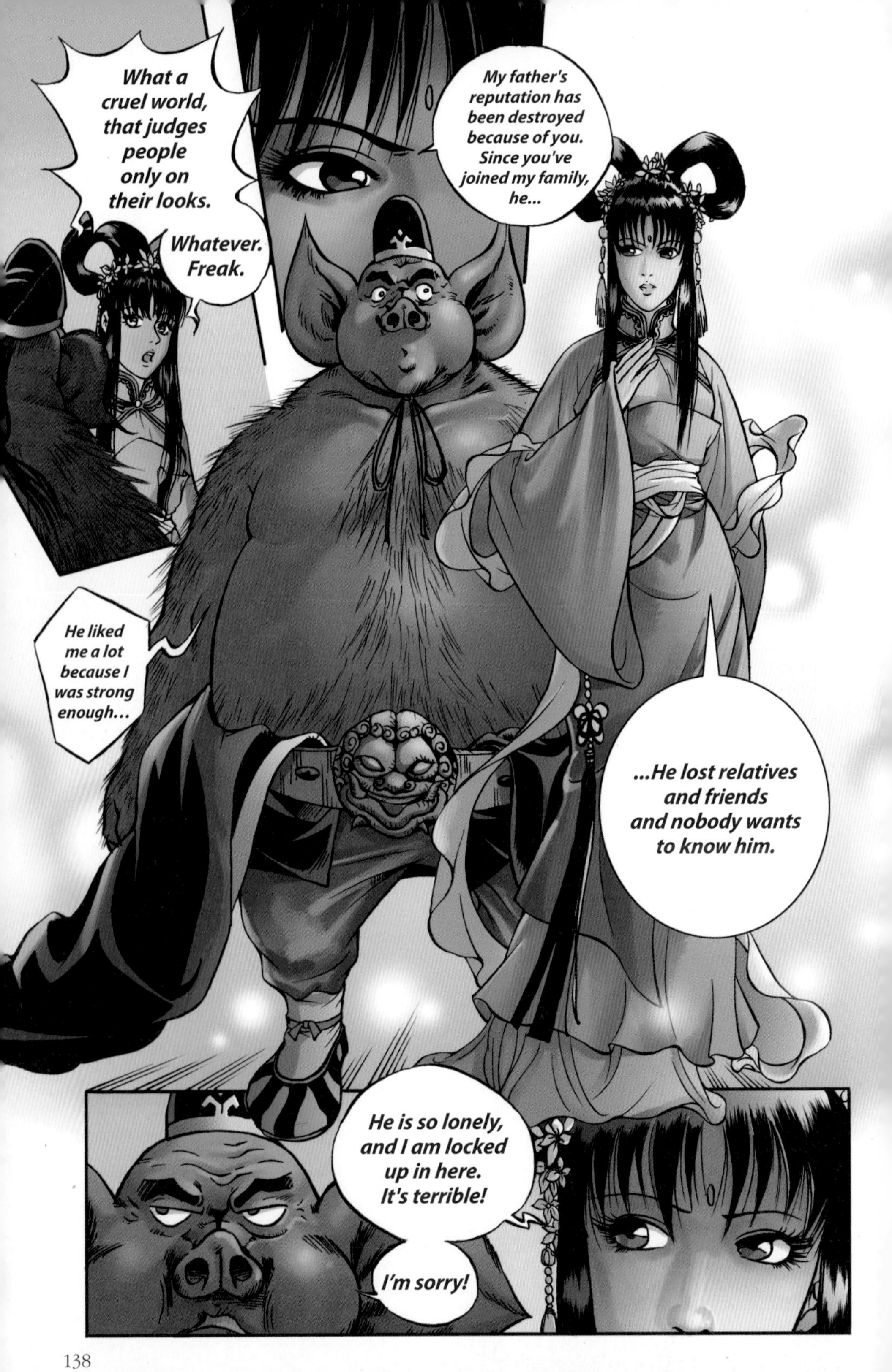
What a cruel world, that judges people only on their looks.
Whatever. Freak.
My father's reputation has been destroyed because of you. Since you've joined my family, he...
He liked me a lot because I was strong enough...
...He lost relatives and friends and nobody wants to know him.
He is so lonely, and I am locked up in here. It's terrible!
I'm sorry!

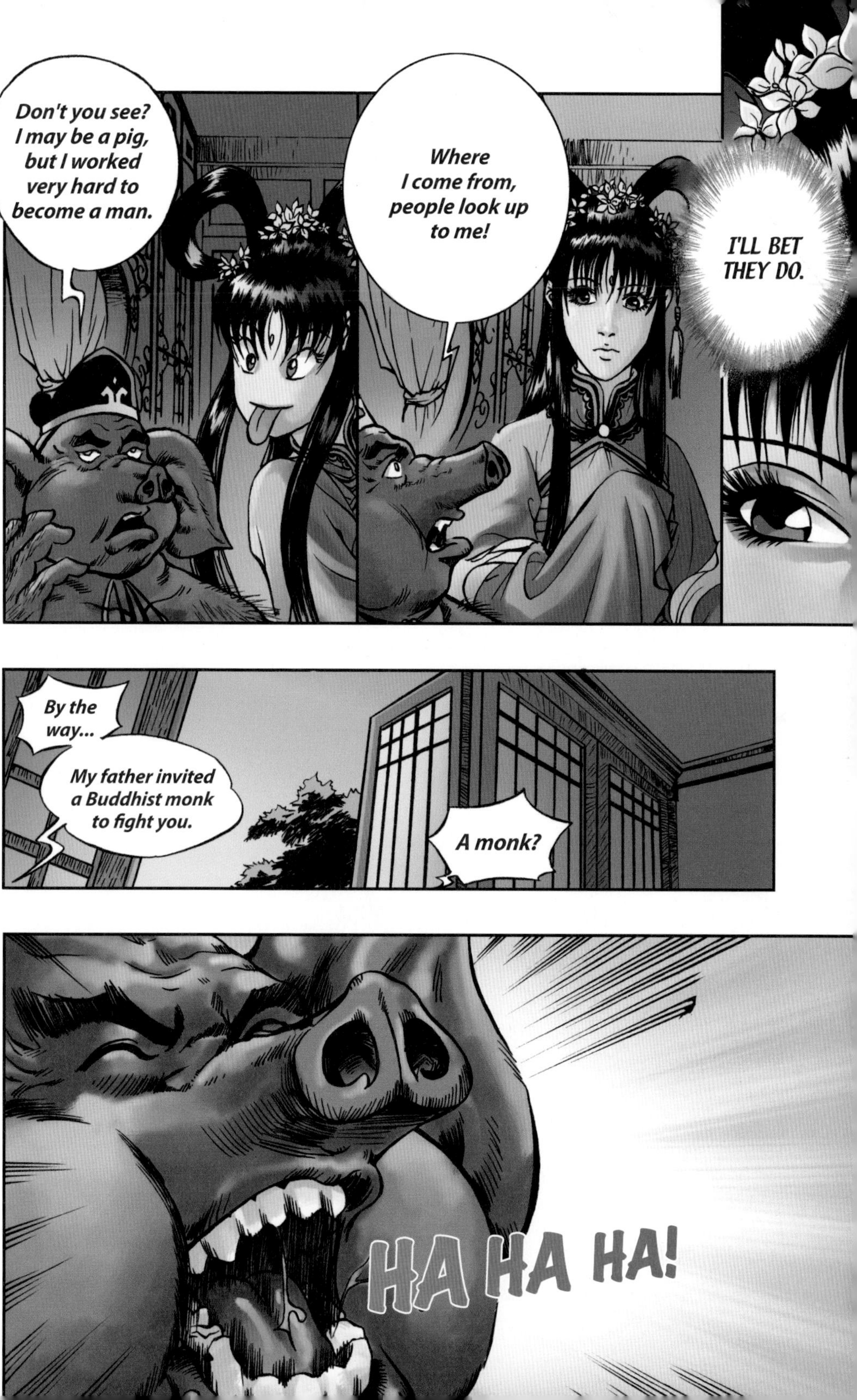
Don't you see? I may be a pig, but I worked very hard to become a man.
Where I come from, people look up to me!
I'LL BET THEY DO.
By the way...
My father invited a Buddhist monk to fight you.
A monk?
HA HA HA!

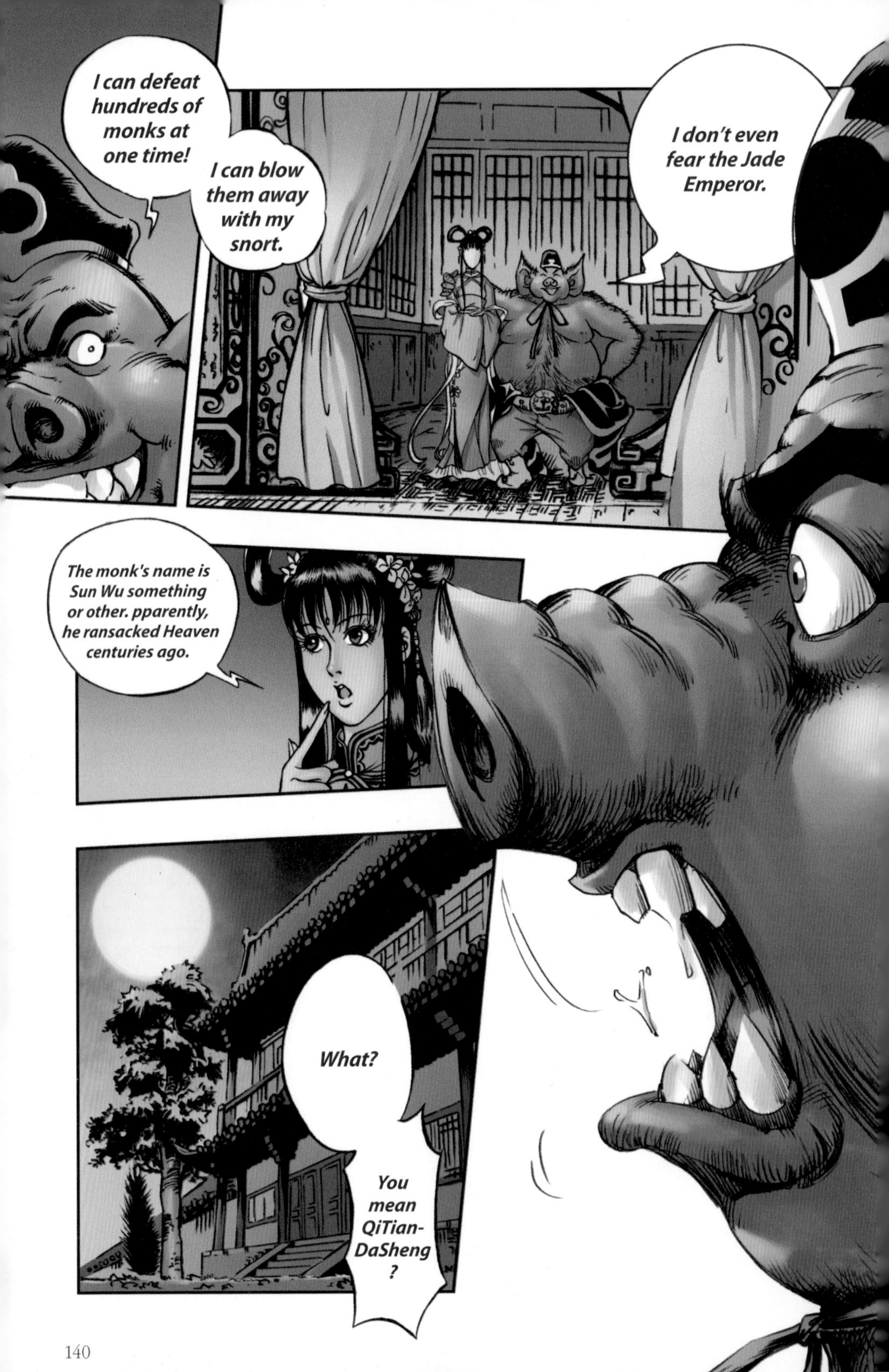
I can defeat hundreds of monks at one time!
I can blow them away with my snort.
I don't even fear the Jade Emperor.
The monk's name is Sun Wu something or other. pparently, he ransacked Heaven centuries ago.
What?
You mean QiTian-DaSheng?

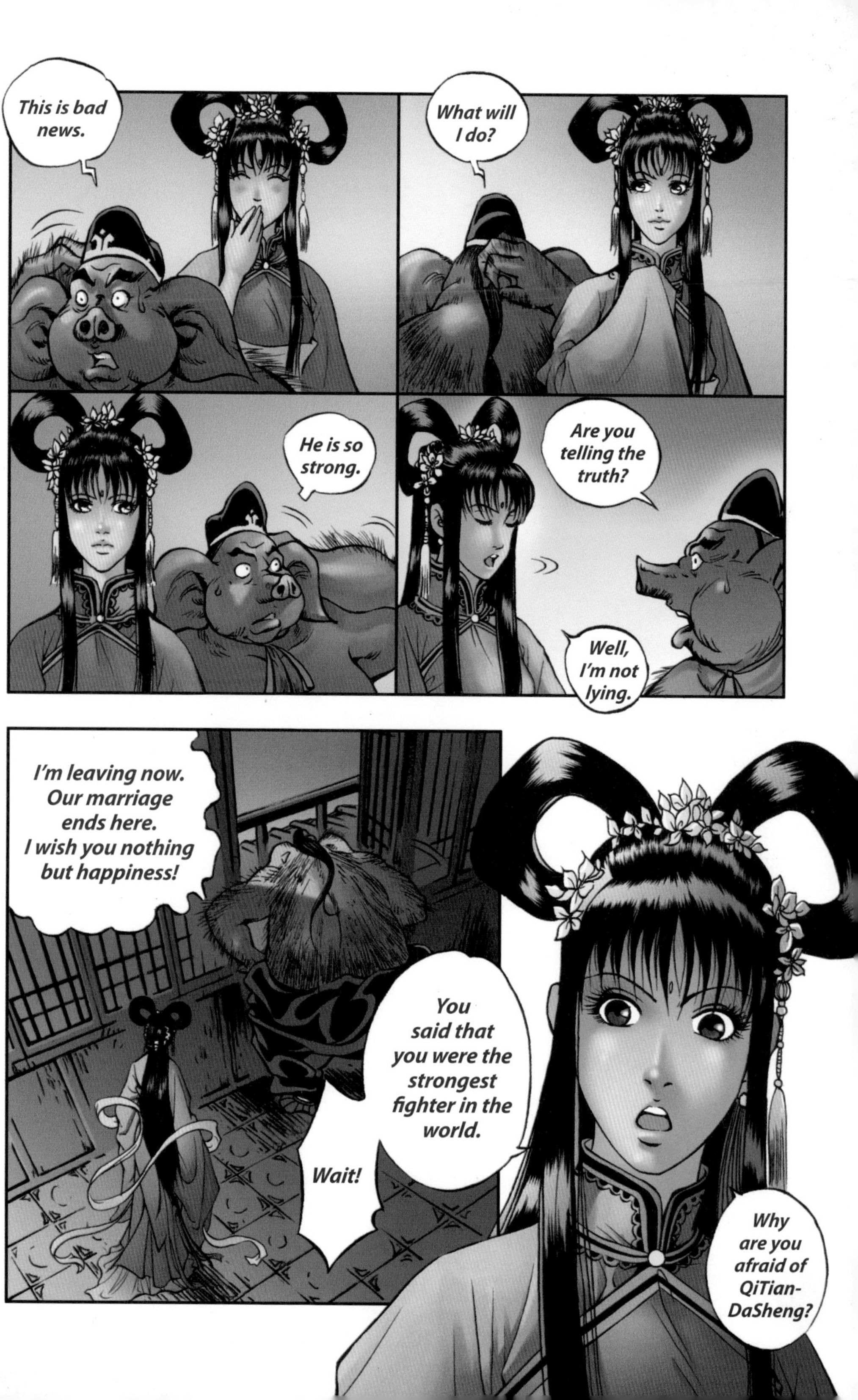
This is bad news.
What will I do?
He is so strong.
Are you telling the truth?
Well, I'm not lying.
I'm leaving now. Our marriage ends here. I wish you nothing but happiness!
Wait!
You said that you were the strongest fighter in the world.
Why are you afraid of QiTian-DaSheng?

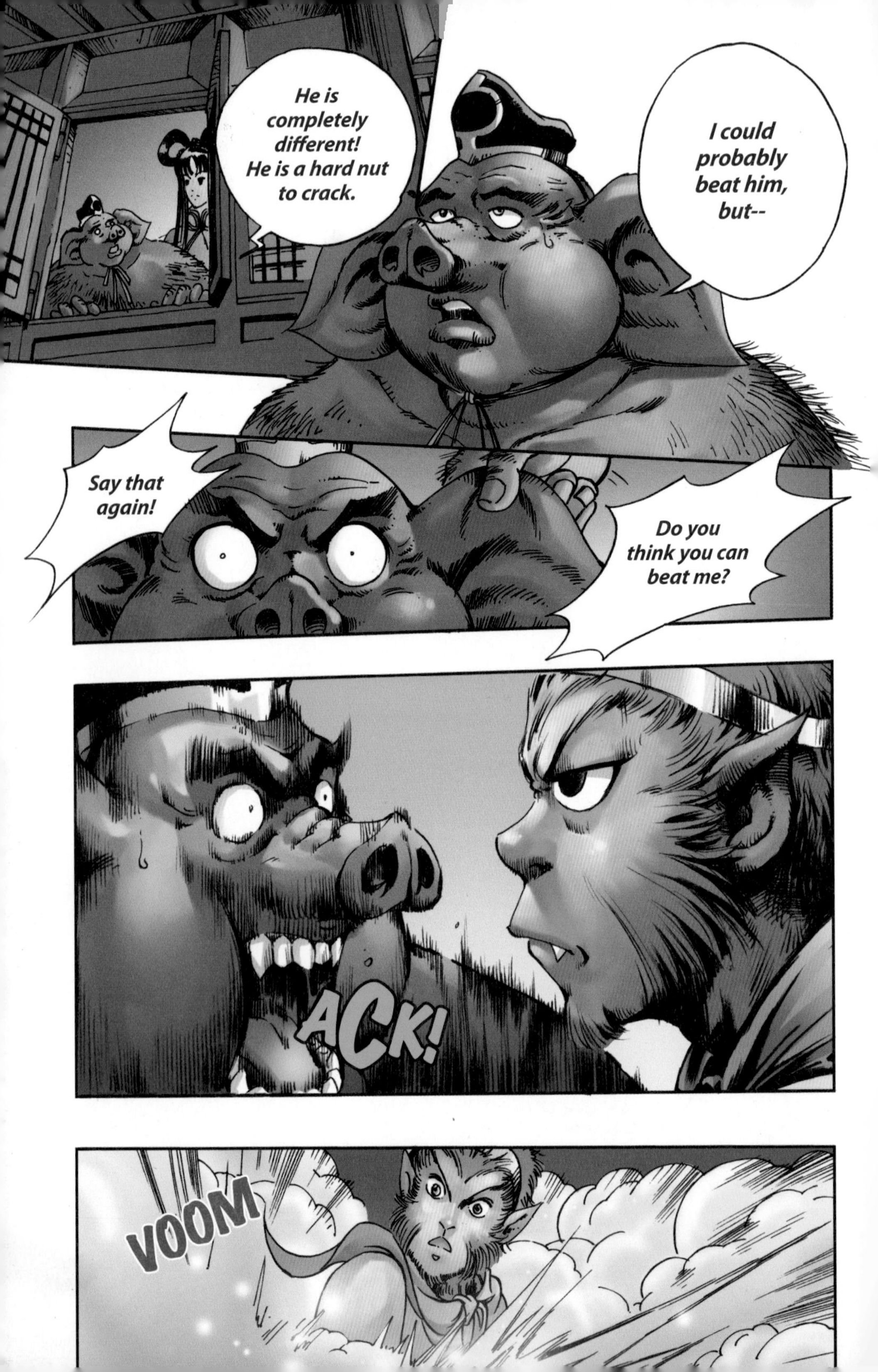
He is completely different! He is a hard nut to crack.
I could probably beat him, but--
Say that again!
Do you think you can beat me?
ACK!
VOOM

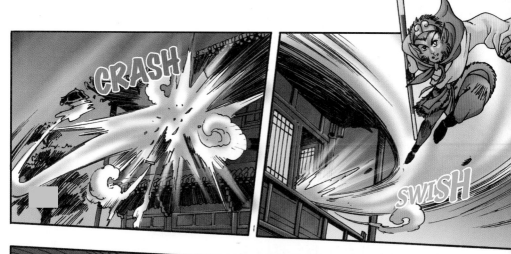

Hey, Pigsy!
Where are you going?
Cui Lan wants a kiss!

I thought
Cui Lan smelled
like a monkey's
cage.

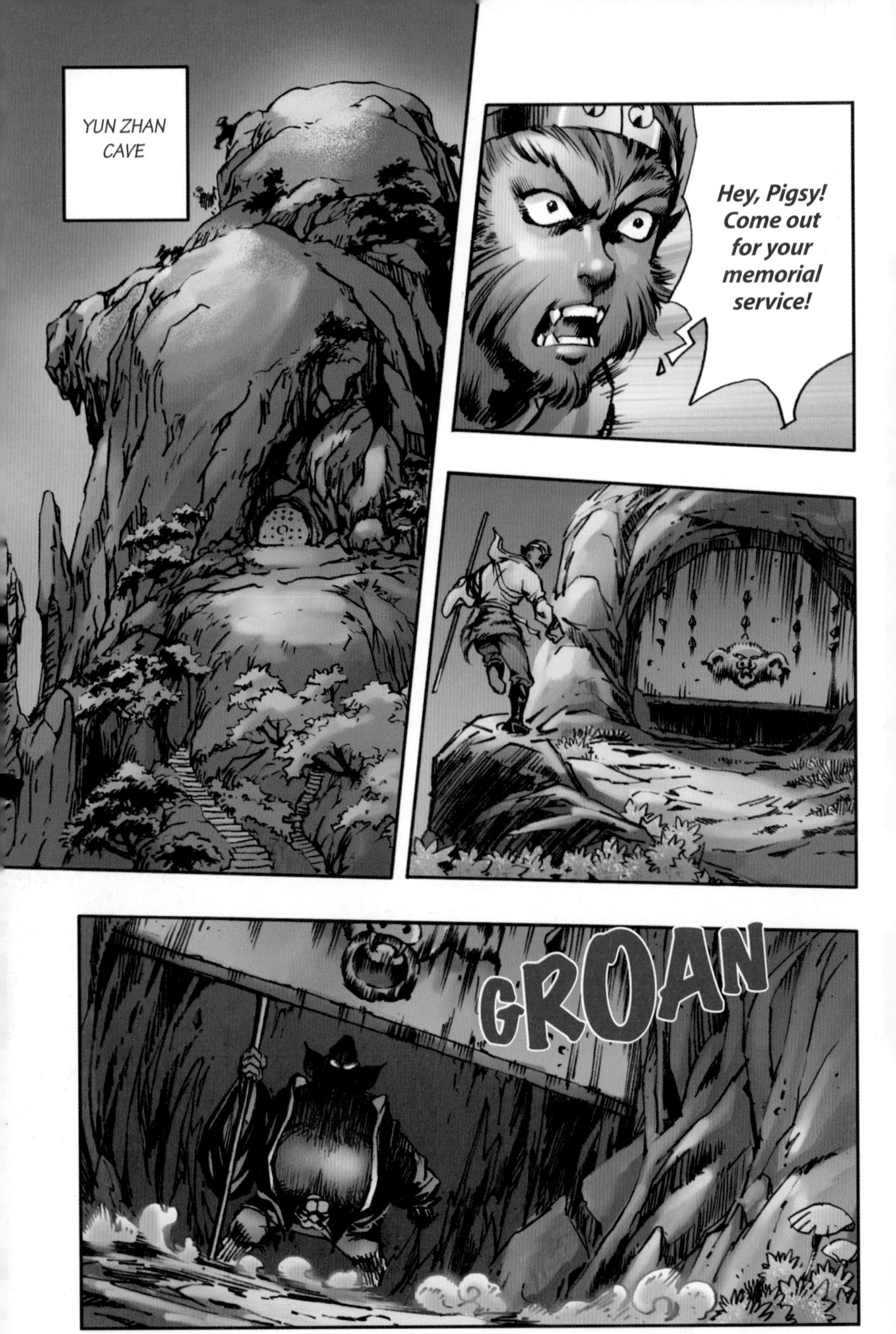
YUN ZHAN CAVE
Hey, Pigsy! Come out for your memorial service!
GROAN

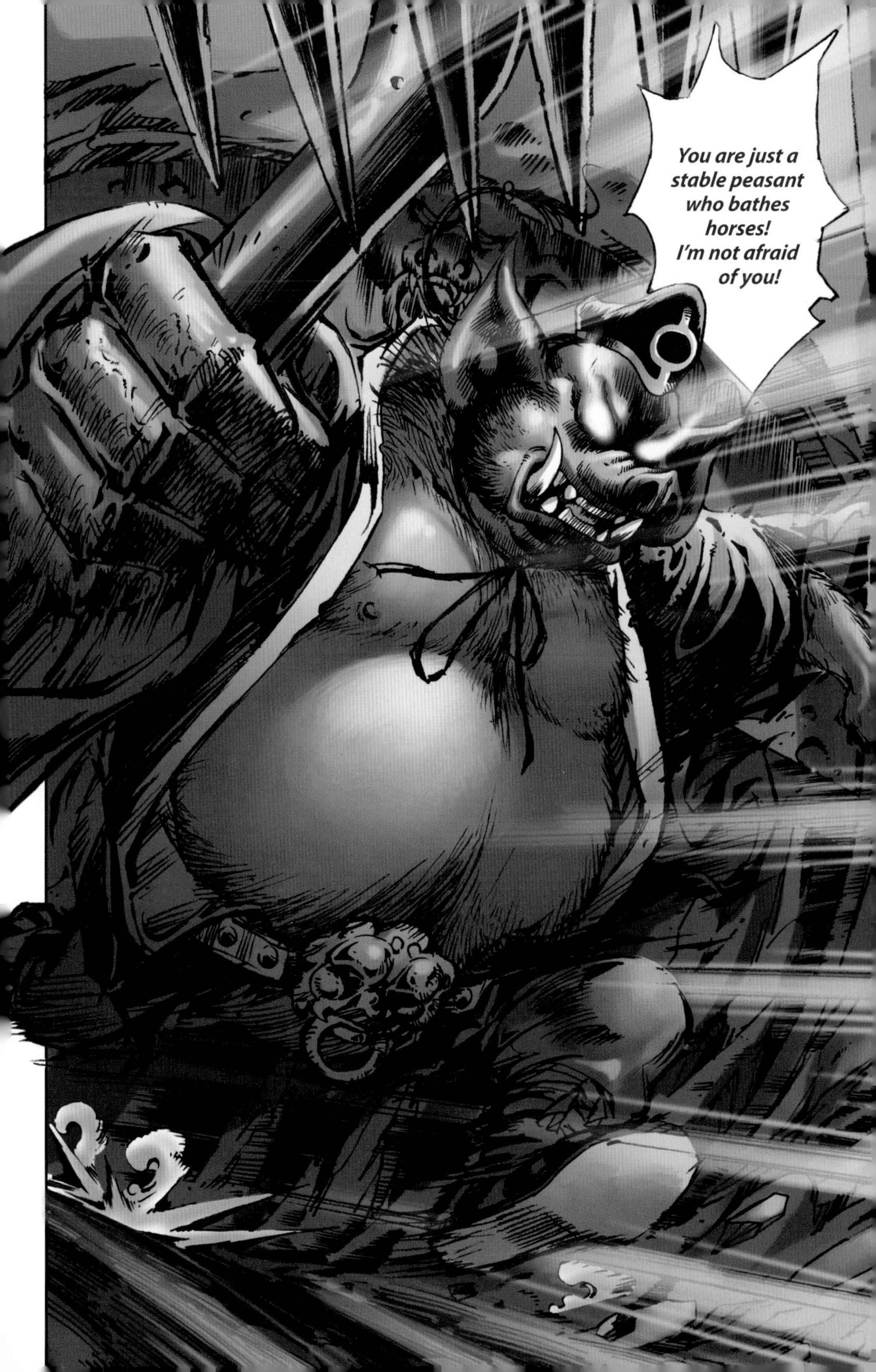
You are just a stable peasant who bathes horses! I'm not afraid of you!

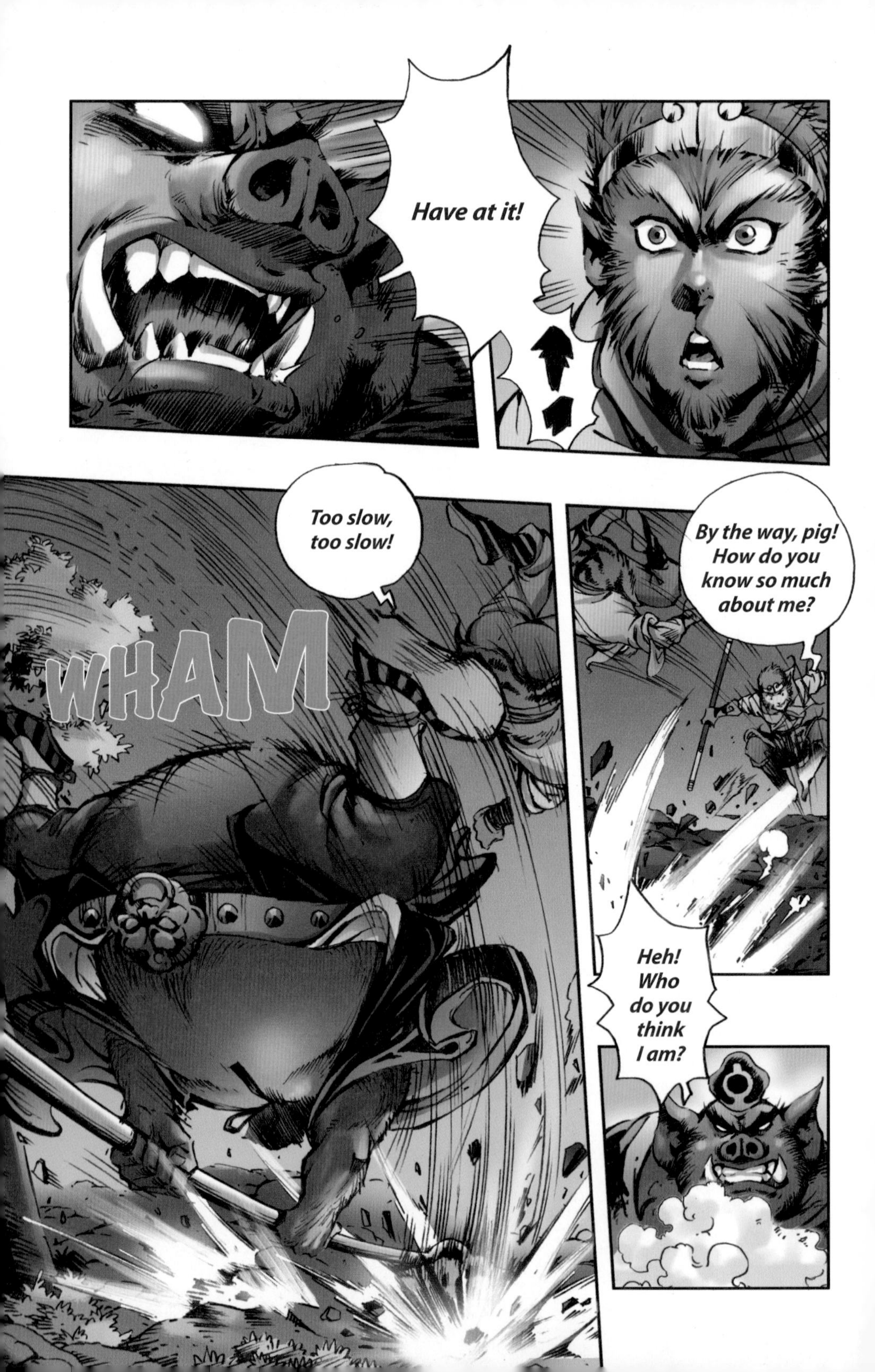
Have at it!
Too slow, too slow!
WHAM
By the way, pig! How do you know so much about me?
Heh! Who do you think I am?

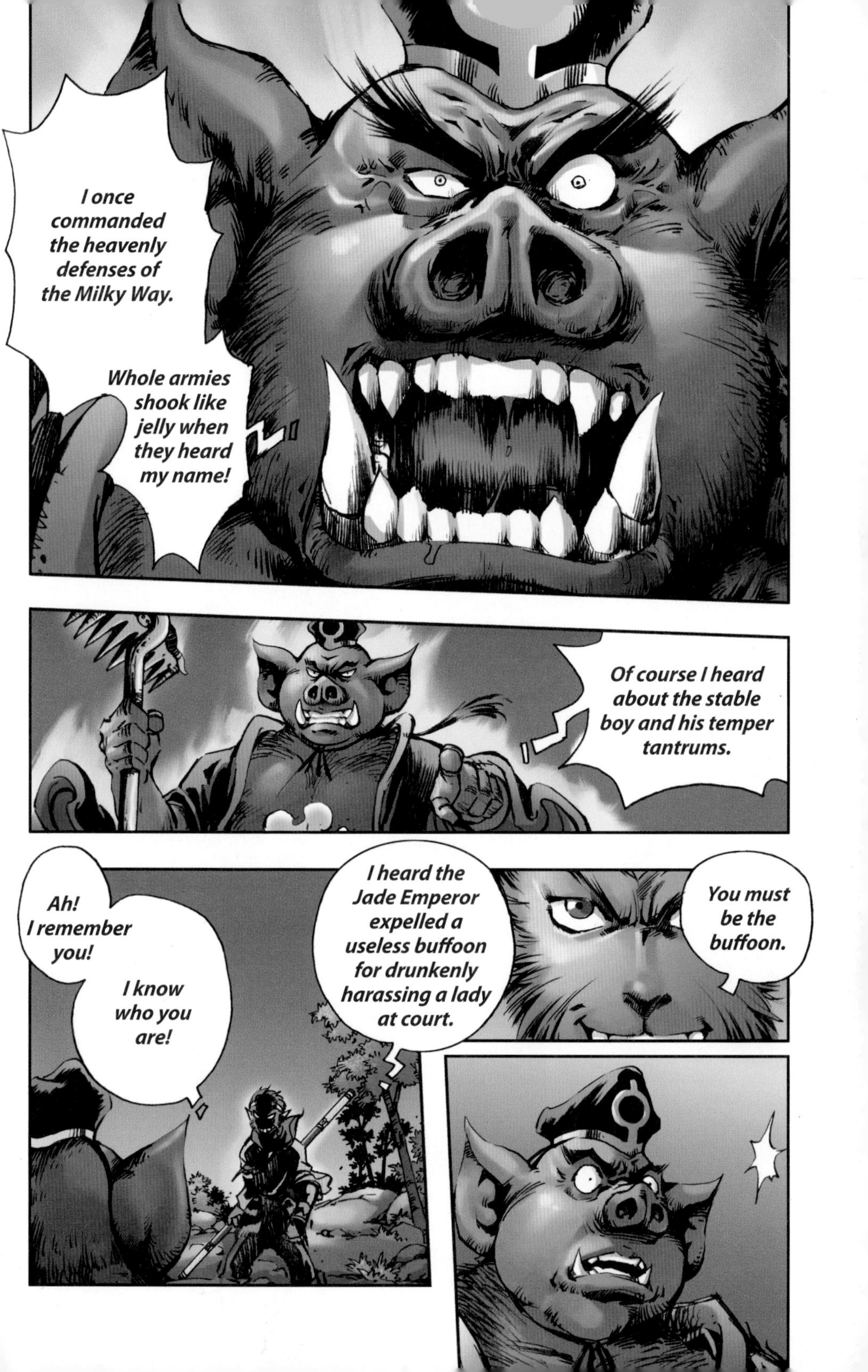
I once commanded the heavenly defenses of the Milky Way.
Whole armies shook like jelly when they heard my name!
Of course I heard about the stable boy and his temper tantrums.
Ah! I remember you!
I know who you are!
I heard the Jade Emperor expelled a useless buffoon for drunkenly harassing a lady at court.
You must be the buffoon.

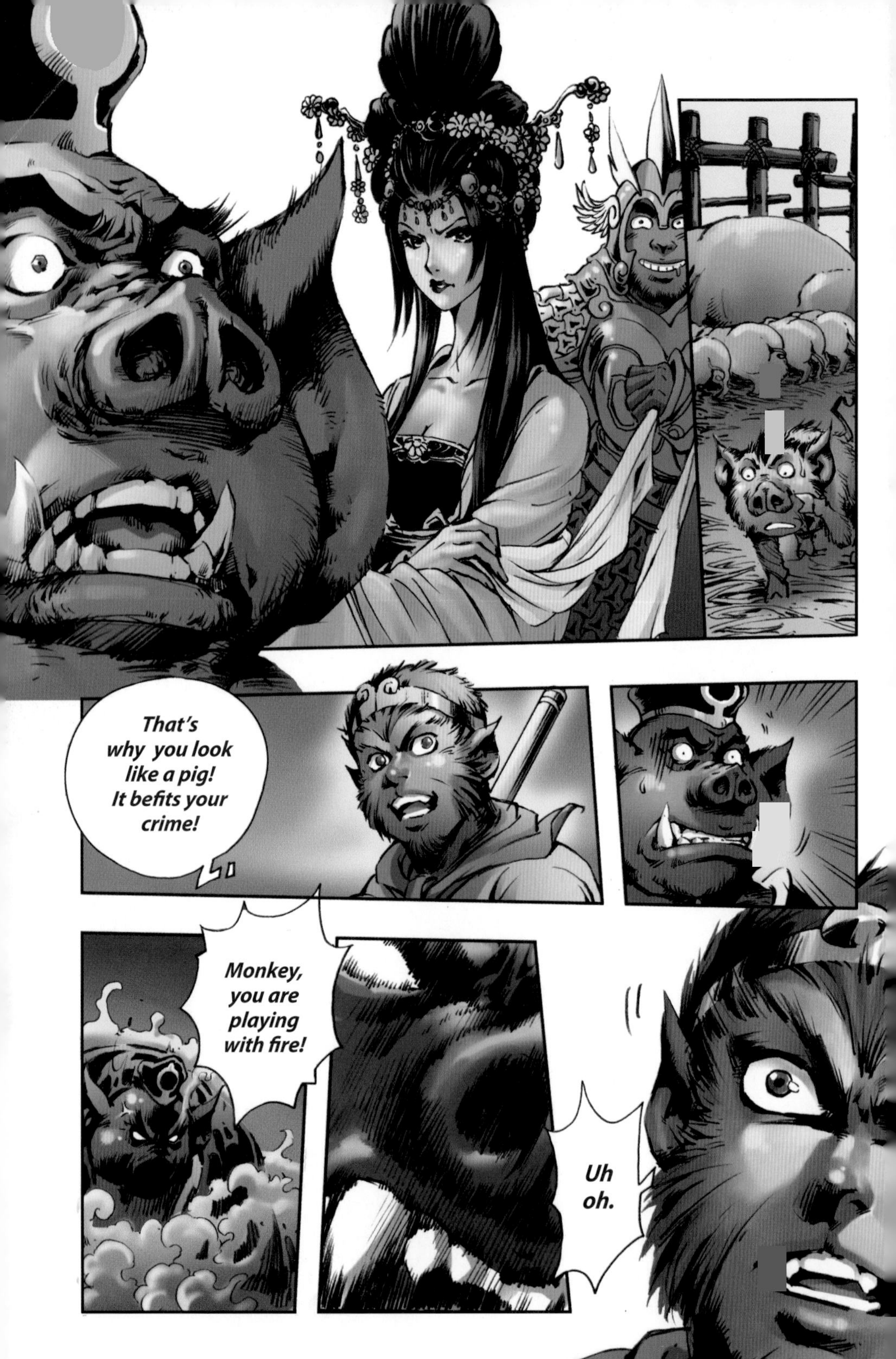
That's why you look like a pig! It befits your crime!
Monkey, you are playing with fire!
Uh oh.

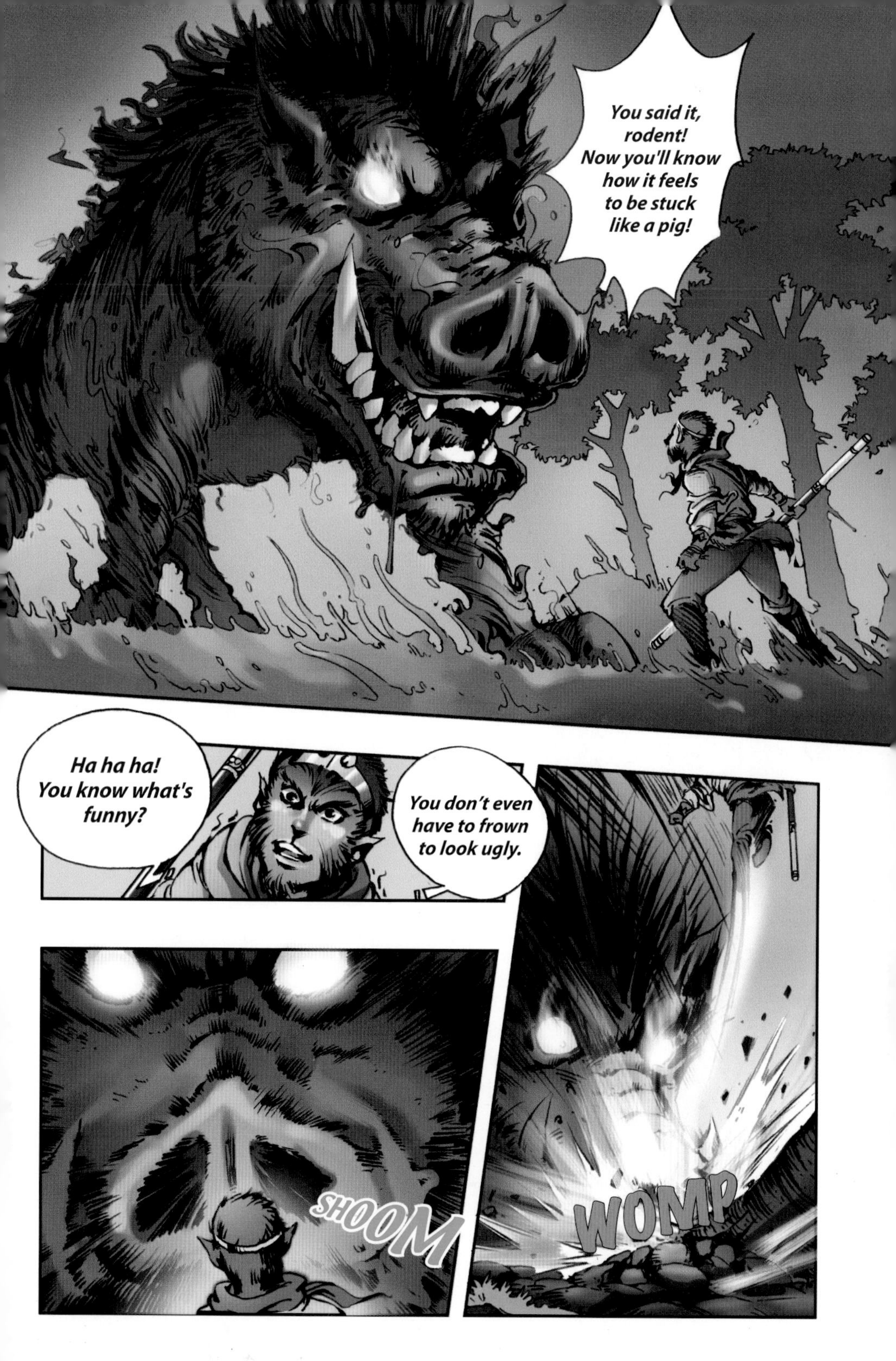
You said it, rodent! Now you'll know how it feels to be stuck like a pig!
Ha ha ha! You know what's funny?
You don't even have to frown to look ugly.
SHOOM
WOMP

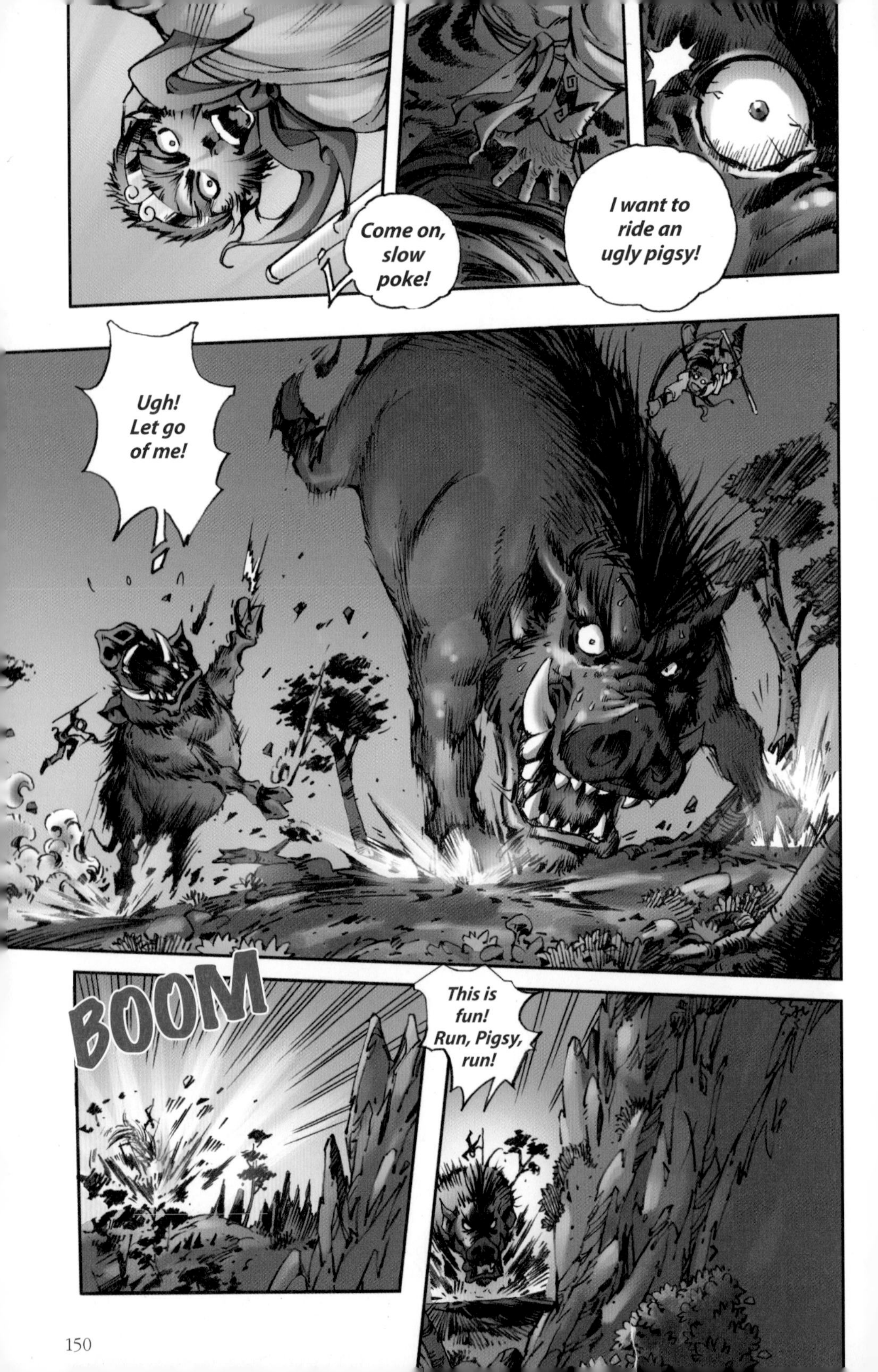
Come on, slow poke!
I want to ride an ugly pigsy!
Ugh! Let go of me!
BOOM
This is fun! Run, Pigsy, run!

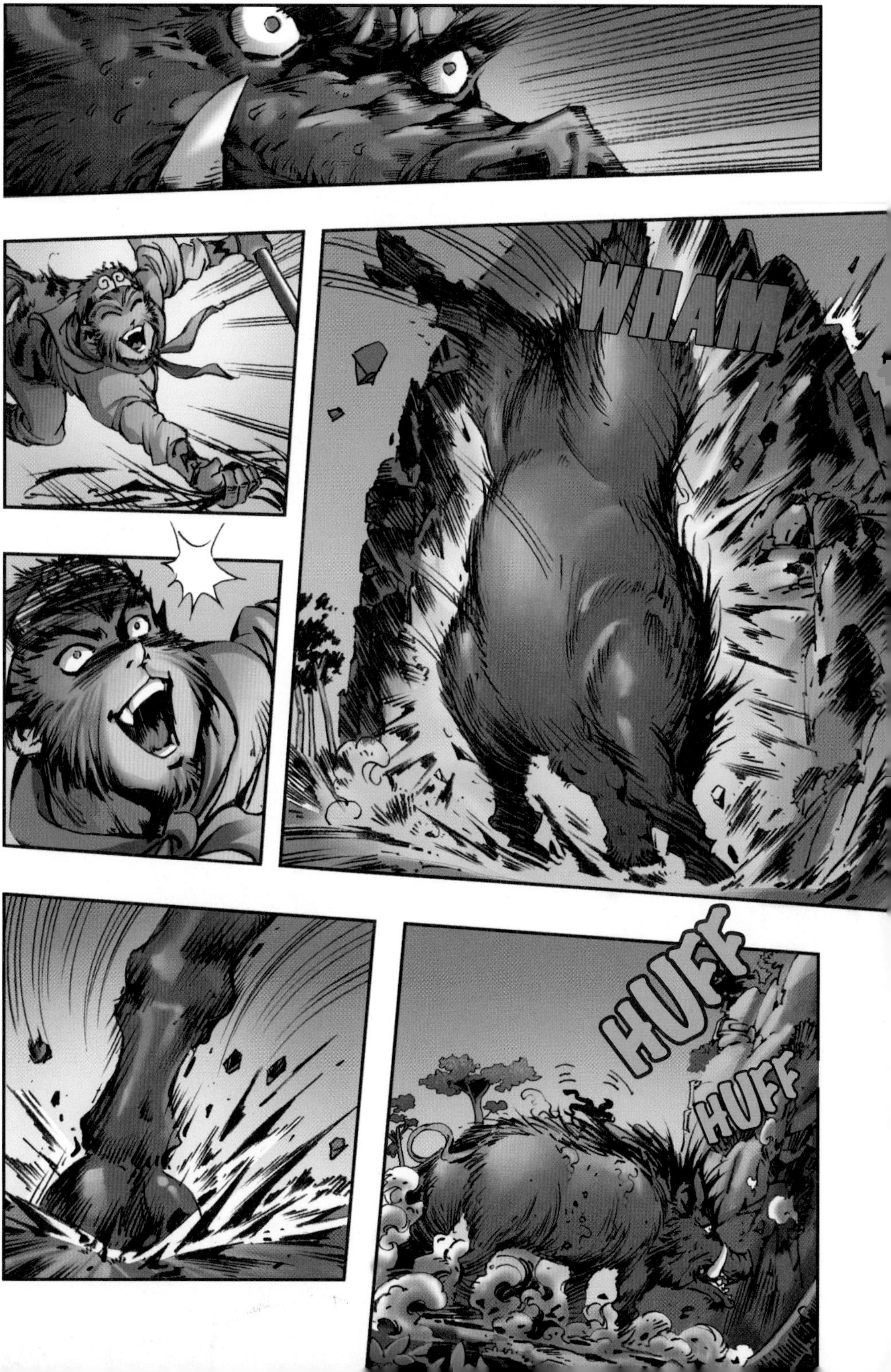
WHAM
HUFF
HUFF

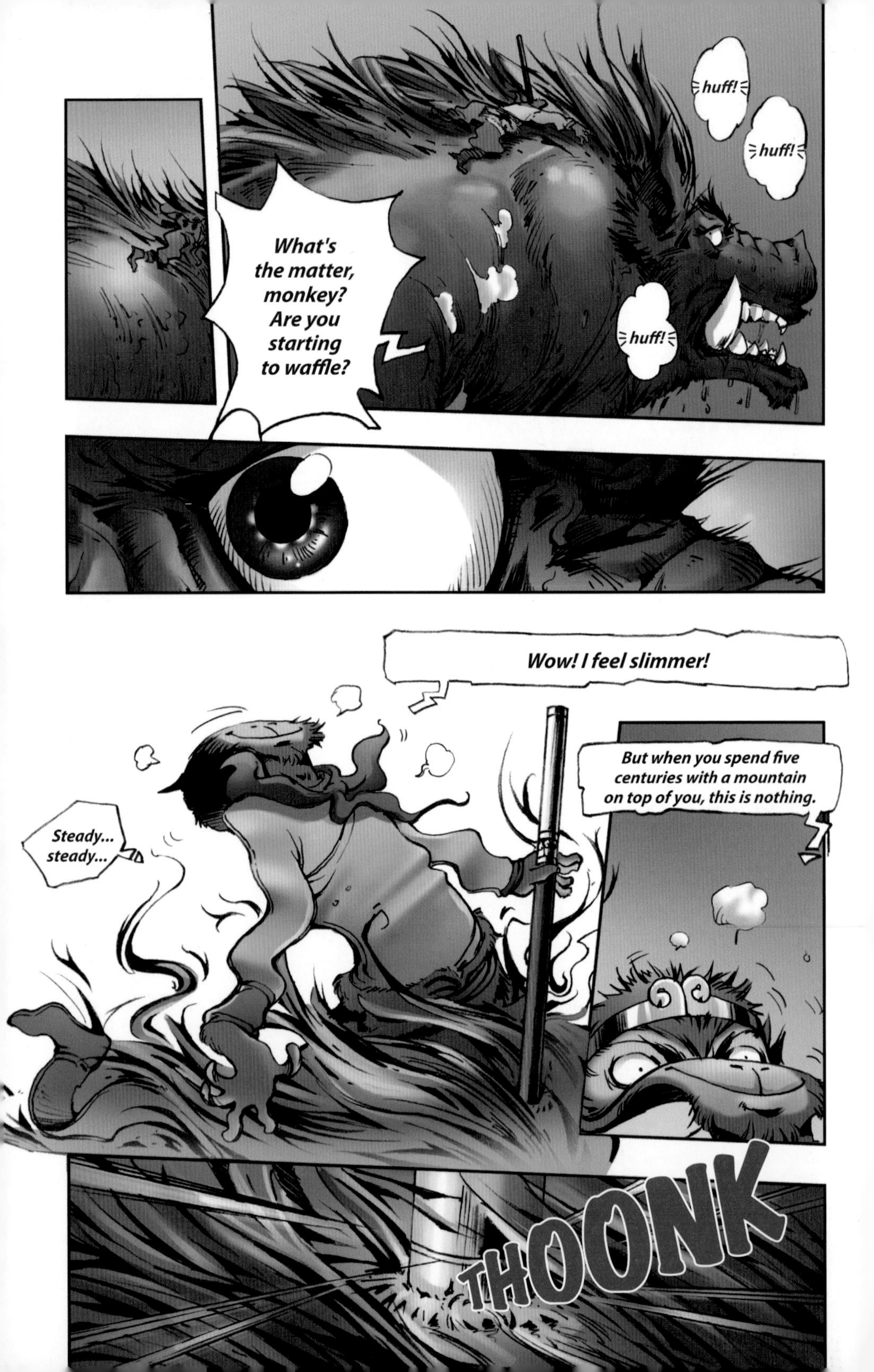

huff!
huff!
What's the matter, monkey? Are you starting to waffle?
huff!
Wow! I feel slimmer!
But when you spend five centuries with a mountain on top of you, this is nothing.
Steady... steady...
THOONK

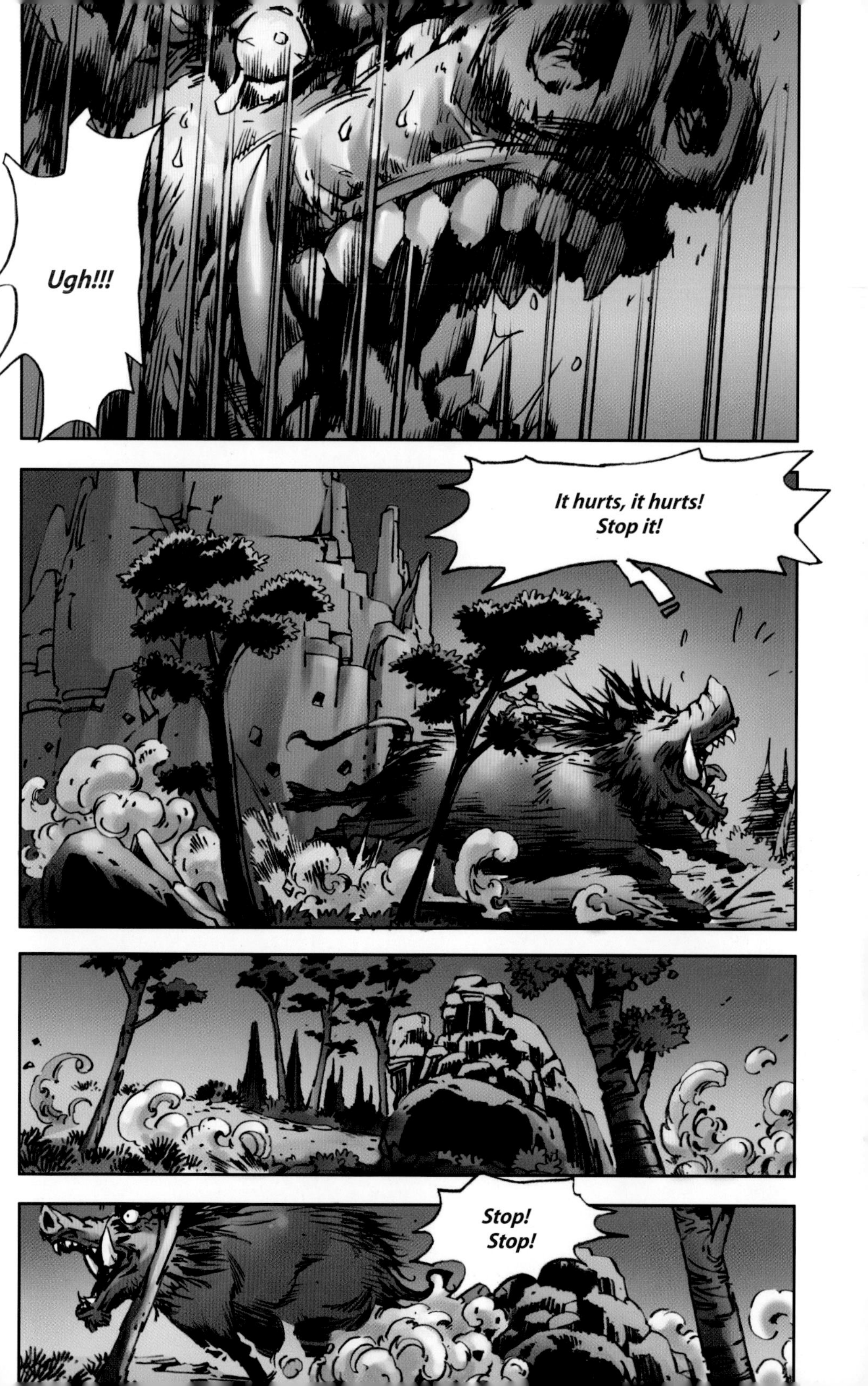
Ugh!!!
It hurts, it hurts! Stop it!
Stop! Stop!

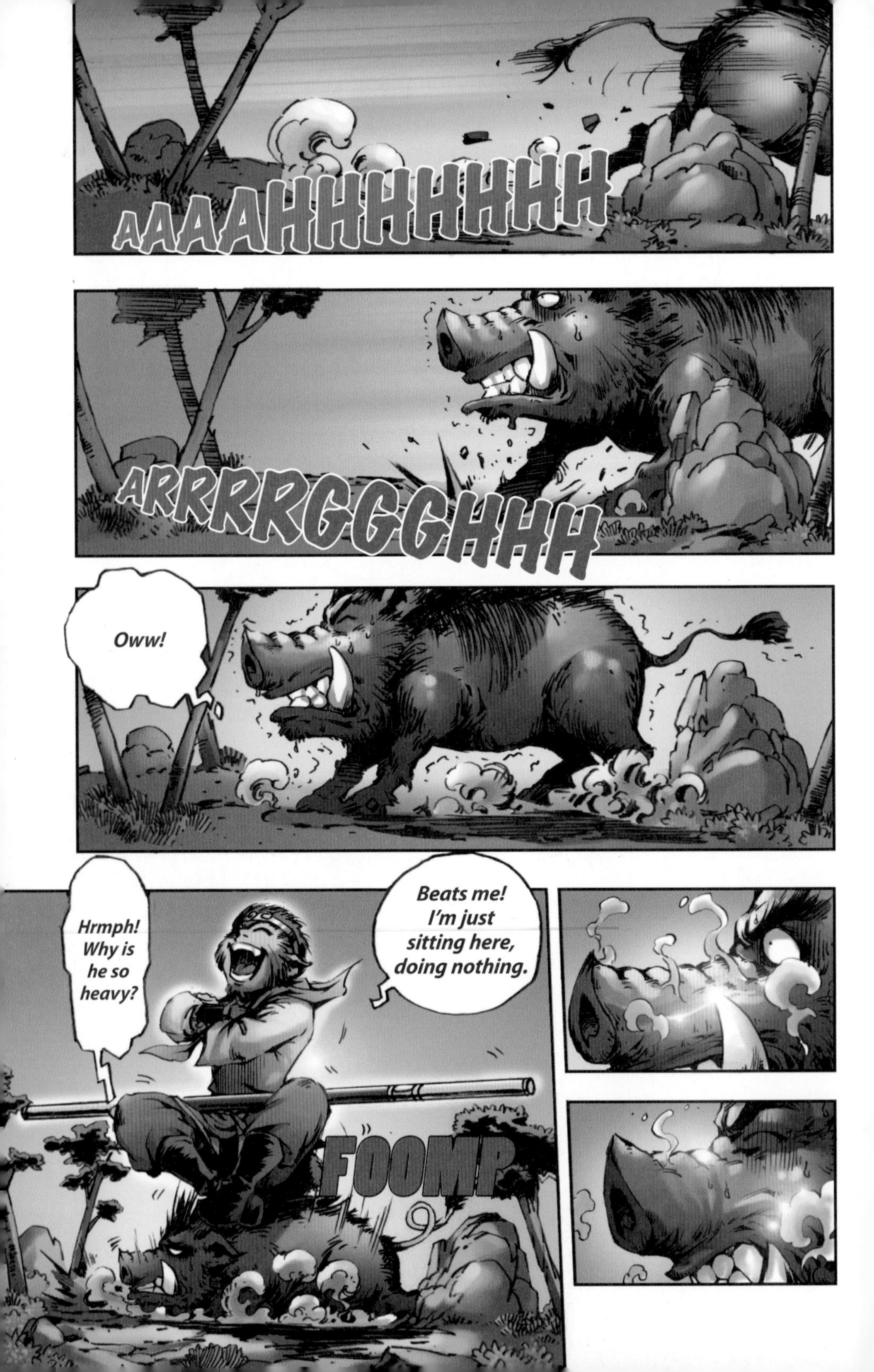
AAAAHHHHHHHHH
ARRRRGGGHHH
Oww!
Hrmph! Why is he so heavy?
Beats me! I'm just sitting here, doing nothing.
FOOMP

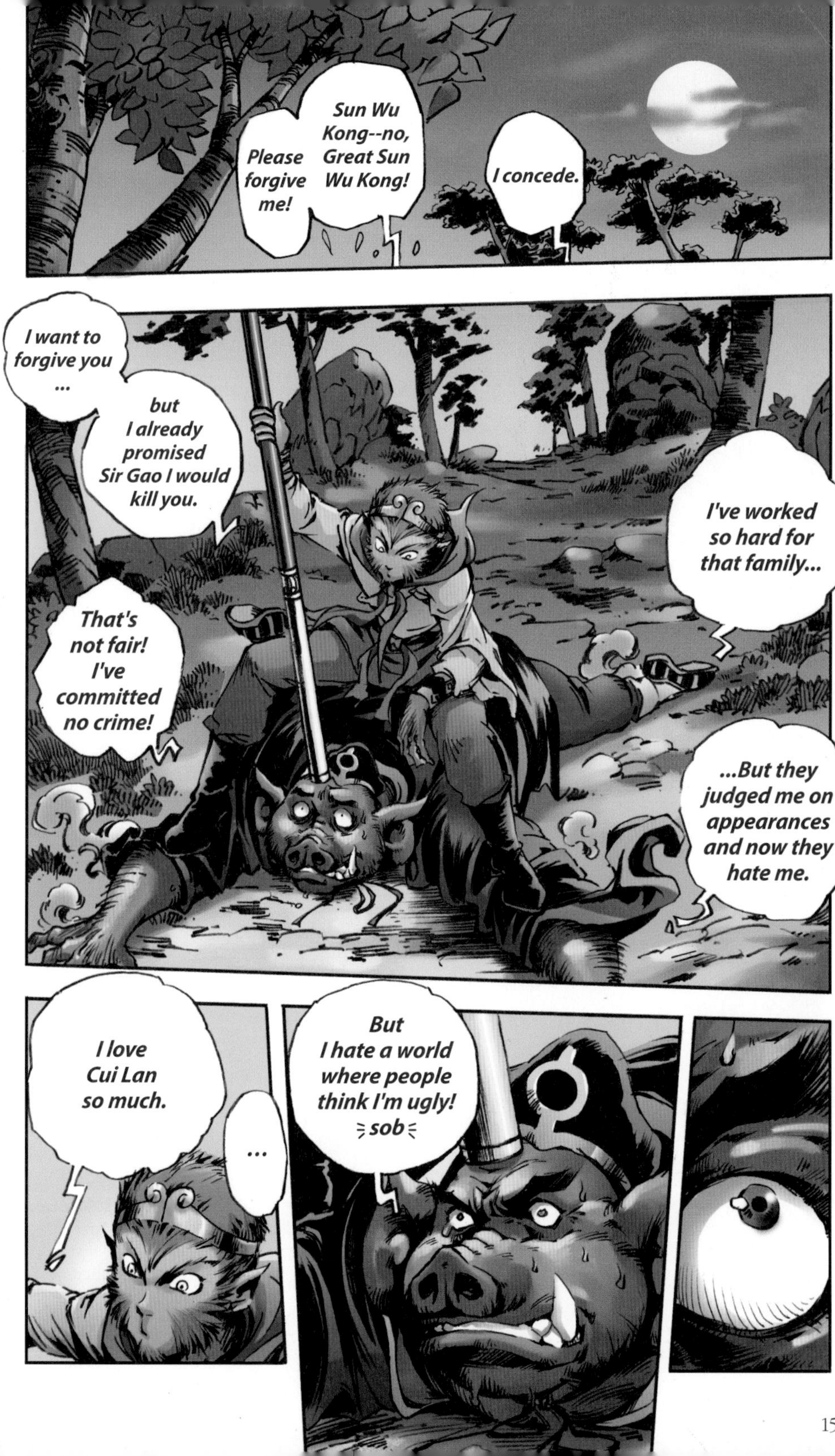
I concede.
Sun Wu Kong--no, Great Sun Wu Kong!
Please forgive me!
I want to forgive you ...
but I already promised Sir Gao I would kill you.
I've worked so hard for that family...
That's not fair! I've committed no crime!
...But they judged me on appearances and now they hate me.
I love Cui Lan so much.
...
But I hate a world where people think I'm ugly! sob

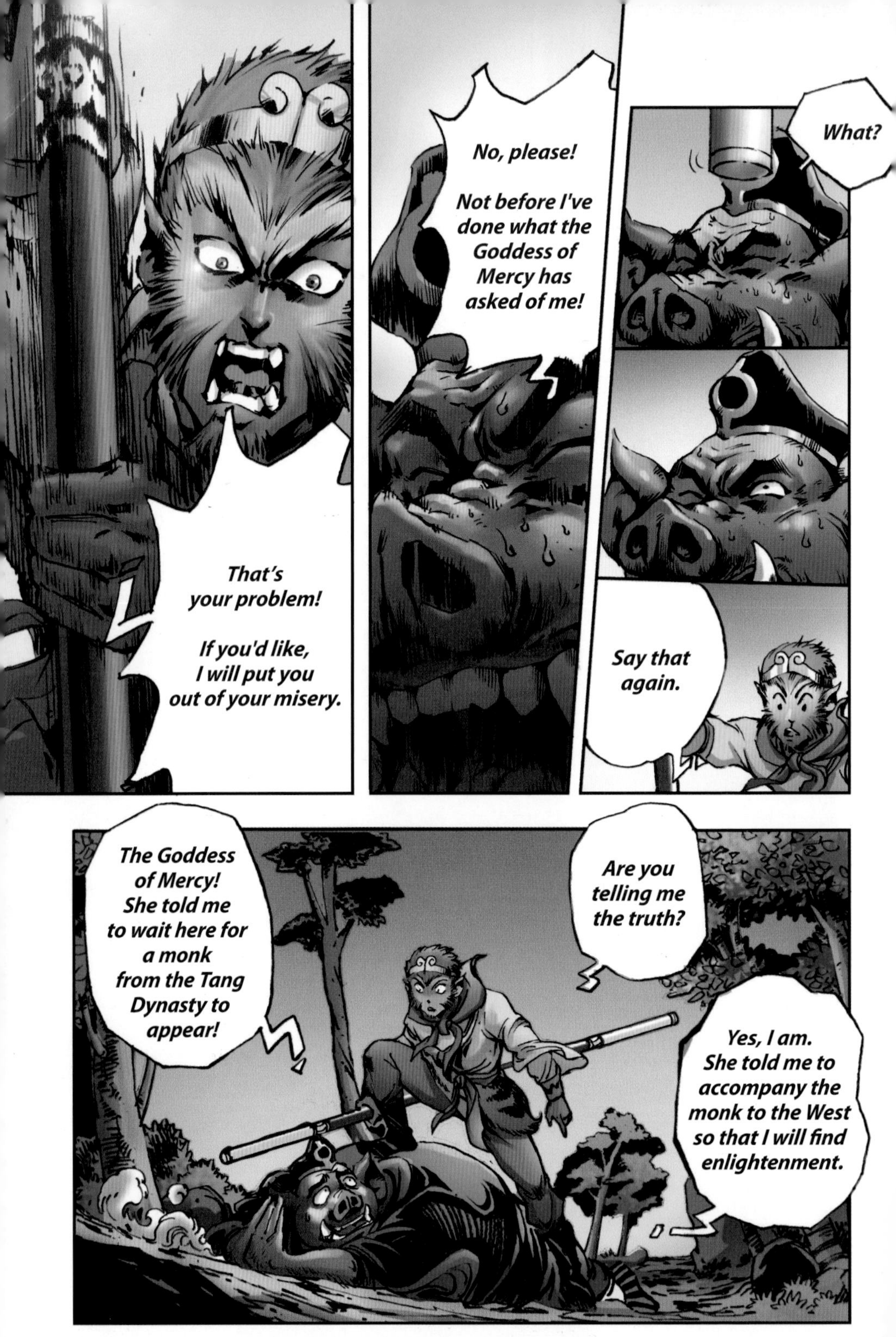
That's your problem!
If you'd like, I will put you out of your misery.
No, please!
Not before I've done what the Goddess of Mercy has asked of me!
What?
Say that again.
The Goddess of Mercy! She told me to wait here for a monk from the Tang Dynasty to appear!
Are you telling me the truth?
Yes, I am. She told me to accompany the monk to the West so that I will find enlightenment.

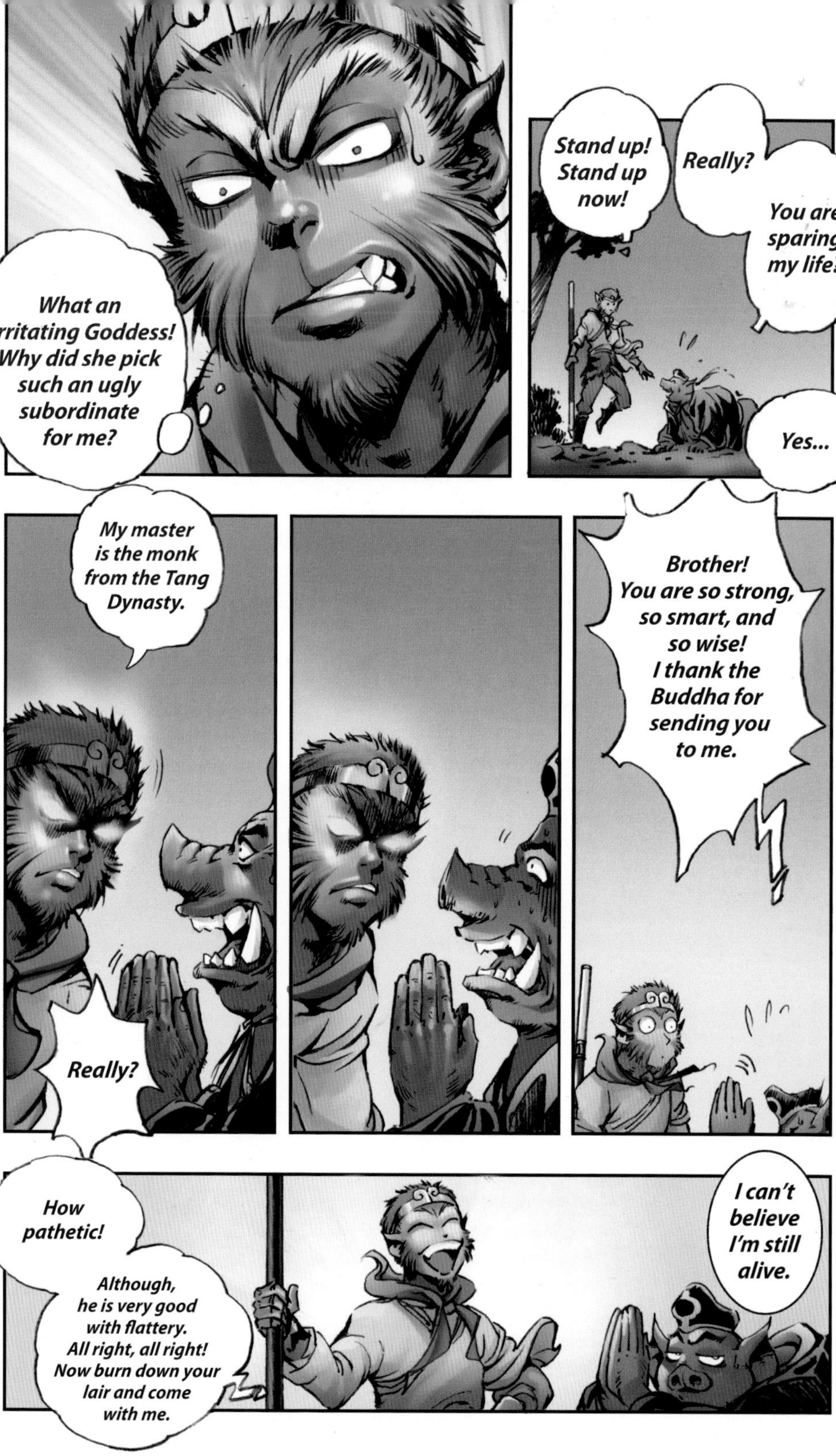
What an irritating Goddess! Why did she pick such an ugly subordinate for me?
Stand up! Stand up now!
Really?
You are sparing my life?
Yes...
My master is the monk from the Tang Dynasty.
Really?
Brother! You are so strong, so smart, and so wise! I thank the Buddha for sending you to me.
How pathetic!
Although, he is very good with flattery. All right, all right! Now burn down your lair and come with me.
I can't believe I'm still alive.

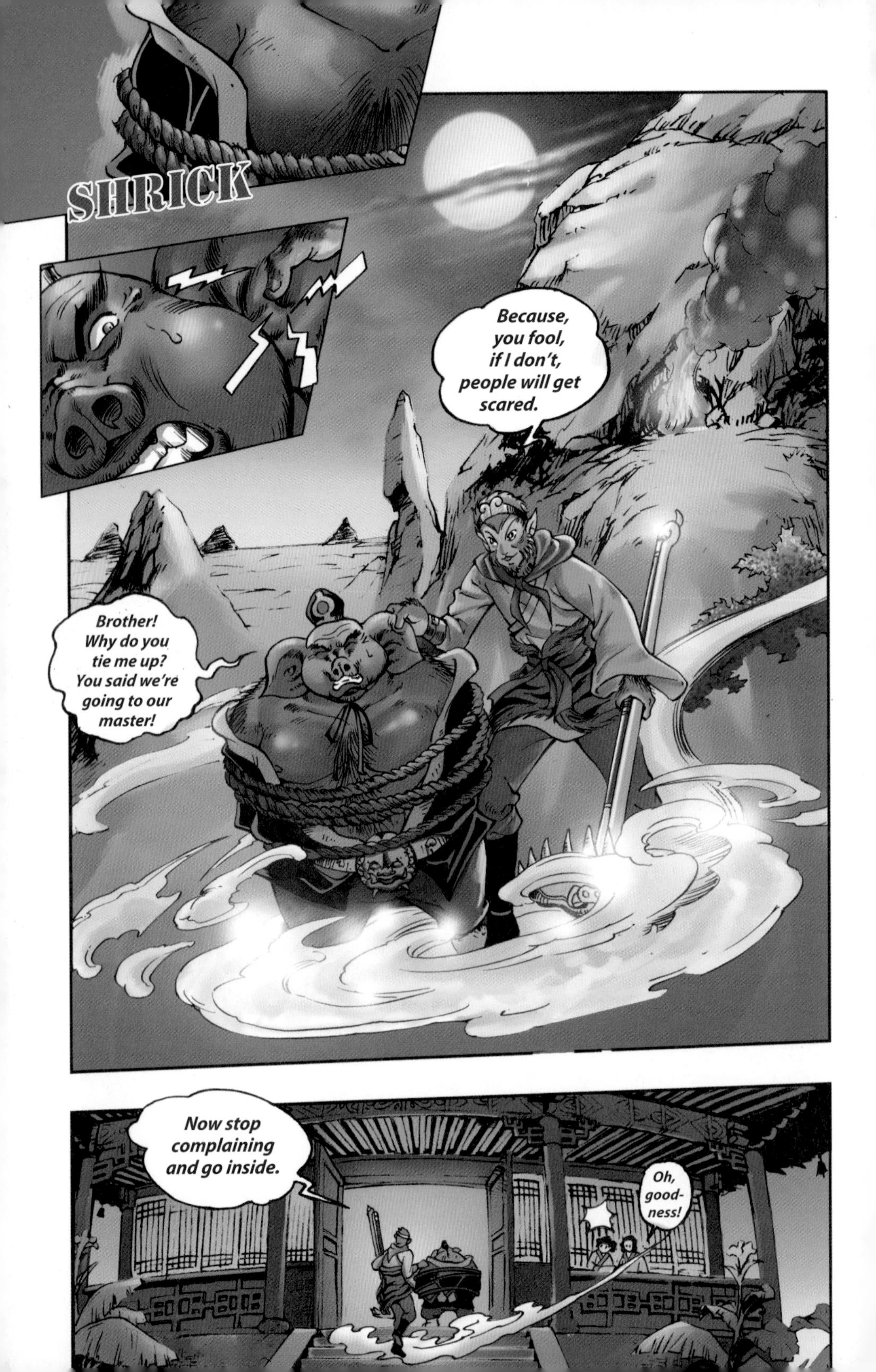
SHRICK
Because, you fool, if I don't, people will get scared.
Brother! Why do you tie me up? You said we're going to our master!
Now stop complaining and go inside.
Oh, good-ness!

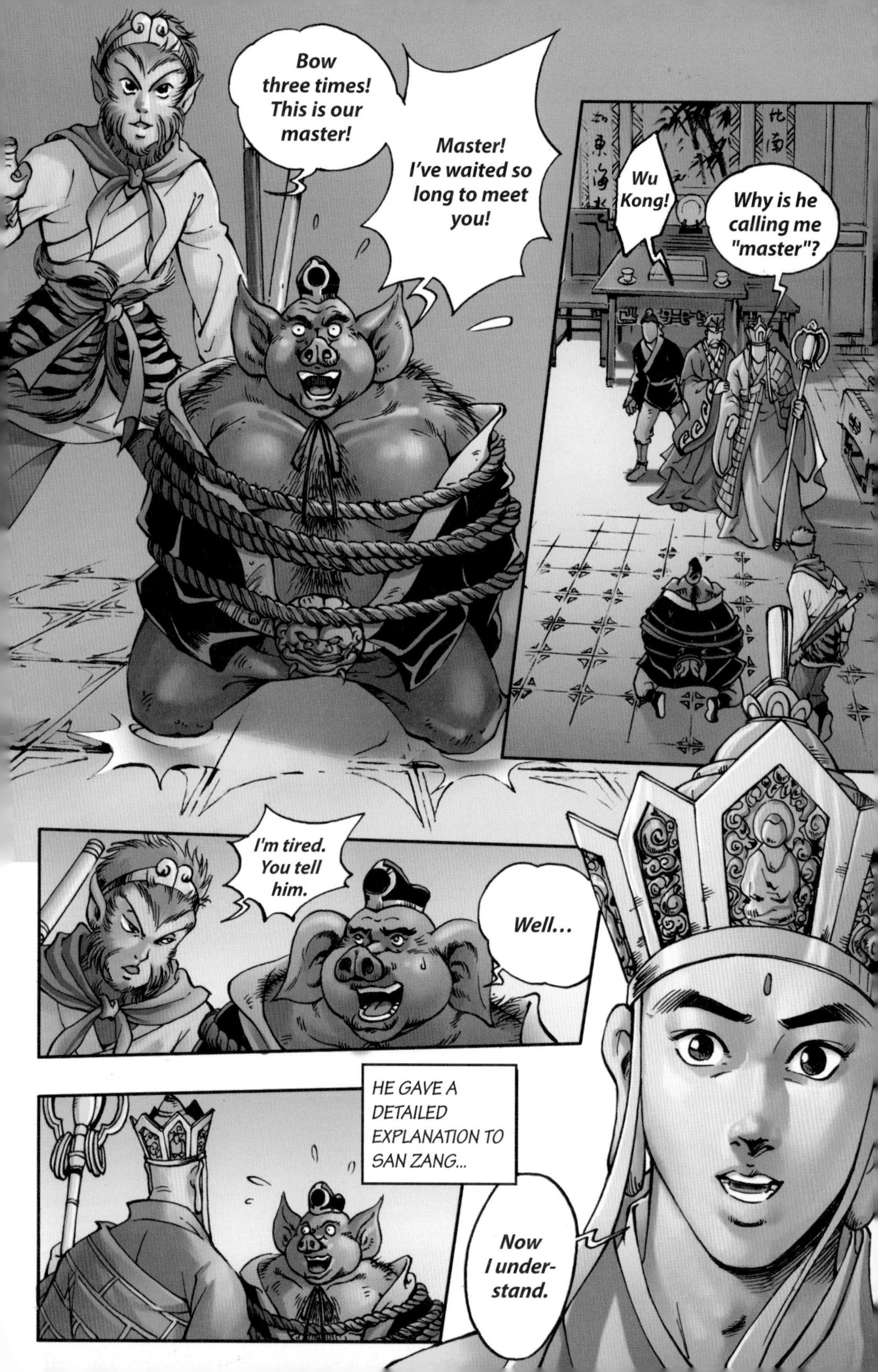
Bow three times! This is our master!
Master! I've waited so long to meet you!
Wu Kong!
Why is he calling me "master"?
I'm tired. You tell him.
Well…
HE GAVE A DETAILED EXPLANATION TO SAN ZANG...
Now I under-stand.

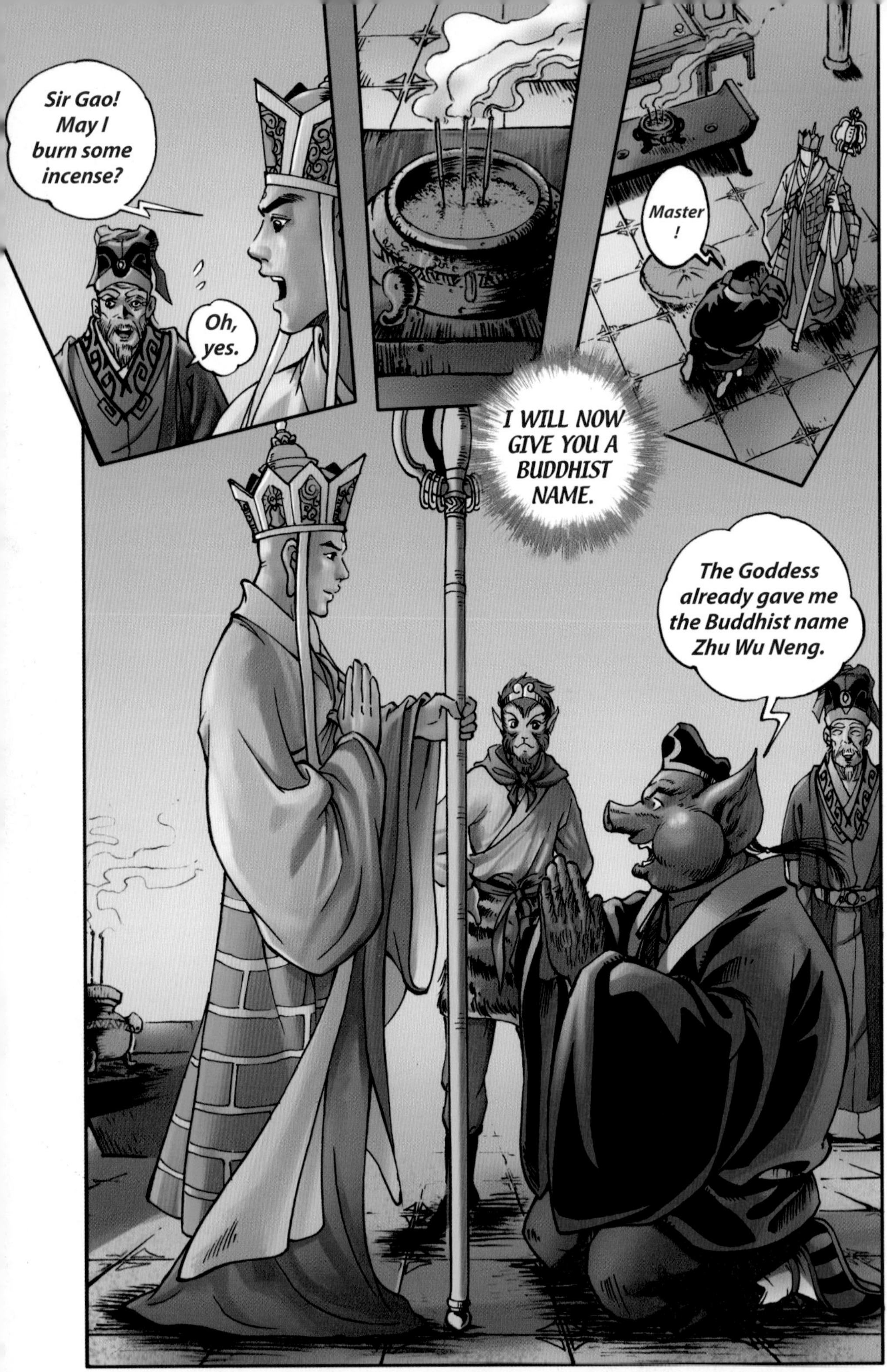
Sir Gao! May I burn some incense?
Oh, yes.
Master!
I WILL NOW GIVE YOU A BUDDHIST NAME.
The Goddess already gave me the Buddhist name Zhu Wu Neng.

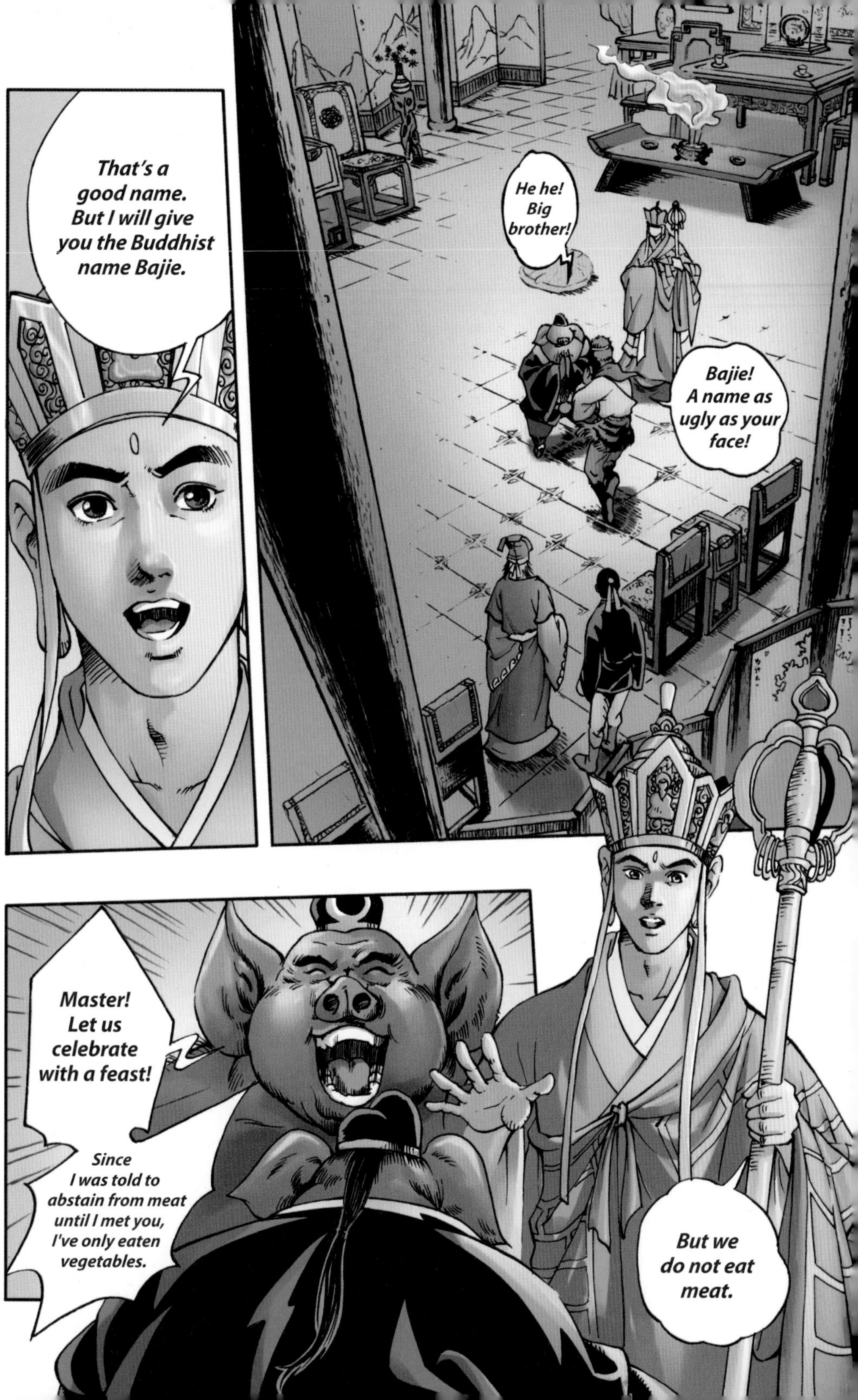
That's a good name. But I will give you the Buddhist name Bajie.
He he! Big brother!
Bajie! A name as ugly as your face!
Master! Let us celebrate with a feast!
Since I was told to abstain from meat until I met you, I've only eaten vegetables.
But we do not eat meat.

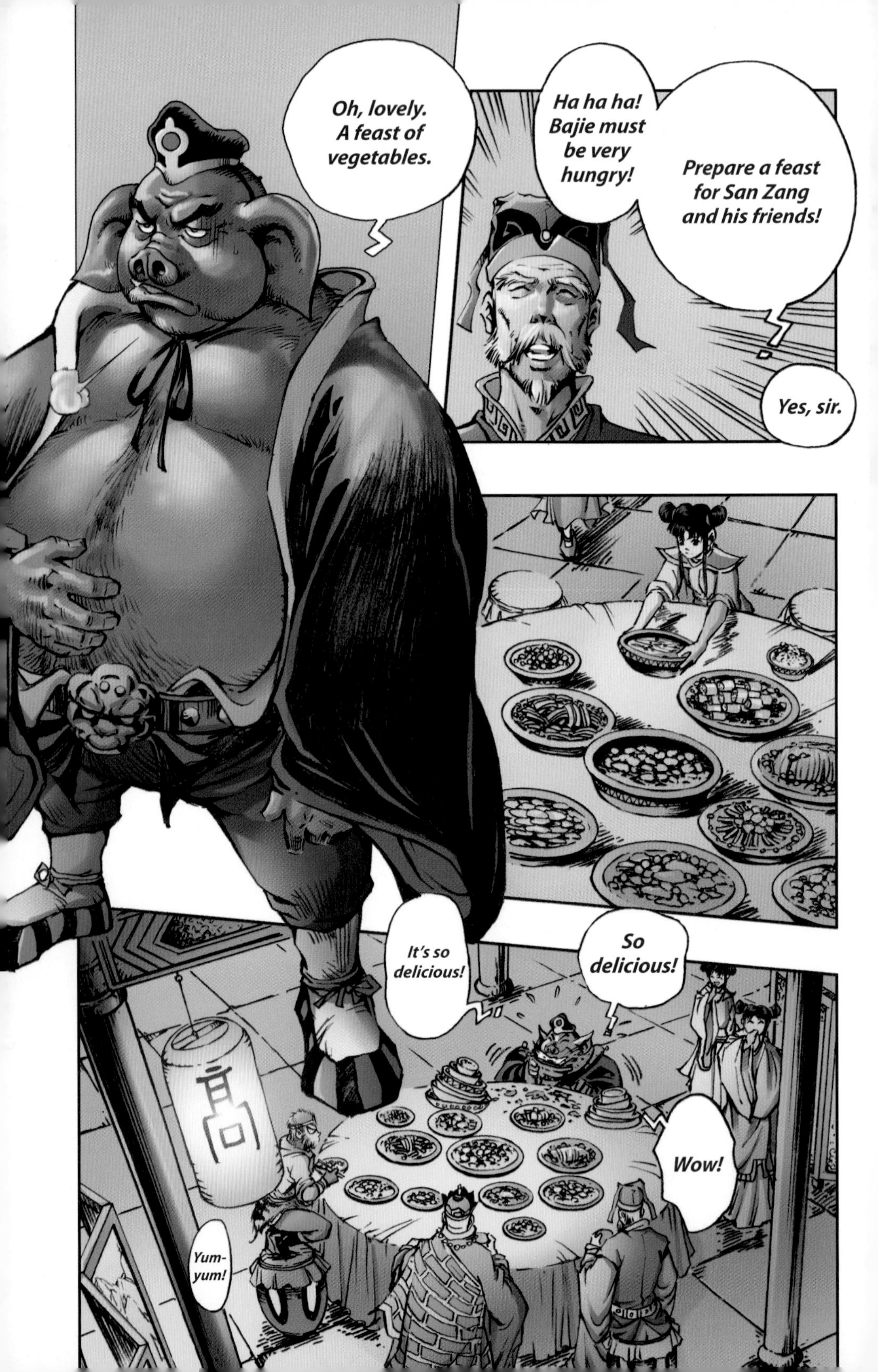

Oh, lovely. A feast of vegetables.
Ha ha ha! Bajie must be very hungry!
Prepare a feast for San Zang and his friends!
Yes, sir.
It's so delicious!
So delicious!
Wow!
Yum-yum!

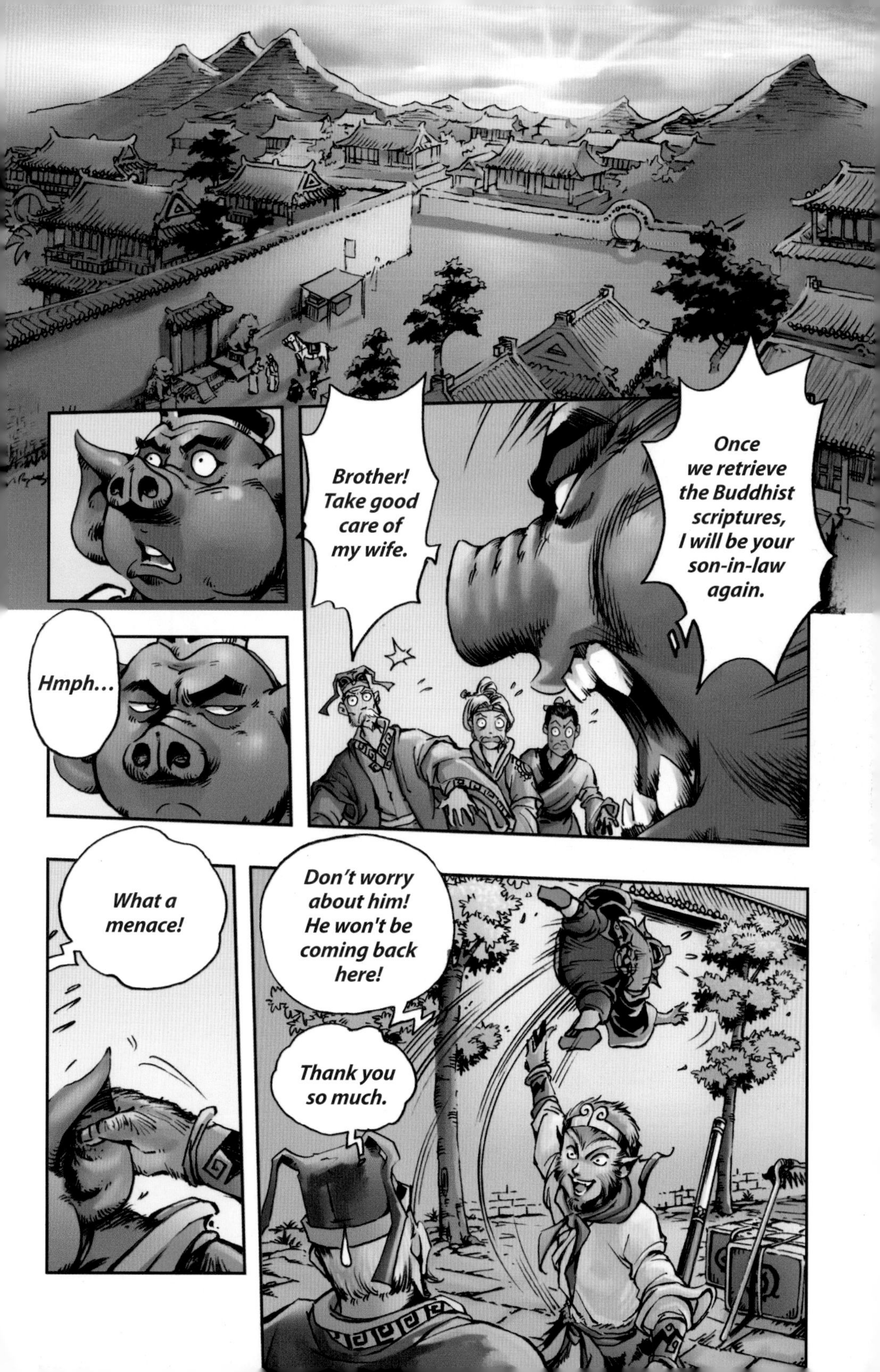
Brother! Take good care of my wife.
Once we retrieve the Buddhist scriptures, I will be your son-in-law again.
Hmph…
What a menace!
Don't worry about him! He won't be coming back here!
Thank you so much.

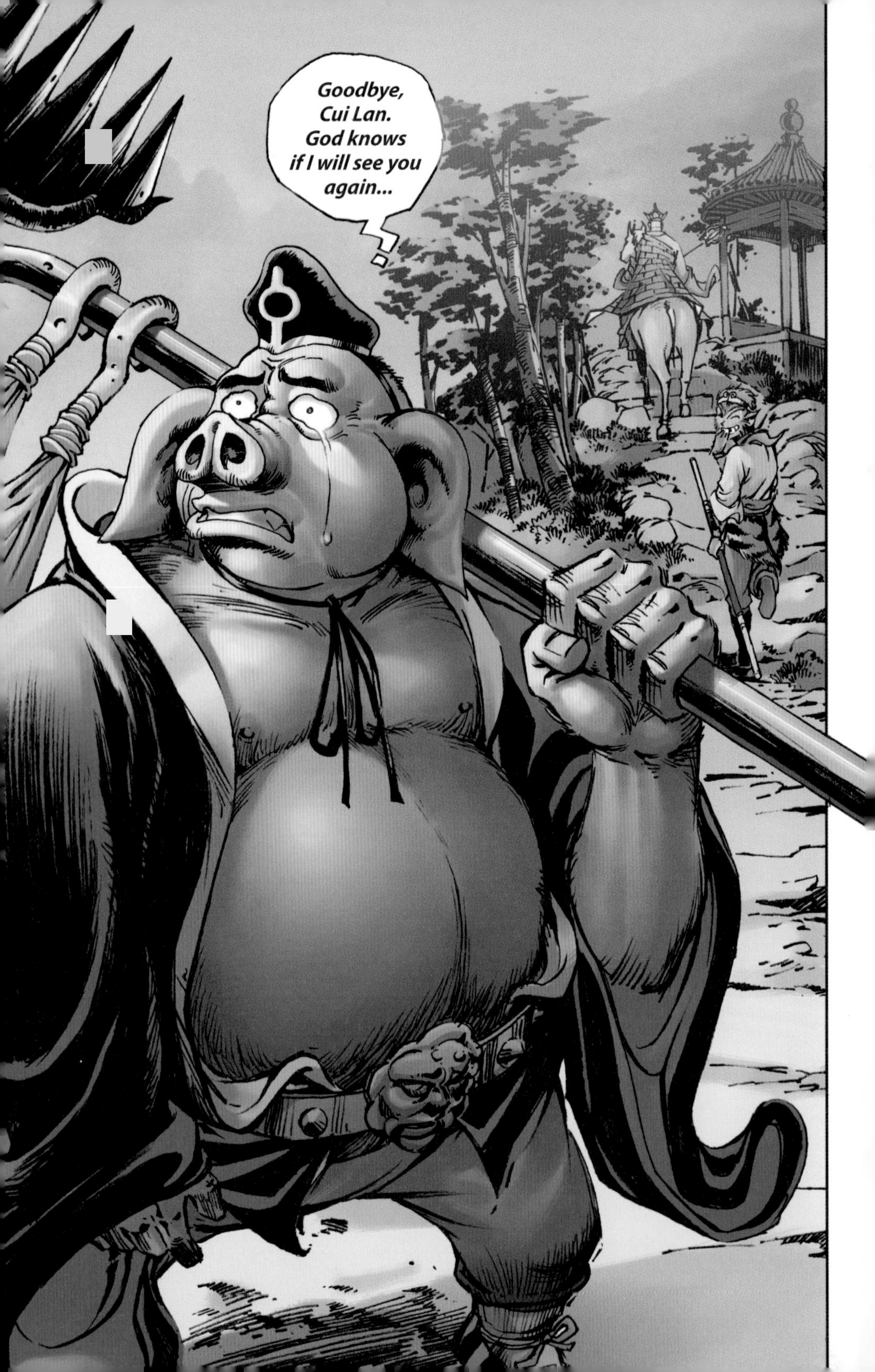
Goodbye, Cui Lan. God knows if I will see you again...

MONKEY KING

Appendix

━━━━

ENEMIES AND A NEW FRIEND

───────

● *One evening, at a remote Buddhist temple, two unlikely companions have requested a place to sleep. One is a Buddhist monk named San Zang, entrusted by Emperor TaiZong to represent the Tang Dynasty. The other is a former monkey king and perpetual malcontent named Sun Wu Kong, who spent five hundred years buried under a mountain, a punishment handed down by Buddha himself. Both have been sought out by the Buddhist Goddess of Mercy to journey to the West, and to retrieve sacred Buddhist scriptures from the lands bordering China. Neither suspects the covetous nature of their hosts.*

Late that night, Sun Wu Kong awakes to the sound of commotion outside their sleeping quarters. The temple's monks, driven mad by jealousy, are attempting to kill San Zang in his sleep and steal a precious robe he is carrying, a robe of unsurpassed beauty given to him by the Goddess of Mercy herself. Knowing how much his master detests the use of violent force, Wu Kong enlists the help of the King of Heavenly Eyes, who loans the monkey BiHuoZhao, a charm that deflects fire. Wu Kong succeeds in preventing the fire from reaching San Zang, but helps the fire to spread elsewhere, completely engulfing the temple in flames. The inferno is visible for miles in every direction, and catch the attention of the Black Bear Demon, who comes to the temple and, while the monks are distracted by the fire, steals San Zang's precious robe.

The next morning, San Zang finds the temple destroyed and the robe missing. He immediately suspects Sun Wu Kong is responsible. When Wu Kong explains what the monks were trying to do, they decide to confront the Chief Priest and demand that he return the robe. However, the Chief Priest has already discovered that the robe has been stolen, and is inconsolable with grief. Once confronted by the journeymen, the Chief Priest takes his own life. San Zang casts the blame for the priest's death on the monkey, saying that if Sun Wu Kong had not so foolishly bragged about the precious robe, the chief priest would still be alive. To punish the monkey, San Zang once more utters an incantation that causes the monkey tremendous pain; the incantation was taught to San Zang by the Goddess of Mercy as a means of subduing the monkey when he got out of hand. The monks of the temple intervene on Sun Wu Kong's behalf, telling the priest that the fire was not his fault, and telling him about the bear demon and the theft of the robe.

After threatening the monks with his miracle staff should they fail to take care of his master, Sun Wu Kong is dispatched to retrieve the robe, and leaves for the Black Bear Demon's lair. Once he finds the right mountain, Sun Wu Kong begins banging on the impenetrable doors to the demon's cave, and then engages the Black Bear Demon in a fight that lasts all morning. Near midday, the bear demon decides he is too hungry to fight, and beats a hasty retreat to his cave. He asks that their fight commence after lunch. Sun Wu Kong goes to the temple to update his master on the situation, and returns to the mountain to resume the fight. Along the way, he encounters a messenger bearing an invitation from the Black Bear Demon to the recently deceased Chief Priest, inviting him to a party at the demon's cave to celebrate the theft of the precious robe. Wu Kong kills the messenger and transfigures into the priest, gaining access to the cave. Wu Kong tries to question the bear demon about the robe, but his cover is blown when the messenger is found dead. Once again, the two fight. Once again, the bear demon calls for a break in the fighting, this time because it's getting late. An angry Sun Wu Kong returns once more to his master, who is growing ever more frustrated by the monkey's failure to retrieve the robe. This time, the monkey decides to ask the Goddess of Mercy for help. Together, they infiltrate the bear's cave: the goddess disguised as a monster friend of the bear demon, and Wu Kong transfigured into a special elixir that is given to the bear demon as a gift. The bear swallows the elixir, and Sun Wu Kong begins reeking havoc on his stomach. The bear, in agonizing pain, agrees to hand over the robe. The Goddess of Mercy then subdues the bear with a headband and incantation more powerful than the one used to subdue the monkey. The bear demon repents his sins and joins the goddess as a protector of Heaven.

Once Sun Wu Kong returns with the robe, he and the priest make haste toward the West in an effort to make up for lost time. They come upon a village whose ruler, Sir Gao, asks for their help in defeating a pig monster who has kidnapped his youngest daughter, Gao Cui Lan, and is holding her hostage. He explains that the pig monster was once his son-in-law, whose true nature was revealed by the incredible amount of food he required. Sir Gao and Sun Wu Kong break in to the manor where Gao Cui Lan is being held and free the girl. Sun Wu Kong then transfigures into Cui Lan and lures the pig monster into a long fight. Sun Wu Kong finally gains the upper hand and is about to kill his opponent when the pig monster reveals that the Goddess of Mercy has recently approached him about becoming San Zang's second companion for his journey to the West. Sun Wu Kong is *annoyed that the goddess has picked such an ugly creature to accompany them, but spares his life. San Zang gives the pig monster the Buddhist name Zhu Bajie, and he joins the two monks on their journey, never to see Gao Cui Lan again.*

MORALITY PURSUED
IN THE JOURNEY TO THE WEST

———

●   *The Journey to the West begins with the birth of one its two central protagonists, the stone monkey, Sun Wu Kong, but the dominant narrative of the story is the journey of the other protagonist, the priest San Zang. The two companions have very different backgrounds, and seem to embody conflicting moral codes. For Sun Wu Kong, a son of heaven and earth, the natural order of Taoism is central to his development: when he was a Monkey King on Spring Mountain, his life was in harmony with the world around him. He ate, drank, and slept to his heart's content, and he was at peace with the natural order of things. San Zang, on the other hand, was brought up in a monastery from the time he was a baby, and has practiced Confucian principals of self-improvement through strict moral cultivation since he was a young boy. But San Zang is not strictly a Confucianist—*

Confucianism is most closely embodied by the heavenly gods. As evidenced by Sun Wu Kong's long feud with the Jade Emperor, when the principles of Confucianism and the principles of Taoism come together, they don't blend perfectly. So what, then, is the moral code of The Journey to the West?

The moral universe of The Journey to the West is difficult to define at first, largely because it depicts both gods and monsters as susceptible to great failings. Sun Wu Kong's failings are well known, and could perhaps be viewed as a criticism of Taoism. But Zhu Bajie, a trusted commander in the Jade Emperor's army, gets drunk, harasses a court lady, and is banished from Heaven—hardly typical for a heavenly being of Confucian morals. He is then reborn as a pig, terrorizes a family, but is still offered repentance by the Goddess of Mercy. Likewise, the chief priest of a Buddhist temple, who has pursued moral cultivation for hundreds of years, fails to find enlightenment and comes undone with greed at the first sight of a precious robe, a greed so overwhelming that the priest decides to kill himself rather than face life without the robe. But despite the heinousness of his behavior, the priest's death is mourned by San Zang because all life, no matter how compromised, is precious.

The central moral conflict of Journey to the West only comes into focus when Sun Wu Kong's Taoist utopia comes into contact with the more hierarchical structure of the Confucian order. The hierarchy instills Sun Wu

Kong with a sense of jealousy, his jealousy leads to greed, his greed leads to anger, and his anger leads him to attempt an overthrow of the Jade Emperor, an act that is a violation of Taoist morals, which promote the harmonious coexistence of all living things. But that doesn't mean that the heavenly gods are perfect beings, or that their morals are better: most of the Jade Emperor's allies look down on Sun Wu Kong and his monkey brothers as second-rate beings. This is why they continually underestimate Wu Kong. The Confucian gods are quick to judge, slow to react, and often seem to not understand the natural world; for all of their wisdom and enlightenment, they spend a lot of time getting very angry.

The need for a resolution to this conflict is where Buddhism comes into the story, and where the morality of Journey to the West becomes clear. Buddhist enlightenment, embodied by the Goddess of Mercy, can be thought of as an intersection between the two opposing ideals. While Buddhist enlightenment demands rigorous moral cultivation, it does so in the name of a moral code that says no one creature, heavenly or mortal, is greater than another, and that we all are bound by the same moral fabric. This is why transfiguring is one of the highest things that can be achieved: because it requires an understanding of the sameness of all things. When the Goddess of Mercy is able to easily impersonate Ling Xizi, it is because there is no difference between the monster and the goddess. The goddess believes that most of the world lacks this moral compass, and that is why she has asks San Zang and his companions to retrieve the Buddhist scriptures from the West. Buddhism becomes the central moral component of *The Journey to the West* because the story exists at the crossroads of natural existence and practiced enlightenment, at the intersection of man's true being and man's true potential.

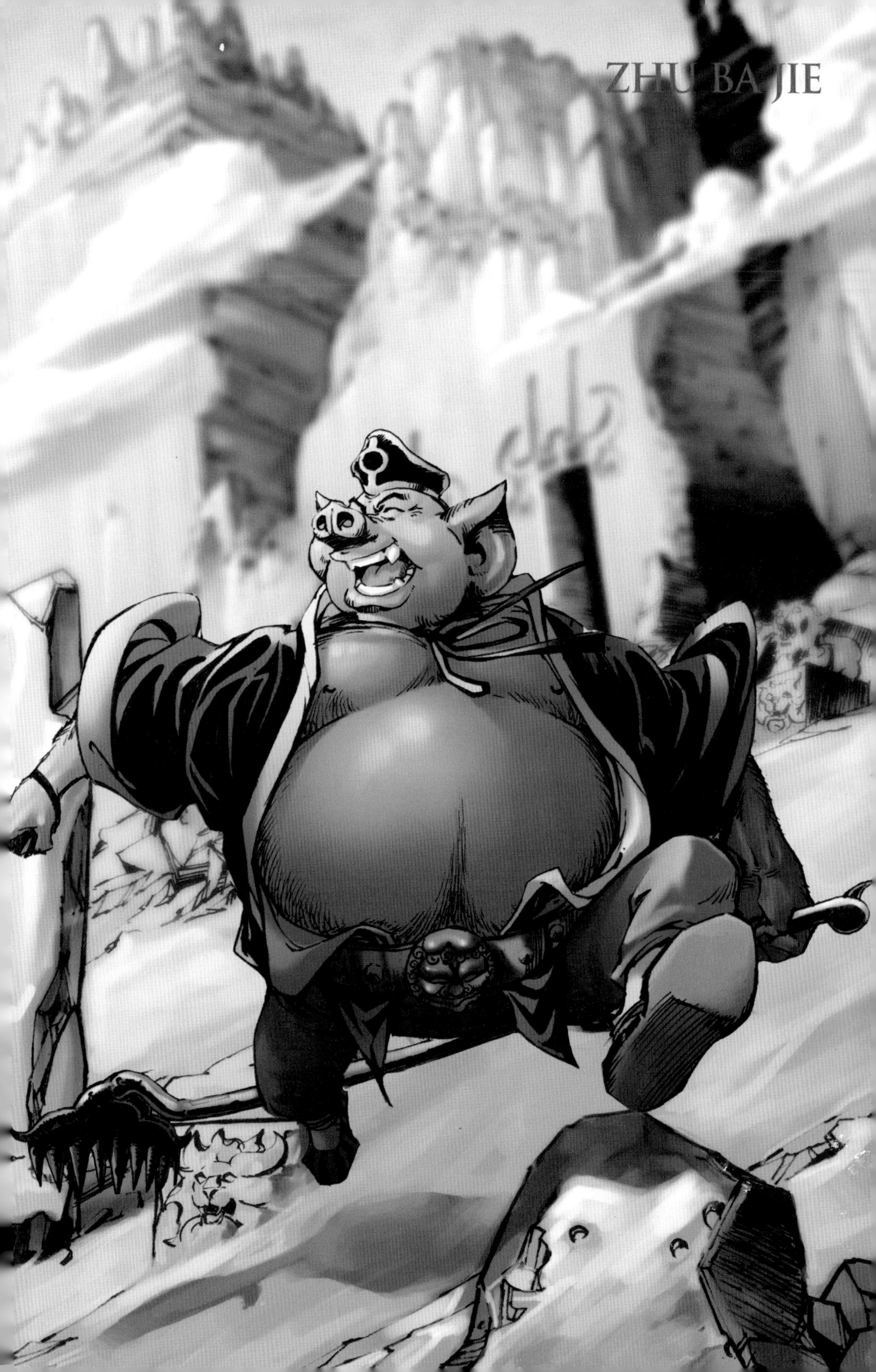
ZHU BA JIE

Adventures from China MONKEY KING

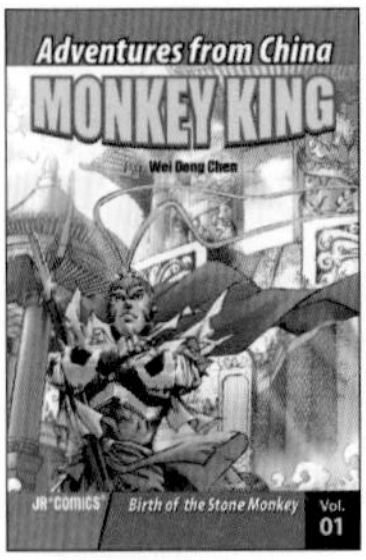
Adventures from China
MONKEY KING
by Wei Dong Chen
JR COMICS
Birth of the Stone Monkey
Vol. 01

Vol. 01

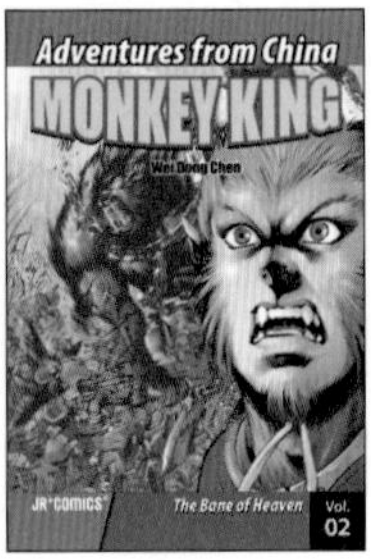
Adventures from China
MONKEY KING
by Wei Dong Chen
JR COMICS
The Bane of Heaven
Vol. 02

Vol. 02

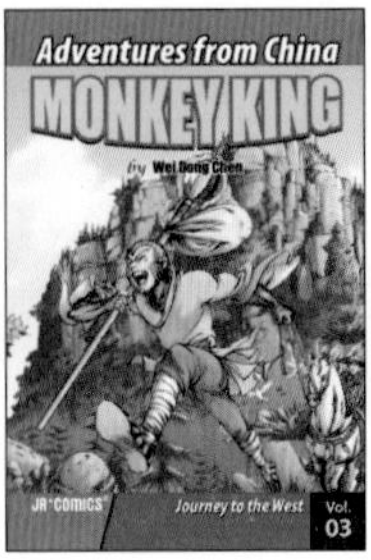
Adventures from China
MONKEY KING
by Wei Dong Chen
JR COMICS
Journey to the West
Vol. 03

Vol. 03

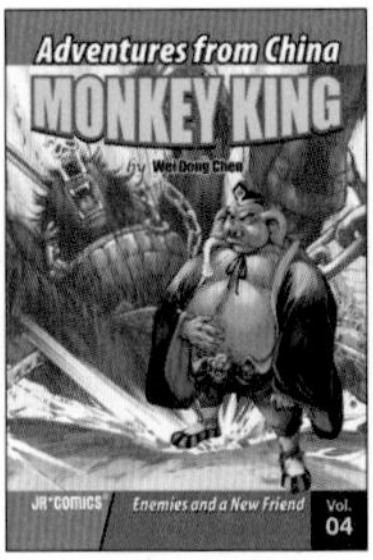
Adventures from China
MONKEY KING
by Wei Dong Chen
JR COMICS
Enemies and a New Friend
Vol. 04

Vol. 04

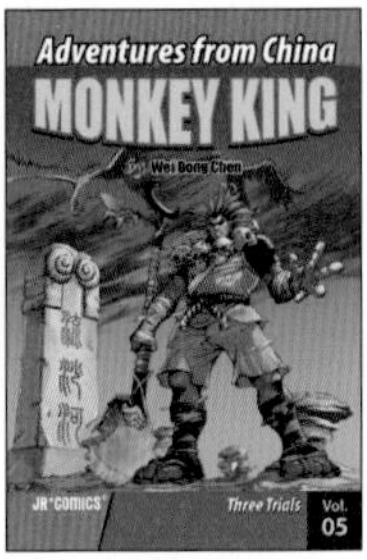
Adventures from China
MONKEY KING
by Wei Dong Chen
JR COMICS
Three Trials
Vol. 05

Vol. 05

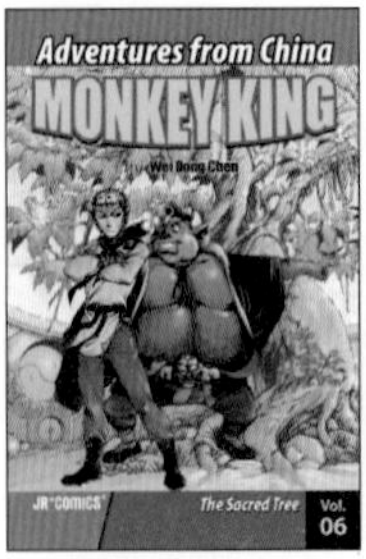
Adventures from China
MONKEY KING
by Wei Dong Chen
JR COMICS
The Sacred Tree
Vol. 06

Vol. 06

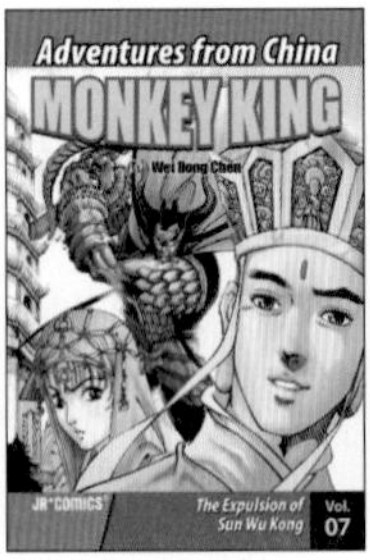
Adventures from China
MONKEY KING
by Wei Dong Chen
JR COMICS
The Expulsion of Sun Wu Kong
Vol. 07

Vol. 07

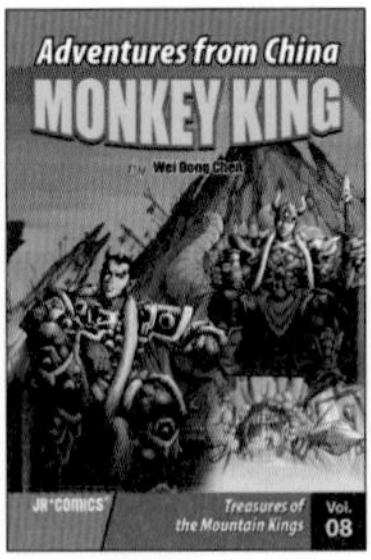
Adventures from China
MONKEY KING
by Wei Dong Chen
JR COMICS
Treasures of the Mountain Kings
Vol. 08

Vol. 08

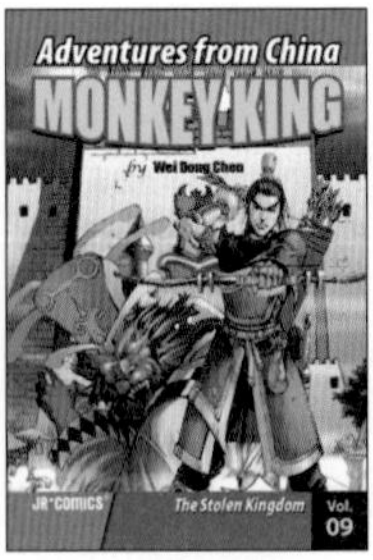
Adventures from China
MONKEY KING
by Wei Dong Chen
JR COMICS
The Stolen Kingdom
Vol. 09

Vol. 09

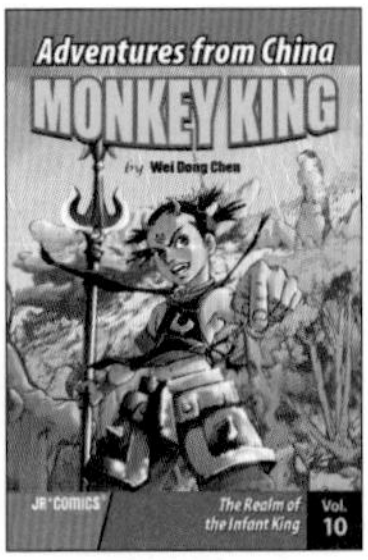
Adventures from China
MONKEY KING
by Wei Dong Chen
JR COMICS
The Realm of the Infant King
Vol. 10

Vol. 10

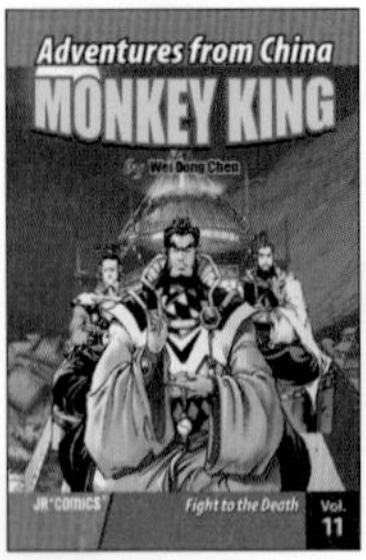
Adventures from China
MONKEY KING
by Wei Dong Chen
JR COMICS
Fight to the Death
Vol. 11

Vol. 11

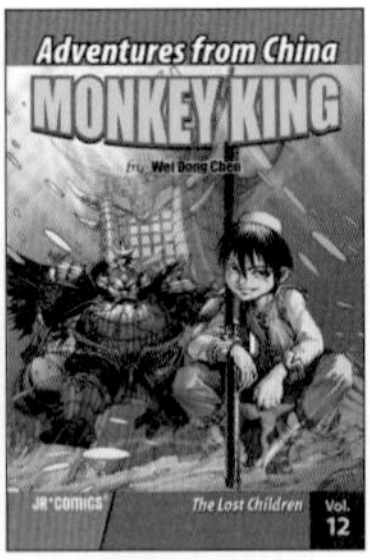
Adventures from China
MONKEY KING
by Wei Dong Chen
JR COMICS
The Lost Children
Vol. 12

Vol. 12

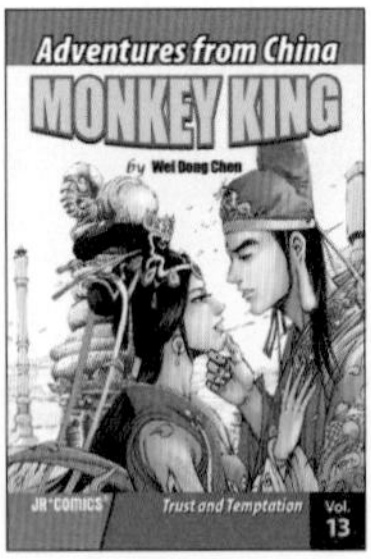
Adventures from China
MONKEY KING
by Wei Dong Chen
JR COMICS
Trust and Temptation
Vol. 13

Vol. 13

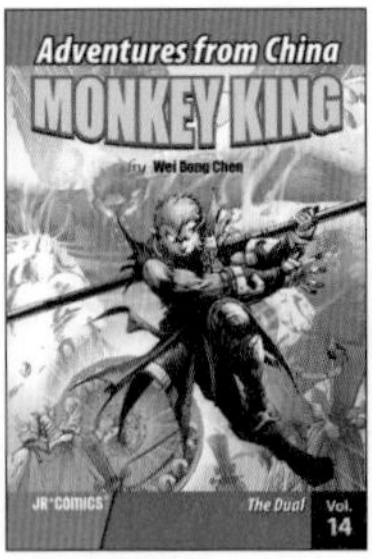
Adventures from China
MONKEY KING
by Wei Dong Chen
JR COMICS
The Dual
Vol. 14

Vol. 14

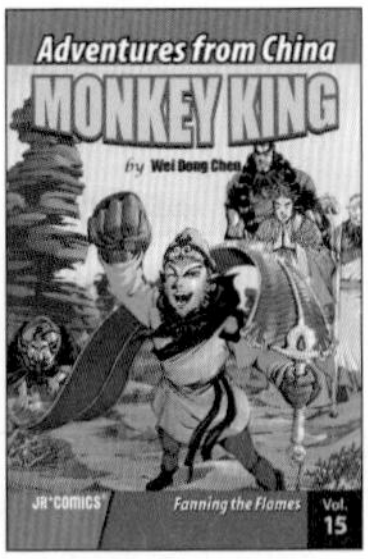
Adventures from China
MONKEY KING
by Wei Dong Chen
JR COMICS
Fanning the Flames
Vol. 15

Vol. 15

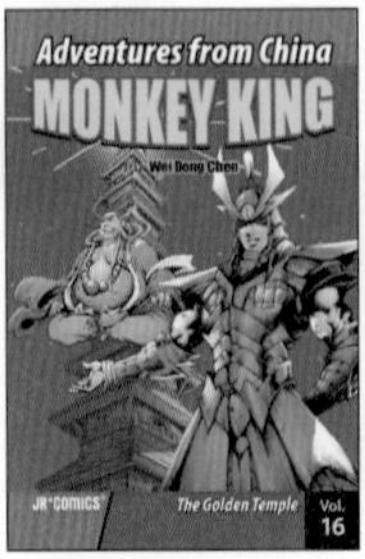
Adventures from China
MONKEY KING
Wei Dong Chen
JR COMICS
The Golden Temple
Vol. 16

Vol. 16

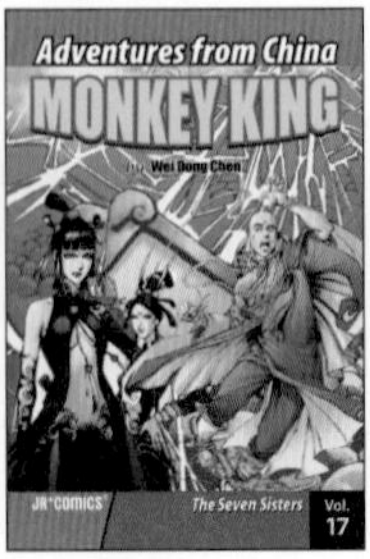
Adventures from China
MONKEY KING
by Wei Dong Chen
JR COMICS
The Seven Sisters
Vol. 17

Vol. 17

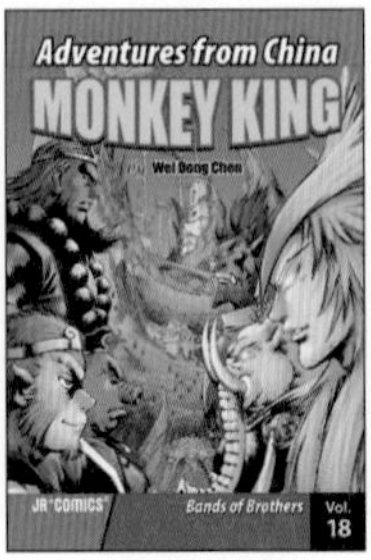
Adventures from China
MONKEY KING
Wei Dong Chen
JR COMICS
Bands of Brothers
Vol. 18

Vol. 18

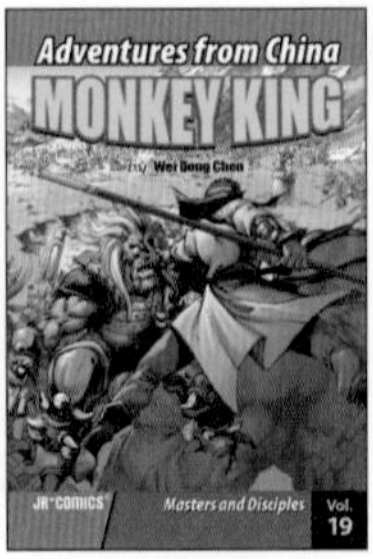
Adventures from China
MONKEY KING
by Wei Dong Chen
JR COMICS
Masters and Disciples
Vol. 19

Vol. 19

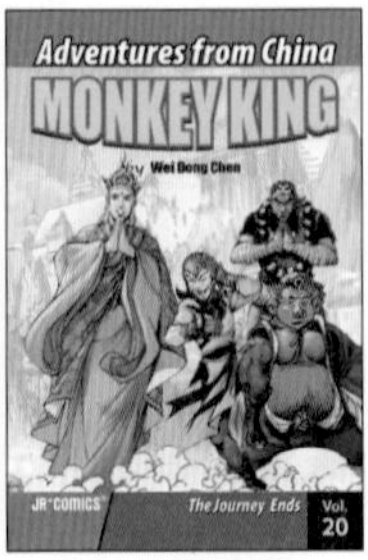
Adventures from China
MONKEY KING
by Wei Dong Chen
JR COMICS
The Journey Ends
Vol. 20

Vol. 20